THE
TAKEOVER

OTHER TITLES BY T L SWAN

THE TAKEOVER

THE MILES HIGH CLUB

T L SWAN

 Montlake

Published by Montlake, Seattle

www.apub.com

Amazon, the Amazon logo, and Montlake are trademarks of Amazon.com, Inc., or its affiliates.

ISBN-13: 9781542017336
ISBN-10: 1542017335

Cover design by The Brewster Project

Cover photography by Wander Aguiar Photography

Printed in the United States of America

I would like to dedicate this book to the alphabet,
for those twenty-six letters have changed my life.
Within those twenty-six letters I have found myself,
and now I live my dream.
Next time you say the alphabet,
remember its power.
I do every day.

Chapter 1

The phone buzzes on my desk. "Hello," I answer.

"Hi, Tristan Miles is on line two for you," Marley replies.

"Tell him I'm busy."

"Claire." She pauses. "This is the third time he's called this week."

"So?"

"Pretty soon, he's going to stop calling."

"And your point is?" I ask.

"My point is we paid the staff out of the overdraft this week. And I know you don't want to admit this, but we are in trouble, Claire. You need to hear him out."

I exhale heavily and drag my hand down my face. I know she's right; our company, Anderson Media, is struggling. We're down to our last three hundred staff, having downscaled from the original six hundred. Miles Media and all of our competitors have been circling like wolves for months, watching and waiting for the perfect time to move in for the kill. Tristan Miles: the head of acquisitions and the archenemy of every struggling company in the world. Like a leech, he takes over companies when they're at their lowest, tears them apart, and then, with his never-ending funds, turns them into huge successes. He's the biggest snake in the snake pit. Preying on weaknesses and getting paid millions of dollars a year for the privilege. He's a rich, spoiled bastard with a reputation for being acutely intelligent, hard as nails, and conscience-free.

He's everything I hate about business.

"Just listen to what he has to say—that's all. You never know what he might offer," Marley pleads.

"Oh, come on," I scoff. "We both know what he wants."

"Claire, please. You can't lose your family home. I won't let that happen."

Sadness rolls over me; I hate that I've found myself in this position. "Fine, I'll hear him out. But that's it," I concede. "Schedule a meeting."

"Okay, great."

"Don't get excited." I smirk. "I'm just doing this to shut you up, you know?"

"Good, mouth officially shut from here on out. Cross my heart."

"If only." I smile. "Will you come with me?"

"Yes, for sure. We'll stick Mr. Fancy Pants's checkbook where the sun doesn't shine."

I giggle at the idea. "Okay, deal."

I hang up and go back to my report, wishing it were Friday and I didn't have to worry about Anderson Media and the bills for a few days.

Only four days to go.

Thursday morning, Marley and I power down the street on the way to our meeting. "Why are we meeting here, again?" I ask.

"He wanted to meet somewhere neutral. He has a table booked at Bryant Park Grill."

"That's odd—it's not a date," I huff.

"It's probably all part of his grand plan." She holds her hands up and does an air rainbow. "Neutral ground." She widens her eyes in jest. "While he tries to fuck us up the ass."

"With a smile on his face." I smirk. "I hope it at least feels good."

Marley giggles and then falls straight back into her coaching. "So remember the strategy," she instructs me as we walk.

"Yes."

"Tell me it again . . . so that I remember it," she replies.

I smile. Marley is an idiot. A funny idiot nonetheless. "Stay calm; don't let him ruffle my feathers," I reply. "Don't say an outright no—just keep him on ice in the background as an insurance policy."

"Yes, that's a great plan."

"It should be—you thought of it." We arrive at the restaurant and stop around the corner. I take out my compact and reapply my lipstick. My dark hair is twisted up into a loose knot. I'm wearing a navy pantsuit with a cream silk blouse, closed-toe high-heeled patent pumps, and my pearl earrings. Sensible clothes—I want him to take me seriously. "Do I look okay?" I ask.

"You look hot."

My face falls. "I don't want to look hot, Marley. I want to look hard."

She scowls as she falls into character. "Totally hard." She punches her hand with her fist. "Iron maiden snatch style."

I grin at my gorgeous friend; her bright-red zany hair is short and punky, and her pink cat-eye glasses are in full splendor. She's wearing a red dress with a bright-yellow shirt underneath with red stockings and shoes. She's so trendy that she's actually edgy. Marley is my best friend, my confidante, and the hardest worker in our company. She hasn't left my side for the last five years; her friendship is a gift, and I have no idea where I would be without her.

3

"Are you ready?" she asks.

"Yes. We're twenty minutes early—I wanted to get here first. Get the upper hand."

Her shoulders slump. "When I ask you if you're ready, you're supposed to answer with, 'I was born ready.'"

I push past her. "Let's get this over with."

We drop our shoulders, steel ourselves, and walk into the foyer. The waiter smiles. "Hello, ladies. How can I help you?"

"Ah." I glance at Marley. "We are meeting someone here."

"Tristan Miles?" he asks.

I frown. How did he know that? "Yes . . . actually."

"He has the private dining room booked upstairs." He gestures to the stairs.

"Of course he does," I mutter under my breath.

Marley curls her lip in disgust, and we make our way up. The top floor is empty. We look around, and I see a man out on the balcony on his phone. Perfectly fitted navy suit, crisp white shirt, tall and muscular. His hair is longer on top, dark brown with a curl. He looks like he belongs in a modeling shoot, not the snake pit at all.

"Holy fuck . . . he's hot," Marley whispers.

"Shut up," I stammer, in a panic that he will hear her. "Act fucking cool, will you?"

"I know." She hits me in the thigh, and I hit her back.

He turns toward us and flashes a broad smile and holds up a finger, gesturing he will be just a moment. I fake a smile; he turns his back to us to wrap up his call, and I glare at his back as my anger rises. How dare he make us wait. "Don't speak," I whisper.

"Can I whistle?" Marley whispers as she looks him up and down. "I totally want to wolf whistle the fuck out of this guy. Asshole or not."

I pinch the bridge of my nose—this is a disaster already. "Please, just don't speak," I remind her again.

"Okay, okay." She does a zip-her-lips-closed gesture.

He hangs up his call and walks toward us, confidence personified. Smiling broadly, he holds out his hand. "Hello, I'm Tristan Miles." He's all dimples and square jaw and white teeth and . . .

I shake his hand. It's strong and large, and I'm immediately made aware of his blazing sexuality. The buzz he gives me makes me take an involuntary step back. I don't want him to know that I find him attractive. "Hello, I'm Claire Anderson. Nice to meet you." I gesture to Marley. "This is Marley Smithson, my assistant."

"Hello, Marley." He smiles. "Nice to meet you." He gestures to the table. "Please take a seat."

I sit down with my heart in my throat—great. As if I wasn't ruffled already; he didn't have to be good looking as well.

"Coffee? Tea?" He gestures to the tray. "I took the liberty of ordering us morning tea."

"Coffee, please," I reply. "Just cream."

"Me too," Marley adds.

He carefully pours us our coffees and passes them over with a plate of cakes.

I clench my jaw to stop myself from saying something snarky, and finally, he takes a seat opposite us. He undoes his suit jacket with one hand and sits back in his chair. His eyes come to me. "It's nice to finally meet you, Claire. I've heard so much about you."

I raise my eyebrow in annoyance; I hate that his voice is husky and sexual. "Likewise," I reply.

I glance down and notice the black-onyx-and-gold cuff links and the fancy Rolex watch; everything about this guy screams money. His aftershave wafts between us. I try my hardest not to inhale—it's otherworldly. I glance over at Marley, who is smiling goofily as she stares at him . . . totally besotted.

Great.

He sits back, relaxed and confident, cool and calculating. "How has your week been?"

"Fine, thanks," I reply, my patience being tested. "Let's just cut to the chase, Mr. Miles, shall we?"

"Tristan," he corrects me.

"Tristan," I reply. "Why do you want to meet with me so badly? What could possibly warrant you calling me five times a week for the last month?"

He brushes his pointer finger over his big lips, as if amused, and his eyes hold mine. "I've been watching Anderson Media for some time now."

I raise my eyebrow again. "And do tell—what have you learned?"

"You are letting staff go every month."

"I'm downsizing."

"Not by choice."

Something about this man rubs me the wrong way.

"I'm not interested in what you're offering, Mr. Miles," I snap. I feel a sharp kick under the table to my ankle, and I wince in pain. *Ow* . . . that hurt. I glance at Marley. She widens her eyes in a shut-up-now signal.

"How do you know I want to make you an offer?" he replies calmly.

How many times has he had this conversation? "Don't you?"

"No." He sips his coffee. "I would like to buy your company, but I'm not offering a free pass."

"Free pass," I scoff.

Marley kicks me again . . . oh shit, that hurt. I throw her a dirty look, and she fakes a broad smile. "Happy, happy," she mouths.

"And what do you mean by a free pass, Mr. Miles?"

"Tristan," he corrects me.

"I'll call you whatever I want."

He gives me a slow, sexy smile, as if loving every minute of this. "I can see you're a passionate woman, Claire, and that's admirable . . . but come on. Let's be serious here."

I roll my lips, willing myself to stay silent.

"The last three years your company has run at a massive loss. You're losing advertising accounts left, right, and center." He steeples his hand on his temple as he stares at me. "I'm guessing the financials are a nightmare."

I swallow the lump in my throat as we stare at each other.

"I can take everything off your hands, and you can take a hard-earned break."

Anger begins to pump through my blood. "You would love that, wouldn't you? Play Mr. Nice Guy and take everything off my hands . . . come in on your horse and save the day like a white knight."

His eyes hold mine, and a trace of a smile crosses his face.

"I will hold on to my company if it's the last thing I do." I again feel a swift kick, and I jump, losing the last of my patience. "Stop kicking me, Marley," I splutter.

Tristan breaks into a broad smile as he looks between us. "Keep kicking her, Marley," he says. "Kick some sense into her."

I roll my eyes, embarrassed that my assistant is kicking the shit out of my ankles.

He sits forward, his purpose renewed. "Claire, let's get one thing straight. I always get what I want. And what I want is Anderson Media. I can take it now from you for a good price that will protect you. Or"—he shrugs casually—"I can wait for six months until the liquidators move in and get it for next to nothing, and you can face bankruptcy." He steeples his hands on the table in front of him. "We both know the end is near."

"You self-conceited prick," I whisper.

He tilts his chin to the sky and smiles proudly. "Nice guys come last, Claire."

My heart begins to beat faster as my anger builds.

"Think about it." He takes out his business card and slides it across the table.

TRISTAN MILES
212-555-4946

"I know this is not how you want to sell your company. But you need to be a realist," he continues.

I stare at him, sitting there all cold and heartless, and I feel my emotions bubbling dangerously close to the surface.

Our eyes are locked. "Take the offer, Claire. I'll email you a figure this afternoon. You will be taken care of."

My sanity rubber band snaps, and I sit forward. "And who will take care of my late husband's memory, Mr. Miles?" I sneer. "Miles Media sure as hell won't."

He twists his lips, uncomfortable for the first time.

"Do you know anything about me and my company?"

"I do."

"Then you'll know that this company was my husband's labor of love. He worked for ten years to build it up from the ground. His dream was to hand it down to his three sons."

His eyes hold mine.

"So . . . don't you fucking dare"—I slam my hand on the table as my eyes fill with tears—"sit there with that smug look on your face and threaten me. Because believe me . . . Mr. Miles, whatever you're dishing out isn't half as bad as losing him." I stand. "I've already been to hell and back, and I will not have some rich, spoiled bastard make me feel like shit."

He rolls his lips, unimpressed.

"Don't call me again," I snap as I push back my chair.

"Think about it, Claire."

"Go to hell." I begin to storm to the door.

"She's just having a bad day. We'll definitely think about it," Marley splutters in embarrassment. "Thanks for the cake—it was yummy."

I angrily wipe the tears from my face as I run down the stairs and out the front doors. I can't believe I was so unprofessional. Tears fill my eyes again. Oh well, at least I stood up to him, I guess.

Marley runs to keep up with me. She wisely stays silent and then looks up and down the street. "Oh, screw this, Claire—let's not go back to work. Let's go get drunk instead."

I stand at the window and stare over New York. My hands are in my suit pockets, and a strange feeling is burning a hole in my stomach.

Claire Anderson.

Beautiful, smart, and proud.

No matter how many times I've tried to wipe her out of my mind over the last three days since our meeting, I can't.

The way she looked, the way she smelled, the curve of her breasts through her silk shirt.

The fire in her eyes.

She is the most beautiful woman I've seen in a long time, and her heartfelt words are playing on repeat.

"So . . . don't you fucking dare sit there with that smug look on your face and threaten me. Because believe me . . . Mr. Miles, whatever you're dishing out isn't half as bad as losing him. I've already been to hell and back, and I will not have some rich, spoiled bastard make me feel like shit."

I take a seat at my desk and roll a pen beneath my fingers as I mentally go over what I need to say. I have to call her and follow up on our meeting, and I'm dreading it. I exhale heavily and dial her number. "Claire Anderson's office."

"Hello, Marley. It's Tristan Miles."

"Oh, hello, Tristan," she replies happily. "Are you after Claire?"

"Yes, I am. Is she available?"

"I'll put you straight through."

"Thank you."

I wait, and then she answers. "Hello, Claire speaking."

I close my eyes at the sound of her voice . . . sexy, husky . . . enticing.

"Hello, Claire. It's Tristan."

"Oh." She falls silent.

Fuck . . . Marley didn't tell her it was me.

An unfamiliar feeling begins to seep into my bones. "I just wanted to see if you were okay after our meeting. I'm sorry if I upset you." I screw up my face . . . *what are you doing? This is not in the plan.*

"My feelings are no concern of yours, Mr. Miles."

"Tristan," I correct her.

"How can I help you?" she snaps impatiently.

My mind goes blank . . .

"Tristan?" she prompts me.

"I wanted to see if you would like to have dinner with me on Saturday night." My eyes close in horror . . . what the fuck am I doing right now?

She stays silent for a moment and then replies in surprise, "You're asking me out on a date?"

I screw up my face. "I don't like the way we met. I would like to start again."

She chuckles in a condescending tone. "You have got to be kidding. I wouldn't go out with you if you were the last man on earth." Then she whispers, "Money and looks don't impress me, Mr. Miles."

I bite my bottom lip . . . *ouch.* "Our meeting was nothing personal, Claire."

"It was very personal to me. Go and find a bimbo to wine and dine, Tristan. I have no interest in dating a cold, soul-sucking bastard like you." The phone clicks as she hangs up.

I stare at the phone in my hand. Adrenaline is pumping through my system at her fighting words.

I don't know whether I'm shocked or impressed.

Perhaps a bit of both.

I've never been rejected before and definitely never been spoken to like that.

I turn to my computer and type into Google: *Who is Claire Anderson?*

Chapter 2

Six months later

I read the invitation in front of me.

Master Your Mind.

Oh God, what a crock of crap.

I need to get out of this—I honestly can't think of anything worse.

"I think this is going to be great for you," Marley says.

I look up to my trusty best friend as she does her best sales pitch, trying to push me out of my comfort zone. I know her heart is in the right place, but this is just going too far. "Marley, I can tell you straight up, right now, that if you think a motivational conference with all those crazies is going to help me, you are more insane than I ever realized."

"Stop it; it's gonna be fantastic. You go away, regroup, and refocus, and you'll come back refreshed, and the company and your life and everything else is all going to fall into place."

I roll my eyes.

"Come on—can we at least agree that you need to change your mind-set?" she asks me as she sits on my desk.

"Possibly." I sigh, dejected.

"And it's not your fault you're flat. You've been through so much: your husband's unexpected death, caring for three boys, and struggling to keep the company afloat. It's been hell. And realistically you've been fighting since Wade's death five years ago."

"Do you have to say it out loud? Sounds even more depressing." I sigh again.

A knock sounds at my office door.

"Come in," I call.

The door opens, and Gabriel smiles broadly. "Ready for lunch, Missy?" His eyes flick to Marley. "Hey, Marls."

"Hi." She smiles goofily.

I smile as well. "Mr. Ferrara." I glance at my watch. "You're early. Lunch isn't for an hour. I thought you said two?"

"My meeting finished early, and I'm hungry. Let's go now."

I look over at the gorgeous Italian, tall, dark, and handsome in his designer suit. Gabriel Ferrara is a rock star in New York, but to me he is just a dear friend. He knew my late husband, and although I never met him when Wade was alive, he got in contact with me not long after his death. He owns one of the largest media companies in the world, and his building isn't far from here. He gives me advice here and there, and we catch up for lunch when we can. It's completely platonic between us—he's a rock that I lean on from time to time.

"Gabe, tell Claire that she needs to go to this conference." Marley sighs in exasperation.

He frowns as he looks between us. "All right . . . Claire, you need to go to this conference," he repeats unenthusiastically. "Now let's eat. Sushi awaits."

Marley's eyes find mine. "Can you just have a week off and go to Paris? Take some time for yourself. Get away from the kids. I can look after everything back here at the office. We had that cash injection—things are okay around here for the moment. Use the time to recharge."

I exhale heavily. I know I need to pull myself out of this funk. My life is so dull; I've lost enthusiasm for everything. My life that was once wild and carefree has been replaced with animosity. Sometimes I'm so furious at Wade for leaving me with this mess that I tell him off in my head, as if he can hear me, and then afterward, I feel so guilty because I know he would have given anything to see his sons grow up and that leaving me would have never been his choice.

Life just isn't fair sometimes.

They say that only the good die young—what about the best? Why did he have to go too?

"Go to the conference," Marley urges me. "You are not going to lunch until you agree to this."

"Hurry up, woman. Yes. It's agreed; she's going." Gabriel tries to finish the conversation. When I don't move, he exhales heavily and falls onto the couch.

"You know I don't know how to do the motivational mumbo jumbo." I stand and begin to pack files away. "The crap that they go on with is next-level batshit crazy."

"I think you need some batshit crazy, because batshit broke isn't a fun place to visit." Marley sighs again.

I smirk.

"This is true." Gabriel smiles as he scrolls through his phone.

I continue putting things away. This *is* true. Batshit broke is not somewhere I want to visit at all. I sit back in my chair and stare at my hopeful friend.

"Go, recharge. It's in Épernay in the Champagne district of France, for fuck's sake. It doesn't get any more beautiful than this, Claire. It's a tax deduction; you either pay for this or pay it in taxes—the choice is yours. At the very least, you can get a massage every afternoon and then drink two liters of champagne every night with your gourmet dinner and fall into bed in a blissful stupor."

"Épernay is beautiful," Gabriel mutters, distracted. "I would go just for the location."

"You've been there?" I ask him.

"A few times. I went with Sophia last summer," he replies. "She loves it there."

I imagine myself alone in a luxurious hotel room. It's been so long since I've gotten away. Five years, actually. "Now, a gourmet dinner and champagne . . . that *is* tempting."

"If the conference part of the trip is boring, just ditch it, and have a week to yourself in France. You need this break," Marley says.

Gabriel stands. "Agreed. You're going. Hurry up; I'm ravenous."

I exhale heavily.

"Will you just go for me?" Marley takes my hand in hers. "Please." She smiles sweetly and bats her eyelashes as she tries to be cute.

Oh God, she's not going to let this go. "Fine." I sigh. "I'll go."

She bounces off my desk and claps her hands in excitement. "Yes, this is going to be so good for you, Claire—just what you need." She rushes toward the door. "I'm going to book flights now before you change your mind."

I roll my eyes as I pick up my handbag. "I'm already dreading it."

"Eep, I'm so excited." She flaps her hands around and rushes out of the office.

"We going?" Gabriel asks.

"Yeah. I'm not feeling sushi, though."

"Fine." He holds his hand toward the door. "You choose, but make it fast. I'm about to faint."

"Okay. Let's go over the details," Marley says as she sips her drink.

I nod as I take a bite of food. We are in a restaurant having lunch. It's the day before I leave for my conference. "Your bags are packed."

Marley gets out her diary and begins to read from her list. "Uh-huh."

She ticks the first checkbox on her list. "Hair done—tick." She continues going through her list. "Appointments cleared," she mumbles to herself as she reads through her list.

I keep eating my lunch, totally unexcited about the next week.

"Oh." She frowns and looks up at me. "Did you get laser?"

I roll my eyes.

"There are a lot of hot opportunities at these kinds of conferences, Claire."

"Are you kidding me?" I stare at her deadpan. "You want me to go to this conference so I can get laid?"

"Well." She shrugs. "Why not?"

"Marley." I drop my knife and fork with a clang. "Sex is the very last thing I want. I still feel very married to one man."

Her face falls, and she puts her pen and paper down. "But you're not, Claire." She takes my hand over the table. "Wade died, honey. Five years ago now . . . and I know for a fact that he wouldn't want you living alone forever."

My eyes drop to the plate of food in front of me.

"He would want you to be living life to the fullest . . . for both of you."

I feel a lump in my throat begin to build.

"He would want you to be happy and cared for . . . loved."

I twist my fingers together on my lap. "I just . . ." My voice trails off.

"You just what?"

"I just don't think I'll ever move on, Marl," I say sadly. "How could any man ever live up to Wade Anderson?"

"Nobody will ever replace him, Claire. He's your husband." She smiles softly. "I'm just saying go on a few dates. Have some fun . . . that's all."

"Maybe," I lie.

"You need to take your wedding rings off and put them on the other hand."

Tears instantly threaten at the very thought.

"No men are coming near you because they think you're married."

"I'm happy with that."

"Wade's not. And when he finds someone that he thinks is worthy of you, he will send him. But you need to be ready."

I stare at my beautiful friend through tears.

"He's still with you. He will always be with you. Trust him to watch over you. You need to let him go, Claire."

My eyes hold hers.

"You didn't die in the accident with him. Live while you can."

I drop my head and stare at my plate on the table, my appetite suddenly diminished.

"I'm going to book you for some laser this afternoon."

I pick up my knife and fork once more. "They're going to need a machete. I've been rocking the full-bush vibe."

She giggles. "Yeah, that mess has got to go."

I pull my car up and stare at the house in front of me.

Our house.

The one that Wade and I built together—the one we planned on getting old in.

Our small patch of paradise on Long Island. Wade was adamant that his children grow up in a semirural area. He grew up in New York City himself, and all he ever wanted for his children was a large patch of land for them to play freely on whenever they wanted.

We bought a block of land and built our home. It's not flashy and fancy. It's made of weatherboard and has a large veranda around the edge, a big garage, and a driveway with a basketball hoop. Four bedrooms, two living areas, and a big rustic kitchen.

It's so Wade. At the time we could have afforded much better, but when it came down to it, he wanted a country home filled with laughter and children.

And that's what we had.

My mind goes back to that early morning when the police knocked on my door.

"Are you Mrs. Claire Anderson?"

"Yes."

"I'm so sorry; there's been an accident."

The hours that followed were monumental and painful. They are so clear in my mind—the way I felt, the words I said, what I was wearing.

The way my heart was breaking.

I get a vision of myself crying over him in the morgue and whispering to his lifeless body, offering him an eternal promise as I brushed the hair back from his face.

"I'll raise our children as you wanted. I'll carry on what we started. I'll keep all your dreams alive . . . you have my word. I love you, my darling."

My face screws up in tears, and I snap my thoughts back to the present. It doesn't do me any good letting that memory linger. If I let myself go back there, it's like I lose him all over again.

The pain never goes away, but some days it feels like it might just kill me. I'm an empty shell. My body functions as it should, but I'm barely breathing.

I'm suffocating in a world of responsibilities.

The promises I made my husband in the hours after his death have come at a heavy cost.

I don't go out at night, I don't socialize anymore, I work my fingers to the bone . . . both at home and in the office.

Devoted to keeping Wade's dreams alive, to keeping his children loved and protected. To keeping his company afloat. It's hard, and it's lonely, and damn it, I just wish he'd walk through the fucking door and save me.

Marley's words from earlier today run through my mind.

"He's still with you. He will always be with you. Trust him to watch over you. You need to let him go, Claire."

In the pit of my stomach, I know she's right. Like a song hanging in the wind, her words are lingering with me. Chipping away at my sensibility.

I stare into space as an empty sadness surrounds me . . . he's not coming back.

He's never coming back.

It's time; I know it's time.

That doesn't make it any less painful.

I couldn't imagine living without him. I don't know how I'm doing it.

I don't want to have to learn to.

I stare down at my wedding rings and grip them with my fingers as I prepare myself to do the unthinkable.

I blink through the tears; a suffocating weight is on my chest, and I slowly pull them off. They catch on my knuckle, and finally they slide free.

I close my hand into a fist. It feels light without the weight of my rings, and I stare down at the white band left on my bare finger. The sun's reminder of what I have lost.

I hate my hand without his ring.

I hate my life without his love.

Overwhelmed with emotion, I put my head down onto the steering wheel . . . and for the first time in a long time, I allow myself to cry.

I throw the last pair of shoes into my suitcase. I leave tomorrow for the conference. "I think that's it."

"Did you get your toothbrush?" Patrick asks as he lies on his stomach on my bed, beside my suitcase. My youngest child is also my wisest. He never forgets a thing. "Not yet. I still have to use it. I'll pack it in the morning."

"Okay."

"So Grandma will be here when you get home from school," I remind him.

"Yes, yes, I know," he says with an eye roll. "And I have to call you the moment Harry's naughty or if Fletcher gets short tempered." He sighs as he recites my orders.

"Yes, that's right." Little do his brothers know, but Patrick is also my tattletale. I know what his brothers have done before they even finish doing it.

I have three sons. Fletcher is seventeen and has taken on the unofficial job as my personal bodyguard. Harry is thirteen, and I swear to God he's either going to end up a Nobel Prize–winning genius or in jail. He is the most mischievous human being I know, always getting into some kind of trouble—mostly at school.

And then there's my baby, Patrick, just nine years old. He's sweet and gentle and sensible and everything his brothers are not.

He's also my biggest worry. He was only four when his father died, and he missed out the most.

He doesn't even remember his dad.

He has photos of him strewed all over his room. He hero-worships him. I mean, we all do. But Patrick's obsession is almost over the top. He asks me to tell him a story about his father at least twice a day. He smiles and listens intently as I relay past events and tell him stories about Wade. He knows all of Wade's favorite meals at restaurants and then always wants to order the same. He sleeps in one of his dad's old T-shirts. I do this too, but I would never let on that I do.

To be honest, I kind of dread story time. We all laugh and make jokes over the memory. Then the children go to bed and fall into a blissful slumber, and my mind goes over the scene time after time.

Wishing we could do it all over again.

Wade still lives here with us, just not in flesh and blood.

He's dead enough that I'm lonely . . . but alive enough that I can't fathom moving on.

I'm stuck in the middle, halfway between heaven and hell.

Madly in love with my husband's ghost.

"Okay, read out my list," I continue.

"Bus . . ." Patrick frowns as he reads. "Bus-in-ess."

"Business clothes."

"Yes." He smiles proudly that he nearly got it.

I mess up his dark hair that is curling up at the ends. "Check."

He ticks the word. "Cas . . ." He frowns, as if stuck.

"Casual clothes?" I ask.

He nods.

"Check."

"Pj's." He hunches his shoulders in excitement. "I knew that one."

"I know—look at you all growing up and reading." Patrick has dyslexia, and reading is hard for him, but we're getting there. I check the suitcase. "Got them."

He ticks and then goes to the next item on the list. "Shoes?"

"Check."

"Ha . . . ha . . ." He frowns, deep in concentration.

"Hair dryer?"

"Yes."

"Got it."

"Dresses."

I puff air into my cheeks and look in my wardrobe. "Hmm, what dresses do I have?" I flick through my clothes on the hangers. "I only have going-out kinds of dresses. These aren't really work-conference outfits. Hmm . . ." I pull out a black one and hold it up against my body and look in the mirror.

"That's a pretty dress. Where did you wear that with Dad?"

"Well." I frown. I have no idea, but I have to make something up like I always do. "Um, we went for pizza, and then we went dancing."

He smiles goofily, and I know he's imagining what I've just told him. "What kind of pizza did you eat?"

"Pepperoni."

His eyes widen. "Can we have pizza tonight?"

"If you want."

"Yes." He punches the air. "We can have pizza tonight," he screams to his brothers as he runs from the room. "I'm having pepperoni, like Dad."

I smile sadly. He would be sorely disappointed if he knew Wade would have had extra-chili-and-anchovy pizza, but I'll let him have his pepperoni pizza with a huge smile on his face.

I take a few of the dresses and throw them into my suitcase; they'll have to do. I don't have time to buy anything else.

I stare down at my packed suitcase and put my hands on my hips. "Okay, I think that's it. Conference, here I come."

The car pulls into the grand entrance of the Château de Makua. "Wow," I whisper as I peer out the window. I've flown almost eight hours, and then my driver picked me up, and it took us another three hours to drive here. I'm dead tired after my early start but suddenly filled with nerves.

The driver takes my suitcase from the trunk, and I tip him and stare up at the big building in front of me.

MIND MASTERS

Even the name of this conference is ridiculous. I wheel my suitcase in and wait in the line at reception.

The building is lovely, old fashioned, and otherworldly. It's luxurious and opulent and feels like I have stepped back in time. The foyer is grand, and a huge circular staircase is the center feature.

"Next?" the concierge asks as everyone shuffles forward. I look around at the people in front of me in the line. I wonder if they are attending the conference.

There are two girls who look like Barbie dolls. Huge silicone lips—and how do they think those ridiculous huge eyelashes look good? Don't their eyes hurt with something that heavy on their lids like that?

One has waist-length bleached-blonde hair with extensions that you can see at the roots. Ugh . . . so tacky. The other one has a dark, curly, thick mane. They're both wearing next to nothing and are done up to the nines. I tighten my ponytail and pull down my linen shirt, feeling extraordinarily uncool. Damn it, I should have worn something a bit swankier.

The blonde notices me standing behind her. "Oh, hi. Are you attending Mind Masters?"

"Yes." I give an awkward smile. "Are you?"

"Yes," she shrieks. "Oh my God, I'm so excited. I'm Ellie. What do you do?"

"Um." I shrug, suddenly feeling very self-conscious. "I'm Claire. I work for a company."

"I'm running my own empire," Ellie says as she widens her eyes in excitement.

"Empire," I repeat, amused. "In what?" I ask.

"I'm an influencer."

I stare at her as my brain tries to keep up. Oh God no . . . one of those twits who gets paid for posting fake crap. "Really? Great."

"I travel the world and model bikinis." She smiles. "If I post an image of myself, the world goes into meltdown."

I bite my bottom lip to hide my smile. Is she for real? "I . . . bet they do."

The dark-haired girl in front of her turns toward us and laughs. "Snap, girlfriend."

"Oh my God . . . you too?" Ellie gasps.

They both burst into laughter. "I'm Angel," the dark-haired girl introduces herself. "I'm going to be an influencer too."

"You haven't started yet?" Ellie asks in a condescending tone.

"Well." Angel shrugs. "Not technically. I still have a few movies left on my contract, but as soon as I finish those, I'm totally into it—all systems go."

"Movies?" Ellie gasps. "What kind of movies?"

"I'm a porn actress. You may have seen my latest, *Anal Mistress with Johnny Rocket Cock.*"

Ellie's eyes widen, "Oh. My. God." She gasps. "I totally recognize you." They begin to laugh and bounce on the spot in excitement.

Oh hell.

I wonder what Johnny Rocket Cock does to her ass.

Or what anyone does to anyone's ass, actually. It's been so long since I've been touched that I've completely forgotten everything, and even when I was, it was never hard-and-fast porn-style sex. It was loving and tender. The kind of sex that married people have.

Safe and real, a world away from being an anal mistress.

What the actual fuck has Marley gotten me into here?

I turn toward the man behind me. Has he heard any of this?

"Hi." He smiles.

"Hello."

He's blond and normal looking. He seems nice. "Are you here for the conference?" he asks.

"Yes."

"Me too." He holds out his hand to shake mine. "I'm Nelson Barrett."

"I'm Claire Anderson." I smile.

"I'm a computer scientist." He looks around at our surroundings. "I'm so out of my comfort zone here it's not even funny."

"Me too." Relief fills me. Someone normal. "I work in media."

"Lovely to meet you, Claire."

"You too."

We both turn to the front and watch the antics of the girls. They are loud and animated and so excited to be here. I smile as I watch them; their enthusiasm is childlike and lovely to watch.

I make an idle observation that enthusiasm like that seems to dissipate around the age of twenty-eight. I predict they have five good years left before life begins to really fuck them up the ass. Relationship breakdowns and debt—that's if they can find a decent person to fall in love with.

I shake my head in disgust.

Look at me being a downer . . . maybe I really do need to be here.

I've never been a negative person before. I hate this part of my personality that has surfaced in recent times.

I don't even know myself anymore.

The line moves forward, and people begin to pile into the foyer behind us. Men and women, all excited entrepreneurs. Apart from Nelson, I think I'm the oldest here.

"Oh my God, we have to go out tonight," Angel says.

"Yes," Ellie says as she jumps up and down. "Oh my God, I'm so pumped." She turns to me and Nelson. "Clara, you have to come out tonight." I smile at her botching my name.

"I couldn't keep up tonight." I smile. "Next time, for sure."

"Okay." She turns back to Angel. "Where will we go?"

I turn and force a smile at Nelson.

"I wonder how many films they make tonight for free," he whispers.

I giggle. "I know. Lucky boys. They might not survive it."

"I know for certain that I wouldn't," Nelson mutters under his breath.

We both chuckle and shuffle up the line, and Ellie begins to check in.

Another four men walk in behind me, all older and quite distinguished looking.

Hmm, maybe this is okay after all.

We all chat in the line for a while. Turns out the guys behind us who just arrived are app developers. I don't feel so silly now. Normal people seem to be here too.

A woman walks in, and all the men's heads turn. She's blonde and beautiful. Stylish and trendy and aged around late twenties, at a guess. "Hello, is this the line to check in?" she asks me.

"Yes." I smile.

"Are you here for the conference?" she asks.

"Uh-huh."

"Me too." She holds her hand out to shake mine. "I'm Melissa."

"Hi, Melissa. I'm Claire."

"Nice to meet you."

The line shuffles forward again, and then another two staff members come to reception, so we all veer into different lines.

Nelson comes up behind me. "See you later. We're having dinner in the restaurant downstairs at seven if you want to come, Claire."

"Oh." I turn to him, startled. "Thank you, but I have work to do. I'll see you tomorrow?" I ask.

"Yes, for sure." He smiles. "Have a good night."

I turn back to the concierge with a smile. I feel more comfortable than I thought I would. I think this may actually be okay.

I sit in the swanky conference room with 120 other people. The room is abuzz with electricity. They're all chattering and have their notepads and other papers with them.

Everyone here is so pumped to try to better themselves.

Me . . . well, I'm just here for the champagne and to have an excuse to take a holiday by myself. But anyway, yay for the pumped ones, I guess.

A man comes onto the stage, and everyone claps and cheers. He holds his hands out and smiles broadly. Hmm . . . I wonder who he is.

He waits for the cheering to die down, and he smiles broadly again. "Welcome," he says. He has a small microphone attached to his shirt. "Welcome to Mind Masters. A place where you will find a better version of yourself." His voice is loud and echoing, as if he's giving a sermon or something. "Are you ready?" he cries.

Everyone cheers.

Oh God . . . so over the top. I clap along with the room as they all lose their shit. They are all standing and laughing as they clap. I frown as I look around at them . . . honestly, calm down, everyone.

This is like a fucking cult.

I glance down at my phone as I contemplate filming this shit for Marley. Even she wouldn't believe it.

"And now, I would like to introduce our opening speaker. Someone that I know a lot of you follow on the circuit. A rock star in the motivational-speaking circuit and the developer of workshops that are changing the lives of people from all walks of life. He's here for one day only, so please, without further ado—with his cutting-edge strategy, *How to get what you want*—welcome to the stage Tristan Miles."

The air leaves my lungs as the crowd goes wild.

Tristan Miles walks out in a navy designer suit and his just-fucked dark wavy hair. He smiles broadly, holds his hands in the air, claps with the audience, and then takes a bow. Everyone is going crazy and yelling and clapping.

My eyes nearly bulge from their sockets . . . *what the fuck?*

I begin to hear my heartbeat in my ears as everyone else in the room disappears.

My fury begins to pump. I can't even stand the sight of him—well, that's not completely true. Damn asshole is a double-edged sword: gorgeous to look at, impossible to tolerate.

"Hello, everyone," he says in the same echoing voice. "Congratulations." He smiles as he waits for silence. Goose bumps scatter across my skin at the sound of his deep voice. He has a slight twang of an accent, a little upper-crust English mixed in with New Yorker. He sounds distinguished and intelligent—I don't know, but whatever it is, it's sexy as fuck.

Ugh . . . I hate everything about him.

29

"Welcome, and thank you for coming. You have taken a very valuable step in your personal development." He looks around the room at everyone as he speaks. "I, for one . . ." Our eyes meet, and he stops speaking as he stares at me and then blinks.

Fuck.

He quickly recovers. "I, for one, am excited for you."

He keeps talking, but I can't hear him. I can only hear adrenaline screaming through the rapids that are my bloodstream. Last time we spoke, he was intent on stealing Wade's company from my sons.

I'm not sitting here and listening to this vile bloodsucker give a motivational speech.

He ruins family businesses for fun.

How pathetic.

Of course he's presenting at a conference called Mind Masters. This is right up his pretentious alley. He thinks he *is* the mind master . . . *what a joke.*

I stand. "Excuse me," I whisper to the person next to me. I begin to shuffle past the people in my row as they sit in their seats.

"Claire Anderson," he calls from the stage.

My horrified eyes meet his.

"Sit back down."

"I . . ." I take another step toward the exit.

"Claire," he warns.

I glance around at the 120 pairs of eyes fixed firmly on me and then back up at him.

"I said sit. Back. Down."

Chapter 3

Fuck.

I fake a smile.

Who in the hell does this asshole think he is?

"I said sit. Back. Down."

Well, I say go fuck yourself, you giant condescending twat. I raise an eyebrow as he glares at me, and I smile sweetly. Then, with deliberation, I walk toward the door.

He narrows his eyes and then recovers and goes back to his speech. "As I was saying," he continues.

I go into the corridor that leads out of the room, just out of his sight, and listen to his speech.

For ten minutes, I fume in silence, unable to concentrate on anything he's saying.

Just the sight of this man brings out a temper in me that I never even knew I had.

I peek around the corner and watch him walk back and forth on the stage. His voice is deep and commanding. One hand is in the pocket of his expensive suit trouser pocket; the other he moves around in the air with animation as he talks.

He's handsome and has this powerful edge to his personality.

He's comfortable taking center stage; in fact, he's probably comfortable on every stage.

The crowd is silent as they all hang on his every word. They take notes and laugh on cue. The women all look up at him in awe, wanting him, and the men all want to be him.

Me . . . I just want to punch him in his pretty-boy face.

I hate that everything comes easy for him. He was born into this entitled family. Wealthy beyond measure and charismatic as all hell. It's just not fair that he is ridiculously handsome to add to the mix.

I get a vision of him and the girls he must have falling at his feet. He must be a real player—probably has five girls on the go at a time.

I go over our last conversation that we had over the phone.

"I wanted to see if you would like to have dinner with me on Saturday night," he asked.

"You're asking me out on a date?"

"I don't like the way we met. I would like to start again."

"You have got to be kidding. I wouldn't go out with you if you were the last man on earth. Money and looks don't impress me, Mr. Miles."

"Our meeting was nothing personal, Claire."

"It was very personal to me. Go and find a bimbo to wine and dine, Tristan. I have no interest in dating a cold, soul-sucking bastard like you."

That was so cool.

I find myself smiling goofily into space. He asked me out. Tristan Miles asked me out, and I know it was just so that he could try to schmooze his way under my radar, but damn it felt good knocking him back.

"Claire Anderson." I hear a voice from the stage.

Huh?

I look up to the stage in horror. Wait . . . did he ask me something?

How can he see me?

He's moved and is now on another stage and in my line of sight. Shit.

He holds his hand in the air, palm up. "Please share."

"I beg your pardon." I frown. "I didn't hear the question."

A trace of a smile crosses his face as his eyes hold mine.

"I asked everyone to recall a time when they felt satisfied. A time when they were really proud of themselves."

"Oh." My eyes widen.

"And, judging by your grin, I'm assuming you recalled something amazing."

I stare at him.

"Please." He rolls his hand out in an overexerted way. "Let us share in your pride."

Asshole.

I glare at him. Is he for real?

He puts both hands into his suit pockets and begins to pace. "We're waiting, Claire," he says in a condescending tone. I feel my underarms heat with perspiration as everyone in the room waits for my answer. Holy shit, this man is infuriating.

"The last time I felt really satisfied was when I refused a date with a cold, soul-sucking bastard. Even if he was the last man on earth," I announce.

Our eyes lock, and he raises an eyebrow.

Game on, asshole . . . don't fuck with me.

"Ah . . . but, Claire, how sad that the best thing you recall about your own life experiences is one that revolved around another. I think that says a lot more about you than it does him. I want a real answer this afternoon. Reflect on it until then."

He smiles out at the audience, completely unfazed.

I step back, infuriated. What in the actual fuck does he think I'm going to learn from reflecting on what kind of person I am? I know who I am, and I'm completely happy with her.

Jerkoff.

This conference is just so typically him.

"And besides." He gives me a slow, sexy smile as he continues to pace back and forth across the stage. "You'll probably be begging that soul-sucking bastard to ask you back out one day . . . not that he ever would."

The crowd laughs, and he moves on to his next victim. "You, the girl with the long blonde hair. What is your proudest memory? And I want you to really dig deep on the answer."

I feel my blood pressure rise. Perspiration begins to bead on my forehead, and I want to march down and kick Mr. Fancy Pants straight up the ass and knock him off the stage.

Damn him . . . can I not have one fucking week away from life and forget who I am?

Why the hell is he here?

Over the next hour, Tristan Miles holds the audience captive, and I stare into space as I imagine myself torturing him to a grizzly death.

I should have stayed in my seat. Not only do I have to listen to his crap—I now have to stand up for it. I'll just look stupid if I walk out now.

Wind it up already.

He's only here today, and then he goes back to New York, I remind myself. I'm so annoyed with myself that I gave him the satisfaction of saying he wouldn't ask me out again anyway.

How uncool can a person be?

God, he's probably happily married by now . . . to a super-model or an Instagrammer.

Ugh, I hate this guy. He turns me into an idiot.

"There will be a short recess now. Morning tea is catered in the lounge, and then we will go into our goal workshops. We set our goals on the first day and then again on day five to see how much you've grown." He looks at his watch. "See you in the Boronia Room in half an hour from now."

I exhale heavily and make my way down to the lounge for morning tea. Everyone is chatting and happy. I make myself a coffee, grab a slice of chocolate cake, and then stand in the corner and take out my phone. I google *massage parlors in this area.*

Screw this; I'm out of here.

My only goal for today is to get a massage and drink two liters of champagne.

I sip my coffee and click on the list that comes up.

Tristan walks into the room, and all heads turn. He has this powerful aura that surrounds him; you can't help but look his way. His dark-brown hair is short on the back and sides, with a bit of length to it on the top. It has that perfect just-fucked look.

His posture is straight, and his jaw is square and strong. He has the biggest brown eyes I have ever seen. His eyes find mine across the room, and he holds me to attention. His stare is potent; I can feel the heat of it on my skin. Electricity bounces between us, and I snap my eyes away angrily.

Damn him for being good looking.

"Hello." A male voice comes from beside me. "Mind if I join you?"

Oh, it's the man I met at reception yesterday. What was his name again? "Not at all." I smile. "Please."

"I'm Nelson. We met yesterday."

"Yes. I remember. Hi, Nelson. I'm Claire."

"Yes, of course. I'll say." He chuckles. "Mr. Miles picked on you a bit in there."

"Oh." I sip my coffee, wishing the earth would swallow me up whole. "Did he? I didn't notice." I try to act casual.

"I mean, I'm not one to openly fawn over someone, but," he gushes, "have you read his portfolio?"

"No." I sip my coffee and glance up, straight into the gaze of Tristan. Our eyes lock for a few seconds, and then one of the five women clambering around him says something, pulling his gaze from me, and I snap my eyes away.

"He's got six degrees and speaks five languages," Nelson continues. "Has an IQ of one hundred and seventy. That's even higher than a genius; that's like a mentalist." He nods, as if he is relaying some life-changing information.

"Wow." I fake a smile.

Oh please, give me a break. I widen my eyes . . . big fucking deal. Go away, Nelson; you're annoying, and I want to google massages. I've got better things to do than talk about mental smart assholes.

Get drunk, for one.

"I'm not actually feeling well," I lie.

"Oh really?" Nelson's face falls. "Are you okay?"

"I have a migraine."

"Oh no."

"Yes, I always get them when I fly. It's so annoying. I'll be fine, but I might have to lie down, so if I go missing this afternoon, you'll know where I am. I'll be fine tomorrow."

"Of course, yes." He thinks for a moment. "I'll let them know."

Three hours later, the strong hands go up the center of my spine and then slowly slide down around my naked hips.

The room is darkened, the relaxing music has a deep sensual beat, and the smell of the masseur's aftershave is doing things to my lady parts.

Pierre's hands slide up my back. He drizzles hot oil, and it gives me a thrill as I close my eyes.

Now . . . this . . . is more like it.

"Is this all right?" he asks in his strong French accent.

"Perfect," I breathe.

Oh man, this is more than perfect; this is spectacular. I'm doing this every day.

Screw the conference.

His hands roam down my back, and I smile into the table.

My phone rings in my bag. It's loud and would be annoying to people in the other rooms. "Oh, sorry." I wince. "It will stop in a minute."

It rings all the way out and then starts to ring again. Shit. "Sorry." We wait for it to stop, and it starts again. Damn it, what if something's wrong back home? "I'm sorry; can you pass me my bag, please?"

He picks up my bag and passes it to me, and I dig around for my phone. I don't recognize the number. "Hello." I lie back down.

"Where are you?" Tristan barks. "You are missing the workshops."

Oh shit. "Umm . . ."

"And don't even think about lying to me, Claire. I know you're not in your hotel room."

I frown at his tone. Who the fuck does this guy think he is? "Excuse me?"

"Where are you?" he sneers.

"I'm getting a massage, actually."

"What?" he gasps.

"Your lecture was intolerable and completely boring. I have better things to do. Goodbye, Mr. Miles."

"Claire Anderson," he begins to scold me, and I press "End Call." I turn my phone on silent and throw it onto the chair in the corner. "Sorry about that. Where were we?"

Pierre's strong hands go down over my ribs and then lower to my hip bones, and I feel a twinge of arousal sweep through me.

I smile with my eyes closed. Hmm . . . it really is fun being a bitch.

Pierre's hands roam over my stomach.

Now *this* . . . is relaxing.

I stand near the bar with my drink in hand. "So then I got another fifty thousand followers from that boost alone," Saba says.

"Wow, that's fantastic," Melanie replies.

I'm standing with four beautiful women, but I'm bored as hell. I fly out first thing in the morning.

My eyes scan the room. *Where is she?*

"So, Mr. Miles, are you married?"

My eyes snap back to the blonde in front of me. "Please, call me Tristan. And no, not married."

"A girlfriend, perhaps?" Saba asks.

"No." I sip my drink. "Very single."

"Really?" Saba says in a sexy voice. "Me too. Talk about great timing."

I fake a smile. "It's always a great time to be single, isn't it?"

The girls all laugh on cue, and I look around the room. If she doesn't come tonight, I'm going to be pissed.

"I just broke off my engagement," Melanie replies.

I look her over. She's blonde and beautiful—my usual type—and I make myself nod as I act interested.

"I just really want to focus on my goals right now, and my ex just wasn't moving in the right circles—you know what I mean? He wanted a house in the suburbs with three kids, and I want more from life than that," she continues. "I want a global empire."

"Oh, totally," the girls all agree.

"I had that too with my ex. Why don't they get it?" one of the other girls says.

Oh fuck . . . get me out of here.

I wave at a colleague. "I'm going to see my friend." I turn to walk off.

"Tristan," Saba calls.

I turn back to her.

"Maybe we could do some revision of the notes I took today." She smiles sexily. "Later, in my room."

"Ahh . . ." I look between the women.

"I mean . . ." She shrugs. "We could all go over our notes together." She pulls her fingers through her hair. "The four of us girls and you. Like a group thing." The girls all smile sexily.

"Could make for a great night," Melanie whispers.

"I have no doubt." I smirk as I look among them. "Let's see how the night goes, shall we?"

I turn and walk over to one of the other lecturers as I hear them giggle behind me. "Hey," Elouise says.

"Hi." I sip my drink.

"Let me guess; they're all throwing themselves at you?"

"No." I keep a straight face. "What makes you say that?"

"Because I've never seen a man so hit on in my life." She grins wryly. "The women you attract are shameless."

I chuckle into my drink. Elouise is a psychologist, perhaps fifty to fifty-five years old. She's at a lot of conferences I go to, as she does the personality-trait testing. She sees a lot on the circuit. "Trust me, Elouise; it gets very boring after a while." I glance around again and see Claire in the corner, talking with a group of men.

She's here.

I watch her as she talks.

Her shoulder-length dark hair is full, and she's wearing a black dress. It's not showy or sexy. She's understated. Sensible and undeniably alluring. So very different from the women I'm used to. My eyes roam up and down her body. She's older than me, but I'm not sure by how much. Maybe a couple of years?

Elouise and I continue to talk, but my eyes stay fixed on Claire Anderson across the room. She's talking and laughing with a man.

Who is he?

Hmm . . .

I'm going to go and talk to her. "Back in a moment," I say as I head off in her direction. Just as I approach her, someone calls me.

"Mr. Miles."

I turn and see an attractive blonde. She already hit on me at lunch. "Oh, hello," I reply, feeling uncomfortable being in earshot of Claire.

"Melissa," she says. "We met at lunch."

"Yes, I remember, Melissa." I smile.

The man who was standing with Claire walks to the bar, and she glances up, clearly hearing the woman and me.

"What are you doing later?" she asks. "Can we meet up for a drink?"

Claire rolls her eyes and turns her back to us.

Fuck . . .

"No, I don't mix business and pleasure." I fake a smile and keep walking to Claire. "Hello."

She looks up at me deadpan, having heard what was just said. "Hi." She sips her drink, unimpressed, and turns her gaze straight ahead.

"How was your massage?" I ask.

"Great." She sips her drink.

God . . . she's so rude.

"Are you going to look at me while I speak to you?" I ask.

Her eyes rise to meet mine, and my stomach unexpectedly flutters. "What do you want, Mr. Miles?"

I stare at her, confused as to what my stomach is doing. "Tristan. Call me Tristan."

"No," she replies flatly. "Calling you Tristan would mean that I want to be on a first-name basis with you." Her tongue swipes over her bottom lip, and I feel it in my crotch. "And I don't."

"Claire."

"Call me Mrs. Anderson."

"Why are you being so rude?"

"I'm not being rude; I'm being honest. Would you prefer that I lie?"

Well . . . blow me down.

"Maybe," I reply.

"It's so lovely to see you, Tris. Let's hang out and sing 'Kumbaya' around a campfire. I've missed your good looks and witty charm," she replies without missing a beat. She smiles sweetly and bats her eyelashes for effect.

I smirk and clink my glass with hers. "Cheers. That's more like it. Glad you're getting into the spirit."

She moves her chin in a come-here gesture, and I lean in, waiting for what she has to tell me. "Go away, Mr. Miles," she whispers.

I chuckle, excited for the first time in a very long time. "No."

Her gaze goes in front of her again. "I see you're still as annoying as ever."

"And I see you're still taking those bitch pills."

"Ah, yes." She sighs. "Let's blame my distaste for you on meds, shall we? There couldn't possibly be another reason why you repulse me, could there now?"

My eyebrows rise in surprise. Women just don't speak to me like this. "*Repulse* is a rather strong word, isn't it?" I say as I join her in staring straight ahead. "I think the word you meant to use is *fascinate*."

Her mouth curls up at the corners, and I know she's struggling not to smile. "Go away, Mr. Miles," she repeats.

"Do I fascinate you, Claire?"

"Call me Mrs. Anderson," she whispers. "And you don't have what it takes to fascinate me."

Our eyes lock, and for the second time tonight my stomach flutters.

She has this aura surrounding her, elusive and enticing.

Controlling.

I bet she'd be fucking wild in bed. I get a vision of us together, naked, and I feel the throb of arousal between my legs. I purse my lips to hide my delight.

"Goodbye." She walks off through the crowd, and I stare after her.

All right . . . I'll admit it.

That woman is insanely fucking hot.

I watch her walk across the room as I troll my mind for a plan. This is possibly the only place I am going to see her. Hmm . . . what to do.

I take out my phone and call my brother. He answers after the first ring. "Hello, Tris."

"Jameson," I say as I watch her strike up a conversation with another man. "Change of plans."

"How so?"

"I was only going to stay at the conference for the opening day."

"Yes."

"I've decided that I'm staying on for the week. There is an . . ." I pause as I search for the right wording. "Opportunity . . . that I would like to investigate further."

"Okay, when will you be back?"

"Monday, next week."

"Yeah, of course. Listen, I'm in a meeting. I'll call you later."

"Okay." I hang up and put my phone back into my pocket, and my eyes rise to watch Claire Anderson across the room once more.

This conference just got interesting.

"I'm just going to get a drink," Nelson says. "Do you want another?"

"Okay, thank you."

"I'll be back shortly," he replies, and I watch him as he walks over to the bar.

He's a nice guy.

I'm surprised—this has actually been a great night. We had dinner, and then there was dancing. I've been chatting with everyone, being sociable. Marley would be so proud of me.

"Ahh, alone at last." I hear a voice. I glance over to see Tristan Miles standing beside me. Great. I roll my eyes.

"Where did your disciple go?" he asks as he sips his drink.

"Who's that?" I frown.

"The boring Goody Two-shoes."

I bite the inside of my cheek so that I don't smile. He hit the nail on the head. "I don't know who you're talking about."

"Nelson Mandela or whatever his name is." He waves his glass in the air toward Nelson.

Unable to help it, I smile. "I have no idea what his surname is, but I'm pretty sure it's not Mandela, Mr. Miles."

"I told you to call me Tristan."

"And I told you to go away."

"You know . . ." He pauses, as if getting the wording right. "If I wasn't at a work conference and being professional, I'd have a lot to ask you."

"Such as?" I question.

"I'm working," he says as he straightens his tie.

Eager to know what he wants to say, I reply, "Consider yourself off the clock. Anything you say to me will be considered a private matter."

"Why do you hate me so much?"

"Well, there's a lot to dislike."

"Such as?"

"You want my company, Mr. Miles."

"No." He sips his drink. His tone makes me think he's annoyed. "I made an honest offer for your company, and you rejected it. End of story. I haven't approached you since, and I have respected your wishes."

Our eyes are locked. I can feel the energy, and it bounces between us. It's almost as if our bodies are speaking to each other without words. I can pretend not to notice it all I want, but the truth is Tristan Miles is a sensory overload.

Feeling foolish for my over-the-top hatred, I reply, "If you must know, I find you rather annoying."

His mouth falls open as he fakes shock. "Are you always so coldhearted, Claire?"

I chuckle. "I think we both know who is coldhearted out of the two of us."

His eyes hold mine, and then he raises his eyebrow. "What about your blood?"

"What about my blood?"

"Does your blood run hot?"

He's so naughty.

Hmm . . . I hate to admit it, but there *is* definitely something about this guy.

I smile broadly at his audacity. "I don't think you need to know about the temperature of my blood."

"Oh, but a man does wonder." He sips his drink with his eyes locked on mine. The air swirls between us. "Perhaps we should talk about it . . . outside." He gives me a slow, sexy smile and then raises his eyebrow. "Off the clock, of course."

"You want to go outside and talk about the temperature of my blood, Mr. Miles?"

"Yes," he whispers as his eyes drop to my lips.

I lean in. "Mr. Miles," I whisper.

"Yes."

"I'm not attracted to you, on or off the clock."

He puts his lips to my ear. "Liar."

His breath tickles my skin and sends goose bumps scattering down my arms.

"Will you stop it?" I whisper as I look around, uncomfortable with my body's reaction to him. *Traitor.*

His eyes hold mine. "Call me Tristan."

"No." I sip my drink. God, I wish I could tip my head back and drain the glass.

"Claire." He leans in to whisper in my ear again.

"What?"

"Don't be scared of calling me Tristan."

I roll my eyes.

"Because one day very soon, I predict that you're going to be moaning it."

I smirk. "Are you always this delusional?"

"Just saying." He gives a casual shrug and then turns and walks off, and I watch him walk through the crowd.

Nelson appears. "Here's your drink."

"Thanks." I take it from him and look across the room to see Mr. Miles arrive at a group of women. They all gush and smile, and then he turns toward me. His dark eyes meet mine, and he gives me another slow, sexy smile before holding his glass in the air toward me, as if to signify the opening of the Olympic Games.

I swallow the lump in my throat.

Jesus, what the fuck does that mean?

Chapter 4

It's late, just past two o'clock in the morning, and I don't know how the hell I'm still here.

The night has flown. It feels good not having to rush home to homework and dinner and responsibilities. I think all 120 people from the conference are still here. The mood is light and jovial. I'm standing at the back of the room near the bar. There are ten of us standing in a group. They're telling stories, and we're laughing and having fun, and every now and then I look across the room and into the stare of Tristan Miles.

He's watching me . . . he's been watching me all night.

The heat of his gaze on my skin is warm like the sun. It makes me wonder if he's this intense in bed. Because right now, he's not just undressing me with his eyes; he's fucking me with them.

Arousal heats my blood, and I find myself imagining what we'd be like together naked.

Like a well-oiled machine, he's working the room. Everyone wants to talk to him; everyone wants to be near him. And I'm pretty damn sure that every woman here is fantasizing about taking him home.

I know I am.

I never would, of course. God no.

But his unapologetic flirty way is definitely appealing . . . even to those who aren't interested.

I let my mind wander for a moment. What would it be like to have wild and carefree sex with a man like him? To know that there is absolutely no chance of a tomorrow?

To live completely in the moment.

I stare down at my straw as I circle it in my drink. My mind begins to tick as it tries to reconcile my thoughts. It's been a long time since I had a thought like that.

Sex hasn't crossed my mind since Wade died.

Five years next month.

I was thirty-three when I lost my husband, just coming into my sexual prime.

I lost a lot that day—and not just him . . . a major part of who I was.

Wade and I met in college. We dated for two years, and then the unthinkable happened. I became pregnant on the pill at the tender age of twenty.

Wade was ecstatic. I mean, he never had any doubts that we were going to be together. He told me on our fourth date that he was going to marry me. He was three years older than me and thought he knew everything.

I smile wistfully—looking back, I see that he did.

I get a flashback of us kissing and laughing . . . rolling around in bed, making love.

And my heart hurts.

I don't just miss him . . . I miss everything that we did together. The way he made me feel like a woman every time he looked at me.

Arousal.

The rush of an orgasm.

I close my eyes in disgust.

Oh God . . .

Here we go.

I need to stop drinking. I remember now—I remember why I don't drink. It makes me sad, like a big dark blanket that comes to rest over my shoulders. One that's heavy and laden with responsibilities. I put my drink down on the bar. "I'm going to get going," I announce as I wave. "See you all tomorrow."

I head over toward the exit and catch sight of Tristan talking to three women—the same three women who have been hanging off him all night. He sees me coming and pushes himself off the wall. "Claire," he calls as he steps into my path.

I can't be rude in front of the girls. "Hi." I smile over his shoulder to his groupies as they look on.

"Are you ready?" he asks.

I stare at him, confused. "Huh?"

"You know." He widens his eyes. "To study."

"Oh." I frown. He must be trying to get rid of these women. "Yes, of course."

"Lead the way." He gestures to the door.

Oh jeez. I take off toward the door.

"But—" one of the girls says from behind us.

"Sorry, girls, rain check," he calls as he runs to catch up with me.

We walk out into the foyer and over to the elevator.

"Thanks." He sighs.

I roll my eyes. "I'm not your scapegoat, Mr. Miles."

"I know." He links his arm through mine. "We really are going to study; didn't I tell you?"

"Does this over-the-top-flirty thing often work?" I ask as the elevator doors open, and we hop in.

He gives me a cheeky grin as the door closes behind us. "Always."

I shake my head as I smile at the ground; his heavenly after-shave wafts around me.

"Are we drinking coffee or champagne?" he asks playfully.

"I'm going to have a cup of tea."

"Tea?" He scrunches up his nose in disgust. "Like English granny tea."

"Yes. Like English granny tea."

"Oh." The doors open, and I step out of the elevator. So does he. We walk down the corridor. Where is his room? He doesn't really think he's coming with me . . . does he?

"I suppose I can try it, just this once," he replies.

"Try what?"

"Tea."

"You are not coming with me," I scoff.

His face falls. "Why not?"

"Because I'm not like that, because I'm too old for you, and because, well . . ." I pause as I think of the right wording. "I vowed to hate you for all of eternity." We get to my door, and I turn to him. "This is me."

He puts his hands into his trouser pockets. "Come on, Claire; it's tea." His mischievous eyes hold mine. "It's not like I'm going to fuck you into next week or anything."

I stare at him, shocked that he's just said that out loud. I'm not used to men talking to me like this.

His crude words penetrate into the dark corner of my sexuality.

I feel something dormant wake up deep inside.

Five years is a long time.

The air crackles between us.

"It's not like I'm going to make you come so fucking hard or anything." He gives me a slow, sexy smile. "It's not like it would be the best sex of your life or anything."

I have no words . . . he's stolen them.

"Admit it," he says softly as his gaze drops to my lips. "You haven't wondered what I'd be like in bed?" he whispers.

"No," I lie. It's the only thing I can think about. "Not once."

"You haven't wondered how big my dick is?" he breathes as he tucks a piece of my hair behind my ear and steps toward me.

Jesus, he's hung. Only a big man would bring attention to the size of his dick.

Not helping.

I swallow the lump in my throat as I get a vision of him naked. "No."

He leans in and puts his mouth to my ear. "Confession."

I close my eyes. Oh man, this is a bad . . . situation. With a bad man.

My heart begins to beat deep and slow, in time with his, as I imagine doing bad things to him.

"You've been on my mind." His deep, hushed voice on my neck begins to send shock waves through my system.

"Why's that?" I whisper, but I don't know why I'm asking—I already know the answer.

He presses his hips forward and pins me to the wall. He's hard and ready. My insides begin to melt.

Oh fuck . . . he feels good.

"Through three lectures and one workshop, all I've done is imagined you riding my cock," he whispers darkly.

I instantly get a vision of me on top of him, naked, our bodies wet with perspiration.

His erection big and deep.

"God . . . ," he breathes as he takes a handful of my hair and grips it hard. "We'd be so fucking hot together, Anderson."

The elevator door pings, and Nelson walks out.

My temporary brain snap dissipates, and I push back from Tristan. "Stop it," I whisper.

Nelson looks between us from the other end of the corridor and frowns. "Hello."

Tristan rolls his eyes and runs his hand through his hair in frustration. "Hi," he mutters dryly.

I turn the key and open my door in a rush, taking the momentary distraction as a godsend. "Good night, Mr. Miles."

"Anderson," he whispers.

I close the door in his face and click the lock. I fall against the back of it and close my eyes. I'm panting, and my body is still reeling from the feeling of him so close.

My phone beeps with a text.

Come on?
I'm leaving tomorrow.

His words repeat in my mind.

"We'd be so fucking hot together."

I put the chain on, and I peek through the peephole to see him roll his eyes and shake his head.

He's pissed off.

He knew he nearly had me.

Oh crap . . . that was close. Another text beeps through.

Claire, come on.
You're killing me here.
There are no prizes for being a good girl.
You only live once.

"Fucking hell," I mutter.

I turn my phone on silent, put it on the charger, and storm into the bathroom, and then I lock that door too. I need to get some distance between me and him.

God, wake up, Claire.

The very last thing I'm about to do is have sex with that soul-sucking bastard. And besides, I wouldn't even know what to do with him. I'm positive the kind of sex that I've had wouldn't be the same type of sex that he has.

I'm into tender loving care, and he's probably a world-renowned anal master.

I shiver at the thought of appearing vulnerable and sexually inexperienced to him.

I imagine him guiding me as to how he likes it, and my blood boils.

No way in hell am I giving him one inch of power over me.

"That's it. No more," I whisper angrily. "Cold shower." I turn the water on with force. "That man is the devil."

I sit and stare into space in the truth circle.

One by one we are being asked a question about ourselves that only we would know. Something that apparently burns a hole in our existence.

"Tell me, Ariana, what is the one thing that makes you angry?" Elouise asks.

Ariana frowns as she contemplates her answer, and we sit in silence as we wait. All of our questions are different, based on our psychological testing. Elouise, the psychologist who is running this part of the workshop, has tailored the session to what we did yesterday morning. We've broken up into small groups of fifteen and are sitting and listening to everyone in our group.

Once again, I zone out into space.

I'm flat today.

Down on myself, for many reasons.

I hate that I'm physically attracted to someone I don't like. I hate that I let him get under my skin. I hate that I wanted him, and, most of all, I hate that the opportunity to have a wild and carefree night with him is gone. He's gone back to New York now.

Tristan fucking Miles.

The reason I haven't slept, the reason I had to get myself off while watching YouPorn last night.

And the reason I feel so fucking sexless today that I just want to cry.

It was nice being hit on . . . being made to feel desirable.

To feel like a woman again.

And it's not him; it's not about him. It's what he represents.

A carefree time in my life that's gone.

I've been thinking about it . . . long and hard—all night, actually. And if there was ever a man whom I should have slept with as a get-back-into-the-dating-game kind of thing, it should have been Tristan Miles.

He is uncomplicated and unavailable, the kind of man you have thoughtless sex with. I was physically attracted to him, and yet there was absolutely no chance that I could have developed feelings for him. He's not the kind of man I could ever fall in love with.

It was the perfect opportunity . . . and I let it go.

Fucking great.

"Claire?" a voice asks.

I look up, dazed. "I beg your pardon?" I ask.

"Let's talk about the hardest thing in your life," Elouise says.

I frown.

"What is the hardest thing that you have had to do?"

I stare at her for a moment. "Little League."

Elouise's face falls, and everyone listens intently.

"Explain that to me."

"Um." I take a nervous, deep breath. "My husband . . . um . . ."
I pause midsentence.

"Start at the beginning." Elouise smiles.

"Five years ago, my husband was riding a bike early one morning." I smile as I remember Wade in his full riding kit. "He was training for a triathlon." I pause.

"Go on."

"He was . . . hit by a drunk driver at five fifty-two a.m."

Everyone watches me.

"He died at the scene. He was thirty-six." I twist my fingers together on my lap. "And I thought that was going to be my worst day." I smile as I try to make sense of what I'm about to say. "But I was wrong." I stay silent for a moment.

After a while, she prompts me, "Go on, Claire."

"Watching my three sons grow up without a father, day in and day out, is far worse." My eyes fill with tears. "Every Saturday," I whisper, hardly able to push the words past my lips. "Every Saturday . . . we go to their games. And when they do something good, they look up into the stands to see me." I stare straight ahead as I pause.

"Take your time, dear."

"They're so proud, and then I watch their little faces fall when they remember that their dad's not here to see it."

Elouise nods quietly.

"So yeah . . ." I shrug. "Little League is the hardest thing about my life."

The group remains silent, and I glance up to see Tristan standing to the side of the circle. His hands are in his pockets, and his haunted eyes hold mine.

I drop my head, wishing I could take the personal words back.

I don't want Tristan Miles to know me, to know anything about me or my children and our daily struggles.

I'm keeping my distance. My attraction to him is just that—a physical attraction.

It means nothing.

"Okay, moving along. Richard. Tell me about your childhood."

It's just around ten o'clock at night when we are walking back from the restaurant.

The group is sleepy and subdued. Unlike last night, everyone is tired.

Today was a hard day and—I hate to admit it—a little cathartic. I had a lot of soul-searching moments and listened to a lot of the others have them too.

An unexpected bond has formed between me and my little group. I'm feeling deep and emotional and somewhat raw. It was unexpected, if I'm honest.

Tristan was at dinner but was sitting at another table with the other lecturers. He was chatting and talking and deep in conversation with another man.

He hasn't been annoying me today, or flirting. In fact, he hasn't come near me since he heard my little truth bomb this morning. It's all a bit real for him, I think.

Even for me, sometimes.

We arrive at the hotel, and I see a convenience store up ahead. I might get some chocolate. A cup of tea and something sweet will end the day on a high. "I'm just going to grab something from the store. See you all in the morning," I say.

"See you," my group calls as they disappear into the hotel.

I cross the street and grab my chocolate and look through the books they have. Hmm. What can I read? I don't read romance anymore, and horror is scary when my kids are on the other side of the world.

Nope . . . nothing interests me. Oh well, it was a nice thought.

I pay the cashier and head back over to the hotel. "Claire!" I hear from the side street next to the hotel.

I glance over and see Tristan standing in the dark. "Hi." I clutch my chocolate tightly in my hand.

"I just wanted to see how you were," he says.

See how I am . . . like a victim?

My face falls, and an unexpected surge of anger rises in my stomach. I hate that he heard my admission of weakness this morning. "I'm fine."

"Do you want to go and get some granny tea?" He gestures up the street to a café. He's not using it as a code for sex; he really means tea tonight.

Suddenly, I'm angry at his change of direction with me. I can handle flirty and fun.

This . . . I cannot.

"No," I snap. "I do not." Infuriated, I storm off, and then, unable to help it, I turn back to him. "You know what? Fuck you," I say.

"What?"

"Don't you give me that look, Tristan Miles."

"What look?" he gasps.

"That pathetic look of sympathy," I sneer. "You can look at me sexy; you can look at me with distaste. But don't you fucking dare feel sorry for me."

He stares at me.

"The one person in the world that I don't want pity from is you."

He steps forward. "What *do* you want?"

"I just want to be treated normal," I snap. "Not like poor Claire Anderson the widow." I throw my hands up in the air. "Like a normal woman who you don't know."

I feel like I'm about to explode, and I suck in deep breaths to try to calm myself down. My eyes search his. "At least when you're an asshole, I know what to expect."

He rushes me and grabs my face in his hands and kisses me. His tongue swipes through my lips, and he pushes me up against the wall.

"Believe me, Claire Anderson . . . the last thing I feel when I look at you . . . is pity."

His tongue dances against mine, and his grip on my face is near painful.

I'm forced forward as he pulls me onto his cock. I can feel it as it hardens.

My insides begin to liquefy . . . oh God.

Something snaps inside of me, and I begin to kiss him back.

I kiss him with everything I have, and God it feels good. Deep, erotic . . . and so long awaited.

He pulls back and looks at me as he holds my face in his hands. His breathing is labored. "What is that kiss, Anderson?"

I stare up at him as my chest rises and falls.

"That's not a granny-tea kiss." His hands grip my face harder, and he licks my open lips. My insides clench at the dominance of his action. "That's a hungry kiss," he whispers darkly and then licks my lips again. The way he's licking my open lips with no regard for what my tongue is doing is making me want him to lick me somewhere else. Every muscle deep inside of me clenches as I imagine his head between my legs.

"Are you hungry, Claire?" he breathes.

Fucking starving.

I put my hand on the back of his head and pull him down to me. I kiss him again. Harder this time, more urgent, and it's as if some kind of sexual rubber band has been stretched beyond repair and has finally snapped in a spectacular fashion.

All bets are off.

I don't want to be a sad widow anymore . . . just for tonight, I want to be a woman.

His hand goes to my breast, and my concentration returns. The arousal fog temporarily dissipates.

Reality sets in. Wait . . . what?

What the hell am I doing?

I step back from him in a rush.

"What's wrong?" He frowns as he pants.

I hold my temple as I try to get a hold on my arousal. "Will you just stop it?"

"Stop what?"

"I'm not interested in you, Tristan. I will never be interested in you. Back off," I whisper angrily.

He screws up his face in disbelief. "What?"

"You heard me."

"I can feel your attraction to me. Stop lying."

"You're delusional," I snap.

"You want me; admit it."

He reaches for me again, and I step back farther, out of his reach. "Leave me the hell alone, Tristan."

"Get back here," he orders.

"Go to hell."

Get back here . . . I wish.

Three words never sounded so hot and so wrong, and fuck me, my body desperately wants to do as he commands.

But I won't let her . . . because she's just horny, and he's a cad.

And I want to be able to live with myself tomorrow.

I march in through the hotel foyer on a mission.

Get the hell away from Tristan Miles.

That man is the devil and as tempting as sin.

Chapter 5

I sit in the crowded auditorium in a detached state. The people are all listening to the lecture on mind-sets and are journaling and actively working on the set tasks.

But not me, because I can't concentrate at all.

I'm in the middle of a sensory overload.

Tristan Miles is circling the room. Like a graceful panther on the prowl, he's walking in and out of the aisles of the audience, helping people when they ask for his input and encouraging them as they think out loud.

I have no idea what's come over me or why the thoughts in my head have suddenly appeared. That kiss last night opened something up inside of me . . . and I have questions.

Carnal questions.

He's wearing a perfect-fitting navy suit and a cream shirt with a yellow-and-gray-checkered tie. He just took his jacket off and slung it over a chair, and every muscle in my body sighed.

His cream shirt is rolled up at the sleeves, revealing his muscular forearms and broad chest. I have a full view of his behind now too . . . it's tight and firm, and his thigh muscles are thick and sculpted. His hair is dark and wavy, and his skin . . . good God his skin—it's bronzed and olive from the sun, and it matches his big brown eyes. I shouldn't even be looking at this man, let alone staring.

But I can't help it, and I can't stop myself, and I'm not quite sure that I want to . . . every cell in my body is begging for him, and Marley's words from the first time she saw him about wolf whistling the fuck out of this guy are taunting me as a dare.

A perfect male specimen.

Complete wolf-whistling material . . . whore-bag material too. I'm pretty sure that Tristan Miles could talk anyone onto their back and have them begging to open their legs for him. I get a vision of him taking his shirt off at the end of the bed, and my stomach flutters. Cheers to the lucky bitches who are able to act on it and drink him down like chocolate.

I smirk at my spot-on analogy as I drop my eyes to the floor. Tristan Miles *is* chocolate. Rich, delicious, and dreamy, he offers a high . . . but in the end, he is detrimental to your health and bad to the bone.

He slowly approaches up the aisle behind me, and a waft of his aftershave surrounds me as he gets closer. As if sensing his arrival, my entire body breathes in. I hold my pen midair as I stare straight ahead and try to focus. As he nears, goose bumps scatter up my arms at his close proximity.

I've never had a sexual attraction to someone like this before. It's strange.

I've thought about him all night—and not the "Oh, he's a nice guy" kind of thoughts.

Thoughts about him throwing me on the bed and giving it to me good.

I don't like him, and yet . . . all I can think about is getting naked with him. This isn't who I am; I'm not the kind of woman who thinks with her vagina.

But something about being wild and carefree with a man like him is so damn inviting.

In slow motion, he crouches down beside me. "Do you need any help, Claire?" he whispers.

My breath catches as I stare into his big brown eyes.

Fuck yes, I do.

"I'm okay," I whisper. "Thanks."

We stare at each other for a beat longer than needed; the undercurrent of arousal is flowing between us. It's there every time we are close to each other.

Does he feel it too . . . or do all women react to him this way?

"Are you coming to the wine tour this afternoon?" he whispers.

I nod, unable to push a word through my lips.

He smiles softly. "I'll see you then." He stands gracefully and, with his perfect posture, keeps walking; his aftershave lingers in the distance behind him.

An unexpected thrill runs through me, and I look down at my notepad, rattled by my body's reaction.

What will I wear?

I shake my head, disgusted that I just had that thought.

No.

Tristan Miles is off limits.

Stop it . . . whatever you are thinking, stop it right now.

My cheeks hurt from laughing, and the heat of the alcohol haze warms my face.

This is our sixth winery, the final destination of our tour, and it's just ten o'clock at night.

With each winery, we've gotten sillier and sillier. The bus pulled up out front here, and we all nearly fell out of it as we laughed out loud. We've had such a fun day.

Who knew this conference would be fun? I most certainly wasn't expecting it.

My eyes go to the man sitting alone at the bar. Tristan.

We've only spoken in a group today, and although our eyes lingered on each other across the circle, not a word has been said about our kiss last night.

"Let's keep going for dessert and port," Jada says. "We'll go to the brewery."

The group laughs and starts chattering as they make plans to move on, but my eyes stay firmly fixed on him as he sits alone.

Screw it . . . just go talk to him. There's no harm in talking to him, and besides, I've come to the conclusion that perhaps he has a different side than what I first perceived.

Although, that could just be the wine talking. The group continues to chatter and laugh, and I take a deep breath and walk over to him at the bar. "Is this seat taken?" I ask.

His eyes come to me, and a trace of a smile crosses his lips. "Be my guest."

I sit down on the stool beside him at the bar, and the waiter approaches me. "What will it be?"

"I'll have another glass of champagne, please."

"Sure." His eyes flick to Tristan. "Another scotch?"

"Please." Tristan stares straight ahead, with his hands clasped in front of him. "Took your time, Anderson," he says.

"What does that mean?"

He glances at his fancy watch. "It's ten p.m."

"Well, if it's too late to talk, I'll leave," I tease. I go to stand.

"Sit. Down." He smirks. "You're lucky it's a quiet night."

The bartender puts the champagne down in front of me, and I pick it up as I try to hide my smile. "Who's lucky?"

He chuckles and taps his glass on mine. "To Épernay."

"To Épernay," I whisper. Our eyes lock, and I sip my champagne. It's cold and bubbly and starts a fire inside of me.

With his eyes fixed firmly on mine, he licks the scotch from his lips. "You should probably stop looking at me like that."

Electricity buzzes between us as everyone else in the room disappears.

"Like what?"

"Like you want to fucking eat me."

My stomach flutters. "That's very presumptuous, Mr. Miles."

"Call me Tristan."

I bite the inside of my cheek to stop myself from smiling. I like this game. "I'll call you whatever I like," I mouth.

He inhales sharply and rearranges his crotch.

Watching him touch his dick does something to my insides, and my sex begins to throb.

"What makes you think that I want to eat you?" I whisper.

His eyes drop to my lips. "Because I want to eat you, and it's manners to reciprocate."

I giggle at his audacity. "I don't have very good manners, I'm afraid."

In slow motion, he picks up his chunky crystal glass and smiles as he puts it to his lips. "So . . . this martyr thing works for you?"

"How am I a martyr?"

"Well." He shrugs casually. "You keep telling me that you're not attracted to me, and yet . . ."

"And yet what?" I whisper.

"And yet I can feel it," he murmurs. "Your body is calling for mine."

Our eyes lock as the air leaves my lungs.

"Every time I'm close to you, I can sense our bodies talking to each other. Don't tell me you can't feel it, because I know you can," he whispers.

We stare at each other for an extended moment, the air swirling between us.

"Are you going to give her what she needs?" he asks as he lifts his glass to his lips.

I drop my head, rattled by his sixth sense. "I'm afraid I can't."

"Why not?"

"Because you're not someone I . . ."

"Like?" he asks, amused.

I hold my tongue, not wanting to be rude.

"Relax, Anderson; you're not someone that I would like either. Don't get ahead of yourself."

I smile, relieved.

"But . . . what happens on tour stays on tour," he adds.

My stomach flutters at the prospect of having secret sex with this man.

His focus moves to straight in front of him, as if he's pondering something, and then he smiles darkly and takes a sip of his drink.

"What?" I ask.

"Well, you do know that one day, we are inevitability going to . . . fuck."

I stare at him as a million pornographic pictures come to mind.

"An attraction like this doesn't go away, Anderson."

Goose bumps scatter up my arms; he *does* feel it too.

"So, as I see it . . . we can use the time away to our advantage."

"Or?" I ask.

His dark eyes meet mine. "Or we can go back to New York until I eventually wear you down—for then I will fuck you on your desk. It will be hard and wet and messy, and who knows who might walk in on us."

I blink, shocked. *What the hell?* "You're so sure of yourself."

"I always get what I want." He gives me a slow, sexy smile. "And what I want is you."

My stomach flutters with nerves. "Why?"

"You see . . . I could pretend that I like you and that I want to explore our friendship or some fucking bullshit." He sips his drink. "Or I could just tell you the truth."

"Which is?" I breathe.

Our eyes are locked.

"The idea of you hating me while I lick you up is a fucking turn-on," he whispers.

I begin to hear my pulse in my ears.

He leans in and whispers in my ear. "I want to hear you fucking moan, Anderson." His breath tickles my ear, and goose bumps scatter. "It's all I can think about; my cock has been weeping for you all day."

Jesus.

"You don't expect me to like you?" I ask, fascinated by his request.

"As a friend . . . who you can trust to take care of you sexually, of course."

"Anything more?"

"Absolutely not."

I sip my champagne as I process his words. "I'm not the kind of woman who does this sort of thing," I whisper.

"And I'm the kind of man that does. You don't even have to talk; I'll do all the work."

The air buzzes between us like electricity.

This is it, the defining moment—an offer to possibly find the woman inside of me whom I've lost. I know that I have two choices. I can go home alone and always regret this moment, or I can have honest sex with a man with whom it's impossible to form an emotional attachment.

"We're going to the cellar," Nelson says jovially from behind us, breaking the spell. "You guys coming?"

I look over at the group as they all stand by the door, waiting for everyone, and I know I need to make a decision. "Um . . . no. I'm going to call it a night and go to bed."

"Oh, okay." Nelson turns to Tristan. "You coming?"

"No, I'm meeting a friend here at the bar. She hasn't arrived yet," he lies without a beat.

Nelson smiles. "Lucky bastard. Have fun for me." He slaps him hard on the back and smiles at the two of us. "Good night, then. See you tomorrow."

"Good night."

The group waves to us, and with a loud chatter among them, they leave the bar.

Tristan's eyes come to me. "Your room or mine?"

"Mine."

I unlock the door to my room as he stands behind me. I can feel his breath on the back of my neck, and I may pass out at any moment . . . or orgasm. Both options aren't ideal or particularly cool.

He kicks the door shut and, without a word, takes my face in his hands and kisses me as he walks me backward toward my bed. His tongue dives deep into my mouth as he holds me close, and goose bumps scatter up my spine.

No matter what happens from here . . . the man can kiss. So . . . well.

Our tongues dance together, and I can't even open my eyes to look at him.

I'm so in the moment that it's just ridiculous.

"Jesus," he murmurs against my lips.

I giggle.

"Hurry up. Fuck." He begins to undo the buttons of his shirt with urgency.

"What's the rush?"

"The rush is I want you naked, and I can't get you naked until I'm naked. It's the naked law."

"There's a naked law?"

"Everyone knows that. Fuck." He rolls his eyes. "I told you not to talk, remember?"

I laugh. Oh man. He's fun.

He tears his shirt over his shoulders, and my breath catches. Broad and muscular, with a scattering of dark hair. He has a rippled abdomen and a V of muscles that disappears into his pants.

Holy shit.

Suddenly, I'm nervous.

Nobody has seen me naked in a very long time . . . oh jeez.

Abort mission.

He takes my fingers and puts them on his zipper. He smiles, with his eyes fixed on mine. "Take it all off," he mouths.

My heart somersaults in my chest, and I slowly slide the zipper of his trousers down. The tip of his cock sits above the waistband of his briefs. Preejaculate is beading on the end of it, and my stomach clenches hard. In fear and anticipation and horror . . . oh hell, so much to clench about. He holds his hands out wide and smiles down at me.

"Do it," he says.

I slide his trousers down and then his briefs. His cock is large and broad, and it hangs heavily between his legs.

Oh . . . shit.

I inhale deeply as I stare down at him. He's a beautiful man. Handsome, built, and well endowed. I have no words as my eyes drink him in . . . just *wow*.

He smiles darkly. "My turn."

I puff air into my cheeks.

"I . . ."

His lips drop to my neck, and I look up to the ceiling. He begins to undo the buttons on my silk shirt, and I wince and slightly pull away from him.

"What?"

"I . . . haven't . . ."

He stares at me, waiting.

"I . . ."

"You what?" He kisses me softly, as if to prompt me to speak.

"I haven't had sex in a really long time."

His face falls as he connects the dots. "Since?"

I shake my head.

"Jesus, Anderson . . . no pressure."

"Why would that make *you* feel pressured?" I stammer.

He throws his hands up in the air. "Because, like . . . fuck." He goes back to work on my blouse and throws it to the side and then stops and smiles as he looks down at me.

I close my eyes, so nervous that I can't even look at him.

He slides my skirt off, and I stand before him in my panties and bra. He unhooks my bra, and then his lips drop to my nipples as he slowly slides my panties down and throws them to the side.

His eyes drop down my body and then up to my face, and he smiles softly.

"Don't," I whisper, embarrassed. "I must be a world away from the women you normally sleep with."

"Why is that?" he whispers as he kisses my lips.

"I'm . . ."

"Oh, you mean this?" His hands run over my thighs. "A little cellulite," he whispers. His fingertips dust over my stomach. "A few stretch marks." He grabs the little pouch of fat on my stomach and gives it a tug, and I smile against his lips. "C-section scar." He runs his finger over the large scar on my lower stomach. His hands go

70

to my breasts, slightly saggy and not full like they used to be before the kids. He tweaks my nipples, which are large from breastfeeding.

My heart races as he touches all my insecurities.

He holds his hands out wide. "Do I look like a man who doesn't like what he sees?" he whispers.

My eyes lower to his large erection, and then I drop my head.

"Claire." He puts his finger under my chin and brings my face up to meet his. "You're beautiful," he whispers as he kisses me. "So fucking beautiful."

He kisses me again, and it's soft and tender and caring and not at all what I expected.

"You wear your insecurities here." He pinches the bottom of my stomach. "Mine are on the inside," he whispers. "Just because you can't see them doesn't mean they aren't there."

"I knew it." I smile against his lips.

He grabs my hips and throws me on the bed and then crawls over me.

"Be gentle, please," he teases. "Don't hurt me."

I burst out laughing, because that is the most ridiculous thing I've ever heard. "You idiot."

He reaches down and swipes his fingers through my sex. His eyes flicker with arousal. "Hmm . . . so wet." He bends and takes my nipple into his mouth and gives it a hard suck as he slides two fingers in deep.

"Oh . . . God." My back arches off the bed as he begins to pump me.

"Spread them."

I open my legs back to the mattress, and he goes slow at first to let me acclimatize. Then he picks up the pace. He really begins to ride me hard with his fingers.

This feels so foreign and new, and I push the fearful thoughts out of my mind.

It's one time . . . just enjoy this.

My entire body jerks up and down on the mattress from the pressure.

Fuck yes . . . I need this . . . I so need this.

The sound of my wet arousal sucking him in is loud in the room, and the look of triumph in his eyes is so fucking hot. "Clench, baby," he whispers. "Give me a taste of what I'm about to get."

I clench hard, and his eyes roll back in his head. He pumps me harder, and I scream out as I come hard. I shudder, and my convulsion lifts me off the bed.

He screws up his face as he pumps me through my body's rippling around his fingers.

He climbs over me with urgency.

"Condom," I stammer through my fog.

"Shit." He bounces up and grabs his trousers and fumbles around in the pocket for his wallet, and then his face falls in horror. "Fuck it. I only have one. How do I only have one?" He opens it and rolls it on.

I look up, surprised. "What kind of player are you?"

"Unprepared, obviously." He lies back down over me and brings my legs up around his hips, and in one sharp movement he slides home deep. His eyelids flutter. "Fucking hell, Anderson," he pants as he slowly slides out.

I smile up at him in wonder.

"Happy to report . . . the vagina is a perfect specimen," he pushes out through gritted teeth. "No insecurities here."

I burst out laughing. "Shut up, you fool, and fuck me."

He widens his knees and slides in deep, and we find a rhythm. He does a circular thing, and it drives me wild. I begin to thrash beneath him.

His eyes are rolled back in his head.

"You have an ugly sex face," I say.

He bursts out laughing. "I told you, no talking."

We both laugh, and then he falls serious and watches me for a moment as he pumps me deep. This just feels so raw and real.

"You need to come. You need to come," he stammers. "I can't stop it. You need to come," he begins to chant. "Anderson." He screws his face up, as if in pain.

"No," I snap. "I'm not ready." I ride his beautiful deep pumps . . . so good.

"Oh . . . fuck it." I feel the telling jerk of his cock, and he moans, deep and loud, and then goes into a frenzy of deep pumps to completely empty himself.

God, I want to do this all night. "Tristan," I whisper. "What the fuck . . . too quick?" I tease. If I'm honest, I love that he couldn't hold it. I love that he was so turned on that he had no control. This isn't about orgasms for me. It's about a connection that I've been missing, but I'll never let him in on my little secret.

"It's not my fault," he stammers in an outrage. "You shouldn't feel so fucking good. That never happens to me."

"One condom," I whisper. "Are you serious?" I pant.

"I have another way to fuck you that won't result in pregnancy." He smiles darkly down at me.

I giggle up at him. Oh, he's fun, all right. "Forget it, Mr. Miles. You only got one go."

I roll over and feel a hand on my naked hip bone, and I frown. Huh? Oh shit.

My eyes snap open. Tristan Miles is in my bed.

We had sex.

I had sex with Tristan fucking Miles.

Shit . . . you idiot.

I shake him. "Tristan," I whisper. I shake him again. "Tristan, wake up."

"Huh?" He frowns and props up on his elbow. "What's wrong?"

"You need to go," I whisper. I don't know why I'm whispering; nobody can hear us.

"What?" He looks around in confusion. "Why?"

"Because it's five a.m., and everyone is going to be up soon, and I don't want anyone seeing you leave my room."

He frowns over at me. "Why not?"

"Because then I'll be the groupie who fucked the lecturer at the conference."

He lies down and pinches the bridge of his nose. "You are the groupie who fucked the lecturer at the conference."

"This isn't funny," I whisper. "Quick. Get out."

"You're hurting my feelings, Anderson." He smirks as he climbs out of bed. "Kicking me out of bed in the middle of the night. I've never heard of such coldheartedness."

"Shut up," I whisper. "Go." I point to the door. "Get out."

He smiles and pulls his trousers up. "How dare you use my body in this manner?"

I flop back down on the bed. "You're such an idiot."

He leans over the bed and smiles down at me. "And you're fucking hot." He kisses me. "Good night, Anderson."

I smile up at him. "It's morning."

He stands and puts his jacket on and turns toward the door. "Mr. Miles."

He turns back toward me.

"I believe it was you that moaned my name first," I say sweetly.

He rolls his eyes. "That's debatable." The door clicks closed behind him, and I smile goofily up at the ceiling.

That was . . . surprisingly fun.

Chapter 6

I wake with a jump and notice it's light—too light for early morning.

Huh?

I scramble for my phone on the nightstand: 8:45 a.m.

What the hell? We started at eight o'clock this morning. My eyes widen in horror.

Oh my God. I dive out of bed and run to the shower.

Shit.

And my clothes need ironing—oh, this is a disaster. Why am I not more organized?

I shower in record time, grab my clothes, and run around like a lunatic dressing. I hop around, putting my makeup on while looking for my shoes.

Tristan's briefs are in the middle of the floor, and I scoop them up and shove them in my suitcase. I look around for my room key. Where is it?

Oh, damn it, I'll get another one from reception this afternoon. I grab my handbag and run.

Ten minutes later I rush into the conference room to find everyone sitting and listening to a woman speak.

I'm puffing and panting, and everyone in the room turns to look at me. "Hi," I huff. "I don't know . . . my alarm didn't go off." I shrug. "I'm sorry I'm so late."

The lecturer gestures to a chair. "That's quite all right, dear. Please take a seat."

I walk through the chairs and slink into a chair in the back row. Damn it. I want the earth to swallow me up. I look so unprofessional.

I glance over to see Tristan biting his bottom lip to stop himself from smiling as he listens intently to the lecture. His eyes don't come to me at all. Completely cool, calm, and collected, as usual. Wearing a dark-gray suit, he looks like he's just stepped off a modeling shoot. Clean shaven, perfectly put together. His dark wavy hair is well kept, with not a hair out of place.

I bite the inside of my cheek to stop myself from smiling like a loon.

I know what's under his suit, and it's pretty fucking delicious.

We sit at the café and drink our coffee during the afternoon tea break.

Tristan is sitting with his three groupies, and I'm talking to Nelson and Peter, one of the other guys.

Tristan hasn't acknowledged last night at all, and I'm beginning to wonder if I imagined the entire thing. Mind you, we haven't been alone at all, but still.

Not even a glance my way.

"So, Tristan," Saba says in her sexiest voice. "Are we on for tonight? You've been promising to party with us girls."

Tristan's eyes flick guiltily to me. "No. I can't. I'm sorry. I'm busy."

I sip my coffee as I watch him navigate this. It's fun watching him squirm.

"Doing what?" Saba frowns.

"I have a project to finish with Claire. We started it last night, and it still needs work."

The girls' faces fall in disappointment.

"No, that's fine, Tristan," I interrupt. "I finished the job myself after you left."

He blinks in disbelief and then narrows his eyes. "Is that so?"

"Uh-huh." I sip my coffee, acting innocent.

He glares at me.

"Yeah, that's probably why I slept so well. Felt so good to finally get the project done, you know?"

"I would have done it better," he replies flatly.

"Oh, well, you didn't." I smile sweetly. "I saved you the job. You should go party with the girls. I'm sure they're going to be great fun."

"Yes." The girls all giggle on cue, and he looks at me deadpan.

The bell rings for us to return, and everyone stands and leaves us alone.

"Finished the job, did you?" he whispers.

I shrug casually. "It had to be done."

He stands and does his suit jacket up with one hand, unimpressed. "You're a smart-ass, Anderson."

"Have fun with the girls tonight," I whisper. "Although, I really don't know how you would handle three?"

"You're going to fucking get it." He marches off toward the conference room, clearly annoyed, and I smile after him.

I feel a flutter in my psyche; it's as if the playful part of my personality is waking up from her deep sleep.

The long-forgotten piece of me.

Tristan makes me remember who I was . . . *before*.

The room is steamy and hot, and I smile sleepily as my head rests on the side of the bathtub. It's just around ten o'clock, and I'm so relaxed that I'm nearly asleep.

I hear the lock on my door click, and I frown. Huh?

Maybe it's housekeeping. The door shuts. "Hello?" I call.

"Hi," Tristan says as he walks into the bathroom. He takes off his suit jacket and throws it over the chair in the corner.

"What are you doing?" I ask.

He continues to undress.

"How did you get in here?" I frown.

"A key?" He kicks off his shoes.

"How did you get a key?"

He unzips his pants. "I did what any self-respecting man who's kicked out of bed in the middle of the night does." He takes off his shirt. "I took yours."

My eyes widen. "You stole my key?" I gasp.

"Borrowed it, and relax, we swap body fluids. What's yours is mine." He slides down his trousers and briefs. "Move over. I'm getting in."

"Tristan."

He steps into the bath, between my legs, and sits down. The water sloshes over the side.

"It's too hot." He winces as he goes to turn the cold water on.

"Don't even think about it," I mutter.

He smiles and then slides down and closes his eyes. The water sloshes over the sides again.

I watch him for a moment. "How was your date?" I ask.

"It wasn't a date."

"Okay, your foursome."

"You'd like that, wouldn't you?" he mumbles. "A reason to tease me for all of eternity." His hair is all messed up, and his boyish charm is at an all-time high.

78

I smile, surprised by who he's turning out to be. I never once pegged him as fun to be around.

He opens one eye to look at me. "What?"

"You really are a very good-looking man, Mr. Miles."

He smirks. "Is that you giving me a compliment, Anderson?"

I nod in slow motion with a big smile.

He runs his hand up my leg. "Did you really finish yourself off last night?"

"Would it bother you if I did?"

"Yes. It would, actually."

I pick up his foot and kiss it and then put it back down between my breasts. "No, Tristan, I didn't."

He stares at me for a moment, as if processing a thought. He massages my breast with his foot. "Are you lying?"

"Why would I?"

"I don't know." He thinks on it for a moment. "You're a very different species of woman to what I'm used to, Claire."

"How so?"

"It didn't bother you one bit that I went out with three women tonight?"

I smile. If we were different, I would no doubt be raging mad, but knowing that Tristan is just for fun and that it could never be like that between us, I'm surprisingly good. "No. Why?" I lift his foot and kiss it again. "Should it?"

"I don't know." He frowns as he contemplates his response.

"Do you want me to act jealous?" I ask.

He gives me a lopsided smile. "Perhaps a little. Couldn't hurt, could it?"

"Tristan," I whisper as I fall into role-play.

"Yes."

"I thought we had something special. How could you do this to me?"

He bites his lip to hide his smile. "That's more like it."

"After all we've been through, I thought I was the one," I whisper.

He smiles broadly. He likes this game.

I slide across and lie on top of him. His big arms come around me, and my lips take his.

"I kind of like you being jealous," he whispers.

I smile against his lips as I circle my sex over his hardened erection. "Did you go to the pharmacy today?"

He chuckles. "I bought in bulk."

The glimmer of perspiration dusts his skin, and he looks up at me with dark eyes.

Tristan.

Tristan fucking Miles.

Sex-god extraordinaire.

I don't know if this is the same man I slept with last night. The man with me tonight is an absolute rock star between the sheets. I'm in awe.

We've been fucking for hours. Like animals, we can't get enough. We finish and talk for a little while, and then he kisses me, and the entire process begins again.

It's like the ultimate marathon.

We're both wet with perspiration, and I've never had sex like this before. "Come on," he whispers. He wants it harder and tighter. I close my eyes and clench. He has my two hip bones in his hands, and he's guiding me over his cock and positioning me where he wants me.

His pumps get harder . . . deeper.

"Yes," he moans. "Fuck yes." His grip becomes tighter.

I close my eyes as I begin to moan. Fuck . . . how many times can the female body come in one night? This is insane.

"Anderson," he growls as I lose focus. "Fuck me."

"Ohh," I murmur as I stare down at the gorgeous man beneath me. His hair is hanging messily over his forehead, his eyes are dark, and his face is alive with satisfaction. This is his element.

Sex is his thing.

There's a reason the name Tristan fucking Miles came to me. It was a premonition.

The *fucking* wasn't silent; it was a verb.

He flips us so that I am on my back. He lifts my legs and puts them over his shoulders and then comes face to face with me.

And we stop still as we stare at each other.

His body is deep inside of mine; the burn of his rough possession holds me captive.

He smiles softly, and my stomach flutters.

Don't look at me like that.

"Kiss me," he breathes. "I need you to kiss me."

I close my eyes to block him out, because damn. This isn't what this is about.

I need some distance between us—this is too much. Too intense, too personal.

Too . . . intimate.

"Open your eyes," he commands.

I drag them open.

"Kiss me," he whispers.

"Tris," I whisper, close to the edge of insanity.

"It's all right, baby." He pushes the hair back from my forehead. "I've got you."

My eyes search his. I feel my resistance leave, and as if he senses the exact moment that I hand over my power, his lips take mine.

We kiss for a long time. His tongue swipes through my mouth, mirroring the thrusts of his hips.

He begins to moan—long, satisfied deep breaths—and my head is thrown back into the pillow. "Fuck, Claire . . . this is so fucking good."

My mouth falls open, and I shudder hard as a freight train of an orgasm rips through me.

His eyes roll back in his head, and then he straightens his arms and widens his legs and slams in deep. He tips his head back and cries out. I feel the telling jerk of his cock as he comes again.

I turn my head to the side to get away. Damn it, he's under my skin, and I need to get him off.

"Hey," he says.

I keep my face to the side as I pant. Tears threaten.

I'm completely overwhelmed.

"Anderson."

I drag my eyes back to him. I like it when he calls me that; it's playful and mindless . . . not deep and emotional, like how I'm feeling. His eyes hold mine for a moment, and as if reading my mind and knowing exactly what I need in this moment, he says, "You fuck all right for an old duck."

That was the most unexpected thing I have ever heard. I smirk, then smile, and then break into a chuckle. Oh Lord. This man kills me. I laugh out loud as I stare up at the ceiling. "Only you."

Unable to hold himself up any longer, he falls on top of me, and he laughs too.

He pulls out of me and kisses me once more and then hops up and goes to the bathroom.

My body is still throbbing from the pounding he has just given it, and I still feel like I'm teetering on the edge of insanity. I lie in the dark, still panting, as a myriad of emotions run through me. I'm sated and full and lethargic, and a strange twinge of fear loiters in the dark corner of my mind. I push it away as fast as I can.

He reappears from the kitchenette in my room and hands me a glass of water. "Here you are."

I sit up on my elbow and take it. "Thanks."

"Well, your voice *is* hoarse from moaning 'Tristan' all night." He shrugs casually. "It's the least I could do."

I giggle. "Feeling proud of yourself?"

He puts his hands on his hips and puffs his chest out. He's soft now and completely natural, but just as beautiful. "Ten feet tall, actually."

I smile up at him and tap the bed next to me. This man is so unexpected; it's like he's two different people. He's hard on the exterior for the world to see, but as soon as he got naked with me, it was like a different side of him appeared. This Tristan is a lot more appealing, and I wonder how many people get to see this part of his personality. "You should be; I'm very impressed."

He gets into bed beside me and pulls me into his arms, and I put my head on his chest. "And before you kick me out in two hours," he says, "I have the morning off, so I'm staying in this bed until everyone has already left for the conference, and then I will leave." He kisses my temple.

"But if you're still here," I whisper, "how will I sneak in my other conference lover for a prebreakfast nooky?"

He reaches down and twists my nipple hard. "Shut up, or I'm going to fuck you into a coma."

I burst out laughing as I try to escape his grip. "You already did that."

"I'm going to do it again."

The group laughs at something the lecturer says as he walks around the room.

It's three o'clock in the afternoon, and I hate to admit it, but Marley was right: this conference was exactly what I needed. I feel refreshed and energized, and of course, that could have a lot to do with the nocturnal company I'm keeping, but whatever it is, it's worked.

I've achieved what we set out to find—a clean and uncluttered mind. Ready to focus and tackle the next six months. I'm even considering signing up for next year's conference as an early bird to get the pricing discount.

"Hello." Tristan's voice comes from the side of the room. In surprise we all turn toward him.

He's wearing a light-blue suit, a white shirt with a paisley tie, and expensive brown shoes, and his hair is perfectly styled.

I want to beam a big smile at him, but I pretend not to care.

"Mr. Miles," the lecturer says in greeting.

"Sorry to interrupt; I just came to say goodbye," he replies, addressing the group.

I glance toward the door and see his black leather suitcase and suit bag waiting for him.

What?

He's leaving?

He walks to the center of the room. "I have an unexpected meeting in Paris that I have to attend, so this is it from me. My flight leaves in a few hours. I'm on my way to the airport." He smiles as he looks around at everyone.

What?

"Congratulations on what you have all achieved this week," he continues. "You should be very proud of yourself for putting yourself out there and attending this conference. Success doesn't just happen; it is a mind-set. And I urge you to put into practice what you have learned and stop and take the time to celebrate the small victories along the way." He puts his hands in his suit pockets, and he walks across the stage. "You only get one life. So you need to grab it with both hands."

His eyes scan everyone in the room as he addresses us, and I wait for them to come my way.

Look at me.

"Put your hands together for Tristan Miles," the lecturer says. "He's a very busy man, and for him to donate a week of his time is almost unheard of in the corporate world. Thank you, Mr. Miles."

Everyone claps, and he does a demure bow. My heart begins to race into a panic. He's going.

Look at me.

He holds his hands up and claps with the crowd and then turns toward the door and takes his suitcase. After one last wave, he leaves without looking back. I stare at the door he has just left through. Not even a goodbye?

I drop my head.

Fuck.

I know that I should have expected this from him. I knew he was a cold, soul-sucking jerk, and yet somehow I'd convinced myself that I was wrong about him.

Seems not.

"Let's discuss the theory that was brought up this morning, shall we?" the lecturer calls.

I want to run out there and tell him off for being so insensitive.

But I won't. My dignity will not allow it.

Like a slap in the face, I'm instantly reminded of who Tristan really is and why I've kept him at arm's length. I knew this about him; I knew all along he was a cold womanizer, but for some reason my mind didn't reconcile it with the man I've slept with.

It doesn't make me feel any better about last night.

I turn my attention to the window and stare outside at the trees blowing in the wind.

I feel . . . like a number, decidedly cheap.

It's ten o'clock before I head back to my room. I trudge up the corridor. My feet are sore, and I am looking forward to a long hot shower. We went for a drink after the day's events, and that turned into dinner. They're all still going, but I'm not really in the mood.

Welcome to the world of casual sex, Claire, where the only rule is there are no rules. I swipe my key and walk into my room and frown. A huge bunch of red roses sits on the table, a small white card carefully pinned on the red ribbon.

ANDERSON

My heart races as I read—it's from him.

I nervously open the card.

WE HAVE UNFINISHED BUSINESS.
COME TO PARIS FOR THE WEEKEND.
XOXOXOX

"What?" I whisper.

I plop down on the bed and stare at the card in my hand.

This is not what I was expecting at all. After mentally throwing daggers at him all day, this is a huge surprise. I read the card again as I consider his proposal.

I can't go to fucking Paris. I have to get home to the kids.

I get a vision of spending three days in a city I've always dreamed of visiting . . . alone with him . . . it could be so fun.

Damn it . . . I want to go.

I just can't. *Stop it, Claire; it is what it is.*

I exhale heavily and make myself a cup of tea.

My phone beeps with a text. It's from Tristan.

Are you back in your room yet?

I smile softly and put the phone down on the coffee table. He's expecting me to call him to say thank you. I go to the flowers and stare at them. I touch the petals—the flowers have huge heads and a strong perfume. French roses. I inhale the beautiful scent.

So unexpected.

Well played, Mr. Miles. Well played.

I decide to check on the kids, and I call my mother. "Hello, dear." I can hear her smile down the phone.

"Hi, Mom. How are you surviving?"

"Oh, we're having a great time. How are you?"

"Good." I pace back and forth. I am filled with nervous energy. "Are the kids home?"

"No, they're all at sports training. They've been angels."

"Listen, Mom." My eyes close. What the hell am I doing? "I've been offered an extension conference in Paris for the weekend." I scrunch my hand up in my hair. "But I don't think I'll go," I add.

"Why not?"

"It's a bit much to ask of you."

"Oh no. Go, honey. The boys and I are having a great time. It's no difference to me when you get home."

"Really?" I frown.

"Yes, I'm loving the quality time I'm getting with the boys. Let off some steam and have some fun, Claire. If anyone deserves it, it's you."

"But what about Patrick? He'll be fretting."

"He's fine and happy, Claire, and, I hate to say it, not missing you at all."

I smile as hope blooms in my chest. "Are you sure?"

"Positive."

"Oh." I pause as my mind wanders off on a million tangents. "I'll think about it. I'll let you know tomorrow; is that okay?"

"Of course. It must be late there. Get some sleep, and call me tomorrow. But I say go for it. Paris is beautiful, and you've never been."

"Maybe." I shrug.

"Goodbye." She hangs up.

In a daze I walk into the bathroom and run the hot water. I need a hot bath to think about this.

An hour later I sit forward and turn the tap off once more. I fill the bath up, let it cool down, let some water out, and repeat the process. My mind is ticking at a million miles per minute.

Tristan is a soul-sucking bastard who left without even a goodbye.

But then . . . he sent roses.

But I don't want roses, because that's not who we are . . . but maybe he was just being nice because he couldn't say goodbye properly?

He's a bastard . . . but he's a fun bastard. Or maybe that was just an act, and I fell for it hook, line, and sinker.

Oh God, I'm so confused.

If I go to Paris, I'm guaranteed laughter and fun.

If I don't go, there's no chance of me getting attached to him.

He's a player. He probably has ten girlfriends. He is not the kind of man you get attached to.

But he's so fun.

Over the last two nights we have laughed and laughed, and it felt good, even if I knew it was only temporary—just in that moment, it felt really good.

There's absolutely no chance of a future or anything; I already know that. We're from two different worlds.

Am I okay to spend a weekend with someone knowing that? I think on it for a moment.

I've had enough heartache. Maybe it's time to throw caution to the wind. Maybe it's time to just . . . no, it's just safer not to go. I mean, what's the point?

Why prolong what was only a one-night thing? We already extended it to two nights. That's enough.

My phone rings, and the name Tristan lights up the screen. Oh fuck.

I close my eyes and answer. "Hello."

"Anderson."

A broad smile crosses my face just at the sound of his voice. "What do you want?" I tease.

He chuckles. "I'm calling to see if you got my gift in your room."

"Oh." I smirk. "I haven't; I'm in Nelson's room."

"What the fuck? You better not be." It's loud where he is, like a bar or something.

I giggle. "They're lovely."

"So?" he asks.

"So what?"

"Come to Paris. Spend the weekend with me."

I stay silent.

"It's one of my favorite cities. I can show you around. We can go sightseeing."

"I thought you were working?"

"Only tomorrow morning." I hear ice tumble into a glass.

"Where are you?" I ask.

"At the hotel bar."

"Trolling for your next victim?" I tease.

"Nobody here has what I want."

I bite my lip as I listen to him.

"You have what I want, Claire."

"You're not going to get all sentimental and needy on me, are you?"

"I don't do sentimental and needy." He chuckles. "Down and dirty is more my thing."

I smile goofily. "I don't know if I can change my flights."

"I'll organize our jet to pick you up."

"You have a plane?" I frown.

"Company plane."

I stay silent as I think.

"Well?"

"Thank you for the roses," I whisper to change the subject.

"That's okay. They were being thrown out from reception, and I didn't want to waste them. My good deed for the day."

I smile at his appalling lie.

"Come on, Anderson; don't make me beg."

"Fine."

"Fine . . . as in it's a chore?" He scoffs. "At least act enthusiastic."

"I can't wait to spend the weekend underneath you, Mr. Miles."

He laughs out loud. "That a girl. I'll call you tomorrow with the flight times."

"Okay."

"Oh . . . and, Claire," he says, as if it's an afterthought.

"Yes."

"Do your Kegel exercises tonight. I want that pussy nice and tight."

I burst out laughing. "You are an idiot."

"Takes one to know one."

"Goodbye, Tristan." I smile.

The phone goes dead.

I throw my phone onto the stack of towels and put my hands over my mouth.

I was supposed to say no.

Oh jeez, that did not go to plan.

Chapter 7

The plane pulls up to a slow halt on the tarmac at the Paris airport, and my nerves are at an all-time high. I already know that this is the stupidest thing I have ever done, and I haven't even done it yet.

Anastacia, the flight attendant, smiles warmly. "I hope you had a good flight?"

"Yes. I did, thank you."

I look around to see if I've left anything. The plane is, in one word, ridiculous. Luxurious on all fronts, and if I had forgotten for one moment who Tristan is, I have been promptly reminded.

A Miles.

Heir to the most successful media empire and from one of the wealthiest families in the world.

And a week ago . . . I hated his guts . . . and maybe I still do.

But there's something about him that makes me want more.

I feel foolish being here. All it took was a few jokes and a little pity, and I fell into his arms and did the unthinkable. If I wanted a future with him, I would leave and play a little hard to get.

But I don't.

I know what this is—one weekend away from routine, a sleazy conference encounter. And that's okay with me. The reality of the situation is actually more than fine.

It's a relief.

I don't have to impress him, I don't have to believe anything he says, and I most definitely don't have to pretend to be someone I'm not.

He's fun and comfortable, and surprisingly he fits like an old shoe. His sexual prowess is just an added bonus.

My stomach drops as a wave of guilt runs through me for being here, for being sexually active with another man.

For loving every hard inch of him and then craving more.

It was supposed to be just one night.

I think back to what Marley said to me before I left. Shouldn't I be living life for Wade and me?

If it were me who'd died, I would never want Wade to be untouched and unhappy.

I would want him to be happy and fulfilled as a man.

After we go home to New York on Sunday night, Tristan and I will never see each other again, and I can go home reinvigorated with enough sex in the tank to last me another five years. To be honest, I'm kind of proud that I'm doing something for myself for once.

This is so unlike me.

"The car is waiting for you, Mrs. Anderson," Anastacia says.

"Thank you." I walk down the stairs and out onto the tarmac. A black car is waiting.

The driver smiles and opens the car door. "Merci," I say as I get in.

He goes around to the driver's side, gets in, and pulls out.

Tristan called earlier, and he couldn't pick me up because his meeting ran late. He's meeting me at the hotel. I smile as I think back to taking his call when I was sitting with his groupies, and none of them had any idea that he and I had hooked up.

It all feels so naughty.

So not who I am.

I clutch my handbag on my lap with white-knuckle force. My breath quivers as I try to calm myself down.

This is the craziest, most spontaneous thing I've ever done.

Half an hour later we pull into the hotel, and I peer out the window at the sign.

FOUR SEASONS HOTEL GEORGE V

Jeez, looks fancy.

"Arrived safely." The driver smiles over at me.

I take my purse from my bag.

"No, no, it's all taken care of," he says as he gets out of the car. He retrieves my suitcase from the trunk and wheels it up to the doorman. He introduces me. "Mrs. Anderson."

The man in a white doorman uniform smiles and nods. "This way, Mrs. Anderson," he says.

"Merci," I say to my driver as he returns to his car.

"Au revoir," he calls.

The man leads me to the reception desk, and I look around. Everything is beige marble, and big exotic artwork lines the walls.

Huge vases of pink fresh flowers are everywhere, and I mean everywhere. It looks like an over-the-top wedding venue.

"May I help you?" the lady at reception asks.

"Yes. I'm here to see Tristan Miles." I clutch my bag.

She types into her computer. "Your name, please?"

"Claire Anderson."

"Yes," she replies. "He's expecting you. Do you have identification, please?"

I pass over my license, and she studies it and types my license number into the computer. She passes me a key. "You are in the

Eiffel Tower Suite on level seven," she says. "We can take you up if you would like?"

"No, that's okay." I smile. "I can go myself." I take the elevator to level seven. Frigging hell, this hotel is next level. Even the damn elevator is fancy.

I let out a low, deep breath. I'm suddenly nervous. I fix my hair in the mirror, and the doors slide open.

Holy hell.

Lush carpet, chandeliers, and insane luxury . . . and this is just the corridor. I walk down until I get to the room number on the key. Do I knock?

No. Just go in.

I swipe my key and am hit in the face with a visual sensation. I feel the blood drain from my face.

It's huge—not a room at all. A whole apartment of over-the-top wealth. A perfectly decorated beautiful space of creams and whites, with french doors going out onto a terrace that overlooks the Eiffel Tower. It's like a movie, only better.

Holy . . . hell.

Huge silver-gilded mirrors hang on the walls, and there are white lounges . . . white? How the heck do they keep white lounges clean? I look around nervously. "Hello?" I call.

I can hear talking out on the terrace, so I put my handbag down and walk to the door. White overlong drapes hang on the french doors.

"Nous devons obtenir une réponse à ce sujet puis-je avancer a ce sujet cette semaine," I hear. I peer out.

Tristan is on the phone out on the balcony . . . speaking French. What the heck? Well, I guess French is among the five languages he supposedly speaks. He glances up and catches sight of me and gives me a breathtaking smile. He holds one finger up to signify he will be just a minute.

I get a flashback of the first day I met him, looking perfect in his expensive suit and pacing with his hand in his trouser pocket as he speaks on the phone.

Déjà vu.

I drop my head as I remember that I don't like who he is and what he does for a living.

God, Claire . . . what are you doing? Couldn't you have found somebody else to get back in the game with?

"Je dois conclure," he says to whomever he's speaking to. He smiles as he watches me and gives me a sexy wink. "One moment," he mouths.

I roll my eyes as I act impatient, but I'm not really. I could listen to him speak French all day. "Come on," I mouth back.

"Malade, je vais vous envoyer un message dans la matinée. Je vais avoir besoin du rapport d'ici lundi s'il vous plaît," he says in his deep sexy voice.

"Hurry," I mouth to tease him.

He bites his bottom lip to stop his smile and holds up his hand to signify that he's going to smack me.

"Promises, promises," I mouth back.

He walks past me into the apartment. "Oui, s'il vous plaît," he says.

He reappears with an ice bucket and a bottle of champagne with two champagne flutes. He holds the phone to his ear with his shoulder as he pops the cork and fills the two glasses.

He leans in and kisses me softly and then hands me a glass of champagne.

"Thank you," I mouth.

He kisses me again, as if unable to stop, and I can hear the other person, a woman, speaking a million miles a minute to him in French.

"Who is it?" I frown.

"My PA," he mouths. He moves his head from side to side, as if she is taking too long to say what she's saying. "Oui, oui, nous en parlerons lundi. Je dois y aller. Au revoir," he replies.

He listens as she keeps speaking, and he rolls his eyes impatiently.

I smile as I sip my champagne. The cool, crisp taste dances on my tongue. Oh yeah. I eye the glass of bubbles—this is the good stuff.

"Okay, je dois y aller. Passer un bon week-end, au revoir," he says. He hangs up and then turns his phone off and turns toward me.

"About time." I smirk.

He takes me into his arms. "Anderson." He smiles down at me as he pumps my hips into his. "Fancy seeing you here."

I smile goofily up at him. He towers above me. He must be six foot three at least. His dark hair is messed to perfection, and his lips are a perfect shade of *come fuck me.*

"Well, I felt sorry for you." I shrug. "This is a pity date." I look around at the grand apartment. "Not sure if I can spend the whole weekend in this dump, though."

He chuckles. "I do love your smart-ass mouth." He pumps me with his hips once more. "I may have to fuck it later."

I giggle as he kisses me again. This one has a little tongue, and it's as if he's licking me there . . . my entire insides clench in appreciation.

He steps back and holds out his hand to the Eiffel Tower. "Welcome to Paris."

"Oui, oui." I smile.

He pulls out a chair and sits at the table. He refills my glass. "How was your flight?"

"Good." I frown as a thought runs through my mind. "You have a French PA?"

"Yes." He shrugs casually. "I spend a lot of time here."

"How much?"

He scratches his head as he thinks. "Maybe four or five months a year," he replies casually, as if this is no big deal.

"You live here for a third of the year?" I ask in surprise.

"Yeah." He sips his champagne. "My brothers Elliot and Christopher and I share the operations of the French, English, and German offices. We take turns so that one of us is always at each place."

"Why don't you just take one office each?" I ask.

"Because then"—he sips his wine—"we would all live alone on the other side of the world from one another. This way, we're all doing the same job and sharing the responsibilities and see each other and talk all the time."

"You're close to your brothers?"

"Yes." He frowns, as if that's a weird question. "They're my best friends. We've been alone together for a long time."

"Alone?" I repeat. "I thought your parents were still alive?"

"Oh, they are. But I mean . . ." He pauses, as if contemplating his answer. "We went to boarding school together overseas from a young age. We shared a room, and it has mostly always been just the four of us."

"Oh." I sip my wine, and I find myself wanting to ask a million questions about his formative years. "How come you went to boarding school?"

"For the languages." He shrugs. "Among other things."

"You are all multilingual?"

"Yes. We need to be in this business." He exhales deeply as he stares out over the view. "We've always been in training to take over Miles Media. There was never a time when we were . . ." His voice trails off, as if he's cut himself short. He seems uncomfortable with the topic.

"Well, that makes sense, then," I interrupt.

"What does?"

"Why you're such a dirty-talking cad. You had no discipline as a child."

He smiles.

"I bet you were all fucking your governesses in boarding school."

He puts his head back and laughs out loud. "Jameson was, actually, come to think of it."

"Really?" I gasp. Jameson is his older brother and the CEO of Miles Media. We both laugh, and his eyes linger on my face.

"So now that you have me here, Mr. Miles, what are you going to do with me?" I ask.

"Hmm." His eyes hold mine. "The possibilities are endless, really."

I smile.

"You have three options, Anderson."

"Yes."

"You can get your smart-ass mouth fucked."

I smile. That sounds pretty good, actually.

"Or you can bend over, and I'll give my own version of the Eiffel Tower."

I chuckle. He's so ridiculous. Where does he come up with this stuff?

"Or"—he sips his drink and casually shrugs—"I suppose I could take you out for dinner and dancing or something equally boring."

I smile over at him.

He raises a sexy eyebrow. "Well?"

I narrow my eyes as I fake concentration. "I'll take dinner and dancing, thank you."

He rolls his eyes. "Ugh, I knew you were going to pick that one. You're boring. Why would you want to dance when you have the opportunity to suck my dick?"

I laugh, loud and free. The conversations I have with this man kill me.

"What?" He smirks.

I stare at his beautiful face for a moment. "Tristan Miles, I have never met anyone quite like you."

"Ditto." He holds his glass up. "A toast."

I take a big gulp of my champagne and touch my glass with his.

"To swallowing semen," he says.

What the hell? I snort and spit my drink out, and it spurts all over the table as I laugh out loud. "You're head obsessed today."

He sits back in his chair; his eyes are alight with mischief. "That's because I can't stop thinking about it."

"Tristan." I lean forward in my chair.

He leans forward, too, mimicking me. "Yes, Claire."

"Be a good boy, and you might get what you want."

He smiles darkly. "Or be a bad boy, and take it anyway."

The air crackles between us; our eyes are locked, and nerves flutter deep in my stomach.

I think those two lines just summed up the entirety of Tristan Miles.

I can kid myself all I want about being in charge.

We both know I'm not.

We're in a busy and bustling restaurant. It's late, after one o'clock in the morning, and we are sitting side by side at the bar.

The mood of the place is loud and jovial, and music is piped throughout the space.

We've had dinner, and I haven't laughed this much since I don't know when.

Claire Anderson is fucking hilarious.

She's tipsy and relaxing more and more by the minute. I like her like this. I mean, I like her anyway, but she is at her best when her defenses are down.

She's wearing a fitted black dress with spaghetti straps and stilettoes. Her thick shoulder-length dark hair is down, and she's wearing minimal makeup.

She has no idea how fucking sexy she is.

It's the weirdest thing—she's everything that I've never found attractive before.

And I don't even know what it is about her, but I find myself hanging on her every word.

"Tell me." She smiles as she takes my hand in hers. "How are you still single?"

I smile and pick up our hands and bring them to my mouth. I kiss hers and then shrug.

"How old are you?" She frowns.

"How old do you want me to be?"

"You only say that if you're a prostitute."

I widen my eyes. "How do you know I'm not? How do you know that Marley hasn't paid me to seduce you?"

Her lips twist as she fights a smile. "How much is she paying you?"

"There isn't enough money in the world." I smirk into my glass as I take a sip. "Keeping you satisfied is a dirty job. I bit off more than I can chew. I'm demanding a pay raise."

The woman at the bar beside us looks at me and then turns to the bar, as if revolted.

My eyes widen. She heard me. Claire tips her head back and laughs out loud.

I tap the woman on the arm. "She's not paying me," I whisper. "I'm seducing her for free." I cross my fingers on my chest. "And I'm not chewing. It's all licking."

Claire really loses it and laughs hard, and I find myself laughing too.

I fall serious and watch her laugh for a moment, because what I told the woman is not even true.

Claire Anderson is seducing me.

"Answer my question," she says.

"I'm thirty-four."

"And you're still single?" She frowns as she contemplates my age. "How is that possible?"

I sip my drink. "I don't know." I shrug. "I've had four serious relationships over the course of time."

"And they didn't work out?"

"Nope."

"Why not?"

"You're very nosy, Anderson."

She giggles. "I know. You ask me a question next."

I smile and clink my glass with hers. "I'll start thinking of one now." I narrow my eyes, as if concentrating.

"Well?" she prompts me. "Answer my question first."

How do I say this . . . I'm fucked up, and something is wrong with me?

That I've been searching for something for years, but I have no idea what it actually is?

Just tell her the easy version.

"I don't know, to be honest. The girls I went out with were all beautiful—perfect, actually." She watches me intently. "But when push came to shove, I didn't want to fight for it."

"Meaning what?"

"Well, as history repeats, I seem to have a time limit for relationships." I smile at her fascination. "Like a use-by date."

"A use-by date," she scoffs. "What does that mean? How many times you have sex with them?"

I laugh at the double meaning. "No, not that . . . for God's sake."

She puts her hand on my thigh.

"I seem to meet someone, and then we fall into a routine and . . ." I pause.

"What?"

"She falls in love with me and wants to move in and have marriage and babies, and I, for some reason, find something wrong with her and begin to back off."

She listens intently.

"I don't know what it is." I sip my drink. "I don't know why I'm like this. The second girlfriend I had was probably the one. I adored her. Was sad for years when we broke up."

"But you didn't love her?"

"I don't know." I put my hand on top of hers on my leg.

"So she left you?"

"No. I left her."

"But if you were sad for years about it, why didn't you just go back to her?"

"I didn't want to."

She frowns as she watches me.

"I mean, what is love?" I bite my bottom lip as I think; how did we get onto this deep subject? "I mean, define being in love with someone, Anderson. Because I can't; for the life of me I can't."

"Well." She thinks for a moment. "I think it's just like having a best friend who you want to fuck."

I smirk. "That sounds pervy."

"It is a bit." She giggles.

I watch her for a moment. "What was your husband like?"

Her shoulders instantly slump. "He was . . ." Her demeanor becomes sad. "He was a great man. Proud." Her focus shifts from me to a spot over the bar. "I miss him every day."

I squeeze her hand in mine. "What kind of wife were you?" I ask.

She smiles at my change of the subject. "I was a great wife."

"Really?" I fake shock. "I find that hard to believe."

She laughs. "Maybe just an all right wife."

"And you have kids?" I ask.

"Uh-huh, three boys."

I scrunch up my nose. "I can't actually believe that."

"Why not?" she scoffs.

"I've never been with anyone who has kids before."

"What? Never?"

"Nope."

"Why not?"

"I don't know. It's weird, come to think of it. I have a very specific type of woman that I'm attracted to."

She laughs and holds her hands up in the air. "Wait, let me guess."

I chuckle as I hold my hand up for another round of drinks. I'm feeling very inebriated. "Please do."

"Hot body."

I tip my glass in agreement.

"Young."

"Affirmative."

She narrows her eyes at me as she thinks. "I'm saying blonde."

"You're nailing me here." I chuckle. "Every time."

Her eyes dance with delight. "So she has to be a natural blonde with a hot body and younger than you."

"Pretty much."

"What else does she have to have?"

I roll my lips as I think. "I like trendy girls."

"Trendy girls," she scoffs. "What does that mean?"

"I don't know why, but I like girls who are into fashion."

"Like . . . models?" She frowns.

"No, not necessarily models, but girls who are into dressing nice and look after themselves."

"Handbags."

I smirk with a shrug.

"You like girls who look good on your arm."

"Possibly." I chuckle at her analogy. "Why, what do you like in men?"

She raises her eyebrows as she thinks. "I don't know."

"What do you mean?"

"I don't know what I like. I only had two boyfriends before Wade and then . . . you."

I smile over at her. I like that there's not many. "And what did you like about me?"

"Well." She falls serious. "I wanted to turn you."

"Turn me." I frown as I take a big gulp of my drink. "Into what?"

"A motherfucker."

I snort, and my drink dribbles onto my chin. "What?" I splutter.

"I want to go down in the history books as the woman who officially turned Tristan Miles into a motherfucker."

I laugh out loud as I take a napkin and wipe my face.

This woman is hilarious. I grab her in a headlock and nearly pull her off her chair. People around us all watch our drunken behavior. "If I had known how fun it was to fuck around with an aged duck, I would have been doing it long ago," I whisper in her ear.

She laughs and punches me under my coat and pulls out of my grip. She fixes her hair in an overexaggerated way. "I'll have you know I'm not even old, Mr. Miles."

"How old are you?"

"I'm thirty-eight."

I smile. "Only four years older than me."

"Why, how old did you think I was?"

"At least"—I smirk as I think of a number—"sixty."

"Tristan!" she cries.

I grab the back of her head and drag her in to kiss me. She smiles against my lips. "Don't try and sweeten the last comment with those magic lips," she whispers.

I put my mouth to her ear so that nobody else can hear me. "What about my magic tongue?"

She smirks.

"Did you know I'm good with my tongue?" I nibble on her ear, and she giggles as she tries to escape me. What must we look like to other people? Carrying on like teenagers.

"I am well aware of your strengths, Mr. Miles."

I hold her face and kiss her. I completely lose focus on where we are, and my eyes close in pleasure.

Oh, this woman . . . she makes me forget everything and everyone. When I open my eyes again, I see her smiling dreamily up at me. "What's that look for?" I ask.

She becomes thoughtful and cups my face in her hands. "In all seriousness, Tris, thank you."

"For what?"

"For making me remember what it feels like to laugh."

I smile softly, and we stare at each other for a moment. Suddenly I'm hit with an urgency to be alone with her. "Are you ready to go home, Anderson?"

"Yes, I am, motherfucker."

I laugh out loud and pull her from the stool. "And just by chance, you're a mother. How convenient."

Chapter 8

It's late, and we've been at it for hours. The arch of Claire's back as she lies beneath me tells me she's close. I'm wet with perspiration and holding myself up on straight arms as I drive her into the mattress.

She whimpers beneath me, and I tip my head back and close my eyes in ecstasy.

Her wet body is rippling around mine, sucking me in, and the sound of skin slapping is echoing through the room.

This is when she's at her best; this is when she has me in the palm of her hand.

On an orgasm high, worn down, and unable to filter what she says.

Vulnerable and soft.

"Tris," she whispers as she reaches out to pull me down to her. "I need you."

Our lips crash together, and it's not just my balls that are about to explode.

It's my fucking head—this woman fries my brain.

She clenches hard, and we both moan as the wave of an orgasm crashes between us.

She clings to me as we pant and half laugh; our heart rates race together.

I go to pull out, and she clings to me. "No, Tris," she whispers. "Stay inside of me."

"Just let me roll you over, baby." I kiss her softly. "I can't hold myself up any longer."

I pull out and roll her onto her side away from me and lift her leg and slide back in. I wrap her tightly in my arms. She smiles sleepily as I kiss her temple. "That's better," she whispers. I kiss her neck as I hold her tight.

We fell asleep like this last night, too, our bodies joined. As one.

Claire Anderson.

The high of the orgasm she gives me isn't half as good as the high after it.

When I'm holding her in my arms like this, intimacy is running between us like a river, and just for a moment . . .

She is mine.

I wake with a huge stretch and a smile. God. It's been years since I've slept this well.

I roll over to see Tristan on his back. One arm is behind his head, and the other is scrolling through his phone. The white sheet is pooled around his groin, and his rippled stomach is on display.

What a sight to wake up to. "Good morning."

He smiles and leans over to kiss me. "Morning." His hand lingers on my jaw as he smiles sexily over at me.

"Why are you awake so early?" I ask.

"Been up for hours. Couldn't sleep," he mutters as he returns to his phone and keeps scrolling.

"Why not?"

"All your snoring. It's like sleeping with a boar cuddling your back. It gives a new meaning to a wild night."

I giggle and rub my eyes as I try to wake myself up.

"What's your name on Instagram?" he asks as he concentrates on his phone.

"Huh?" I glance over at him.

"I've been looking for you for a good hour. What's your name?"

"You woke up early to stalk my Instagram?" I frown.

"Name," he replies flatly as he continues to stare at his screen.

"I have a private account."

"And?"

"And . . . it's private."

His eyes flick over to me. "You're not going to give it to me?"

"No." I smile. "I have like fifty followers, and they are mostly family. It's me and my kids, personal stuff. Nothing exciting, I can assure you."

He sits up on his elbow. "What? And I can't see it?"

I smile at his outrage. "Tristan, why would you want to?" I sit up and climb out of bed. "It's just my kid stuff. Sports, birthdays, pets . . . crap like that."

"Well . . . maybe because I spent half the night inside your body, I assumed I would be able to see what your kids look like."

I smile at his annoyance. "No. You can't, actually." I throw my robe on around my shoulders. "My kids are off limits and not up for discussion with you." I walk into the bathroom and close the door. "Trust me, Tristan," I call through the door. "It's not like all your girlfriends' Instagram accounts. Stalk them instead." I go to the bathroom and come back out to find him still on his phone. He's glaring at it, as if he's annoyed.

"What are we doing today?" I ask.

"Hmm," he grunts, unimpressed. "I'm going to steal your phone, take a shot of my cock, and post it on your"—he holds his fingers up to air quote—"'private Instagram' with the heading *Paris, hashtag loving-the-cock*."

I giggle. "That's a great hashtag."

He throws his phone to the side and rolls me over onto my back. "You wound me, Anderson." He kisses me. "Why can't I see your kids?"

I run my fingers through his dark stubble. "You know why." I kiss him softly. "We aren't like that."

He stares down at me for a moment and then blinks, as if processing my words.

"Well?" I ask. "What are we doing today?"

"Stuff," he mutters dryly as he rolls off me onto his back. "Lots of stuff."

I frown as I watch him. "What puts you in this mood today?" I ask.

"Nothing." He puts the back of his forearm over his eyes.

"Tris." I pull his arm off his face.

His eyes hold mine.

"Look at you getting all needy."

"I am not getting all needy," he snaps, insulted.

"What's this, then?"

"This is . . ." He frowns as he tries to articulate himself. "I'm not fucking needy, Claire. I've never been needy in my entire life."

"If you say so." I smile and kiss him. I run my fingers through his hair to try to calm him. "Take me sightseeing, Mr. Miles. Show me Paris through your eyes."

He regains his composure and rolls me onto my back and holds my hands above my head. "The only way you're going to be seeing Paris is on the end of my dick."

I giggle. "You're a sex maniac."

He bites my bottom lip and stretches it out. "We already established this."

The candlelight flickers on our faces.

We are in Tristan's favorite restaurant in Paris. He's ordered for us, and I swear every time he talks to someone in French, I lose a little more of my mind.

What a dreamy day. We went to the Louvre and then to the Eiffel Tower. Then we strolled down the Champs-Élysées, a strip of gorgeous shops. We visited the Arc de Triomphe and then went to the ruins of Notre Dame. At one point, I thought Tristan was going to burst into tears. He loves that chapel and had been there many times before it burned down. I take his hand over the table. "Thank you, Tris. I've had the best day."

He smiles warmly over at me.

"Seriously, like one of my favorite days ever in my entire life."

His eyes glow with tenderness as he squeezes my hand. "I'm glad. It's a beautiful city."

"Oh . . . it really is," I gush. "The Eiffel Tower and, oh, the Louvre." I shake my head as I go over the day. "I can't believe I'm even here, you know?"

He sips his red wine as he smiles over at me. "And it's not over yet. I got you a surprise."

"You did?" I smile.

"Tickets to Moulin Rouge tonight."

My mouth falls open. "Are you serious?"

"You can't come here and not see it." He smiles sexily.

"Oh," I gush over at him. "You are the best tour guide ever. You know so much about this place."

"I've spent a lot of time here."

"Do you always stay at the same hotel?"

"Always, and the same room."

"You always stay in the same room?"

"Yes." He chuckles. "Makes me feel more at home if I have familiar surroundings."

"What's it like?" I frown. "What's it like traveling the world on your own?"

"I'm not alone. I have friends everywhere I go. I just pick up where I left off with them last time I was here."

I watch him for a moment. "Do you have a lady friend here?"

"No one steady."

That shouldn't make me as happy as it does. "Where do you live in New York?" I ask.

"I have a penthouse in Tribeca."

"Oh." I frown.

"Where do you live?" he asks.

"I have a house in Long Island."

"Long Island?" he gasps. "You commute every day?"

"Yeah." I shrug. "We wanted the kids to have a house with a yard growing up."

"Hmm." He thinks on my answer for a moment and rests his chin on his hand with his elbow on the table.

"I don't know if I want to go to Moulin Rouge with you," I say, deep in thought.

"Why not?"

I shrug bashfully. "All those beautiful young girls with their boobs hanging out."

He smiles over at me.

"I might get jealous." I smile as I sip my wine. "You must date some beautiful women."

He sips his wine but doesn't reply. The question hangs in the air between us. "What was your favorite thing you saw today?" He changes the subject.

"Honestly?"

"Of course."

"It was you."

Our eyes lock.

"You were the most beautiful thing I saw today, Tristan Miles."

The air swirls between us, and he takes my hand again over the table. "Do you know how you can really impress me, Anderson?"

"How?"

"You can strip down to a G-string, go topless, and get onstage tonight at the Moulin Rouge and dance for me."

I giggle as I imagine the horror. "I don't want to evacuate the establishment."

He drops his chin back onto his hand and gives me a slow, sexy smile. "The other women would all pale to your beauty."

I smirk at his ridiculous statement.

"On any stage," he whispers as his eyes hold mine.

An unwelcome flutter happens in my stomach.

The air between us is electric, and I know that I shouldn't be feeling this . . . whatever this is . . . but when he says sweet things, I can't help but feel something in my chest.

All day we have laughed and held hands and carried on like kids in love.

I'm not sure that Tristan Miles is as hard as I once thought he was.

"And the answer was no," he says softly.

"To what?" I'm confused as to what he's talking about.

"I don't remember if I dated any beautiful women."

I frown.

"Because," he whispers as his eyes drop to my lips, "at this moment, all I can think about . . . is you."

My heart beats faster as we stare at each other, and I want to go around to his side of the table and take him into my arms and kiss him.

But I can't.

I can't imagine that this is more than it is, that his pretty words are more than just pretty words. Because he's a fantasy man, and we can't be anything more than a weekend away. Our lives are too different—*we* . . . are too different.

I know that.

"What's going to happen tonight when everyone sees me naked on the stage at the Moulin Rouge?" I ask.

"I'll be fighting the men off." He chuckles. "Probably the women too."

I giggle and pick up my wine. I hold my glass out and clink it with his.

"To naked brawling," I whisper.

His eyes twinkle with a certain something. "Naked anything, where you're concerned."

This poor, deluded man. Since when did cellulite and stretch marks become hot? I bet he never thought he would see the day. I giggle. "You must be sick of seeing me naked, Mr. Miles."

"Anderson, I'm just getting started."

We walk out through the departure lounge of the private part of the airport. Tristan is wheeling both of our suitcases behind him, and we walk in through large glass doors from the tarmac. One lone lady is checking and stamping passports to let us into the country. "Hello, Mr. Miles." She smiles.

Jeez, he flies so much that the staff all know him.

"Hello, Margarete," he says. "Where's Boris?"

"On day shift today."

She opens his passport. "How was Paris?"

"Parfaite." He smiles.

She giggles on cue, and I smirk over at him.

Flirt.

She stamps our passports, and we look into the eye-scanner thingy.

This is so much more civilized than standing in the queue for an hour.

"Goodbye, Margarete," he says as he pulls our two suitcases through another huge door. When we walk out, I look around, disoriented. Oh, we are in the foyer of the airport. I never knew that these doors into this private part of the airport were even here.

"Where are you parked?" Tristan asks.

"Over in long term, level one."

"Okay, I'll just drop my bag at the car and walk you up."

"You don't have to."

"I want to."

We walk out through the front doors, and he walks to the left with our two suitcases and stops at a black limo. The driver gets out. "Hey, Tris," he says.

I stop on the spot, shocked. He has a limo . . . what the heck?

"This is Claire," he says to introduce me. "This is Calvin."

"Hello." He smiles.

I give a weak wave.

Calvin grabs his suitcase, and Tristan takes my hand. We walk toward level one.

"I can wheel my suitcase."

"Let me act like a gentleman, please," he says as he walks.

"You have a limo?" I frown.

He shrugs, as if it's no big deal. "Miles Media has limos. It's not personally mine."

I'm suddenly reminded of who he is. *A Miles.*

We walk for a while, and I feel anxious. I don't want to let him go, but I know I have to. I went to France to fill my well—I got the ocean instead.

Tristan Miles is beautiful, smart, and witty, and he makes me laugh, which is not an easy feat, and that's just on top of the amazing sex. But more than that, he makes me feel like I'm the most beautiful woman in the world. Never once, not even for a second, did I feel insecure about my body. He constantly had his arm around me or was holding my hand, kissing me. Listening to everything I said and giving me great conversation. I think we talked the entire weekend; never once did it feel forced or uncomfortable.

He's going.

I exhale as reality begins to seep through my bones. The man I was away with doesn't really exist. He is a very small piece of who Tristan Miles is. Sadly, my first instincts are in fact his reality, and even though we've had an amazing time together . . .

It ends here.

I can't even fathom being with someone like him long term.

We take the elevator to level one, and he's quiet too.

"This is me." I smile as we get to my car.

I pop the trunk, and he puts my suitcase in and turns to me. Now it's awkward . . . now it feels forced.

"Thank you so much for a great weekend." I smile.

He takes me into his arms. "Are you sure you can't stay at my house tonight? It is late."

I give him a sad smile. "I have to get home to the boys."

He nods and inhales sharply.

We stare at each other, and it's as if we both have something to say but are holding our tongues.

"Goodbye."

He kisses me, long and deep. Our eyes close at the contact. He holds my face in his hands, and my feet float from the floor. "Call me when you get home so I know you got there safe?" He pushes my hair behind my shoulders.

"Okay." I smile up at him.

With one last big hug and another kiss, he lets me go, and I climb into my car.

He puts his hands into his jeans pockets as I pull out, and with one last sad wave, I drive off. My eyes watch him in the rearview mirror as I drive toward the exit of the parking lot. He's standing still and watching my car disappear.

"Goodbye, Tristan." I sigh. All good things come to an end . . . damn it.

Why do you have to be him?

An hour later I pull into the driveway at home.

I sit and stare at it for a while. There's a bike on the porch and a basketball left on the ground near the hoop. Shoes are scattered everywhere, and no matter how many times I tell them to pack their crap away, it always looks like this.

I smile at the familiarity. *I'm home.*

I pick up my phone and text Tristan.

Arrived home, safe and sound.
XOXOX

I climb out of the car, and the front door flies open. Patrick and Harry come flying out. "Hello." I laugh. They both nearly tackle me to the ground as they wrap their arms around me.

"Hello, my darlings. I missed you." I cuddle them both and squeeze them tight.

"Did you bring us presents?" Patrick asks.

"Yes, hello, Mom," I correct him.

"Hello, Mom," Patrick repeats.

"Mom, Fletcher is out of control," Harry says. "He didn't rinse the dishes before he put them in the dishwasher, and now it's clogged."

"Oh." I frown as I pop the trunk.

"Him and Grandma are trying to fix it now."

"That doesn't sound good," I mutter as I grab my suitcase. Harry takes it from me and starts to pull it up the driveway.

"Let me do it," Patrick says.

"No," Harry snaps. "You're too little."

"I am not too little," Patrick yells at the top of his voice as he swings a punch at his brother.

Harry pushes Patrick, and he falls over. "Oww. Mom, he pushed me!" he yells.

I roll my eyes. Ugh. I haven't missed their bickering. "Shh, it's late," I whisper. "Keep your voice down. Poor Mrs. Reynolds will wake up."

I glance up at the window next door. If the truth be known, Mrs. Reynolds is already watching us. She knows what happens in the street before it actually happens.

We walk up to the front porch. "Why are everyone's shoes everywhere?" I ask. "The shoebox is for shoes."

For God's sake. I stop and throw all the shoes into the shoebox as the boys continue dragging my suitcase into the house. We must look like slobs to the rest of the street.

Every day, fifteen pairs of shoes are scattered everywhere. Every single night, I put them all back into the shoebox. Yeesh.

I walk into the house and through the living area out to the kitchen and frown as I take in the sight.

The dishwasher is pulled out from the wall, and Fletcher is on his back underneath it.

There are tools scattered all over the kitchen floor, and he is shining the flashlight on his phone up into it. "Hi, Mom," he calls. "I'm fixing the dishwasher."

"Great." I frown at my mother. "Does he know what he's doing?" I mouth.

"No." She widens her eyes and shrugs. "He doesn't."

God.

"How was it, love?" Mom smiles as she pulls me into a hug.

"It was wonderful. Thank you so much for watching the kids." Woofy, our dog, comes flying around the corner with a huge cone on his head. "What the heck happened to Woofy?" I ask.

"Oh, he chased a squirrel under a metal fence and cut his back," Mom says.

"Oh no. Is he okay?" I bend and pull my faithful friend's face to mine. "Are you okay?" I ask him.

"Yes, but he got stitches, and now he needs to wear a cone so that he can't chew them out."

"Ugh, why didn't you tell me over the phone?"

"Because we wanted you to relax. I'm going to take a shower, and then I want to hear everything." She disappears upstairs.

"Okay." I exhale heavily as I look around at the chaos.

"Where are my presents?" Patrick asks.

"They're wrapped up. You can have them tomorrow. I have to unpack my entire suitcase to find them, and it's too late now," I say.

"Aww." He frowns as he puts his hands on his hips in disgust. "I've been waiting up for this."

"I thought you were waiting up for me." I smirk as I tickle him and pull him into a hug.

"I was, really—I was just pretending." He corrects himself for being insensitive.

I glance over and see Harry sitting on the couch. He never demands my attention but needs it more than anyone. I go and sit beside him, and Patrick flops on my lap.

"What have I missed, Harry?" I ask.

"Everything," he says, clearly unimpressed. "You've been gone too long, and I don't want you going away again. I was getting out of control at school with you not here."

I smile and mess up his hair. "Okay, no more trips."

"Do you promise?" he asks.

"I promise."

Fletcher climbs up from underneath the dishwasher and turns it on. "I fixed it, Mom," he announces.

I smile. Fletcher likes to fix things. I think he thinks that's what he should do as the man of the house. "Thanks, buddy." I hold my arms out for him, and he comes and hugs me. "I missed you." I squeeze him tight. "Thanks for taking care of everyone."

I'm not joking; I'm really not going away again. I missed them desperately.

The dishwasher begins to churn, and Fletcher smiles proudly. "Told you I fixed it."

"I never had any doubts." I smile.

"Harry and Patrick, upstairs to clean your teeth. I'll come up in a moment. You have school tomorrow."

They moan and walk upstairs.

Fletcher packs up all the tools into the toolbox. "I'm taking them out to the garage."

"Thanks, buddy."

He disappears outside.

I go to the bathroom and then turn the television channel. I'm walking over to the fridge when I feel something wet on my foot. Huh?

I glance down, and my eyes widen in horror.

Water is flying out of the bottom of the dishwasher; the entire floor is flooded, and it is running into the next room.

"Ahh!" I yell. "Fletcher. Turn the water off." He doesn't reply, and I run to the linen closet and grab whatever I can to stop the house from flooding. "Fletcher!" I scream as I throw blankets onto the floor. "Quick."

He appears, and his face falls in horror as he sees the flooding.

"Don't just stand there!" I yell. "Turn the water off."

He runs outside.

The water is spurting out of the bottom of the dishwasher now like a fire hose.

The kitchen is four inches deep, and the living area carpet is all wet too.

What the fuck did he do? "Ahh," I cry as I try to make a dam so it won't go farther.

The water turns off, and I pant as I work fast to try to stop the carnage.

Fletcher comes running back in. "What do I do?"

"Get some towels; help me mop this up, honey." He runs off, and we get to work.

"What the hell happened?" I hear Mom cry. I look to the top of the stairs and see my mother sopping wet and wrapped in a towel with a headful of shampoo. "I can't rinse off the shampoo. The water stopped. What am I supposed to do now?" she cries.

For fuck's sake.

I pinch the bridge of my nose. *Back to reality.*

It's Monday morning, and I walk into the office. I can hardly wipe the satisfied grin from my face.

"Well, hello there." Marley smirks as she looks me up and down. "Look at you, all glowy and shit?"

I pull her into a hug. "Thank you for forcing me to go. You were right; I really needed it."

"You liked it?" She frowns in surprise.

"I loved it. I even booked in for next year."

"Yes." She pumps her fist. "I fucking knew you would love that motivational shit."

"Who knew?" I smile and walk past her into my office and take a seat.

"Do you want a coffee?" Marley calls.

"Umm . . ." I frown as I dig my phone out of my bag.

"You're going to need it. You have like a thousand emails to answer."

I roll my eyes. "Yeah, okay, thanks."

I plug my phone in to charge, and the screen lights up.

Five missed calls, Tristan.

Shit, when did he call me? I scroll through to the missed calls. Last night.

Hmm. I was so exhausted after I mopped up the lake-size flood in the house, and by the time the emergency plumber left, I didn't even check my phone.

Oh well. I turn it on silent, put it down, and boot up my computer. I smile broadly. I honestly feel like I haven't been here for a month. So rejuvenated.

My stomach growls, and I glance at my watch. Eleven thirty. Marley was right; I haven't even come up for air this morning.

A knock sounds at the door, and I glance up at it. Where's Marley?

"Come in," I call.

I keep reading an email, then glance up to see Tristan standing there. Navy suit, pale-pink shirt, and crimson tie—looking as gorgeous as can be. "Tristan," I stammer. "What are you doing here?"

He gives me a slow, sexy smile. "Well, you're not answering my calls, so I had no choice." He walks over to me and bends and kisses my lips.

I jerk back from him. "What are you doing?"

"Kissing you hello."

"Don't."

"Why not?" He frowns.

"Tristan." I stare at him for a moment. He can't be serious. "The dirty weekend was just that. One weekend. I don't want anything with you."

Chapter 9

He screws up his face. "What are you talking about, Anderson?" he scoffs. "Get your stuff. We're going to lunch."

What?

"Are you listening to me, Tris?" I stand up.

"No. I'm not. You're talking shit." He puts his hands on my hips and smirks down at me. "Why wouldn't we see each other when we get on so well? That's the most ridiculous thing that's ever come out of your mouth."

The door opens, and we both turn suddenly.

Marley's eyes widen in horror as she sees me in Tristan's arms. "Oh . . . sorry." She winces.

Shit.

Tristan steps back from me, clearly annoyed at the interruption.

"That's okay." I force a smile. "What is it, Marley?"

"I was going to see if you wanted lunch, but . . ."

"No, she's having lunch with me," Tristan asserts.

My eyes flick to him. "I'm fine for the moment, Marley. Thank you."

Marley's wide eyes dart between Tristan and me, and I can almost hear her brain ticking . . . just great. How the heck do I explain this?

Tristan glares at Marley and raises an impatient eyebrow.

"Oh," she stammers, all flustered. "I'll just be at reception."

Tristan's nostrils flare in annoyance. "Okay."

She points outside with her thumb. "If you need me—"

"Thank you, Marley," he interrupts her.

She smiles broadly and closes the door, and his eyes come back to me. "Where were we?"

I smile and rub my hand down his arm. "Tris. We can't see each other anymore."

He brushes my hand off. "What?"

"We can't see each other."

"*You're* dumping *me*?"

"Nobody is dumping anybody," I say softly. "I really, really like you. The guy I went away with was perfect."

"So why can't we see each other?" he scoffs.

"Because of the obvious."

"Like what?" he snaps. His anger is building.

"Tristan, because you are Tristan Miles, and I'm too old for you. I have children and responsibilities, and you like young blondes who are into fashion."

He narrows his eyes. "Don't be fucking funny, Anderson."

"I'm not. You told me that yourself." I take his hand in mine. "Tris, if circumstances were different and you were . . ." I pause as I try to articulate what I want to say. "If you were older than me and say . . . had been divorced and had a few kids, we could maybe try and see each other."

"What?" he snaps again. "You won't see me because I don't have children? That's fucking ridiculous, Anderson. Can you hear yourself right now?"

"Don't raise your voice at me," I warn him.

"Shut up, and come to lunch with me." He takes me into his arms, and his lips drop to my neck. Is he for real? "Tristan." I sigh. Jeez. "Stop it."

"Don't tell me you don't like me, because I know you do."

"I do. I'm not denying it. I adore you."

"So?"

"I don't like you . . . like that."

He stares at me, as if trying to process my words. "Like what?"

I'm just going to have to come out with it. "Tris, you aren't exactly boyfriend material for me."

"What?" he snaps in an outrage. He points to his chest. "*I'm* . . . not boyfriend material?" he whispers. "I'm great fucking boyfriend material, Claire."

I exhale . . . here we go. He's angry now. "No. You're not."

"If anyone around here is not partner material, it's you."

I cross my arms and watch him as he begins to pace, furious at my rejection.

"You, Claire Anderson . . . are too old for me."

"I know."

"And you"—he points at me—"have too many children."

"Precisely."

"And I'm not into kids. Especially when they aren't mine."

I hold my hands out wide. "Like I said."

"And I don't want to be with someone who can't be spontaneous, anyway."

"Good. You shouldn't." I smile.

"Don't be fucking condescending, Anderson."

I roll my eyes. "Are you finished?"

"No. I'm not," he growls. "You piss me off."

"I gathered that."

"Stop it."

I pull him into my arms and run my fingers through his dark hair. His big beautiful brown eyes search mine, and he puts his hands on my hips. "You really are a beautiful man, Tris," I whisper.

He pulls me closer.

126

"You deserve the best." I kiss his lips as I run my fingers through his stubble. "I'm not her; I'm sorry. I wish I was. I really do. We are at different stages of our lives. You are just about to settle down and start a family, and I am finishing with mine."

"Stop talking."

"We both know that this isn't going anywhere. I'm not a casual-sex kind of person, and you are."

"Shut the fuck up, Anderson." He kisses me softly and with just the right amount of tongue. My stomach flutters. "One last time?" he whispers against my lips.

God, it's so tempting . . . "No."

He pushes me up against the wall and slides his hand up my skirt. "Let me fuck you on your desk." His mouth drops to my neck, and I giggle as I look up at the ceiling. "I told you I was going to do it. Right here, right now."

"Tristan." I laugh as I push him off me. "You gave me an option: France or my desk. I took France. You don't get the desk. Now you need to go."

He stares at me for a moment. "You're actually serious about this?"

"Yes."

"You don't want to see me ever again?" He frowns.

"No."

His mouth falls open. He really is shocked. "But we had the best weekend."

"I know. It completely sucks that you're a soul-sucking bastard player." I turn him and push him toward the door. "Now, I need to work."

He chuckles, amused at my description. "This is the stupidest thing you've ever done." He smirks.

I laugh and keep pushing him toward the door.

"You're missing out on some magical dick." He grabs his crotch.

"Undoubtedly."

We get to the door, and he turns toward me. We stare at each other for a moment, and he steps forward and pins me to the door. He grabs my face in his hands, and his tongue swipes through my open lips. My knees weaken, and he grinds his hard cock up against me. He turns my head and puts his mouth to my ear. "Guess what, Anderson?" he whispers.

"What?" I smile.

"We're not over . . . till . . . I say we're over."

He pulls off me and leaves. The door clicks, and my chest rises and falls as I stare at the back of it. A broad smile crosses my face.

Tristan fucking Miles.

I sit back down at my desk and get back to work, and five minutes later my door bursts open. "Are you serious?" Marley gasps as she closes it behind her. "What the fuck did I just see?" she whispers.

"Nothing." I open my email. "Forget you saw it."

"Claire Anderson. I demand to know what the hell is going on with that god."

"He's not a god. He's just a random guy." I hit my keyboard with force. Who am I kidding? He's totally a god.

"And so how did it go from hating his guts to him groping you in your office?"

I continue typing. I can't even look at her. "He may have been in France."

"No way," she says.

"We may have . . . hooked up."

"Holy hell." She puts both of her hands in her hair.

"A little bit."

"Ahh . . . get the fuck out of here," she cries. "Are you frigging kidding me?"

"I wish I was."

"What happened?" she whispers as she leans in. "I need all the details."

There's a knock at the door. "Yes?" I call.

An employee named Alexander pokes his head around. "Don't forget we have that meeting in five minutes."

"Oh." My face falls. I completely forgot all about it. "Yes, of course. See you in the conference room."

Alexander closes the door, and I turn to Marley, who is waiting patiently for the details. "I don't want to talk about it here. Let's finish work early today and go to a bar for a staff meeting."

She smiles mischievously. "Yes. We need to discuss Miles Media in great detail."

Marley sits down at the bench table and puts my glass of wine in front of me. The bar is crowded and bustling with a four-o'clock rush. It seems everyone wants a drink before they head home.

I sip my wine, and Marley stares at me. "And?"

"And what?"

"Don't you hold out on me, Claire Anderson. I need all the fucking details."

I drag my hand down my face. "God, Marley," I whisper. "It was like a movie."

She listens intently.

"I got to the conference, and he was the opening speaker. I went to walk out, and he said, 'Claire Anderson, sit back down.'"

Her eyes widen.

"Then we had banter for a few days, and I was still hating him. But surprisingly, he's witty and funny."

"I knew he would be," she interrupts. "Smart guys are always witty."

"Anyway, one night on the way back from dinner, he kissed me."

She holds her hands up and dances on her chair.

"He wanted to come back to my room, and I said no and locked him out."

"You idiot," she gasps. "Are you fucking crazy? Have you seen the level of hotness of that guy?"

I raise my eyebrows and smirk.

Her mouth falls open. "Don't tell me."

"Yep."

"And?" she gasps.

"Off-the-hook hot," I whisper.

She grabs my arm and squeezes it hard. "You had sex . . . with Tristan fucking Miles?"

"Shh, keep your voice down," I whisper as I look around at the people surrounding us. "Yes. A lot of sex. In fact, I fucked his brains out."

She puts both hands over her mouth in shock. "What the hell, Claire?"

"I know." I sip my wine. "But then he came into the conference and said that he had to leave unexpectedly and said goodbye to the group and didn't say goodbye to me."

She frowns. "What? I'm confused . . ."

"But then I got back to my room, and there were red roses and a card asking me to go to Paris for the weekend with him."

Her eyes widen. "Fuck, this story is just getting better and better. Did you go?"

"Yes."

Her eyes nearly pop from their sockets. "And?" she cries.

I shake my head, unable to believe this story myself. "It was incredible. We had the best time."

"Oh my God, this is . . ." She shakes her head as she tries to reconcile what's happened.

"But today, he showed up unexpectedly, and I ended it."

"What?" She screws up her face. "Why?"

"Oh, come on, Marley. We both know it's not going anywhere." She stares at me.

"He's young and handsome and a player. I'm in bed at nine o clock on Saturday night, dead tired. He doesn't do long term, and I can't really do anything else."

"So?"

"No." I smile sadly. "He's beautiful, but he's at a stage where he is going to want to settle down soon, and I'm not the person. We are at different stages of our life."

"Why can't you just fuck him for fun, Claire?" she mutters flatly.

"Because . . ." I think on my answer for a while. "You know, I realized something about myself this weekend."

"What's that?"

"I quite liked having someone there, you know. Talking, laughing, having sex."

She smiles sadly as she listens.

"And I might want to pursue dating again."

"Why can't you just date Tristan?"

"Tristan doesn't date. All he would do is tie me up so I don't meet anyone else."

I smile as I remember him dancing naked at the end of the bed. "Perhaps if he were older and had a few kids with another woman, I would follow it up. But we are at different stages of life, and I'm not holding him or myself back by pursuing something that will never go anywhere. Trust me; this is shitty for me, too, but he isn't someone I want to date long term."

Marley exhales heavily. "Yeah, I guess you're right. Fair enough."

I take her hand in mine and smile sadly. "One weekend was enough, and you know what? It did the trick. I feel like a weight has been lifted from my shoulders, and for the first time in a long time, I'm kind of looking forward to what the future may bring. Thank you so much for making me go. Honestly it was so needed."

We sit in silence for a moment, and her eyes come to mine. "Put me out of my misery; was it good?"

"Ridiculously so." I smile. "He has a body built to please a woman. I didn't know that virile men like him existed in real life."

Marley tips her head back to the ceiling. "God, he's so hot . . . I can't stand it," she moans.

"I know." I sigh. "He really is. And fun, so fun. Honestly I've never been with a man who is so fun. I was in an orgasm high the entire weekend."

Marley sips her drink, deep in thought. "Maybe he could just fuck me for a while to take his mind off you."

I throw my head back and laugh out loud.

"I'm not joking, Claire. I need some fucking fun in my life," she mutters dryly. "I'm having a fun famine. It's depressing, actually."

"Tristan is off limits." I clink my glass with hers.

She rolls her eyes. "You're such a spoilsport. He was totally into me."

"I don't doubt it." I giggle. "Tristan Miles is into everybody."

The drive home from work is long, but for once, it doesn't seem it.

Every day this week I have daydreamed about Tristan Miles the entire way home.

Thinking of the funny things he said, the places he took me in Paris, him speaking French, the way he touched me. The way I touched him . . . our laughter.

God, so much to think about where he is concerned.

Since I saw him on Monday, I've had trouble focusing. I'm just grateful that we had that week together.

I wonder what kind of woman he will end up with. I smile sadly. Lucky bitch, whoever she is.

I think about my life and how blessed I am now that Mom and Dad have moved to be closer to us and help me with the kids.

Wade and I relocated here when he started Anderson Media. Neither of us had family close. And now because of work I can't move. We are effectively here alone for good. It took a long while for Mom and Dad to realize that I was staying put. I think they were secretly hoping I would pack up and move back to Florida, but when they realized I wasn't, they sold their Florida home and bought a house not far from mine.

I pull into the driveway and stare at the house. I exhale heavily. It's extra messy today. It looks like a junkyard. Bikes and skateboards and shoes everywhere.

Frigging kids. Ugh.

I grab all of my things and walk into the house, and Fletcher comes marching out from the kitchen. "What is this?" he cries as he holds his hand up in the air.

"Huh?" I glance over at Harry and Patrick. They both look scared for their lives.

What in the world?

"What are these?" Fletcher bellows. I can see he has something in his hand, but I have no idea what.

"What are you talking about, Fletcher?" I frown.

"Whose jocks are these that I found in your suitcase?" he yells as he spins Tristan's briefs on his finger.

My eyes widen.

Oh shit.

"Yes, Mom. Who left their damn underwear in your suitcase, and what exactly were you doing in fucking France?"

My mouth falls open. "Do not use that language with me, young man. How dare you? What were you doing looking through my suitcase? You're grounded."

"You're grounded, Mom," he cries. "What the hell were you doing in France?"

I narrow my eyes and go to snatch the underwear from him, and he snatches it away.

"Did you even go to France, or was that a lie too?"

My mouth falls open. "You self-centered little . . ." I stop myself before I call him a name. "How dare you."

"Oh, I dare, all right. Who is he?" he yells. "I'm going to kill him with my bare hands."

Fuck's sake. I march into the kitchen with him hot on my heels. I pour myself a glass of wine as Fletcher carries on and waves the underwear around like a lunatic.

"I mean it," he yells. "I want his name."

I pinch the bridge of my nose . . . God . . . I do not need this shit.

I pull the car up and frown as I peer at the house. This can't be it. I search for the address that Sammia found for me, and I frown. This is the right address.

Huh?

There are bikes and shit all over the front yard. I sit in the car for a moment and stare at the junkyard.

There's no way she would live here.

I'm not giving up this easily. We are not over until I say we are over.

Oh well, guess there's only one way to find out. I get out of the car and walk up to the front steps. Five bikes are strewed across the front yard, along with basketballs and catcher's mitts. I look around at all the shoes. Does a fucking centipede live here or something?

How many children does she have?

I peer in through the screen door. I can hear yelling coming from the kitchen.

That's weird.

I knock on the door.

"Hello?" I call.

I hear Claire's voice. "That is enough, Fletcher," she snaps. "I'm not having this conversation with you."

Huh?

"Hello?" I call again.

"Hello," a boy says as he appears in front of me.

I stare down at him. He's little and has dark hair. "Is this the Anderson house?" I ask.

"Yes."

I frown. What the fuck—she does live here? "Is . . . Claire Anderson here?"

"Yes. That's my mom." He swings his arms from side to side as he looks up at me, totally clueless.

I wait for him to go and get her. When he doesn't, I ask, "Um . . . can you get her for me, please?" *What the hell, kid?*

"Yeah, okay." He walks off, and I stand at the door . . . uneasiness fills me. This was a bad idea.

Another kid comes to the door. He has curly light hair, and he glares at me through the screen. "Who are you?"

"Tristan." I smile.

"What do you want?"

Jeez. I frown . . . these kids are rude. "I'm here to see your mother."

"Go away." He closes the door in my face.

I frown and step back . . . what?

I wait for him to open it back up. He doesn't. Okay . . . what just happened?

"Harry." I hear Claire's voice. "Don't be rude." She opens the door in a rush, and her eyes widen as she sees me. "Tristan," she whispers as she steps out onto the porch and quietly closes the door behind her. "This is a really bad time. You need to go," she whispers.

I can sense something is wrong with her. "What? Why?" I whisper back.

The front door opens up in a rush. "Is this him?" a big teenage kid yells.

Claire's face falls, and I frown as I look between them. "Huh?"

"That means yes," he growls. He turns his attention to me. "You!" the huge kid screams. The veins are sticking out of his neck in anger. What the hell? He looks like the Hulk.

"You!" he yells again at the top of his voice. "I'm going to kill you with my bare hands."

My eyes widen in horror, and I step back and stand on something—a skateboard. It rolls out from underneath me, and my ankle turns, and I step back as I fall. Then I tumble down the six stairs. "Ahh!" I cry as I hit the ground with a thud.

Claire runs down the stairs. "Oh my God, Tristan."

Ouch . . . a searing pain rips through my ankle.

The huge kid comes running down the stairs and starts whipping me with something across the head. "Stay the hell away from her." He continues to hit me. "Stay. The. Hell. Away." He whips me again and again.

"What are you doing?" I cry as I try to shield myself from his onslaught.

"Fletcher!" Claire screams. "Go inside the house. Now."

He holds something up to my face. "Are these your underpants?" he sneers.

My eyes widen . . . oh, hell on a cracker. This is the fucking twilight zone.

"Are they?" he cries. He holds them up to my face, and when I don't answer him, he gets infuriated and begins to suffocate me with them as he tries to stick them in my mouth.

I thrash on the ground as I fight for survival. "Claire!" I scream. "What the actual fuck?"

"Fletcher. Get into the house!" she screams as she pushes him off me.

The crazed lunatic is panting, gasping for air as he glares at me. "Don't push me . . . pretty boy." He pegs the underpants as I cover my head with my forearms to shield myself from another attack, and he storms inside. The screen door bangs hard.

The second-oldest boy disappears into the house as well, and Claire and the little one kneel down beside me.

"Tristan, I am so sorry," she whispers. "He's in so much trouble you won't even believe it."

I stare at her as I pant . . . what the actual fuck just happened right now?

I go to stand up, and my ankle gives way, and I nearly fall.

"Oh my God, you're hurt," she whispers.

I stare at her deadpan. "I wonder why."

"Because Fletcher tried to put underpants in your mouth so you would choke," the little kid says. "Choke to death," he adds.

"Enough, Patrick," Claire says to him.

They help me up, and I can't put any weight on my ankle.

"Come inside, and let me get some ice," Claire says.

"You have to be kidding," I snap as I pull my arm from her grip. "I am not going in that house. That kid is deranged. He almost killed me."

"He has anger-management issues," the little kid says.

"Tris, come on. You can't drive anywhere like this," Claire urges. Eventually I hop up the stairs, and they both help me in and lead me, and I fall onto the couch.

Claire moves the ottoman over to me and puts my foot up and takes my shoe and sock off.

"What is he doing in my house?" the Hulk kid says as he comes storming into the room.

"He is my guest. Go to your room," Claire growls.

"But—"

"So help me, Fletcher, I have never been so angry with you. Go to your room now!" she screams.

He gives me one last death stare and stomps up the stairs.

"I'll get some ice," Claire says. "I have to go out to the garage freezer. Back in a moment." She disappears, and the youngest kid comes and sits beside me. So close that he's nearly sitting on top of me. I edge myself away from him.

I look around the house in horror. The furniture is all moved to the side, and there are huge-ass fans going, facing down to the floor. The carpet has huge wet patches . . . what happened there? Are they washing out a bloodstain?

The television is blaring a really loud game show, and there is some kind of art project sprawled over the coffee table. It's messy and chaotic . . . not what I expected at all. Pain sears through my ankle, and I wince.

A cat jumps up on the couch. It's big and ugly, and it comes over and tries to sit on me. Eww. I lean away from it.

"Muff. Get down," the kid says.

I look at him. "Your cat is called Muff?"

He smiles and nods proudly. "He's naughty. He pees on things." The cat jumps onto the ottoman and begins to lick my foot. I jerk it away. Ugh.

I pinch the bridge of my nose.

Good grief.

The middle kid comes out and stands in front of us. "I'm watching you," he whispers. He slices his finger across his neck as he narrows his eyes.

Huh?

Fuck's sake . . . she's breeding serial killers here.

I begin to feel faint.

"My name is Patrick," the little kid says.

"Hi, Patrick," I reply as I keep my eye on the serial-killer kid, and I gesture to him. "What's your name?" I ask.

"Your worst nightmare," he whispers darkly in a monster voice.

I frown . . . what the hell is up with this kid? "What a stupid name," I whisper back.

"His name is Harry," Patrick says.

"Yeah, well, Harry is psychotic," I reply with my eyes locked on Harry. I tap my temple. "Weirdo," I mouth.

Harry makes crazy eyes and puts his hands around his own throat and begins to choke himself as I watch. He makes choking noises and falls to the floor and then plays dead.

What the . . . ?

I stare at his lifeless body on the floor.

I'm not even joking; this kid is fucking deranged.

Claire comes rushing in from a room at the back. "Oh my God, Tris. I didn't have any ice, so we will have to use a bag of peas."

She places them on my foot. My ankle is now the size of a football and throbbing like a bitch.

"Get up, Harry," Claire says as she tends to me. He gets up and runs out of the room, and I stare after him. I don't trust that kid. Something is seriously off here.

I need to keep my wits about me in this house . . . the end is near.

The corner of the bag of peas is open, and they spill all over the floor. A dog comes running through the house with a bucket tied to its head and begins to eat the frozen peas off the floor. "Woofy," Claire calls. "No, boy."

I frown as I watch in horror.

What is this godforsaken place?

Savages . . .

The middle child—what's his name, Harry?—comes back into the room with what looks like a dressing gown cord and a teddy bear. He sits opposite me, and I frown as I watch him. What the hell is he doing now?

"I'll drive you home, Tris," Claire says.

My eyes are locked on the evil kid. He ties the cord around the teddy bear's neck.

"You'll have to leave your car here," Claire continues.

The kid stands on the couch across from me and lets the bear drop. It hangs by the noose. "Broken neck . . . he's dead," he whispers.

Get out . . . get out . . . get out of the fucking house.

I stand in a rush and trip over the dog, who is eating the peas. "Fuck," I cry in pain.

"Tristan, you can't drive," Claire gasps.

"Well, I'm not fucking staying here," I stammer. I hop out the front door and take one last look around.

I never knew what hell looked like.

Now I do.

"Tristan, come back."

I hop out onto the porch. "Goodbye, Claire," I call. *It was nice knowing you.*

Chapter 10

I lie on the couch with my foot raised. I have an ice pack on it, and it's throbbing and swollen.

This is just great. How in the hell am I supposed to work when I can't even get a shoe on? The swelling had better go down overnight. I'm sure it'll be fine.

I rearrange the ice pack and lie back down.

My mind goes over this afternoon and what I saw at Claire's house.

I have no words.

None that will make me less shocked, anyway. When she said she had three sons, I was picturing cute little kids who play with LEGOs.

How wrong could I be?

Her children are nearly grown men—angry grown men . . . ones who hate me.

I get a vision of the house and the pets and the psychotic kids, and I shake my head in disgust.

She said we were at different stages of our lives, and I really didn't understand what she meant.

I get it now.

We have nothing in common . . . apart from our sense of humor, of course—but as a whole . . . it's not enough, and to be honest, it pisses me off.

We could have had something. We could have had something fucking great. Claire Anderson is near perfect. However, the life she has . . . is not, and I don't want to be around those feral kids for even ten minutes. I hate that she has to deal with them alone. She has so much weight on her shoulders, and I don't know how she bears it. What must it be like to be her?

It's not your problem.

I get a shiver as I picture the middle child, and I hate to admit it, but the violent oldest one seemed almost normal compared to that serial killer in the making.

I get a vision of him hanging the teddy bear. What the hell was that about?

Did I imagine it?

My phone dances across the coffee table, and I pick it up to see the name Claire.

Shit. "Hello," I answer.

"Hi, Tris." My face falls into a sad smile at the sound of her voice.

Fuck it . . . why does she have kids . . . animals—whatever the hell they are?

"I called to see if you're okay," she says.

"Yeah, I'm fine." I sigh.

"Oh my gosh, Tristan, I am so sorry."

I stay silent.

"He's just super protective over me and had just found underpants in my luggage. They must have gotten mixed up when I had my laundry done," she lies, and I know he must be listening. "He had a momentary slipup with his temper."

143

"Yeah, I was there, Claire. I saw it, remember? Firsthand, actually. Have the ankle to prove it."

"Anyway, he wants to speak to you," she says.

"No, that's . . ."

"Hello," he says.

I roll my eyes. "Hello," I reply.

He exhales heavily, and I get a vision of Claire standing over him, making him do this. "I'm sorry. I was out of line this afternoon," he says. "I don't know what came over me."

"I could have you charged with assault," I reply.

He stays silent.

"I'm just your mother's friend from work. You jumped to the wrong conclusion. It was completely out of line."

No answer.

"Anything else?" I snap in frustration.

"Nope."

"So that's your apology?" I frown.

"Yep."

"Is your mother there making you call me?"

"Yep."

"Are you really sorry?"

"No."

I narrow my eyes . . . what I really want to blurt out is *I screwed your mother every which way, and she fucking loved every inch of my cock, you little shit.* But I won't. I'll be the adult here.

"Do you want to speak to Mom again?" he asks.

I frown as I contemplate the question, and I close my eyes in regret. Eventually I reply, "No, that's okay. Thanks for calling." I hang up.

I stare at the phone in my hands for a moment.

I get a vision of Claire on the other end. Did she want to speak to me?

My mind goes over how much she has on her plate: work, financial difficulties—and that's aside from bringing up on her own three boys who have obvious troubles.

I feel for her.

I throw my phone onto the couch and drag myself up. I put my foot down to test it, and a shooting pain sears through me.

Fuck's sake, stupid kid.

It's eleven o'clock the next morning when I hobble in to work on crutches.

Jameson is standing in reception. His face falls when he sees me, and he follows me into my office. "What happened to you?"

"Don't ask." I fall into my seat, annoyed.

"What have you done?"

"Torn ligaments. Pulled a piece of bone off when it snapped."

He winces. "Ouch. How did you do that?"

I drag my hand down my face. "A kid beat me up with underpants."

"He what?"

I smile and pinch the bridge of my nose. "I went to the twilight zone yesterday, Jameson."

"How so?"

"Let me set the tone of the kind of people I'm dealing with here."

He frowns in question.

"They have a cat called Muff," I say.

He stares at me flatly.

"What kind of deranged, sick, fucked-up, twisted person calls a family pussy . . . Muff?"

"What are you talking about?" He frowns.

"So I met this chick at the conference in France." I exhale heavily. "She was perfect."

He rolls his eyes. "Here we go," he mutters dryly.

"Ticked boxes that I didn't even know existed. Smart and funny. Hot as fuck." I turn my computer on. "Small problem, though—she has three kids."

He winces.

"So we get back here. She tells me she's ending it because of her kids. Saying that we come from different worlds, blah, blah, blah." I roll my eyes.

Jameson smiles and takes a seat at my desk, his interest piqued.

"I don't believe her reasoning, so I followed her home from work yesterday."

"What? You followed her home?" He frowns.

I shrug. "Little bit. Well, Sammia found her address, actually. Anyway, I get to her house. It's like a junkyard; there's shit everywhere." I wave my hands around as I try to explain the enormity of the mess. "Shoes and bikes and fuck . . . everything under the sun."

He frowns as he listens intently.

"So her kid comes rushing out, but he isn't a kid." My eyes widen. "He's a fucking man-child." I hold my hands up to show him how tall. "He starts whipping me with a pair of underpants that I left in her suitcase."

Jameson's eyes widen, and he smiles.

"So I step back in shock, tread on a skateboard, and go flying down the stairs."

Jameson chuckles.

"Only to have that crazy motherfucking kid jump on me and try to shove my own underpants in my mouth."

Jameson tips his head back and laughs out loud.

"There's more," I stammer. "That's not even the worst part."

Jameson is laughing hard now.

"They take me inside. She sends that child to his room, and then she goes to get ice, and then another kid comes out." I picture his face, and my eyes widen. "This kid . . . is fucking evil, man, I'm telling you."

"What's his name?"

I try to remember it. "Same as that nerdy wizard kid . . . the one with glasses." I click my fingers as I try to think.

"Who? Harry Potter?"

"Yes, that's it. His name is Harry."

Jameson smiles broadly.

"He starts slicing his neck with his finger."

Jameson stops laughing, shocked.

"Then he puts his hands around his throat and begins to choke himself until he fakes his death," I whisper.

"What?" Jameson screws up his face. "That *is* weird."

"Oh, you think?" I stammer. "Then he runs away and comes back with a tie thing and a teddy bear, and I watch as he ties a noose around its neck and then hangs it."

Jameson's eyes hold mine for an extended time. He's as confused as I am. "He did what?"

I cross my fingers over my chest. "As God is my witness. This shit really happened."

Jameson laughs out loud in shock.

"And the dog," I cry. "The poor fucking dog."

"What's wrong with the dog?"

"They have a fucking bucket thing tied to its head."

"What for?"

"To torture it . . . why else?"

His face falls, and he stares at me. "What?"

"I'm not even joking . . . I got out to the car and considered going back in on a mercy mission and stealing the poor bastard to save it. He was eating peas, Jameson. Fucking peas, I tell you."

Jameson tips his head back and laughs hard.

I put my head into my hands. "I'm sorry, Woofy."

"His name is Woofy?"

I nod sadly.

He howls with laughter as he really loses control. "What did you do?"

I exhale heavily. "I did what any self-respecting man does when his life is in danger."

"What's that?"

"I got the fuck out of there."

"You drove home with that ankle?" he asks in surprise.

"Sped the entire way."

Jameson laughs hard.

"No more MILFs for me." I hold my hands in the air. "I'm done." I turn to my computer. "In fact, I don't even think I want kids now. I'm scarred for life."

A melancholy comes over me. "You know, I knew she was a widow and had it tough, but I never imagined it was this bad."

Jameson watches me. "She was probably thinking of you when she ended it."

"Yeah, I guess." I sigh. "Anyway, in another life she's the perfect woman. It's her circumstances that have fucked it."

It's ten o'clock on Thursday morning, and someone knocks on my office door.

"Come in."

Sammia walks in, and I smile. Sammia is my brother's PA and the sunshine of our office. She works out at reception and keeps us all in order. "Tris, your intern interviews are here."

I keep typing. "Okay, what number did we narrow it down to?"

"With all the testing and the two interviews they have already done down on level forty, there are three final candidates."

"Yes, okay, which one do you like?" I ask.

"I like Rebecca," she says. "I think she has what it takes."

"Well, to get this far, they all have what it takes, but let's see who interviews the best." I take out the intern-interview file. Every year we take just one on in the management level. It's the opportunity of a lifetime. Kids travel across the States to be taken under our wing. All our past kids have gone on to great success, and most of them are in managerial positions. "To be honest I haven't even had time to go through any of the interview notes," I admit.

"That's okay." Sammia smiles. "It's not like it's your first rodeo."

I chuckle. "Send the first one in."

"Okay."

I open the file and take out the relevant questions that I need to ask. I ready my notepad and pen.

A light knock sounds at the door.

"Come in."

The door opens, and I glance up. My face falls.

It's him.

The underpants attacker. Our mouths fall open in shock at the same time.

"*You're* . . . Tristan Miles?" he gasps, horrified.

"Are you kidding me?" I snap. "I can't even fucking walk because of you, and now you turn up here looking for a damn job?"

"Trust me. I didn't know it was you," he snaps back.

"Or you wouldn't have attacked me?" I gasp.

"No, I would have still attacked you; I wouldn't have come today."

I throw my head back in disgust. "Are you kidding me?"

He folds his arms and narrows his eyes. "So . . . you were lying."

"About what?"

"You don't know my mother from work at all."

"Yes, I do, and why the hell are we talking about your mother now?"

"Why did you come to my house to see her? Why didn't you just see her at her office?"

"First of all . . ." I point to the chair. "Sit down," I snap as I grab my crutches and move them out of his way. He falls into his seat. "Second of all, last time I looked, it's your mother's house. And thirdly, it's none of your business why I wanted to talk to her. My ankle is completely fucked, by the way; thank you for asking."

He smirks.

"You think this is funny?"

"No, I think you're a lying jerk. They were totally your underpants, and you can stick your job up your entitled ass. I don't want it anyway."

I shake my head. Why am I not surprised by his attitude? "I will."

We glare at each other.

"Don't tell my mom that I came here today."

I frown. "She doesn't know?"

"No, and I would appreciate it if she didn't find out."

"Why didn't you tell her?"

"I was going to surprise her if I got the job."

I stare at him as I process his words. "Why wouldn't you tell her you were going for this? Applications have been going on for months."

His eyes drop to the carpet. "I didn't want her to be disappointed when I didn't get it."

"She wouldn't be disappointed if you didn't get the job. I know that for a fact."

His jaw clenches as he stares at the carpet in front of us.

"Why would you want this job?" I ask.

"I want to learn what to do and take over Anderson Media." He pauses. "So she doesn't have to work so hard."

I stare at him.

"She does enough." He scuffs his shoe on the carpet. "I don't want her to have to worry anymore."

My heart drops. "You think you have to protect your mother?"

"I don't think it; I know it." He stands. "It's okay." He exhales deeply. "I won't waste your time."

He's right; he does have to protect her. She's worth protecting.

I watch him for a moment, and I hate to admit it, but I'm strangely impressed by his loyalty to Claire.

"Sorry about your ankle," he says.

"Are you really?"

"Nope." He stares at me. "Don't tell me you wouldn't do the same if you found someone's underwear in your mother's bag."

"No, actually, I wouldn't," I mutter dryly. "Because . . . I'm not psychotic."

He rolls his eyes. "Whatever." He walks toward the door.

"Intern interviewees usually shake my hand," I call after him.

"Not this one." He turns and leaves. The door clicks quietly behind him.

I stare at the door he just left through for a moment, and then finally I push the intercom. "Sammia, send in the second interview, please."

"Sure thing."

My eyes drop to look at the interview-rating-system sheet in front of me, and I exhale heavily. How the fuck do I even rate that?

I stare at my computer screen. It's been five days since I interviewed the three finalists. Five days of me fighting myself over who I want to hire.

Rebecca is fantastic. She would be an asset to any business, and I will be offering her a position regardless of whether she gets this role.

Joel, the other candidate, was perfect on paper. His psychometric testing was spot on, and he blitzed every question with a practiced perfection.

Then there was Fletcher Anderson. He didn't even want to do the interview. He wouldn't shake my hand and near fucking killed me with barely an apology. He's crazy and wild and everything I don't have the time or energy to train.

He also had more passion in his little finger than the other two had combined.

No matter how hard I try to talk myself out of it, he's the one I keep going back to. He's the one with loyalty to family, albeit. . . mishandled. Media is in his blood, and he has a real opportunity to take over Anderson Media one day as the CEO

. . . that's if the company holds out that long. I know it will. Claire's got this. With his passion and temper and the right training, we could make him the best damn CEO in New York.

I exhale heavily as I go over the pros and cons of each candidate again, hoping by some miracle to find something good about the other two—and there is, but there's just an untapped quality that Fletcher has. But then he has major anger issues, and I will perhaps be forced to fire him down the track anyway.

Two steps forward, one step back.

I even tried to call Rebecca to offer her the position yesterday, but when it came to making the call, I couldn't do it.

My head says he's too hard and to let it go; my gut is telling me he's the one.

Decisions, decisions.

Patrick lies on my bed as I fold the washing and stack it all around him in piles. "Read that line again, Paddy," I say.

"The house was in the ha . . . ha . . . ha . . ." He frowns as he concentrates.

"Sound it out," I remind him.

"Ham-p-tons." He accentuates the *s* at the end.

"Yes, you got it."

He smiles proudly and keeps going. Patrick has just this year been diagnosed with dyslexia. And to be honest, once we got that diagnosis, it was a huge relief for me. His teachers and I couldn't work out why he couldn't read and why some tasks at school were so hard for him when he's obviously so bright. In the end, I took him to a therapist, and she discovered it.

"All al . . ." He frowns. "Long," he continues.

Fletcher walks into the room. He's fighting a smile.

"What?" I ask as I keep folding.

"I've decided that I'm deferring university."

I throw a newly folded towel onto the pile. "Well, that's not happening."

"Yes, it is. I'm eighteen next month, Mom. I can do what I like."

"Fletcher Anderson, you are way too smart to have a year off doing nothing. I'm not even discussing this with you."

"I got an internship."

My face falls. "What do you mean?"

"I applied six months ago and made it to the final three."

"What?" I stare at him. "Why didn't you tell me?"

"I didn't want you to get your hopes up."

I smile and take his face in my hands. "Fletch, when are you going to stop worrying about me?" I fold another towel. "So when is the final interview?"

"I already had it."

My face falls again. "What? When?"

"Wednesday, in New York."

I stare at him. "How did you do this without me knowing?"

"Caught the train. Anyway, I didn't think I had a chance after Monday and the way we met."

I screw up my face in confusion. "What do you mean?"

"It's with Miles Media."

"You got an internship with Miles Media?" I gasp.

"Yep." He smiles proudly. "Tristan Miles is my new boss."

My eyes widen in horror. "What? No," I snap. "You can't work with him." I throw the next towel on the pile with force. "Forget it."

"Mom, they're the best media company in the world. It's a big deal for me to get this. They had over four thousand applicants."

"You tried to shove underpants in his mouth, Fletcher," I cry. "How can you walk into that office and not be ashamed of yourself?"

"It's okay. I apologized, remember?"

"No, it's not okay. It will never be okay. It's the most embarrassing thing I've ever witnessed. You can't work there; I forbid it."

Fletcher's a firecracker. I don't want him embarrassing me further. I get a vision of him losing his temper at work, and I shiver in mortification. This is my worst nightmare.

"I am," he snaps. "You can't stop me."

"I can and I will," I cry.

"I want to learn from the best. I want to run Anderson Media one day; they can teach me how."

"All they are going to teach you, Fletcher, is how to be ruthless."

"And that's exactly what I want to learn."

I glare at him. "You call Tristan Miles back and tell him to stick his job where the sun doesn't shine." I'm so angry with that man for going behind my back on this that I can't even stand it.

155

He should have called me to tell me about the interview.

Ever since he met my kids, I haven't heard from him. Not that I wanted to, but anyway, it's the principle of the situation. And now, for him to not call me but to offer my son a job as some kind of poor excuse for him being a wimp who hates kids? He was so hot for me and came to my house, and after one meeting with my children . . . boom. Cold as ice.

I should have known to expect it—actually, who am I kidding? I did.

The beautiful man I met in France isn't the cold man who lives in New York. They are worlds apart. The man in France I adore; the man in New York I despise.

I don't want him near Fletcher, and I most definitely don't want Fletcher to learn business ethics from him.

The notion is preposterous.

I fold my towels with force. I don't care about Tristan Miles anyway. It's not like I wanted anything, but he definitely put a dent in my ego. I know he's brilliant, and I know that Wade would be supporting this. But Tristan Miles is cold and calculating in the business world. I don't want Fletcher's first position to be with him. He's so impressionable, and I don't want him thinking that the cutthroat Miles Media's focus is normal. It's a disaster waiting to happen.

"I start on Monday," Fletcher snaps.

"Over my dead body."

Chapter 11

I straighten Fletcher's tie. "Now remember, ask for help if you don't know what to do."

"Yes, Mom."

I dust his shoulders off. After a weekend of tantrums and tears, I have conceded. Fletcher is starting work with Tristan this morning, and I have never felt so sick in my life. "And make sure you drink lots of water. If you get dehydrated, you won't be able to concentrate."

He rolls his eyes.

"Now, I've packed you a lunch. Don't get into the habit of buying it. You will waste a fortune."

"Mom." Fletcher gives a subtle shake of his head.

"Because . . . you know? What you start doing in this first job will lay the foundation for your entire working career. I want you to build good habits. This is an opportunity to learn, Fletch. Watch and learn, but always remember that you are an Anderson." I pull my fingers through his hair.

He smiles down at me. "I will."

"Being smart in business doesn't mean you have to be cutthroat," I remind him.

"I know; we talked about this." He sighs.

"Your father was such a good man, Fletch, with the highest of morals."

He smiles broadly.

It's my greatest fear that Tristan is going to rub off on this young and impressionable boy. My eyes fill with tears at the mere prospect.

"Mom. Stop."

I put my hands over my mouth as I stare up at my handsome son. "I'm sorry, honey. I'm just so nervous for you."

"Why?"

"Because this is a big deal, and I don't want you to mess it up."

"Mom." He sighs. "I stuffed underpants in the boss's mouth before I even got the job. I'm pretty sure I've already messed it up as much as physically possible."

I hold my forehead as I stare at him. "God, please don't remind me. That will forever be the most mortifying moment of my life." I go back to fiddling with his tie to distract myself.

"Worked out."

I frown. "What does that mean?"

"Well, he never came back." He smirks.

"We were just friends, Fletcher. He was never coming back any-way . . . long before you did that. Don't flatter yourself. If he and I were actually a thing, do you really think that would deter him?"

"Hmm." He shrugs, not believing me.

I'll never admit the truth—that he's right, and just as he planned, it really did work. Tristan never contacted me again after that fateful day. He went from coming to my house to pursue me . . . to never calling again. It says a lot about him and the gumption he has—or lack of it. Anyway, who cares?

Good riddance. I'm actually grateful that Fletcher scared him off. Saved me the job and stopped things from dragging out.

"Just remember to be professional," I remind him.

"I know."

"And use your manners."

He rolls his eyes.

"And if you get into trouble, what do you do?"

"Go to the bathroom, and count to ten to calm down." He sighs.

I smile as I fix his hair. "That's it, Fletch." I smile up at him. "You're going to be great."

I keep straightening his hair, and he swats me away. "That's enough already, Mom."

I grab his face hard in my hands and bring his eyes to mine. "Do you know how proud your father and I are of you?"

He shrugs sadly. "Thanks."

I smile. "And call me on your lunch break."

"Oh my God. Stop nagging me. I'm not going to have time."

"One minute—you have one minute."

With one last eye roll he walks downstairs, and I follow and grab my keys. "Let's go."

This is the longest day of my entire life. I pick up my phone and check it again. "It's one thirty p.m. Why hasn't he called?" I sigh.

"He probably forgot," Marley replies.

"What if they didn't give him lunch?" I say. "He can't handle not eating. He might faint."

Marley rolls her eyes. "It will be fine, and it isn't a prison camp. Miles Media has one of the best reputations for treating their staff well."

"Will you stop telling me that everything is going to be okay?" I snap. "Because I have a reason to be concerned, and I'm really worried about him."

"Oh my God, you're driving yourself crazy—and me, for that matter."

"When you have a child who is going to work for the biggest bastard in the world, you let me know how you go."

"Okay, fine." She smiles my way. "This wouldn't have anything to do with the fact that Mr. Miles hasn't called you, would it?"

I screw up my face in disgust. "What, as if I'm annoyed that he hasn't called me? I had already broken it off with him—not that we actually had anything to break off. It was just one week, Marley, and besides, Tristan Miles means nothing to me. But I have serious suspicions as to why he would've hired Fletcher in the first place. Something feels off. Fletcher tried to bash him with his own underpants, for God's sake."

Marley giggles. "Oh Lord, how I wish I was there to see that. I bet Tristan Miles has never had that before."

I smile as I remember that momentous day. I've never been so horrified and yet so amused at the same time. Not that I would ever admit that to anybody, not even Marley.

"I'm just gonna text him. I can't be going crazy like this for any longer." I type.

Hi Fletch, how's it going buddy?

A reply bounces straight back.

I hate this job. I hate this man, I'm not coming back tomorrow.

My eyes widen in horror. "Oh no, Marley. This is going to be worse than him not even starting. I can just see it."

I text back.

Why what's happening?

He texts back.

Talk to you tonight I've got five minutes left for lunch.

I look up at Marley, my stomach sinking. "What's happening over there? I don't believe this."

Marley rolls her eyes. "I do, actually. Let's face it, Claire. Fletcher doesn't exactly take orders well."

I blow out a big deep breath. "Hopefully his afternoon will be better."

Marley smiles. "It will be. Don't you remember what it was like to start a new job? Everybody's first day at a new job is bad, Claire."

I shrug. "I guess you're right."

"Everything is going to be fine. Relax, and let him go. He's nearly a man. He needs to find his own way."

"Yeah, I know." I sigh. I pick up my pen and try to get back to work. Nightmare images of my poor little baby all alone in that big cranky corporate office are flying through my mind.

Why couldn't he just go to university?

I stir the cheese into the large pot of spaghetti bolognese. I finished early today, and although I wanted to pick Fletcher up from work, I let him catch the train home. I'm really trying my hardest to give him a little tough love. He wants to be a big boy and work; he needs to learn how to be self-sufficient. I look at the clock. Where is he?

I glance up at my other two sons, who are sitting at the kitchen counter. "How did it go at school today, Harry?"

"Okay."

"How was Mrs. Parkinson?"

"A witch, as usual." He sighs.

"I don't think it's very nice to be calling your teacher a witch."

"Yeah, well, if she stopped acting like one, I wouldn't have to call her one."

"Just stay out of trouble, please, Harry. You're on your last warning at that school. I need you to behave. You need to show everyone how smart and charming you really are."

Harry rolls his eyes. Patrick smiles goofily up at me.

"Now let's be nice when Fletch gets home. He's had a really bad day. And I want you boys to try and make him feel better."

"And how are we supposed to do that?" Harry asks with an eye roll.

"Just talk about things and take his mind off it. Make him laugh. Try and make him see that things aren't as bad as he thinks."

Harry smiles. "I think they are as bad as he thinks. Imagine working with that pompous donkey."

"You don't even know him," I snap. "You can't say that; he's a nice man. And he's Fletch's new boss, so you show him some respect."

We hear the front door bang, and Fletcher comes into view. His hair is messed, his tie is askew, his jacket is off, his shoelaces are undone. He looks like he's been to hell and back. I bite my lip to stifle my smile as I give him a hug. "How is my big working boy?"

"It was literal hell."

My face falls. "Why? What happened?"

"Basically, I ruined everything I touched."

"That's okay. You're only new; they can't expect you to know everything. Nobody knows everything on the first day." I smile as I watch him. "What was the last thing that he said to you?"

"Don't you dare be late tomorrow."

I frown. "Didn't he say 'Thanks for your first day'?"

"No, Mom. I told you he's an asshole."

"Hmm. Well, let's just see how tomorrow goes."

"I'm not going back."

162

"Yes, you are, Fletcher," I snap. "You're going to work two weeks there. I will not have you embarrassing me. If you don't like it after two weeks, you can stop, but you will ride it out and at least give it a chance."

Fletcher rolls his eyes and sits at the table, and I put his spaghetti bolognese down in front of him. "I made your favorite."

"I'm too tired to eat it."

I fake a smile and run my fingers through his hair. "I know, baby, me too."

I sit at the table and wait for Fletcher to arrive home from work. Honestly, who knew having a child start work would be so stressful? I can't think, I can't sleep, and I've been leaving work early every day so that I can get home well before he does and cook his favorite meals.

Tristan is giving him hell, and I know that he may need it. But the mother in me is worried that Tristan is just trying to teach him a lesson over the way they met. I close my eyes in horror. I can't even think of that day without cringing. *Whipping him with underpants and then trying to stuff them in his mouth . . . oh, the horror.*

What on earth was Fletcher thinking?

But you know what? I'm proud of Fletch. I'm proud of him for making it above all those other candidates, for taking the job in the first place, and then for having the courage to stick with the job and go back day after day.

The door bangs open, and I smile and pick up the chocolate cake I just made him. He comes around the corner, and I force a smile, even though I feel like bursting into tears at the sight of his sad face. "Hi, Fletch."

"Hi." He yanks off his tie aggressively.

"I made you chocolate cake." I hold it toward him. "Your favorite."

"Thanks." He sighs. He sticks his finger out and swipes it through the frosting and shoves it in his mouth.

I brace myself to ask the dreaded question. "How was your day?"

He slumps into a chair. "Hell."

"Really?" I whisper. Damn it. I really want this to work out. "Why? What happened today?"

"I'm just not very good at it, Mom."

"Honey, you're not supposed to be very good at it. You're just new."

He exhales heavily and swipes his finger through the icing once more.

"What's Tristan like?" I ask.

"Mean."

"Mean?" I frown. "Like how?" I watch him for a moment. "Give me an example."

He puffs air into his cheeks. I've never seen him so deflated. "Well." He pauses as he gets it right in his head. "We do this thing where he goes and visits all the managers on each floor, and I follow him around like a puppy and take notes. Today there was a meeting of everyone together."

"Yes, okay, that's standard."

"Well, today we got down to the fortieth floor and into the meeting, and I realized that I left my pen up on my desk."

"Yes." I frown as I listen to him. "Go on."

"There weren't any other pens there, so I just sat and listened to him talk along with everyone else."

I nod as I listen.

"Halfway through the meeting he noticed I wasn't taking notes and asked why. I told him I left my pen behind, and he completely lost his shit, screamed at me in front of everyone, and kicked me out of the management meeting."

"What? He was screaming at you?" I frown.

"Like a madman. Saying that he won't put up with my laziness or sloppiness, and if I have no desire to learn, then I may as well leave Miles Media right now."

My mouth falls open in surprise. "What? Over a pen?"

"Mom, that's not even the half of it. He yells at me the entire day. Everything I do is wrong."

Anger simmers in my stomach. "He yells at you?"

"Screams the fucking place down. Even Jameson, the CEO, had to come and rescue me today. He told him to settle down." His eyes widen. "And Jameson Miles is known for screaming at everyone all the time, Mom, so I know Tristan mustn't scream at anyone else like he does me." He throws his hands up in the air. "Sammia, Jameson's PA, even bought me a cupcake today. She feels sorry for me too. She told me not to worry about him—that I was doing a good job." His shoulders slump. "He just hates me."

My eyes narrow as I feel anger twist in my gut. "Just ignore him, buddy." I fake a smile. "He'll settle down." *Or else.* "Just keep your head down, and do your job." I cut him a piece of cake and hand it over.

"Cake before dinner?" He frowns.

"Cake *for* dinner, if you want." I watch him eat it and stare into space as adrenaline surges through my body.

Tristan fucking Miles . . . don't push me.

"What do you think, Marley?" I ask. "Should I be worried?"

"Hmm, it's a tough one." She sips her Coke. We are at a restaurant eating lunch. "On one hand, you want Fletch to be taught the right way."

"Yes, but he's screaming at him, Marl. In what job is that okay?"

"It's not; I agree." She shrugs. "It's so not okay in any workplace."

"God, I'm going crazy over this. What if he just hired him to put him through hell for the way they met? What if he's purposely being nasty to teach me a lesson for ending it?"

"It's completely possible." She shrugs again. "But this job will set Fletch up for life, so more fool him, you know?"

"But at what point is it enough? Like how far do I let it go?" A text comes in. It's from Fletcher.

Hi.

I smile. "Fletch is on his lunch break." I text back.

Can I call you?

He texts back.

Yeah.

I dial his number, and he answers on the first ring. "Hi, Fletch." I smile. "How's it going?"

"Pretty shit." He sighs.

"Why?"

"Well, apparently now I'm stupid."

My hackles rise. "He called you stupid?"

"Yep."

"That's it." My anger explodes. "Don't go back after lunch."

"Mom."

"I mean it," I snap. "He can't call you fucking stupid, Fletcher; that is unacceptable."

Marley's eyes widen in horror as she listens. "What?" she mouths. "He called him stupid?"

"No job is worth your self-respect, Fletcher. Do not go back."

"Mom, shut up. You're making it worse. I shouldn't have even told you."

"Fletcher."

He hangs up.

"That's it," I snap. "He's gone too far this time." I down my drink and slam my empty glass on the table and stand. "Meet you back at work. I have an appointment with Tristan fucking Miles."

"Oh shit. Good luck." She winces.

I punch my fist. "Bail me out of jail, will you?"

She giggles and raises her glass at me. "Yes, okay, what account do I take the bail money out of?"

"You'll have to rob a bank."

"Roger that."

I storm out of the restaurant on a mission. Tristan Miles is looking for a fight, and he just found one.

Nobody calls my son stupid and gets away with it.

I march up to the reception desk in the Miles Media building.

"Hello, may I help you?" The young girl smiles.

"I'd like to see Tristan Miles, please."

"Did you have an appointment?"

"No."

"I'm sorry; that will be impossible."

"You tell him Claire Anderson is here to see him."

"I'm sorry—" she continues.

"Tell him," I interrupt her. "I'm not leaving until I see him."

She and the other receptionist exchange glances, and she dials a number. "Hi, Sammia. I have a Claire Anderson to see Tristan Miles in reception."

She listens and then holds the phone down. "She's just checking."

I can hear my pulse as it pumps boiling blood around my body. Boom . . . boom . . . boom.

"Okay, thank you." She types something and hands over a security card on a lanyard. "You can go up. Hector will accompany you."

"I can find it myself," I snap.

"Nobody goes to the top floor without a security guard."

He's going to need one. "Fine."

She waves over a security guard, and he comes over. "Can you please escort Mrs. Anderson to see Tristan Miles, please?"

"Sure thing." He smiles at me. "This way, please." He gestures to the elevator, and I bite the inside of my cheek to stop myself from speaking. I'm so mad that I can't put two words together.

I glare straight ahead at the doors as I go over in my head what I'm going to say.

The doors open, and I storm out. My step falters as I see the floor.

What the fuck?

Expansive views all over New York. White marble. Contemporary luxury at its finest. Of course his office looks like this . . . it only boils my blood more.

The pretty receptionist smiles. "Hello, I'm Sammia. You're here to see Tristan?"

"Yes, please." I remember my manners and force a smile. "Hello, I'm Claire Anderson."

"Are you . . ." Her voice trails off.

"Yes, I'm Fletcher's mother."

I see the exact moment that she realizes why I'm here—her eyes widen. "Oh, I see." She stands and puts her hand out. "This way, please."

We turn left and go down a wide corridor. I can see the sprawling New York skyline at the end, and offices are all to the left. "His office is at the end," she says.

I keep following her, and we get to a large room, another reception area, and I see Fletcher sitting at a desk. Two girls are at desks beside him: one looks younger.

Fletcher's face falls when he sees me. "Mom, what are you doing here?" he stammers in a panic.

"Just visiting Tristan." I fake a smile. "Thanks, Sammia." I barge open Tristan's door and close it behind me.

I find him sitting at his desk. He looks up and runs his tongue over his bottom lip and sits back in his chair, as if amused.

Arrogance personified.

"Claire Anderson." He smiles.

I narrow my eyes.

"And to what do I owe this pleasure?" he says, pen in hand.

"Oh, I think you know," I sneer.

He raises an eyebrow. "No. Actually, I don't."

"What the hell are you doing to Fletcher?"

"What do you mean?"

"I mean," I bark, "how dare you call him stupid? How dare you scream at him in front of other staff? Or at all, for that matter."

He tilts his chin to the sky defiantly. "Did he run to Mommy, did he?"

"Tristan," I whisper angrily. "I understand that you met in terrible circumstances, but it's clearly obvious that you only hired him to make a fool of him. And I won't have it."

He narrows his eyes and sits back in his chair. "Is that what you think?"

"That's what I know."

He stands and comes around in front of me. "I'll tell you what I'm doing with Fletcher Anderson. I'm teaching him work ethic. He's lazy and needs discipline."

"You are not training him; you are belittling him," I fire back.

"I'm teaching him to have some respect," he replies calmly. "Something that he quite obviously hasn't learned at home."

"Why on earth would he respect a jerk like you?" I whisper angrily.

"Because I'm his boss, Claire, and I am not putting up with his excuses," he replies.

"By calling him stupid," I snap.

"I did not call him stupid. I told him to stop acting stupid. There's a big difference. He's intelligent, Claire, a lot more than you give him credit for. He doesn't have anger issues; he has a fucking attitude issue, and I'm getting rid of it."

"By making a fool of him?" I gasp.

"By making him learn from his mistakes. If he is not punished as he does them, he will keep doing it. You don't learn a lesson unless it makes you uncomfortable."

"You yelled at him for forgetting a pen, for Christ's sake," I stammer.

His face contorts in anger. "How many CEOs do you know that don't take a pen to a meeting, Claire?" he sneers. "Rule number one." He holds his finger up to accentuate his point. "Be prepared. Do not turn up to a meeting unprepared."

The door opens, and Fletcher comes into view. He closes it behind him.

Tristan glares at him. "You run to Mommy when you get into trouble?" he asks.

Fletcher stares at him.

"You going to run to Mommy when someone steals your business or your girlfriend?" he asks. "Is that what a man does? Run to Mommy?"

"How dare you?" I whisper angrily. "Get your things, Fletcher; we're leaving. You don't have to put up with this."

170

"Get back to your desk, Fletcher, and finish that report," Tristan snaps.

Fletcher looks between us, unsure what to do.

"Fletcher Anderson," Tristan asserts. His voice rises along with his anger. "That report is to be on my desk before you leave today. I don't care if we don't get out of here until midnight."

"He's coming with me," I snap. "Stick your report up your ass."

"Mom," Fletcher interrupts. "Don't."

"Fletcher, let's go," I urge.

"Do you want to know why I'm riding this kid so hard, Claire?" Tristan asks.

I stare at him.

"Because Fletcher Anderson has more potential than I've seen in a very long time. He's super intelligent."

Fletcher's chest rises as he fights a crooked smile.

"But he's also a little shit, and he's lazy and lacks discipline," he adds.

I continue to stare at Tristan.

"I can give him the tools that he needs, but they don't come easy. There are no shortcuts to this, Claire. I'm the only person who can give him the tool kit. So don't you barge in here and ruin everything for him. You are killing this kid with kindness, Claire. He's not a child. He's a man. He needs to grow the fuck up and take responsibility for his own shortcomings."

Fletcher drops his head.

"Why the hell are you still standing here, Fletcher?" he bellows. "Go and finish the report."

"See you at home, Mom," Fletcher says. He turns and scurries from the office, and Tristan goes back to sit behind his desk.

We glare at each other for an extended time.

The air between us is electric—only this time it's fueled by anger.

"I'm watching you," I whisper.

"I'll tell you who to watch: that middle child of yours. The wizard."

"The middle child of mine is none of your concern," I sneer.

The nerve of this man. This is exactly why I don't want him anywhere near my kids; he's cold and judgmental and lacks any type of empathy.

A fucking asshole.

"Goodbye, Tristan."

He raises an eyebrow in a silent question.

"What?" I snap.

"Is that it?" He holds the pen in his hand. "Is that all you want to say to me?"

I narrow my eyes. Any minute I'm about to explode.

"I've got nothing more to say to you."

He gives me a sarcastic smile. "Liar."

Fucking hell. This man makes me thermonuclear. I want to dive over the desk and punch that sarcastic smile off his face.

Before I lose my temper, I turn and storm from the office with my blood boiling in my veins.

I can't believe I was actually attracted to that jerk.

What a fucking joke.

The television drones on in the background. The children are squabbling among themselves as they sit on the floor doing a jigsaw puzzle. Woofy is chasing Muff around the house, and I'm curled up on the couch, pretending to read.

My mind isn't here, though.

It's in Paris . . . *with him.*

I hate that I'm thinking about such an asshole.

What's worse is I can pretend that I don't like him. I can lie to his face about my wants. I can act like being in his arms for six days didn't mean a thing.

Because if nobody knows my inner fears, then they can't come true.

I turn the page of my book on autopilot. I haven't read a word, but the habit of pretending is strong and down to my bones.

I picture the roses that he left me in Épernay and the card that I have safely tucked in my purse.

WE HAVE UNFINISHED BUSINESS.
COME TO PARIS FOR THE WEEKEND.

I exhale heavily. We did the business, fair and square.

Fucked it to hell and back, actually.

So why does it still feel unfinished? I have this haunting feeling that it isn't over. But then I know it is.

Tristan Miles is lingering in my soul . . . and the bastard won't leave.

He was supposed to be my get-out-of-grief card, my comeback into society.

What he was, was an intoxicating drug and an addiction that I don't need.

So now, instead of one man lingering, I have two.

My beautiful husband, Wade, the one I planned a life with . . . the one whose wishes I'm honoring.

And then there's Tristan, the gorgeous soul-sucking bastard from New York . . . who has a fun, tender side underneath.

But does he really?

Does he have a tender side, or is that just who he pretends to be when he's alone with a woman? Was that all a plot to get under my guard?

It worked, if it was.

The man I spent time with was beautiful.

I drag my hand down my face. I'm sick of this. Why the hell am I always the one who suffers?

If the truth be known, Tristan is probably in bed with another woman right now.

She'd be blonde and beautiful and would be able to be spontaneous and fun.

"Give it back," Harry snaps, interrupting my thoughts as he snatches a puzzle piece from Fletcher.

I look around at my chaotic surroundings, and I know that Tristan doesn't belong here in my world. He will never belong here. This is as far from his reality as he could possibly be.

My stomach twists at the thought.

I get a vision of the two of us rolling around in the sheets, laughing and making love.

The tenderness between us felt so real and intimate.

Did it mean anything to him at all?

I turn the page of my book . . . obviously not.

"I think that just about wraps it up," Michael, our lead accountant, says as he looks up from his spreadsheets.

I smile, optimistic for the first time in a while. "That's great; thank you."

"As long as we keep gaining traction on the advertising, we should be able to pull out of this."

"I agree." I look around at the board members. "Thank you all so much for pulling together and working through the issues. Your advice is so appreciated."

"We'll get through this." Michael smiles. "It's just a rough patch."

"I know." I nod. "Thanks again."

The group of ten stands, and we chatter as we leave. They wait for me to lock up our office, and we make our way downstairs in the elevator together.

It's late—nine o'clock on Thursday—and we've had our monthly board meeting. The figures are finally turning around. I don't have to let anyone go this month, and I think we're actually going to be okay.

"I'll see you next month?" I ask.

"For sure. Bye."

"See you. Do you need a lift?"

"No, I'm fine. Thanks anyway."

I always stay in a hotel here in New York on the nights we have a meeting. By the time I got home, I'd have to turn around and come straight back. It's not worth the two-hour drive.

My phone rings, and the name Gabriel lights up the screen.

"Hi, just finished," I answer.

"I'm across the street in Luciano's."

"Fancy finding Gabriel Ferrara in an Italian restaurant," I tease.

"Shocking, isn't it," he mutters dryly. "I'm coming out now."

"On my way." I cross the street and begin making my way down to my trusty friend. Gabriel always meets me for drinks on the nights I stay in New York.

We don't paint the town red or anything like that, but we have a good time just the same.

I see him walking down toward me, and I smile and kiss his cheek. "Hello, Bella." He smiles.

"Hello."

He holds his arm out, and I link it with mine. "The usual?"

"Uh-huh, sounds good."

We walk the two blocks to our favorite bar. "Oh, did I tell you that Fletcher started an internship?"

"No, you called and told me he wanted to, but I haven't seen you since."

"Oh." I roll my eyes. "In the end, I couldn't talk him out of it."

"You know, I think it will be good for him," he says as we walk arm in arm down the street.

"Hmm, yes, I think so too. Time will tell. I still think he's too young to be in an office environment."

"He's eighteen, Claire."

"I know he is. I guess he will always be a baby to me."

He rolls his eyes as we continue walking. He doesn't know my children personally—only through what I tell him. I purposely haven't told Gabriel where Fletch is working. It's no secret how much he hates Miles Media. Ferrara Media and Miles Media are archenemies, and their power struggle is played out in the media.

If he knew that I spent that week with Tristan, he would lose his living shit.

Oh well . . . it doesn't matter anyway, I guess.

We walk into the bar. It's busy and bustling with people in suits who have come straight from work. "You grab a table, and I'll get some drinks," Gabriel says. "The usual?"

"Yes, please."

He walks off, and I find a bench seat near the window. I perch up onto the stool and quickly text my mom.

Hi,

Everything okay with you guys?

A reply bounces straight back.

Yes love,

176

Kids are all in bed.
Goodnight,
xoxox

I text back.

Thanks Mom,
What would I do without you?
Love you
xox

My mom is a godsend. I don't know what I would do without parents.

I hear a loud burst of laughter from the other side of the bar, and I glance over to see a group of men, and my eyes widen. A man has his back to me and is being animated as he tells a story. Everyone is listening and laughing as he speaks.

Fuck . . . I'd know the back of that man anywhere.

Expensive designer suit, wavy dark hair, broad shoulders, and perfect posture. Tristan Miles.

And I'm here with Gabriel.

Double fuck.

I glance over to the bar to see that Gabriel has just ordered, and the bartender is making our drinks. Oh no . . . too late to leave.

I shuffle my stool around so that my back is to Tristan. Hopefully he won't see me.

We'll have one quick drink, and then I'll sneak out of here.

Eight million people live in New York City; what are the damn chances of being in the same bar as him?

I hear the loud burst of laughter again, and I peer over to see Tristan laughing out loud with the other men.

I do not need this shit tonight; can't I just have a relaxing night with my friend without him turning up?

Gabriel returns to the table and passes my glass of wine over. "Thanks." I take it from him a little too eagerly. I'm suddenly thirsty like a camel.

"How was your meeting?" Gabriel asks.

"Good." I smile, grateful to take my mind off the gorgeous elephant in the room. "The advertising has picked up, and the figures this month were good. Hopefully it will continue."

Gabriel's eyes hold mine. "You know, I've been thinking."

"Did it hurt?" I smirk into my wineglass.

"Why don't you let me help you?"

"And how would you do that?"

"I could buy fifty percent of Anderson Media and take over half the debt. We could work together. I could even be a silent partner, if that's what you prefer."

"What?" I frown. This is the first time he's ever mentioned anything like this.

"I'm serious. I have the contacts, and we could really build it up for the boys."

I stare at him.

"And then"—he sips his drink casually—"when you got back on your feet, you could buy my portion back from me."

"You'd do that?"

"Of course, anything for you. You know that."

I frown and sip my drink.

"Claire Anderson," the familiar voice says from behind my back.

Fucking hell.

I turn and see Tristan standing beside the table. "Oh, hi," I stammer. I look between Gabriel and Tristan as they glare at each other.

"Drinking on a school night?" he asks.

"She's on a date with me," Gabriel snaps.

Tristan smiles sarcastically and pulls up a stool, as if undertaking a silent dare.

"Is that so?" He sits down and turns his attention to me.

The blood begins to drain from my face . . . get me out of here.

"Ah, Tristan, do you know Gabriel?" I ask nervously.

Tristan smiles and puts his hand out to shake Gabriel's hand. "Hello, I'm Tristan Miles."

Gabriel glares at him but doesn't shake his hand. "I know who you are."

Tristan smiles broadly and winks at him. "No handshake?"

Arrogance personified.

Fuck.

He's my son's boss. I have to be civil, and he knows it. Bastard.

"Tristan, if you don't mind . . . we are in the middle of a business meeting," I reply.

"I thought you were on a date?" he replies calmly.

"She is. We are," Gabriel fires back.

Tristan steeples his hands in front of him, as if amused. His eyes are alight with troublemaking mischief.

"What do you want, Tristan?" I snap.

"I need to talk to you, Claire."

"About?"

He sips his drink, clearly amused at his bastardly arrogance. "Fletcher."

"What the fuck do you want to talk about Fletcher for?" Gabriel snaps.

Tristan turns his attention back to Gabriel. "Do you mind with the coarse language? Fletcher is my intern, and I need to speak to his mother. So if you don't mind . . ."

"Fletcher is . . . ?" Gabriel's face falls. "Fletcher is working for Miles? Why, Claire?" he gasps.

"He wanted to work for the best." Tristan smiles sweetly. His eyes hold Gabriel's in a silent dare.

I haven't seen Tristan Miles in full swing yet. He's so arrogant that it's a joke, and I hate to admit it.

It's fucking hot.

"You want to talk to me now?" I ask.

"Yes. Now." He looks over at Gabriel. "Goodbye. This particular meeting is of a private nature."

"I'm not going anywhere," Gabriel snaps.

Tristan's eyes come back to mine. "I could always come to see you in your office tomorrow, Claire . . . on your desk."

"You mean at her desk," Gabriel replies.

Tristan gives me a slow, sexy smile. "I know what I meant."

Oh . . . fuck a duck.

I feel the blood drain from my face. He's going to let Gabriel know that we've been together. Shit. I need to defuse this situation right now before there's an all-out fight. "Gabriel, just give me ten minutes to speak to Tristan about Fletcher. Why don't you go and order us some more drinks?"

They glare at each other for what feels like forever, and finally Gabriel stands. "You have five minutes," he warns him.

Tristan smiles, unfazed by the threat, and then he turns his attention to me. His face drops, and he stares at me flatly.

"What are you doing?" I ask.

He sits forward, unable to hide his anger. "What are *you* doing?"

"I'm having a drink with a friend."

"You're friends with Gabriel Ferrara?" he scoffs.

"Yes, I am, actually," I fire back.

He sips his drink as he glares at me. "What kind of friend, Claire?"

"That's none of your business."

"So let me get this straight: you don't want to see me because of what I do for a living . . . but you are—"

I cut him off. "I don't want to see you because you're a coward."

"How the fuck am I coward?"

"One meeting with my children, and you run for the hills," I blurt out before I put my brain-to-mouth filter on.

He clenches his fists, barely able to control his anger. "You told me you didn't want to see me before I even met your children. Do not fucking lie to me, Claire," he growls.

I sit back, affronted. I hate that he can see through me.

"I know who the coward is here, Claire, and it isn't fucking me."

"You arrogant prick. Have you ever considered that maybe I just don't like you?"

"No. I haven't. Because I know you do."

I screw up my face in disgust. "I know that you think that every woman in the world is in love with you, but I can assure you, Mr. Miles, I am not."

His eyes hold mine, and he gives me a slow, sexy smile, as if he knows a secret.

"What?"

He leans in so that only I can hear him. "I know for a fact that if I wanted to take you home, I could have you riding my cock all night."

I get a vision of myself naked and on top of him, his thick body deep inside of mine, and my body clenches in appreciation.

"The hell you could," I sneer.

He leans closer and puts his lips to my ear. His breath sends goose bumps down my spine. "It wouldn't bother you that I didn't like your children if you didn't want me."

I clench my jaw, annoyed with myself for saying that out loud. "Fuck you."

He smiles darkly. "Admit it, Anderson; you think about me . . . just as much as I think about you."

Shocked by his admission, I swallow the lump in my throat. "You think about me?" I whisper.

"All the fucking time. You're driving me insane."

Electricity buzzes between us . . . and I hate that it does.

"On that note"—he stands—"I'll let you get back to your date."

Don't go.

"It's not a date. He's just a friend," I blurt out.

Our eyes lock. "Prove it."

The air between us is heavy with anger and want; it's a heady combination.

"Call me in two hours," he replies.

"Why would I do that?"

His dark eyes hold mine. "Because I've never needed to please a woman as much as I crave to please you . . . let me."

I get a vision of his head between my legs, his thick tongue taking what it needs from me, and arousal begins to heat my blood.

I don't want to want him . . . but God, I really do.

This isn't good.

Without another word, he turns and walks off, back to his friends on the other side of the bar.

I stare into the space he just left. Every cell in my body is tingling, every inch of me craving what he has to give.

Good God, the devil really does wear Prada.

I'm totally fucking screwed.

Chapter 12

I take deep breaths as I try to ignore the feelings that Tristan Miles arouses in me.

Maybe that's it—it's just a bad-boy thing.

Yes, all women experience this at least once in their lives. I'm just doing it a little later than most.

Of course.

That is totally it. Why didn't I realize this before?

I know I shouldn't want him, and so therefore I do. Maybe if he were the perfect model citizen, I wouldn't even want him at all.

I sip my wine in celebration about my epiphany. God . . . and I thought I really liked him. Stupid idiot. This is actually a relief.

My phone vibrates on the table as it receives a text. Tristan. Here we go.

Let me guess,
Gabriel Ferrara is offering to
help you financially?

I frown. What? Angered, I text back.

Gabriel is a good friend.
I'm offended.
Stop texting me before I block you.

A reply bounces back.

If you block me, who's going to
nail you through the mattress tonight?

I bite my lip to stop myself from smiling. I write back.

I am on a date with another man.
I wouldn't get too cocky if I were you.

An answer bounces back.

You don't like him,
I know you don't.

I roll my eyes; the arrogance of this man is next level.

Okay Siri,
if you say so.

I smirk as I hit send.

Siri?

I glance over to see him sitting on a stool, smirking back as he texts me.

Bastard. I like this game, and I really shouldn't. I reply.

Well you seem to know everything,
so I assume you moonlight as Siri.

I look over to see him smile broadly as he reads my text. I bite the inside of my cheek as I act uninterested.

Lose the prick
and come buy me a drink.

I giggle before I can stop myself. Of all the nerve.

I don't buy random men drinks.
Jealous?

I glance over to see him smiling as he texts back.

Of him?
You must be joking.
And you will do whatever I say.
Make it Scotch.

My eyes glance over to the bar at Gabriel as he waits. This is insane. I feel so naughty. I write back.

You are delusional and strange.
When I'm delusional I just
imagine I'm in Hawaii
drinking Mimosas.
Scotch is not a dream drink.

Gabriel walks back through the crowd with our two drinks and places them on the table. "Here you go."

"Thanks."

He takes a seat. "Are you serious?"

"Gabriel." I sigh. Here we go—an hour-long lecture. "Fletcher wanted to work for them."

"Why wouldn't he come and work for me?" he snaps. "I'm offended. Ferrara Media is where he should be."

"He applied without me even knowing. I have to let him choose his path."

"With him?" he snaps again.

My phone beeps with a text. I glance at the screen.

> **That's a great idea,**
> **let's go to Hawaii for the**
> **weekend.**
> **We can practice tantric sex.**

A stupid grin crosses my face before I can cover it up.

Stop it.

I bring my focus back to Gabriel. "Look," I say guiltily. "It's only twelve months, and I know that it isn't ideal, but it will be good for him to get out of his comfort zone. And besides, he's giving them a run for their money, so he might not even last without being fired."

"Why didn't you tell me?"

"Because I knew you would react like this."

A text bounces in, and I pick up my phone off the table to shield it from Gabriel's eyes. It's a cartoon Kama Sutra image of people in a sexual position with the heading ROCK-A-BYE BOOTY.

I glance over and see Tristan's shoulders bouncing as he laughs and watches me.

Oh hell.

186

"I'm not impressed at all, Claire. I don't like him being around them," Gabriel continues, completely distracted.

"You know as well as I do they are good businesspeople," I argue. "I wasn't impressed at first, but the more I thought about it, the more it made sense." My phone beeps with a text, and I open it discreetly on my lap. It's another cartoon Kama Sutra drawing of a woman crouched between a man's legs, his dick in her mouth. The heading is THE MOTHERLOAD.

What the hell?

I burst out laughing. I glance up, and Tristan's eyes are alight with mischief as he chuckles.

"What is so funny?" Gabriel snaps.

"Oh, Marley is having boyfriend trouble. She's just relaying their latest tiff," I lie.

"No wonder," he mutters into his drink. "That woman is a nutjob."

A waitress arrives at our table. "Here you go—two mimosas." She carefully puts the two drinks down in front of us.

"What are these?" Gabriel frowns.

"On the house," the waitress replies. "Enjoy." She walks off, and I stare at the drinks in front of us.

Don't look over at him . . . don't look at him . . . don't look at him. That's what he wants.

I cannot believe the gall of this man.

Most men would be rattled seeing a woman out with another man.

Most men aren't Tristan Miles.

He's unrattle-able . . . is that even a word? And I hate to admit it, but confidence in a man is very fucking appealing.

Gabriel picks up his mimosa and takes a sip. "Hmm, not bad." He shrugs.

I smirk as I stare at my clueless friend. If he knew who bought that drink, he would be choking on it. "I'm just going to go to the bathroom," I say.

I get up and make my way through the bar and into the ladies' bathroom. I take my time and mentally prepare myself to ignore Tristan for good.

I need to stop this flirty game we have going on.

But he's so fun.

No . . . enough is enough.

I open the door, and before I know it, someone grabs my hand and pulls me around the corner and pins me to the wall.

"Tristan," I whisper.

His lips drop to my neck. "Hello, Anderson, fancy meeting you here." He smiles against my skin as his teeth skim my neck.

"What are you doing?" I whisper as goose bumps scatter up my arms.

"Accosting you in the hallway—what does it look like?" He bites me hard, and I tingle to my toes.

"What if I really was here with Gabriel?" I stammer.

"Then I'm about to steal his girl." He smiles as he takes my face in his hands.

My God, he's so naughty.

"Stop it," I breathe.

"No." He kisses me, soft and slow. His tongue gently coaxes mine to come out and play. My eyes close in pleasure. Damn it, why does he have to kiss so well?

"Tris," I breathe as I feel my resistance begin to wane.

"One last time."

He sucks on my tongue, and I go weak at the knees.

"We shouldn't," I whimper as my hands go to his muscular behind.

"We totally fucking should." He pins me to the wall, and I feel his rock-hard erection up against my stomach.

My insides begin to liquefy . . . fucking hell, he's so damn hot that I can't stand it.

Burning inferno.

"Go out there, and tell him you're going home."

"Why would I do that?"

"Because you are going home. With me."

"Tristan."

"Or I can come and drag you from the table. It's your choice." He shrugs casually. "I need you." He grabs my hip bones and drags my body over his hardened cock. He does need me; every cell in his body needs me. I can feel it.

His hands are in my hair, and our kisses become frantic. Deep, long, and passionate.

Oh hell . . .

I need you too.

"Last time," I pant against his open lips.

"For real." His eyes are closed in pleasure.

What must we look like?

He's fighting this too. He knows we are wrong for each other, but the physical attraction between us is just too strong.

One time . . . one time won't hurt . . . will it?

The damage is already done. One more time won't hurt, surely?

"Go out there, and tell him you're leaving," he says as he straightens my skirt and tucks in my blouse.

"I'm finishing my drink, and then I will."

He kisses me tenderly; his lips linger over mine. "Stay at my house."

"No, I have a room booked."

"Where?"

"The Edison at Times Square."

"Meet you there. Tell the desk that your husband is picking up a key."

I nod, unable to verbally agree to this lunacy. My voice box must know that this is a bad idea.

He tucks a piece of hair behind my ear, smiles, and kisses me once more. He really is a gorgeous man—there's no denying it.

"It's good to see you, Anderson," he whispers.

I smile softly up at the forbidden fruit . . . *it's so good to see you.*

His dark eyes hold mine. "I can't fucking wait to get you naked."

He turns and, without another word, walks back out into the bar as if nothing has happened.

I stare after him. My hair is messed up, and my body is tingling from head to toe. My chest rises and falls as I try to regain my composure. Jesus, what did I just agree to?

Tristan fucking Miles.

I switch the channel on the television and glance at the clock. Where is he?

It's been over an hour. I raced back to my hotel room, showered, and got all irresistible, and now he hasn't even come . . . what if he doesn't show up?

My eyes widen in horror as a possibility comes to mind. What if he was just pulling a power play to prove that he can have me if he wants me? No . . . he wouldn't.

Oh my God, he totally would . . . it's Tristan. What did I expect?

I hear the door click, and I quickly rearrange myself in the bed. *He's lucky.*

The door opens, and he closes it behind him. He turns, and then his eyes float over my naked body. He gives me a slow, sexy smile. "Anderson."

I'm lying on the bed, naked, my legs slightly parted. If I'm going to do this whore-bag thing, I'm going hard core. Don't mess with me tonight, fucker; you have something I need.

You're going down . . . literally.

His eyes fix on mine. "Playing hard to get, I see?" He jerks his tie hard as he undoes it.

"I am hard to get." I tap the bed beside me. "But tonight, I'm easy to fuck."

He chuckles as he sits beside me. "How convenient. I happen to be in the fucking market myself." He bends and kisses me, and I smile against his lips.

His hand runs up the inside of my inner thigh and then swipes down and through my wet sex . . . this all feels so natural.

Too natural.

As if he was always meant to touch me . . . as if he always has.

No. Not tonight. I want some power in this exchange. He's doing what I want. He's pleasing me.

I arch my back and spread my legs. "Feeling hungry?" I ask.

His eyes flicker with arousal, and he smiles darkly. "Fucking oath I am." He stands and tears his jacket over his shoulders and throws it to the side with urgency. "Starving, actually." He grabs a paper bag from the inside pocket and then pulls out a box of condoms. "Do you know how many fucking pharmacies I just went to to find these?"

I chuckle.

"I couldn't find one. I even contemplated going into the brothel on the corner and offering them a hundred dollars for a box."

"I'm not going to ask you how you know that there's a brothel on the corner." I raise my eyebrow.

He frowns, realizing what he's just revealed. "Shut up, Siri." He unzips his trousers and pushes them down, revealing his hard, thick cock.

My stomach flutters, and I giggle in excitement. It's like Christmas morning, and I'm watching my presents being unwrapped.

This time with him is different. I'm not nervous or scared. I'm excited, because I know how good this night is going to be.

He drops to his knees beside the bed and pulls me over to him and then spreads my legs and studies me there.

My breath catches as I watch him. This is strangely intimate . . . but it's okay, because it's him. And I know how much he loves my body.

I don't have one insecurity when I'm naked with him. He wouldn't let me even if I did.

"Ohh," he whispers darkly. "I missed this pretty pussy." He kisses me there with an open mouth, and I reach down and put my fingers in his hair. His thick tongue swipes through my flesh, and I smile as I watch him.

Tristan Miles doesn't go down on women for them . . . he does it for himself.

He loves it.

It's his favorite thing; he could do it for an hour, and I would still have to drag him up to me.

My back arches in pleasure, and I whimper. His licks are hard and slow, measured for the perfect pressure.

We get into a rhythm, and my body begins to shudder. He smiles into me.

He links our fingers on my thigh. Our eyes are locked and . . . oh God.

He's perfect.

The way he holds my hand as he eats me. The way he looks at me.

The way he enjoys it.

No wonder I'm addicted to this man; he's the world's greatest lover.

He begins to flick his tongue in a practiced move, and I convulse.

Shit.

I have no defense against him when he does that. I begin to moan.

He spreads my legs farther apart, his hands on my inner thighs. His entire face is wet with my arousal now, and I begin to writhe under him.

It hits me like a freight train, and I scream out in wonder. He smiles into me as his eyes close in pleasure once more.

The shock waves of the world's strongest orgasm shudder through me, and then he picks me up and throws me over onto my knees. I hear the telling rip of the condom packet, and then he twists my ponytail around his hand and pulls me back onto his cock.

Oh God . . . he's in that mood . . . he's going to ride me home . . . literally.

He hisses as he slides in deep, and my body shakes, still too sensitive from his tongue.

I drop my shoulders into the mattress, unable to hold myself up, and he jerks me back up onto his cock by the hair and slaps my behind. "Up," he commands in a growl.

I smile. Oh, I love him like this.

He slowly slides in . . . and then slides out. In and then out. He gives his cock a delicious deep circle, taking his time to stretch me. No matter how turned on he is, he's always careful to prepare my body. He knows he's a big man, and his experience shows. "You all right?" he breathes.

I nod.

"Answer me."

"Yes," I whimper. But I'm not all right; sex with Tristan is not all right . . . it's a blinding light. So much more than all right.

It's everything.

He slides out, and the sound of my wet arousal sucks in the air. "It's time for you to learn a lesson, Anderson," he whispers.

I smile. "Siri to you."

He chuckles and slams in hard, and I cry out.

Ouch.

He gives me a few hard pumps.

"What's the lesson?" I whimper, his grip on my hair near painful.

"You don't get to break up with me." He pumps me hard, and I nearly bounce headfirst into the wall. "We don't end . . . until we both decide." He slams me hard again, and it's so good that my body begins to ripple around him once more.

He jerks me by the hair, and I smile up at the ceiling, his cock riding me in hard, measured strokes.

"Do you understand me?" he pants.

"No." I giggle.

Slap. His hand comes down on my behind.

"Ouch," I whimper.

His hips pick up the pace. "We don't end . . . until we fucking end." The bed begins to hit the wall with force. His grip is painful.

"Tell me you fucking understand," he moans.

Butterflies flutter deep in my stomach. Hearing the arousal in his voice does things to me. "Yes," I pant.

"Yes what?" he growls.

"I understand."

He lets go and really lets me have it, and it's beautiful and blinding, and I'm sure the concierge is going to be knocking on the door any moment because the bed is hitting the wall so hard that I'm positive we're causing structural damage.

"*Fuck,*" he moans, his voice deep and guttural. "Anderson . . . fuck me," he growls, losing control. "Fuck me harder." His grip tightens, his pumps get harder, and God, this is next-level incredible.

I screw up my face as I try to hold it, and he slaps my behind again. I scream out, and I clench as I come in a rush. He holds himself deep, and I feel his cock jerk hard inside of me.

He lets me go, lays me down, rolls me onto my back, and then slides back into my body. His lips take mine with a tenderness I've never known.

We stare at each other for a prolonged moment, and I can feel his cock gently pulsating inside of me as it tries to completely empty itself.

"I missed you, Anderson," he whispers as he brushes the hair back from my face.

I stare up at him, shocked. An unwelcome emotion overwhelms me, and I blink to stop the tears.

This isn't how this is supposed to go.

I expected a booty call, but this feels special and intimate.

We kiss, and I feel my heart constrict in my chest. This was a bad idea.

I want to go home.

Chapter 13

I wake to the feeling of gentle kisses dusting my shoulder, and I smile sleepily.

He's here.

There's no mistaking waking up next to Tristan.

His cheek comes to mine from behind. "Morning." I smile.

"Anderson," he purrs.

I chuckle and turn toward him so he can kiss the side of my face again.

What a night.

Ecstasy doesn't come close to where this man takes me. His touch is otherworldly.

"I've got to go, babe," he murmurs. "I have a meeting in like half an hour on the other side of town."

"Okay." I smile. I roll over to face him, and we stare at each other for a moment. I bring my hand up and run it through his dark stubble.

"When will I see you?" he asks.

My heart drops. I know this isn't going anywhere, and I have to rip off the Band-Aid. "You won't. This can't go on, Tris."

His eyes hold mine, and a frown crosses his brow, but he stays silent.

"I wish things were different," I say softly as I lean in and kiss his lips. "I really do." I concentrate on my fingers in his stubble. They distract me from my heart telling me to stop talking.

"I have my kids, and I don't do casual, and I can't do a relationship. And even if I could, it's not the life you want."

He exhales deeply, knowing I'm right. His eyes drop away from mine.

"We're so good together," I whisper as I pull his face back to me. "In . . . in another life, we could have been great. Just not this one."

His eyes search mine, and I feel like he has so much to say but is choosing to remain silent.

"Promise me something."

"What?" He sighs, unimpressed.

"Promise me . . . that sometimes . . . you'll think of me."

Our eyes are locked. "No, I can't do that, Anderson . . . if I can't have you, I don't want to think about you."

I smile sadly and lean in and kiss him. Our faces screw up together.

This is goodbye.

We stare at each other, and he runs his fingers over my face, as if memorizing every inch. "I wish things were different," he whispers.

"Me too."

He frowns, and I know he wants one last time. He goes to lie over me.

"I can't, Tris." I shake my head, emotional overload threatening. "I just can't."

He clenches his jaw and gets out of bed in a rush. He dresses in silence as I lie and watch him.

"You know I'm right," I whisper.

He does his tie, refusing to look at me.

"Are you going to say anything?" I ask.

"Nope." He pulls his jacket over his shoulders and retrieves his expensive watch from the bathroom and pats his pockets as he makes sure he has everything. He goes to the door, and I hold my breath as I watch him.

"Tris."

He turns back to me.

"Can . . . can you say something, please?"

"What do you want me to say, Claire?"

Tears threaten. "Anything?"

His eyes hold mine for a beat, and finally he speaks. "Goodbye."

I swallow the lump in my throat . . . not that.

He turns and leaves. The door clicks closed, and I stare at the back of it.

He would have fought me if he wanted it.

He didn't.

And now I know.

I stand under the hot water and let it stream over my head. I've had the worst week.

Busy at work, and I've been moping around about Tristan, and I don't know why. I did the right thing.

We were never going anywhere, and I knew that, but it still stung.

I just wish he wasn't so perfect.

Maybe with kids I'll just never meet someone, and I get it. I'm a lot to take on—any single mother is.

Maybe my happiness won't come until they all move out . . . I just have to be patient.

My phone dances around on the bathroom vanity, and I peer out to see the name Marley light up the screen. I jump out and answer it. Something must be wrong. "Hello."

"Hi, oh my God. You will never guess who I am looking at right now."

I frown. "Who?"

"I'm in Portabella's, the Italian restaurant we've been wanting to come to."

"Who with?"

"My aunt. Guess who's here?"

"Who?"

"Tristan Miles."

I frown.

"Guess who he's here with?"

"Who?" Don't tell me—I really don't want to know.

"Avril Mason."

"The fashion editor?" I frown.

"Yes, they're on a date. She grabbed his hand over the table before."

My heart drops. "Oh well, I don't care." I act brave.

"Yeah, I know. Just thought you would want to know."

"Not really." I close my eyes as the walls close in. "I'm in the shower. I'll see you tomorrow? Thanks for the update."

"Yeah, sure thing."

I hang up and get back under the shower and exhale heavily.

Well, that's it. He's moved on. Didn't take much.

I should have gone out on a date with a less dangerous option.

A man I couldn't fall for.

Oh well, it is what it is.

"Well?" She smiles sexily. "Tell me." She sucks on her finger seductively. "How many times a day do you think about me?"

I stare at the woman sitting across the table from me. Avril Mason: she's beautiful, ticks all the right boxes. Natural blonde, killer body, twenty-eight, a successful fashion editor—she has been on my radar for years, but we have never been single at the same time. I went on one date with her before I went to France for the conference. After that I thought we were going somewhere. Not so much now. I should be obsessed with her; I should be chasing her around New York and falling hopelessly in love.

What I'm doing is neither of those things.

I'm dreaming of a fiery brunette. That woman has gotten under my skin.

I can't get Claire fucking Anderson out of my head. This is my third date with Avril, and every damn time I've spent the entire evening dreaming of Claire. It's getting to where I have to either step up and do the deed with Avril or stop seeing her. This is not my style. I fuck whomever I want, whenever I want. Doing the deed is never an issue. Especially with someone I know I want.

Usually, I close the deal on the first night or, at the least, the second. This is my third date with Avril, and as she sits across from me—and as usual—I find myself wondering what Claire is doing.

What is it about her that has me captivated?

She's wrong for me . . . in every sense. There is nothing that we have in common, and she's right—we live different lives in different worlds.

Avril picks her phone up and pouts and takes a selfie. She instantly posts it on her Instagram and tags the restaurant.

I watch her in a strange detached state.

Why is she so unattractive to me, when I know for a fact that she's beautiful?

What did that fucking Claire Anderson do to my sex drive?

My dick may as well have shriveled up and died. He doesn't want anybody but her.

And I don't get it, because I've dated some beautiful women over the years and yet have never had this happen before. I've always had to try to rein in my sex drive, control it to be loyal. It's been a conscious decision.

But now, nobody seems to be good enough to make him even think about wanting to come out and party. Now my traitorous body has only one woman on its mind.

I sip my red wine, annoyed with myself.

Snap the fuck out of this.

Claire Anderson is no good for you. Stop thinking about her. Witch.

If I had my time again with Claire, I'd give it to her good. I'd break her in half. I get a vision of her riding my cock the other night, and I clench in appreciation . . . so fucking hot.

What am I doing here?

"Well?" Avril asks.

Huh? I glance up from my daydream. Did she say something? "I'm sorry?" I ask.

"I said, let's go back to my place," she whispers. "I've made you wait long enough; it's time."

I smirk, amused that she thinks she's made me wait. Poor deluded woman.

I don't want this.

"I have to be up early tomorrow . . . rain check?" I ask.

201

"Are you serious?"

I hesitate, hardly able to believe it myself. "Yeah, I am." I sigh.

Her eyes hold mine. "You're just not into me, are you?"

I puff air into my cheeks, feeling guilty. "It's not you. It's me." I sigh. "I'm sorry." I shrug. "I have no excuse, because you're perfect."

She gives me a lopsided smile. "Do you want to talk about it in bed?"

I chuckle and sip my red wine. "As tempting as that is . . . no."

"So this is our last date?"

I wince. "I think so."

"I really thought we had something." She pulls a whiny face, and as I stare at her, I remember Claire teasing me with that exact line, as if she knew I heard it often.

And I do . . . but I never knew how it felt to hear it from someone I cared about.

It sucks.

I read the report as Fletcher stands in front of me, nervously waiting for my opinion.

A smile crosses my face. He's worked hard on this; I can tell. "This is good, Fletch."

"Really?"

"I like it. I would have perhaps added a little more information on projected earnings for the first quarter." I look up at him. "But it's good. You did well this week."

He smiles. "Thanks." He turns to walk out, and I notice it's dark outside. I kept him later than usual. "How are you getting home?"

"Subway," he says.

"I can give you a lift if you want."

He frowns. "You want to drive me home?"

"No. I'm offering you a lift because it's Friday night, and I know you've missed your usual train. And besides, your mother will have a conniption if something were to happen to you."

"Ah." He thinks about it.

"Contrary to what you believe, Fletcher, I'm not the devil. I have no plans to kill you and bury you in a ditch on a deserted road."

And besides, I want to see your mother.

"See, the fact that you said that . . . is just creepy," he mutters dryly.

I chuckle. "Was a little." I turn off my computer. "Okay, let's go."

Twenty minutes later we arrive at my parking space, and Fletcher's eyes nearly pop out of his head. "This is your car?"

"Nice, huh?" The lights blink as I unlock it.

He whistles as he walks around it. "A brand-new Aston Martin."

"Uh-huh."

"In sapphire black." He gasps in awe.

"You got it." I smile. "You like these cars?"

"I love these cars."

I smile. "Maybe if you get your license, you can have a drive of it."

"Really?" His eyes widen in excitement.

I shrug. "Sure, why not?"

Fletcher has grown on me. He's not a bad kid after all. Smart and funny, like his mom.

He flashes me a broad smile and climbs into the passenger seat. I pull out of the parking lot with speed, and he smiles goofily through the windshield.

She better be home.

A long hour later we pull into his street. "Just up here on the left," he says.

"I have been here before, remember?" I smirk.

He gives a subtle shake of his head, embarrassed.

My eyes flick over to him. "You know, I hate to admit it, but you impressed me that day."

"Why would that impress you?"

I shrug. "I like the way you look after your mom."

He smiles. "Yeah, well, she's pretty amazing."

She sure is.

I pull up out front and park the car. "I might just pop in to say hello to her—clear the air, so to speak?" I say. I think quickly on my feet. "We were angry with each other last time we saw one another in my office."

He looks at me for a bit, as if carefully considering my request. "Yeah, okay, I suppose."

We get out of the car and walk up to the house. I notice that there is no crap everywhere, unlike last time. The door opens in a rush, and Claire stands there, as if not realizing we were on the other side. She's wearing a black dress, and her hair is up. She looks beautiful.

"Oh. Tristan." Her face falls when she sees me, and she stares at me for a beat. "Hello," she forces out.

"Hi." I smile. Nerves dance in my stomach.

"What are you doing here?" she asks.

"I drove Fletch home."

Her eyes flick between me and Fletcher. "Did you forget about tonight, Fletch?" she asks. She seems nervous.

"What?" he says.

"Remember?" Her eyes widen. "I'm going out, and you're babysitting Patrick for me."

"Oh," Fletcher replies. "Yes, I did. With Paul from Pilates. Sorry I'm late."

What?

"That's me," a voice says from behind us. We all turn to see some blond dude walking up the path toward the house. He's all dressed up.

I stare at him as my brain misfires. *Huh?*

"Hello." He smiles. "I'm Paul."

"This is Tristan, Fletcher's boss," Claire interrupts before I get a chance to say something.

"Hello," I bark. I shake his hand and then turn to Fletcher and widen my eyes.

Are you just going to stand there?

Fletcher smirks and kisses his mother on the cheek. "Have fun, Mom."

"Thanks, darling." She turns to Paul. "Are you ready?"

"Sure am." Paul puts his arm out, and she links it with hers.

I put my hands on my hips in disgust.

What the actual fuck is going on here? She's dating someone else?

Are you fucking kidding me?

Don't cause a scene in front of Fletcher . . . don't cause a scene in front of fucking Fletcher. You are not dating her . . . you shouldn't be pissed.

I am.

I want to cause a fucking scene.

"Won't be late, sweetie. Bye, Tristan." She forces a nervous smile, and I glare at her.

I watch as they walk out, get into his car, and drive away.

I turn to Fletcher. "What are you going to do about this?"

"Nothing. Why?"

"Why aren't you attacking him with underpants?" I snap, annoyed. "What good are you if you're not going to be consistent?" I hit his chest with the backs of my fingers. "Consistency is key, Fletcher. If your mother isn't allowed to date, she isn't allowed to date anyone."

He shrugs, uninterested. "You coming in?"

"Yes, I am, actually." I walk into the house, angered that I've been discriminated against so abysmally.

She's on a fucking date . . . of all the nerve.

I raise my chin in defiance. "I didn't get a chance to talk to her yet. I better wait for her to get home." I look around the house. "Where does your mother keep her wine?"

"Hi." The little dark-haired boy smiles up at me. "You came back."

"Yes, I did." I smirk. This kid is my favorite—cute and innocent.

"What's your name again?" He frowns.

"Tristan." I smile. "I remember your name."

He bites his bottom lip. "What is it?"

"Patrick."

His eyes widen in excitement. "It is." He smiles proudly.

I look around nervously. "Where's that other brother of yours?"

"Who?" He frowns.

"The Harry Potter one."

"Oh, he's at school camp. He gets back in the morning," Patrick replies.

"Great." One less crazy fucker to worry about.

"No way," Fletcher gasps as he looks at his phone.

"What?" I frown.

"Oh my God." He puts his hand over his mouth. "Alita VanDerCamp just messaged me."

"And?" I frown.

"She's the hottest girl in school." His eyes are wide with disbelief.

"Hmm, okay." I shrug as I open a kitchen cupboard. I need a fucking drink.

"Where are the wineglasses, and who the hell is Paul from Pilates? He looks like a real tool."

Patrick smiles goofily up at me as he climbs onto a stool at the counter.

"Hey," Fletcher says as he types.

"That's it?" I pour a glass of wine, having found what I was looking for. "That's what you're going to write? You can't write *hey*." I screw up my face. This kid must be stupid.

"Why not?"

I roll my eyes. "Don't tell me you are clueless with women too."

"Well, what would you write?" he asks.

"I wouldn't text a girl back unless I had a plan."

"A plan." Fletcher frowns. "What the hell does that mean?"

I swear, I need to drink out of the bottle in this house. Do they have any tequila? "If a girl texts you, she's looking for more than a fucking *hey*."

Patrick's mouth drops open.

Oh shit. I point at him. "I swear sometimes. Don't tell your mother."

"Okay." He shrugs. "Harry swears too."

Hmm, I bet he does.

"So?" Fletcher frowns in fascination. "Like . . . what kind of plan?"

"Like, do you want to get something to eat, do you want to go to the movies . . . something like that. Strike while the iron's hot. If she texted you first, she's into you. Move fast, before she changes her mind." I sip my wine. "Girls are changeable, man. One day they like you; the next day they don't."

"Oh." His face falls. "So I'll call her tomorrow, then?"

"No, aren't you listening?" I roll my eyes. "Call her now."

"But I can't do anything tonight."

"Why not?"

"Because I'm minding Patrick."

"On the off chance she says yes, I'll stay with him." I pour the wine so fast into my glass that it sloshes over the sides.

Fletcher looks between Patrick and me.

"I'm waiting here for your mother anyway. I don't mind." I give Patrick a playful soft punch in the arm. He smiles and punches me back as hard as he can in the thigh. It nearly knocks me over, and I double over in pain. Ahh, fuck's sake . . . dead leg. "Ow, ease up." These kids are so violent. "You got a good hook on you, kid."

"I know; I made Harry cry the other day," he announces proudly. "I pulled his hair and punched him in the neck."

I smirk. This one is definitely my favorite. "Hmm, not sure if that's okay, but . . . well done."

Fletcher begins to pace. "So . . . I say hi." He waves his hands around in the air as he thinks. "And then . . ." He turns back to me. "What do I say then?"

I sip my wine. "Hello, my name is Fletcher, and I don't know where I keep my balls, so call someone else," I mutter dryly.

Fletcher throws his phone onto the bench. "I can't do it. I'm not calling her."

"Call her."

"No. I don't know what to say."

"Call her," I demand as I point to his phone with my wineglass.

"I can't."

"Yes, you can." I grab Patrick's shoulder and lead him into the living room. "We're going out here. Do it now."

"What if she says no?" he stammers in a panic.

"Who cares?" I shrug. "The world is full of hot girls, Fletcher."

"Not as hot as her."

"So why are you wasting time talking crap to us, then?"

Fletcher's eyes hold mine. "Okay, I'm going to do it."

"Good."

"I'm going to call her right now."

"Less talking, more action," I call.

"Okay." He begins to pace again, and I roll my eyes. Heaven help him if he actually gets the chance to do the deed . . . he's as green as a fucking tree. Hell, I was fucking twenty-five-year-olds at his age. What in the world has this kid been doing all this time?

I sit on the couch next to Patrick. "Do you want to watch a movie while we wait for pizza?" he asks.

"There's pizza coming?"

"Uh-huh." He smiles and picks up the remote and begins to flick through the movies.

I glance at my watch. "What time did your mother say she was coming home?"

"She's just having dinner. Not late."

"Has she been out with Paul from Pilates before?" I ask.

"Yes, but she has to hide from Harry. She can only go out when he's not home, because he's very rude and embarrassing."

I sip my wine as I act uninterested. That evil fucker is good for something after all.

Who knew?

This isn't their first date? What the fuck? How long has she been seeing him?

I begin to see red.

Fletcher comes rushing back into the room. "She said yes."

"She did?"

"We're going to get food."

"You are?" I'm as shocked as he is. "Great."

His eyes widen in fear. "What will I wear?"

"Oh Jesus." I roll my eyes, and Patrick slaps his forehead. "Just wear something nice. And have a shower. Girls like dudes who smell nice."

Fletcher stares at me, as if I am an alien. "Since when?"

I screw up my face in disgust. "What does your mother actually teach you about girls?"

"Nothing." He widens his eyes. "She thinks I'm too young to date."

I tip my head back to the sky in disgust. "And anyway, how come you didn't attack Paul from Pilates? Why is she allowed to go out with him?"

"Oh." Fletcher shrugs. "He's gay."

I narrow my eyes in delight. "Oh, he is . . . is he?"

"Well, I don't actually know that for sure." He shrugs casually. "But he isn't Mom's type, so . . ."

"Why isn't he your mother's type?"

"Because she does Pilates with him. Nobody does Pilates with a guy they like . . . do they? And besides, he wears a pink sweatband around his head. He's odd. Weird, even."

"Hmm." I think on this as I tap my chin. "That's a very good point, Fletcher. Nobody does date a guy who wears a pink sweatband around their head at Pilates," I say, thinking out loud.

"Precisely." Fletcher turns to go take a shower.

"Oh . . . and, Fletch?" I call after him.

"Yeah."

"Spank the pony in the shower."

He sticks his head back around the corner. "What?"

I nod. "Do that . . . you know, the thing."

Fletcher frowns. "What for?"

"Do you want the whole restaurant to know how happy you are?" I widen my eyes and look at his crotch. "You want to appear as least . . . excitable . . . as possible."

He frowns in horror. "This is a thing?"

Patrick frowns. "Wait, what? There's a pony in the shower?"

"It's a song," I mutter, distracted. "This is *the* thing, Fletch. Nobody goes on a date without listening to 'Spanking the Pony' before they go. Everybody knows that. It's the dating rule number one." Except me, of course, the first time with Claire . . . *damn it.* I got sloppy and didn't even remember the basic rules.

"Are you serious right now?" He frowns.

I roll my eyes. "Trust me on this one."

He shakes his head and mutters to himself as he walks up the stairs. I turn to Patrick. "What do you want to watch?"

"*Godzilla?*" he asks.

"Yeah, that's a good one." I nestle back into the couch. "I hope the pizza hurries up. I'm starving."

Patrick smiles up at me like this is the best night of his life. "Me too."

Where the fuck is she?

I get a vision of her laughing at dinner with him, and my blood boils.

Finally I hear the car pull up, and I glance at my watch: 10:45 p.m.

What time do you call this?

I slide out from underneath Patrick's legs as he sleeps, and I walk over to the window and peer through the side of the drapes.

They're talking in the car.

If you kiss him, you're in deep shit, woman.

He's leaning his arm on the steering wheel and looking over at her while they chat.

He's not gay. No way in hell would he be looking at her like that if he were gay.

Damn Fletcher's gaydar is off, way off.

Get the fuck out of his car, Claire.

Right.

Now.

Don't fucking push me.

She climbs out of the car and closes the door . . . no kiss.

I dive back onto the couch and put a sleeping Patrick's legs back over mine.

Moments later, the door opens, and Claire walks in and around the corner. Then her face falls when she sees me. "Tristan."

My anger is bubbling dangerously close to the surface, and I glare at her, unable to hide it.

She looks down at Patrick sprawled all over me, asleep. "What are you doing here?"

She seems pissed. Well, she's got nothing on me. I'm fucking fuming. "I babysat for you tonight. I believe you owe me a thank-you," I say through gritted teeth.

"What?" she snaps.

"Fletcher had to go out."

"To where?"

"That VanDerCamp girl that he likes texted him, and I said I would stay with Patrick. Fletcher is home now, though, asleep in bed. He wasn't gone for long at all. I'm assuming the date didn't go well."

"Are you kidding me? He left you here alone with Patrick?" she whispers angrily. "Oh, Fletcher is in so much trouble you wouldn't believe."

"I told him to go," I reply. "I don't mind. Do you mind telling me who the fuck Pilates Paul is?"

"None of your business." She gestures to the door. "Now . . . good night."

"Well, that's not a very nice way to treat your babysitter, is it?"

Her mouth falls open. "You are not my babysitter," she whispers. "You're a pain in my ass."

"Me?" I scoff as I point to my chest. "What did I do?"

"You annoy me," she snaps as she storms into the kitchen.

I carefully move Patrick and then jump up and follow her. "And why do I annoy you?"

"Go back to your carefree dates, Tristan. Stay the hell away from my kids."

Oh . . . this is about me dating other women.

She opens the refrigerator with force and then pulls out the nearly empty wine bottle and holds it up. Her eyes flicker with rage.

"It was nice . . . actually. Went with the pizza and all that."

She looks at me deadpan. "You drank my wine?"

"Don't change the subject. Why does me dating other women annoy you?"

"It doesn't," she snaps angrily. "I don't have time for your shit tonight. Go home."

I put my hands onto my hips. "I can't drive. I've been drinking."

"My wine," she growls.

I cross my arms and look her up and down with a smile. "You're in a very bad mood. Am I right in assuming Paul from Pilates is responsible?"

"No, you're not, actually. Tristan Miles is responsible." She storms out of the room.

My mouth falls open. Of all the nerve. I rush in behind her. She goes to Patrick on the couch. She bends to pick him up in her arms.

"I'll do it."

"No." She slaps me out of the way. "I don't want you anywhere near my devil children."

"Oh." I roll my eyes as she struggles to pick Patrick up. "This is about what I said about the wizard."

"His name is Harry, and yes, I do take offense to some pompous, spoiled asshole telling me that my children are misbehaved when he knows nothing about what they have been through," she whispers angrily. "Get out of my way," she says as she struggles with Patrick's weight.

I step to the side. "You're especially bitchy tonight."

She brushes past me and walks upstairs, and I follow her.

"What are you doing?" she whispers.

"Following you. What does it look like?"

"I swear to God, Tristan, I'm going to push you down the stairs in a moment. Go home."

"I see where they get it, Claire."

She turns back to me. "Get what?"

"This violent streak you have is very unbecoming."

She stops where she is and walks back down a step toward me, and I shrink back from her. "Tristan."

"Yes, Claire."

"Shut your mouth."

"Or what?"

"Or I'm going to shut it for you."

"Violent," I mouth as I follow her upstairs and watch from the doorway as she lays Patrick down in bed and takes his shoes off. She brushes his hair back from his forehead and kisses him good night. She then turns the light off, and we walk back out into the hallway.

"Where's your bedroom?" I ask.

"A place that you'll never get to. Go downstairs."

I roll my eyes. "I don't want to go there anyway, Claire."

Her eyes hold mine. "Good."

"Yes, good," I blurt back. "We're over, remember?"

"Exactly, so why bother coming here?"

We stare at each other, and that feeling comes over me, the one where I want to push her up against the wall and kiss her senseless.

Her eyes drop to my lips, and I know she can feel it too.

"Well, where am I going to sleep?" I ask. "I can't drive."

"Call your limo driver."

"He's off tonight."

"Why not call an Uber?"

"They ran out of cars."

She narrows her eyes. "I know what you're doing."

"What's that?"

"Don't play dumb with me, Tristan." She brushes past me and rushes back down the stairs as I stay hot on her heels.

"So where will I sleep?" I ask.

With you?

"I suppose you can have Woofy's bed, and he can sleep with me."

My face falls in horror. "You would rather sleep with the dog than with me?"

"I would, actually."

"What happened to the fun, hot Claire who fucks me senseless?"

Her eyes meet mine, and the look on her face is murderous. "She woke up to herself," she whispers. "When she realized what a fucktard you are."

My mouth drops open as I feign shock.

She walks forward toward me, and I walk backward. "You barge into my home, uninvited, and then drink my fucking wine. Not to mention—" She cuts herself off.

I shrug as I nearly trip over the couch behind me. "Well . . . apart from those things."

"Go home, Tristan."

"Is this about me going out with that other woman?"

"I don't care who you date."

"Is that a lie, Claire? Because you seem to care."

"Go home," she snaps.

"I can't. I'm over the limit."

"Fine, you're on the couch."

"Can we talk about this?" I reply.

"No." She goes to a cupboard and retrieves a blanket and pillow and throws them at me with force.

I catch them midair. "You're not very hospitable, Claire," I huff. "You really should work on this."

She rolls her eyes and goes to the stairs. "I hope Muff pees on your head." She stomps up the stairs.

My face falls as I process her words. "What?" I look around and catch sight of the mangy cat sitting on the couch. We lock eyes. "Is that a possibility?" I call.

Silence.

"Claire?"

Silence.

"I'm allergic to cats, Claire. I need to sleep with you," I call. "In your bed."

Her bedroom door slams.

I scratch my head as I stare at the cat. He stares back. I point at him. "You come near me while I sleep, Muff Cat, I'm putting you outside," I whisper. "You'll be bear food."

I spread my blankets out on the couch and put the pillow down. Damn this. I want to go home, but I want to speak to Claire in the morning more. I climb in and wriggle around as I try to get comfortable.

Fuck, this couch is made of concrete.

Two hours later

Tick, tick, tick, tick, tick, tick.

"What the hell?" I whisper as I glare at the clock on the wall. What kind of sick fuck has a clock that ticks this loud? No wonder everyone's crazy around here.

Tick, tick, tick, tick, tick, tick.

I can't take it anymore . . . I'm at a breaking point.

"That's it." I throw the blankets off and sit up in a rush. I stand on the couch and take the clock off the wall. "You're going in the trash, motherfucker." I storm out to the kitchen, clock under my arm, and look around in the dark. "I can't see shit." I flick on the light and walk over to the back door and open it in a rush.

It's pitch black and eerily quiet. I peer out. "Where's the trash can?"

Hmm.

I hear a noise and then a bang, and I frown as I look out into the backyard. "Who's there?"

Silence.

Shit . . . this is fucking creepy. I close the door and go back into the house. I'm not risking my life for a ticking time bomb—no chance.

Tick, tick, tick, tick, tick.

Although . . .

"Shut up, shut up," I whisper as I shake it. I stare down at the stupid clock as it taunts me. I imagine myself throwing it hard against the wall and it smashing into a thousand pieces.

Tick, tick, tick, tick.

That's it. I can't take it anymore. I look around the kitchen for somewhere quiet, somewhere that will shut this thing up, and I see the perfect plan.

Diabolical.

I open the freezer and stuff the clock in there and slam the door. I smile as I dust my hands together. "That's taken care of you."

I walk out into the living room and stand at the bottom of the stairs. I wonder what she would do if I just sneaked up there for a little bit of spooning. I smile as I imagine myself slipping into her bed.

I'm missing her.

I come back to earth with a thud, and I roll my eyes. I know that's not going to happen.

I lie back down on the couch and nestle in as I try to get comfortable.

One hour later

"Meow."

I scrunch my eyes shut . . . no, make it stop.

Purr . . . purr . . . purr. "Meow." I try to block it out. "Meow."

Oh hell, a night in this godforsaken place is worse than being on *Survivor*.

"Meeeooowww."

"What?" I whisper angrily as I sit up in a rush. "What the fuck do you want, Muff Cat?"

Purr, purr, purr. The cat jumps on top of me, and I wince. It crawls onto my lap and sits there.

"What?" I snap.

The cat looks up at me.

"There aren't a thousand other places to sit in this house? You have to fucking sit on me?"

"Meow."

"Shut the fuck up." I push it off me and lie back down and turn my back to it.

"Meow."

I close my eyes tight, and I feel something hitting my face. I open my eyes to see the cat tapping me with its paw. "Are you serious?" I whisper. "Fuck off, Muff Cat."

"Meow."

Oh hell, the wizard is probably sleeping pretty at camp. My eyes snap open as I have a realization.

His bed is empty.

Yes, I'll sneak up there and sleep in his bed. Great idea. I gather my blankets and pillows and make my way upstairs and creep down the hall with the flashlight on my phone.

Must be this room, the only one with the door open.

I shine my torch in, and an empty single bed comes into view. Perfect.

I close the door and climb into bed. It's comfortable and warm. I find myself instantly relaxing and slowly drifting off to sleep.

I hear a scratch at the door. "Meow."

I put my pillow over my head. "Shut. Up."

This is unbearable.

I roll over and inhale deeply. Finally I'm relaxed.

Sleep is a wonderful thing. It's morning, but I don't care. I'm too exhausted.

I think I got two hours at the most.

I snuggle back in, and I get a strange feeling that someone's watching me.

I open one eye. The wizard is standing over me; the look on his face is murderous.

"What the hell are you doing in my bed?" he growls.

Chapter 14

I sit up with a start and flinch. "What are you doing here?" I snap.

"This is my room," he barks.

I lie back down and pull the blankets over myself. "Well, I'm sleeping here. Get out."

"Why, you—"

I sit up like the devil himself. "Listen, kid," I whisper through gritted teeth. "I've had a really bad fucking night, and if I get up now, I'm probably chucking you out the window."

"Are you going to make me cry?" he whispers in a baby voice. "Mommy doesn't like big scary men picking on me."

I narrow my eyes. Why, you conniving little shit. "You cry to your mother, and see what happens to you," I whisper angrily. "Don't push me, kid."

"Don't push *me*," he growls.

"Get out," I whisper.

"This is my room. You get out."

I glare at him. "I'm not moving." Our eyes are locked, and then, as if having an epiphany, he smiles darkly, turns, and storms out.

I lie back down and stare at the ceiling for a moment . . . what was that evil smile for? What is he up to?

Claire.

I sit up in a rush and nearly run down the hall to her room. The door is shut, and I put my ear to it and listen.

Is he in there?

I swear, if he tells on me . . . he's dead meat.

I can't hear anything. I look left, and I look right. Nobody's around. I slowly open the door, and I find Claire fast asleep. I slip in and close the door behind me and flick the lock.

I creep toward the bed. Claire is sleeping on her back, her hands above her head. I find myself smiling as I watch her. She's like an angel.

She's so beautiful.

I look around the room. Her presence is so strong in here. God . . . I just want to take her in my arms and kiss her.

But I can't . . . can I?

I raise an eyebrow as I watch her.

Maybe?

I slink into her bed and lie on my side, facing her. I watch how her lips part as she inhales. Her dark hair is messed up, and her eyelashes flutter. My eyes drop lower, down over her neck, her perfect décolletage . . . down lower to her floral nightdress and the tiny patch of white skin that disappears beneath it.

I've never known a woman as beautiful as she is.

She's perfect—everything about her is perfect.

Her eyes flutter open, and she frowns at me, as if trying to focus.

"Hey," I whisper. I pick up her hand, and I kiss her fingertips. She watches me in some kind of dazed state. "How did you sleep?"

"Tris." She frowns.

I smile. She's back; my soft girl is back. "Yes, baby, I'm here." I lean closer to her.

I hear a bang, bang, bang on the door. "What are you doing in there?" the wizard screams through the door.

She jerks back from me and seemingly comes to her senses. "Oh my God." She looks around with wide eyes. "What are you doing?" she stammers.

"What am I doing?" I snap. "Shouldn't you be asking what the fuck *he* is doing?"

Bang, bang, bang sounds on the door as he pounds it with his fist.

"Tristan," she whispers.

"I nearly died last night, Claire, between the cement couch, the clock, the cat, and now the fucking crazy nut outside."

She jumps out of bed.

"But it was all worth it . . . just to see you wake up," I say.

She stops. Her eyes meet mine, and I smile softly.

"Tristan," she whispers. "What are you doing here?"

I shake my head, lost for words because I don't even know. "We need to talk."

"I'm going to rip you apart with my bare hands," the wizard yells.

Oh my God . . . this kid is cramping my style.

"You have to go," she whispers. "This is not the time, Tris."

Bang, bang, bang echoes through the solid door.

For fuck's sake.

"That's it." I get up and storm to the door and open it in a rush. He falls in because he was leaning on it. "What are you doing, you psychopath?" I bark.

"Tristan," Claire warns me.

"What are you doing in here?" Harry yells.

"Getting my keys." I look around. "Nope, can't find them. Not in here." I march out and down the stairs, away from Claire.

That kid is a fucking cockblock.

223

I go down and snatch the overnight bag I'd brought in from my car and walk toward the bathroom.

The wizard steps in my way. "I'm warning you," he sneers, "stay away from my mother."

I glare at the self-righteous little shit in front of me. "I've got two words for you." I hold up two fingers.

"What are they?"

I lean in real close. "Boarding. School."

He narrows his eyes. "You're going down, pretty boy."

I grit my teeth. "Bring it." I storm into the bathroom. I have no idea how to handle this little shit. I'm going to have to try to talk to Claire when I can get her on her own. There's no point staying here with him carrying on like this. If I lose my shit with him, that's it—I can kiss her goodbye for good.

Although, kissing Claire and her house of horrors goodbye would be the much smarter option right now. What the fuck am I even doing here?

I clench my hands together as I imagine myself wringing the little fucker's neck. Finally I throw on some clothes and walk back out to find Claire in her dressing gown. She has the kettle boiling and is standing in the kitchen.

Calmness sweeps over me, and I smile. "What are you doing today?" I ask her.

"Mom stuff," the wizard snaps from behind me.

"That's enough, Harrison," Claire snaps back.

Fuck this.

"I'm going to get going." I sigh. This pit bull of a kid is chasing me out.

"Okay." She forces a smile.

"Are you sure you can't escape for a lunch date?" I whisper.

"We're very busy today, Mom," Harry interrupts.

I clench my jaw. I wasn't joking—boarding school could be in this kid's very near future.

She smirks. "Does it look like I can do lunch today, Tris?"

I stare at her deadpan. "Fine . . . I'll see you later?"

"Okay." I slowly walk to the door, and she follows me.

I turn toward her, and we stare at each other for a moment. So much I would like to say . . . to do.

Harry steps between us, forcing me back from her. "Do you mind?" I ask.

"Not at all," he snaps.

I glare at him. "If you want to do something useful, keep Paul from Pilates off the property and away from your mother. He's no good, that guy."

Claire tries to hide her smile and fails abysmally. "Goodbye, Tristan."

Harry's eyes widen in horror. "Who's Paul from Pilates?" he says as he looks between us.

I smile at Claire and give her a wink.

She narrows her eyes in return. "Nobody that you need to worry about," she says. "Tristan is delusional."

"Goodbye," I say, feeling pleased with myself.

"Oh, Tristan," Harry calls, and I turn back toward them. "Tick. Tock." He smiles darkly, as if he has a secret.

I narrow my eyes . . . what the fuck does that mean? I shake it off. "Goodbye, Claire. Goodbye, Wizard."

I walk out to my car, and I hear a little voice call, "Tristan?" I turn and see Patrick running out after me. He's all messed up and just woken up. His hair is standing on end.

"Hey, buddy." I smile.

His face falls. "Where are you going?" he asks.

"I have to go home."

225

He catches his lip with his teeth, as if worried. "Well, are you coming back?"

"Of course I am."

"When?"

"Um." I glance up and see Claire standing at the door, watching us. "Soon." I ruffle his hair and smile. "Thanks for hanging out with me last night. Next time I get to pick the movie."

He swings his arms happily. "Okay." He turns toward his mother and smiles proudly.

With one last wave, I get into my car and drive away.

Half an hour out on the highway, and my car begins to shudder. I turn the radio down to listen to the engine. I accelerate, and it shudders again.

What's going on?

I slow down and continue to drive, but the car seems to have no power.

What in the world?

It begins to shudder violently, and it limps along for a while. I eventually pull the car over and turn it off.

I sit for a moment and then turn it back on. It won't click over.

The engine ticks as it tries to start, but it just won't. "Oh, come on. You've got to be kidding me."

This car is fucking new.

I try to start it again and again.

Screw this. I get out and slam the door shut.

I take out my phone and google *tow trucks*.

This is the last thing I need.

Claire

I type the email.

> Mr. Scott,
> It was lovely meeting you

I'm interrupted by my phone ringing. The name Paul lights up the screen.

Oh no. I exhale heavily. I don't even want to speak to him. Our date on Friday was the longest night of my life.

It's Monday, and I know he's calling to see if I'm going to Pilates tonight. Damn it.

Now it's just going to be awkward. What a stupid move to date someone from my favorite Pilates class.

My mind goes to Tristan. I can't believe that he was waiting for me to come home from my date. I smile at the thought of him at home alone with my kids.

Oh well . . . at least he survived, I guess.

I ignore the call and go back to my email. Then . . . knock, knock.

"Come in," I call as my eyes stay glued to my computer. The door opens and closes.

"Anderson," I hear the deep, flirty voice purr.

I look up to see Tristan Miles in all his glory. Perfectly fitting dark-navy suit, a crisp white shirt, and a navy tie. His hands are in his pockets, and he looks very much like the Miles Media heir that he is. His dark hair is messed to just-fucked perfection.

"Tristan."

Our eyes meet, and my stomach flutters. He's so damn gorgeous that I can't stand it. "Hello." He smiles.

"Hi." I turn back to my computer, unsure what to say. "What are you doing here?"

"I came to take you out for lunch."

I keep typing.

"Claire," he asserts. "Look at me, please."

I drag my eyes to meet his. The funny, flirty expression I'm used to has been replaced by one of new determination.

"Why would you want to take me out to lunch?" I ask.

He walks around to stand in front of me. He takes my hand and pulls me up out of my chair and into his arms. "Because I can't fight this anymore. I can't pretend that I don't want you. Because I do."

His body is hard and strong against mine, and as I stare up at him, I lose my ability to speak. He leans down and kisses me softly. His lips hover over mine.

"Tris," I whisper.

"I'm sick of playing these stupid fucking games."

"Such as?"

"Stop acting dumb, Anderson; it doesn't suit you at all." He tucks a piece of my hair behind my ear. "I don't want you to go out with that Pilates fuckwit again."

"Why?"

"Because I want you all to myself."

"And yet you expect me to share?"

"No. I won't see anyone else either."

I stare at him for a moment as I try to keep up with the conversation. "Speak English, Tristan. What are you proposing?"

"Casual monogamy."

"Casual monogamy?" I smirk. "Is that a thing?"

He pulls me close and bumps me with his hips. "We'll make it a thing."

"And may I ask how?"

"Well . . . I'll only see you, and you'll only see me."

"I don't know if I can do that." I smile against his lips as he moves closer and kisses me.

"Too bad." Our lips crash together as he holds my face in his hands. "I don't have a choice in the matter, so we need to do this."

"Why don't you have a choice?" I ask.

"Because I only want you."

I pull into the loading zone and give Fletcher a wave. He smiles as he sees me and runs over and jumps in. He's carrying a suit bag and is rustling around and not closing the car door. "Hi," I say as I put my indicator on. "Quick, I'm not allowed to pull in here."

He slams the door, and I pull back out into the traffic. "Hi," he replies.

"Hi." I smile over at him and rub his leg. "Look at you, my big working boy." I glance into the back seat. "What's in the bag?"

"Oh." He smiles proudly. "Tristan bought me a present."

My eyes flick over to him in surprise. "What?"

"He said I've been working really hard, so he wanted to reward me."

"Are you serious?"

He nods with a proud smirk.

"Fletch, I'm so proud of you for trying so hard." My eyes swing to the back seat. "What is it?"

"A new suit."

I frown over at him. "How much did that cost?"

"Like three thousand dollars."

"What?" I scoff.

"Mom, I tried to tell him it was too much, and he told me I can't wear cheap suits if I want to be taken seriously."

229

I frown as I watch the road, and my heart drops. Wade would have loved to have bought Fletch his first nice suit. Annoyance fills me. I know I should be grateful, but I feel like Tristan has stepped over the line. This was something that I wanted to do.

I'm his mother . . . it should have been me.

"Him and Sammia took me. Sammia told me to let him buy it because he has the money, and it's true—I have been working very hard."

"Wow." I widen my eyes as I act enthusiastic. "Remind me, who is Sammia?"

"She's Jameson's PA. Her and Tristan are good friends."

"Oh." I remember her. She's gorgeous.

"Yeah, I thought they were going out for a while."

My eyes flick over to him. "Why did you think that?"

"Oh, they go to lunch together a lot. I just assumed."

I grip the steering wheel as an unexpected burst of jealousy runs through me. I glance back over at him. "So . . . are they going out?"

"No. I met Sammia's fiancé this week. Turns out they really are just friends."

"Oh." Relief fills me, and I frown as I assess my emotions. Hmm . . . I really shouldn't care what he does.

Turns out that maybe I do. "Do you like Tristan?" I ask him.

"Yeah, he's kind of growing on me."

"Why is that?"

"Well, he's not the bastard he pretends to be. Put it that way."

My eyes dart between him and the road. "Why do you say that?"

"I don't know," he says casually as he stares out the window at the people rushing by on the sidewalk. "He's not who I thought he was."

"How come?"

230

"I don't think he's a bad guy in a good suit like I first thought. I think he's actually a good guy in a good suit." He takes out his phone and starts to scroll. "He's actually pretty funny."

I bite my lip to hold my tongue. I want to ask him a million questions about Tristan Miles, but I know I can't be obvious, and besides, he and I are effectively just friends, so it doesn't matter anyway.

My mind goes over what he said to me in my office earlier today.

"So . . . sleeping with only you . . . isn't a problem for me." His lips touched mine. *"However, not sleeping with you is a torture I won't tolerate."*

I smirk to myself as I drive. I like the fact that he doesn't want anyone else, and I know that this is probably a disaster waiting to happen, but I'm going with the oblivious approach.

I'm just not going to think about it.

What will I wear tomorrow? Nerves flutter in my stomach at the thought of having him to myself for an hour.

For the first time since Paris, I find myself being a little excited.

Marley walks into my office. "What do you want to have for lunch?"

"Oh, um." I pause. Shit. "I have an appointment today on my lunch break. Sorry." I spin toward her in my chair. It doesn't feel right lying to my best friend, but this really needs to stay between Tristan and me. "What are you going to get?"

"Hmm . . . not sure, really. I'm feeling like sushi, but then"— she grimaces—"I can't be bothered to walk to the good place."

"Yeah, I know. It's a trek." I think for a moment. "What about Denver's?"

She screws up her face, as if I'm stupid. "Don't you remember last time we went there?"

231

"No, what happened?"

"Death by risotto." She widens her eyes. "We nearly died that day, Claire."

I giggle. "Oh, that's right. How could I ever forget that?" We had risotto, and it upset our stomachs so bad that we were lying on my office floor groaning for an hour.

"What appointment do you have?"

"Oh." I try to think on my feet. "Doctor. Just an annual checkup." My phone beeps with a text, and I see the name Tristan light up the screen. I turn it over so that she can't see his name.

"Cool," she says as she walks toward the door.

"What are you going to have?" I call. "Death by risotto or good sushi?"

She shrugs. "Hmm, probably mediocre sushi from around the corner. Save my feet."

"Mediocre sushi is better than no sushi at all," I reply.

"This is true." She disappears out the door, and I read my text.

Anderson,
Your lunch date is at
Dream Downtown at 1pm.
Tris.
xo

I smile and glance at my clock. Hmm, that's a weird place to have lunch. Must be so that nobody sees us. One hour until I get to see him.

I walk into the foyer of the Dream Downtown hotel right at one o'clock.

"Hello." I hear his deep voice behind me.

I spin toward him, and my heart catches in my throat. He's wearing a gray suit and a cream shirt with a navy tie. His dark curled hair is unruly, and he looks completely edible. "Hi." I smile.

His hungry eyes drop down my body. "I've already ordered lunch for us."

"You have?"

He glances toward the reception desk, as if guilty of a sinister crime. "Yes, it's in the private dining room."

"Oh." I frown.

"This way, please." He turns and walks off toward the elevator, and I follow him. We get in. He pushes the number seven, the doors close, and we begin to go up.

"Where is this . . . private dining room?" I ask.

"I can't tell you," he says dryly. "It's private."

"So it's a super-private dining room?"

"Precisely." He continues to look straight ahead.

"How did you know how to find it if it's so private?" I ask as I play along.

"My uncle's sister's husband's brother's mother-in-law told me about it," he replies without hesitation.

"Oh, I see." I smile and put my head down. This man kills me. The doors open, and he strides down the hallway on a mission and presents a key from his pocket at one of the doors. "This isn't a private dining room; this is a hotel room."

He winks darkly. "Semantics."

"How so?"

He turns the key and opens the door. "You will be eating, and . . . it's private." He stands back to let me in. The room is quaint with a king-size bed and a lovely bathroom.

The curtains are drawn, and it's dark, lit only by the lamps. A platter of food covered with a silver lid and a bottle of champagne are on the table. I turn toward him. "You've already been up here?"

"Well, I had to organize your lunch." He rolls his eyes, as if I'm stupid. "This is a dining room."

I look around the room. "And you drew the curtains for me?"

"Yes." He steps toward me. "Didn't want to scare you with my member. Thought I would ease you back into the saddle."

I burst out laughing. "Your member?" His lips dust mine, his tongue slowly sliding through my lips as he takes my face in his hands.

Oh man . . . the way he kisses.

I open my eyes to see his are closed. He's totally in the moment with me. "Do you know how fucking horny I am, Anderson?" he whispers against my mouth.

I smile. "Probably as horny as me."

"No. I win. I've jerked off three times today in preparation for this. You'll be lucky if I have anything left for you."

I burst out laughing. "Oh, I missed your sense of humor."

We fall serious for a moment as our eyes search each other's. I missed more than his sense of humor, but I'll never admit it. "I need you naked," he whispers. His concentration drops to my blouse, and he begins to slowly unbutton it.

My heart is beating so fast as I stand before him. How is this happening? We've been in the room together for all of two minutes.

This is lust . . . pure, unadulterated lust.

"What were you thinking about when you jerked off?" I whisper.

His eyes hold mine. "You."

My heart constricts in my chest as my eyes search his again. I know this is casual and probably sleazy sex. But damn it, it feels like more. It feels like a lifetime since I've been in his arms. He undoes my last button and slides my blouse over my shoulder and carefully places it over the back of the couch. His lips go to my neck as he slowly unzips my zipper and slides my skirt down.

He nips my neck with his teeth and then takes my skirt fully off and carefully places it on the chair. "We don't want any creases in your clothes when you go back to work."

I frown. How many times before has he had this kind of lunch date?

He knows the drill . . . I push the thought to the back of my mind.

Don't go there.

He steps back from me; his eyes drop down my body, and I close my eyes to block him out. My nerves are at an all-time high. I know I am nothing like the women he's used to. "You know . . . ," he whispers.

I stare at a spot on the carpet—anything to take myself away from the intensity of his gaze on my body.

He drags my face to his. "I had forgotten how beautiful you are, Anderson."

If I could answer him with something witty, I would. But I can't. I'm overwrought with the feelings he brings out in me.

He bends and kisses my clavicle and then one by one takes my nipples into his mouth through my bra.

I hold my breath to try to stop it from quivering, to try to at least act a little cool.

He drops lower to my stomach. He trails kisses lower and lower and then drops to his knees in front of me. He nibbles my sex through my panties, and I close my eyes as I nearly combust.

Oh, dear God . . .

He pulls my panties to the side and kisses me softly there . . . oh fucking hell.

I feel his exhale on my skin, and I hold my breath as I wait for a reaction.

He inhales sharply and then, as if unable to help it, licks me deep with his thick tongue. He moans in appreciation, and it sends a rumble through my sex. My legs nearly cave in under me. I glance up and catch sight of us in the mirror.

Me in my black lace underwear. Him in a full suit and tie, on his knees in front of me.

I look down at him, and his eyes are closed in pleasure, as if he might die if he doesn't get to taste me. Impatient with licking around my panties, he slides them down, throws them to the side, and then walks me backward over to the bed.

He slowly takes my bra off and then lays me down and spreads my legs wide.

His eyes roam over my flesh. I'm completely at his mercy.

Here for his pleasure.

We stare at each other as the energy swirls between us like wildfire.

When Tristan Miles has me naked . . . nothing else matters.

All I care about is pleasing him.

He bends and takes my thighs in his hands and holds me wide as his tongue begins to swirl deep in my sex.

My back arches off the bed, and I writhe beneath him. My hands twist in his wavy hair, and I drag his face up so I can look at him. His lips glisten with my arousal, and his eyes are a beautiful shade of "come fuck me."

"Get up here," I whisper.

He licks me again, his eyes closing once more, and it becomes very clear that he isn't in control of his actions anymore. He's working on instinct now, sheer male instinct. His body has taken over; it doesn't matter what I ask for. He needs to do it his way . . . at least this time, anyway.

He keeps eating me, deeper and deeper as he loses all control. His face thrashes from side to side, and his whiskers burn my sensitive skin.

Fucking hell . . . so good.

My back begins to arch in pleasure; my face contorts as I try to hold it. "Tris," I whimper as I pull his hair between my fingers. "Up here. Come up here." I want to kiss him.

I desperately want to kiss him.

He grazes his teeth against my clitoris, and I cry out as I burst into orgasm. I shudder hard as he softly licks me through it. For five minutes he continues as I stare at the ceiling and shudder and see stars.

I think that's the hardest I've ever come. God damn, he's so fucking good at this.

I come to my senses and realize that he's still completely dressed in his suit.

I sit up with a renewed determination and crawl onto my knees. "Stand up," I breathe.

His eyes flicker with fire, and he stands up as I unzip his trousers. His cock is rock hard and sitting above the waist of his briefs. Preejaculate is beading on the end. I should undress him. I should take my time.

What I want is to suck him . . . hard. I want to make him blow, fully dressed in his expensive suit.

I kiss his dick, and he runs his hand tenderly through my hair as he looks on.

What is it about the two of us together?

We don't even need to speak; it's like we have a secret language. I can tell what he's thinking, just by his touch. I begin to lick him with a flat tongue. Our eyes are locked.

He loves this.

He pulls my hair back into a ponytail on top of my head as he watches, and I smile around him. He wants in my mouth—that's why he's pulling my hair back from my face.

I lick everywhere, but I won't put him completely in my mouth, and he begins to move my head by the grip he has on my hair to try to get in.

I lick up the length of his shaft, and then I whisper, "Fuck my mouth, Mr. Miles."

He inhales deeply and pushes his cock down my throat. His preejaculate is salty, and the grip he has on my hair near painful. He slides out and then pumps back in as his eyes roll back in his head. "Fuck," he moans.

"Harder," I whisper around him.

He pushes in deep again, and this time I flick my tongue. His cock jerks, and he staggers forward.

He's close already.

We find a rhythm. His hands grip my hair, and as I kneel naked on the bed, he fucks my mouth. Long and deep, the moans coming out of him are the hottest sounds I've ever heard.

His grip becomes painful as he slams into my mouth, and he tips his head back. With a deep moan, he comes in a rush. The hot semen fills my mouth, and I drink it down like a pro.

He struggles for air and tips his head back to the ceiling, and I lick him up as I continue to empty his beautiful body.

Then I stand and take his jacket off, and I undo his tie and slowly unbutton his shirt.

He looks on in a strange detached state, his face full of awe.

I slide his shirt over his shoulders and am blessed with a view of his thick, muscular chest with its scattering of dark hair. "Tristan," I whisper as I kiss his chest. "I've missed your beautiful body." I kiss lower and take him into my mouth again, and he pulls me up.

He kisses me, and it's tender and meaningful and everything that a hotel hookup is not. "Fuck me," he whispers. "You need to fuck me, Anderson."

I pull his pants down in one quick movement. He disappears and grabs a handful of condoms with urgency. He throws them on the side table and rolls one on. He pushes me backward, and I fall onto the mattress with a giggle as he climbs over me.

In one hard pump he slides in deep. Our mouths fall open as we stare at each other.

Our hearts racing hard in our chests.

He pulls out and slides back in deep, and my body ripples around his as it tries to deal with his size.

Not all men are created equal. Tristan Miles is bona fide proof of that.

Sex with him . . . is otherworldly.

"I've been looking forward to wrecking your vagina all day, Anderson," he whispers. I burst out laughing, and he slams in hard. "Get your fucking legs up."

The water runs over my back, and I smile as my head leans against his broad chest.

"You know, when I teased you about drinking granny tea, I had no idea how granny you could actually get," he mutters dryly.

I giggle. "You are a lucky boy." I'm wearing a shower cap so that I don't go back to work with wet hair. "You know, this is a very expensive lunch for you every day. How much does this hotel cost, anyway?"

He smiles down at me as he readjusts my granny shower cap. "Worth every penny."

It's Friday, and contrary to the two lunch dates a week we agreed on, we have spent three lunch breaks together here this week. I've lied to everyone in my office about where I have been.

I'm a bad boss doing bad things with a bad man.

We can't get enough of each other.

"I've got to go, baby," I whisper.

"Hmm." He holds me tightly in his arms. "Don't leave me," he teases.

I smile as I kiss him. "I have to." I drag myself from his arms and dry myself as he stays in the shower. "Are you not going back to work?" I ask as I dress.

He begins to wash his hair. "No. How did you know?"

"You have an overnight bag with you today."

"Oh, I'm going to the gym."

"Okay." I frown as I remember something. "Did you get your car back?"

"Hopefully I can pick it up this afternoon. If not, I have another lined up for the weekend."

"Okay."

"Can we do Monday lunch?" he asks as he rinses the shampoo from his hair. "Wednesday is too far away," he adds.

I stare at him for a moment, and he's right: Wednesday *is* too far away. "Yes, perhaps. I'll call you."

What's happening here?

I dismiss my questions and lean in and kiss him. "Goodbye."

"Can you pass me my conditioner out of my bag before you go, please?" he asks.

I go out and retrieve his conditioner from his bag and notice his phone is lighting up. I hand the conditioner over. "Your phone has been ringing." I put it on the bathroom counter.

"Bye, Tris."

"Bye, babe." He gives me a sexy wink, and I smirk as my eyes drop down his naked body.

Hmm, I've died and gone to lunch-break heaven.

I listen to the door bang, and I smile as a warmth floods through me.

Claire Anderson makes me happy.

Stupidly fucking happy.

To the point where I'm nearly driving myself insane with my goofy grin.

I put the conditioner in my hair and screw up my face. Oh God. That shit stinks. I don't remember it smelling like that before. I lean out of the shower and throw the small bottle into the trash can, and I see my phone dancing on the counter. The name Mechanic lights up the screen. Yes . . . my car. "Hello," I answer, trying not to drip on the phone.

"Oh, hello, is that Tristan?"

"Yes. Speaking."

"Hello, it's Steven from Aston Martin calling."

"Is my car ready to pick up?"

"No, unfortunately not. We've only just been able to discover what's wrong with it. It's had us baffled all week."

"Oh." I sigh. "Okay, what is it?"

"Um." He pauses. "I don't know how to put this."

I frown.

"Someone has put sugar in the gas tank."

"What?"

"Someone who had access to your key has put a shit ton of sugar in your tank. It seized the motor."

I screw up my face. "Are you kidding me? Who would . . ." My voice trails off.

The wizard.

"Okay," I snap. "That's fine. Just fix it, and let me know when it's ready."

"Sorry, sir."

Anger boils my blood, and I run my fingers through my hair. My scalp burns.

Oww. I pull my hand down and see it's full of hair. My eyes widen.

What the fuck?

I grab my hair, and it comes out in chunks. "I've got to go," I stammer.

"Okay, sir, so—"

I hang up on him and run to get back under the shower. My scalp is burning to fuck, and my hair feels like jelly as I try to rinse it out.

I think back to the words Harry said to me when I last saw him. *"Tick. Tock."* My eyes widen in horror. That evil wizard has put hair-removal cream in my conditioner . . . and fucked up my car.

I wash my hair like a madman. I'm going to be bald. My anger erupts like never before.

"Tick. Fucking. Tock. Prepare to die, motherfucker."

Chapter 15

For half an hour, I stand under the water. I get out briefly and google *How to stop hair-removal cream from working?*

Water and shampoo remove hair-removal cream.

I go to use my shampoo, and then I eye the bottle suspiciously. Fuck that. I reach out and throw that bottle into the trash as well. Who knows what that shit of a kid has done to anything? I use the hotel's cheap and nasty shampoo.

I rinse my hair for another twenty minutes, and then I get out and look in the mirror. My hair feels like fairy floss—some places worse than others . . . but all in all, it's fucked.

I dial Jameson's number.

"Hey," he answers.

"Meet me out front of the building in ten minutes."

"I can't."

"Jameson," I whisper through gritted teeth. "Meet me, or else prepare to bail me out of prison tonight for killing a minor."

"What?"

"That kid." I pinch the bridge of my nose, unable to believe it. "He put sugar in the gas tank of my Aston Martin."

"What?"

"Oh, it gets better. He also put hair-removal cream in my fucking conditioner bottle."

"He did not."

"Jameson," I whisper angrily. "My hair looks like singed pubes, so you either take me to a fucking bar, or that's it . . . I'm going crazy." My eyes nearly bulge out of their sockets. "And I won't be held responsible for my actions," I snap.

He bursts out laughing. "Are you fucking serious right now?"

"Deadly."

"Jesus Christ, Tris. Who is this fucking kid?"

"Someone on my hit list. See you in ten." I hang up and look in the mirror at my fuzzy hair. I try to part it and push it to the side, but it's all fuzzy and sticking up on end.

I make a fist at the mirror. "When I get ahold of you, kid . . ." I storm out and grab my bag. I take out my toiletry bag and throw the entire thing in the trash.

Who knows what that fucker has done?

I sip my beer and glare at my infuriating brother across the bar table.

Every time he looks at me, he bursts out laughing. He's been doing this for half an hour.

I shake my head in disgust. "If I could run my fingers through my hair in dismay, I would. But I can't . . . because it will fucking fall out." I sigh deeply. "This is not going to work for me. My hair is an asset," I splutter. "How will I walk around like this?" I widen my eyes as a vision comes through. "How will I face people in meetings?" I pinch the bridge of my nose. "Hi, I'm here to take over your company. Don't mind me. I got fucked up by a thirteen-year-old."

Jameson puts his head into his hands and laughs hard. His shoulders and back are racked with giggles.

I sip my beer, unimpressed. "Go ahead; laugh all you want," I mutter dryly. "This is fucking hilarious."

"It actually is," he says with a laugh. "I would say hysterical."

I glare at him, and when he finally stops laughing and comes back to earth, he says, "In all seriousness, what are you going to do?"

"Well, I want to go over there and rip him a new asshole." He laughs again.

"But I won't, because Claire will kick me out."

"And that's a problem?"

"Yes. It's a fucking problem. This woman has me by the balls," I whisper angrily. "You know what I'm doing tonight?"

"What?"

"Unbeknown to Claire, I'm driving an hour to watch movies with her youngest boy . . . who is actually a pretty cool little kid, mind you, but whatever. While I pretend to the other two kids that I am just her friend."

He frowns.

"Then, if I'm lucky, I'll be allowed to sleep on the concrete lounge so that the Muff Cat can piss on my head."

He drops his head and laughs once more.

"Will you stop fucking laughing?" I snap.

"I can't help it." He chuckles. "So this kid is the one who attacked you with the underpants?"

"No, this is the kid who hanged the teddy . . . the serial-killer one."

Jameson puts his hand over his mouth to stifle his laugh once more. "This is fucking hilarious, Tris. I swear to God you're being punked or some shit. I couldn't make this shit up if I tried."

I run my fingers over my lips as I agree with his theory. "It's like an elaborate plan to set me up to fail."

"Well, that's what he's doing. He wants you to stop hanging around. He's effectively pushing you out. Quite smart, if you ask me, and very effective."

I narrow my eyes and punch my fist.

"Anyway, it's easily fixed." He shrugs as he sips his beer. "Leave. Move on. She sounds like more trouble than she's worth."

"Nope, not happening."

He screws up his face. "You really like this girl?"

I shrug. "I do."

"Realistically, though, where is this going to go? I mean, long term you aren't going to be with her. Why put yourself through hell with her kids if you and she aren't suited anyway?"

"Look, I don't know what's going on with us, but I do know that I want to be with her in the right now, and a fucktard little kid isn't winning and keeping her from me."

"What would happen if you go over there accusing him and going out of your mind like you want to?"

"She'll kick me out. Hands down, I come second to the kids. Actually . . . I probably come third after Woofy. No, fourth, after the Muff." I sip my beer. "It's not even a question. I don't even have a fucking rank." I take another sip. "I am rankless in that house."

He smiles into his beer, and we both sit there for a moment in silence as we think.

"You know, we would have pulled this shit when we were kids if Mom tried to date someone else. Can you imagine what we would have collectively done?"

"I guess." I sigh into my beer.

"We'd always conspire to get rid of our governesses. They were dropping like flies for a while there."

"Then there was Maria." I smirk. "She put a stop to that."

Jameson chuckles. "Hottest fucking nanny I ever saw . . . I wonder what ever happened to her?"

I shrug, and we sit in silence for a while as I troll my mind. "Unless . . . ," I murmur as a plan takes shape in my mind.

"Unless what?"

I smile broadly. "Do you know where there's a hardware store in New York? I need a few things."

"Why?"

I stand with renewed determination. "Jameson . . . if you can't beat them, join them."

He pinches the bridge of his nose. "Oh Jesus. Here we go."

I wink.

"Whatever you are thinking, it's a bad idea."

I slap him on the back. "Let's go. We're doing this!"

"I'm not involved."

I smile broadly. "Oh, yes you are."

Claire

I drive down the state highway with a smile on my face. I've had a wonderful week, with lunch dates made in heaven, and the kids' things have been running smoothly.

Well, maybe it's not so much that the kids are running smoothly as it is that I'm not stressed, and things aren't getting to me like they sometimes do.

It's amazing what laughter and orgasms do for the soul. My mind goes to Tristan and the way he makes me laugh. I've never met anyone like him before. He's hard, handsome, and professional on the outside and playful and caring on the inside.

Insanely hot right through.

I get a vision of us meeting throughout the week and how he has ordered my favorite food and drinks for lunch. How he bought me a shower cap so that my hair wouldn't get wet when I showered. How he pulls the drapes before I get there because he wants me to feel comfortable in my skin. He doesn't know that I notice these things, but I do.

How could I not?

He's always making sure that I'm taken care of. There's a gentle, caring side to him that I adore.

I call Harry, putting my phone on speaker in the car. "Hey, Mom," he says.

"Hi, honey. How was your day?"

"Hmm, okay," he says. "Can I go to Justine's party tomorrow night?"

I scrunch up my face. Damn it. Justine is a girl he knows whose parents go away every weekend and leave her home alone with her elder sisters. The only problem is Justine's sisters aren't even home most of the time. "What's the party for?"

"It's her birthday. She's fourteen."

"Are her parents going to be home?"

He hesitates. "Um . . . yes."

I roll my eyes. That means no. "I'll see how you behave."

"Can I, Mom, please?" he begs. "If I behave, can I go to the party?"

I roll my eyes again. "I'm not bargaining with you to behave, Harry. You should want to behave anyway. You're thirteen, not two."

"Well, can I go?"

"I want you to clean up the porch for me. Put all the shoes back in the shoebox, and straighten things up."

"Oh, Mom," he moans. "They aren't even my shoes. I'm not putting everyone else's shoes away. That's not fair."

My anger simmers. "Goodbye, Harry."

"So can I go to the party?"

I narrow my eyes. God, it would be so much easier to barter with this kid, but I know there'll be alcohol at this party, and if he starts drinking and goes off the rails now at this young age, I have absolutely no chance of reining him back in. He's too strong a personality. "Harrison, you want to be treated as an adult, but you act like a baby."

"Mom," he moans. "I'm going," he snaps.

"Clean the porch, and do your jobs, and we will discuss it," I snap back as I lose my patience. "Where's Patrick?"

"I don't know. Goodbye." He hangs up.

I shake my head. That little twerp. He drives me mad.

I call Patrick. I had to give him a phone so that he could contact me whenever he wanted and so that I could call him. "Hi, Mama," he says happily.

"Hi, buddy." I smile. "I'm on my way home."

"Oh, okay."

"Where are you?"

"Nancy and I are at the park."

Nancy, our babysitter, gets the boys off to school for me in the mornings and stays until five thirty in the afternoons. She works a night job, so she has to leave right on time. I'm usually home fifteen minutes after she leaves, so it works out well. "Okay, darling, see you soon."

"Bye, Mama. Love you."

"Love you too. Bye." I hang up and smile. My sweet, placid child. I had to get one out of the three, I suppose.

Although Fletcher has really turned the corner since he started this internship, and I hate to admit it, but I think that Tristan has had a lot to do with it. His tough love approach has worked wonders with Fletch, but of course, it could just be the fact that he's growing up too. Fletcher is a good kid, and his only crime is that he's too protective of me. To the point where if Harry is giving me grief, Fletcher goes ballistic, and I have to break them up from a fistfight.

Harry, on the other hand, is an entirely different kettle of fish. He's naughty wherever he goes and no matter who he's with. His teachers are constantly calling me about his behavior, and last year he even nearly got expelled from school. I've had him at therapy. I've had him at behavioral psychologists. You name it—I've done it.

Diet, exercise programs, no blue lights on screens . . . nothing has worked. It pains me to admit it, but Harry needs his dad. More than the other two, and I'm so out of my depth that I have no idea what to do with him.

At this point, my only goal is to get through each day without an all-out war. If I can get into bed at night, and I haven't had a call from school about him, and we haven't had a run-in, it's been a very good day.

I let him get away with a lot more than I should, simply so that Patrick and Fletcher don't have to put up with his dramatics and my screaming.

It's not fair to them to have to live with it, so I tiptoe around Harry to keep the peace.

It's not right, but at this point, it's all I can do.

"Hello," Fletcher calls as he answers the door. "Mom, Tristan is here."

"What?" I hear Patrick call. He goes running through the house to the door like a maniac. "Tristan!" he cries in excitement.

"Hey, buddy," I hear Tristan's deep voice reply.

What's he doing here?

Nerves dance in my stomach, and I walk out to see Patrick hugging Tristan's leg.

Fletcher rolls his eyes in a "he's so embarrassing" way, and I smile at the beautiful man before me. "Hi."

Tristan's eyes hold mine. "Hello, Claire."

The air buzzes between us.

It's there again, like it is every time we're together—this feeling between us where I want to take him into my arms and kiss him. It doesn't feel natural being platonic.

Tristan Miles was made for touching.

He's wearing jeans and a T-shirt and a navy cap. I love him dressed like this, all casual and hot.

"I came to watch movies with Patrick," he announces.

What?

Patrick's eyes widen in amazement. "You did?" Patrick looks to me. "He came to see me, Mom."

I smile at my baby's over-the-top excitement. "Thank you. That's very nice."

Patrick grabs Tristan by the hand and pulls him to the living room. "What do you want to watch?" He gasps. "Oh, Mom." He turns to me, and it's obvious his little mind is going a million miles per minute. "Do we have popcorn? Can you go and get some for us?" His eyes widen as he remembers something else. "Oh. Tristan, do you want pizza? I know it's your favorite. Mom, can we have pizza, please?"

Tristan messes up Patrick's hair. "I'll have whatever you're having." They fall onto the couch together, and Patrick sits so close he's almost on top of him.

What is he doing here? It's Friday night. Surely he has better things to do than hang out with my kids.

Maybe he wants to be here . . . excitement runs through me.

Stop it. Play it cool. He's probably just being nice . . . *so* nice.

"Give Tristan some room, bubba," I remind him.

Patrick's face falls as he realizes what he's doing, and he moves back. Tristan grabs him and pulls him close again. "It's cool. Stay close, brother."

Patrick smiles goofily up at him, and I bite my lip to hide my smile as my heart swells. Seeing Patrick with Tristan is chicken soup for my soul.

So. Cute.

Harry stomps down the stairs and stops still when he sees our visitor. "What are you doing here?" he snaps.

"Harry," I warn him. Tristan puts his hand up to silence me.

"I'm here to visit Patrick and your mother and Fletch. What are *you* doing here?"

"I live here," Harry gasps, indignant.

"We're watching movies. Go away, Harry," Patrick barks as he flicks through the channels with the remote.

Harry glares at Tristan, and Tristan winks back with a smirk.

"I thought your car broke down," Harry blurts.

"Oh, it's at the police station."

"What for?" I frown.

"It turns out that somebody put sugar in the gas tank, but it's okay. They're getting the fingerprints from the car now that we know what is wrong."

Harry stares at him.

Tristan smiles and casually looks at his watch. "They should be making an arrest tonight sometime."

"Oh, what are they going to do?" Harry scoffs.

"Vandalism is a crime, Harrison. Google the jail time. I'm not making this up."

I frown as I look between them. What's going on here? Have I missed part of the conversation?

Oh dear God, no . . . it wasn't Harry, was it?

Harry scratches his head and looks around nervously. "Mom. I . . . I . . . can I go to Brendan's house?" he stammers. "It's urgent."

"Okay, yes, but only for half an hour."

"Okay." He runs out the back, and the door slams hard behind him.

"Wonder what's wrong with him?" Tristan asks.

"I don't know." I look out the window and see him run into the garage. "He looks like he saw a ghost."

Jesus.

"What do you want to watch, Tricky?" Tristan asks.

Patrick frowns. "Tricky?"

"Well, your name has the word *trick* in it."

"It does?" he gasps.

Tristan frowns. "Yes, it does. You know that."

Patrick's little face falls in disappointment that he doesn't.

"Patrick has dyslexia," I announce.

Tristan's face falls. "You do?"

Patrick twists his little hands together nervously on his lap. "I'm getting better at it." He looks to me. "Aren't I, Mom?"

I smile broadly. "You are, baby. I'm so proud of how hard you're working."

Tristan's eyes hold mine, and I know he wants to ask a million questions but is holding his tongue.

Patrick taps his leg and seemingly brings him back to the moment. "What do you want to watch?"

"Ahh!" We hear Harry scream from outside. I hear something hit the side of the house with force.

"What in the world?" I frown.

Harry comes stomping in like a madman. His face is murderous.

"What's wrong?" I ask.

"This." He holds up his skateboard.

"What about it?"

"The wheels are missing."

All four wheels are missing from his skateboard. Patrick's mouth falls open in horror. "Oh no," he whispers.

"That's terrible," says Tristan casually. "Who on earth would have been in your garage, Wizard?"

"That's what I want to know," he snaps. He storms back out of the room and out into the yard. "When I find out . . ." he calls.

"What are we watching?" Tristan asks Patrick.

"*Jurassic Park*?"

"One or two?" Tristan asks. "I prefer two."

"Okay." Patrick bounces in excitement. "We'll watch two."

"Shall I order pizza?" I ask.

This is turning out to be the best night ever.

"Yes, please." Tristan smiles. His naughty eyes hold mine, and they have that tender glow in them that he gets sometimes . . . I find myself quite giddy.

Could this man be any more gorgeous?

"Would you like a glass of wine?" I ask him.

"I won't be able to drive if I do."

"You can stay on the couch," Patrick splutters hopefully. "Can't he, Mom?"

"Tristan probably has somewhere better to go, bubba," I reply.

Tristan's eyes hold mine. "No. I'm exactly where I want to be. I'll stay, if that's okay."

Hope fills my chest. Okay . . . what the heck is going on here?

"You have got to be kidding me," Harry cries from outside.

I glance to Tristan and see him close his eyes, as if to stop himself from laughing.

Harry bursts through the door. "The wheels of my bike are missing too."

"What?" I frown.

"All the bikes' wheels are missing," he cries. "Someone has broken into our garage and booby-trapped everything!" he yells. "When I find out who it is—"

"You should call the police," Tristan says as he raises an eyebrow at Harry.

"Yes." I frown. "Maybe I should."

"No," Harry stammers. "It's fine. It will be one of my friends playing a trick. I'll find them." He takes off into the backyard again. "Fletcher!" he calls. "Come outside and help me."

Tristan and Patrick return to the television, and I walk into the kitchen to get our wine.

This feels so weird having him here.

Like normal . . .

"Claire, what's the Wi-Fi password?" Tristan calls.

"Hang on. I'll find it." I rattle through the drawer and call it out. "Do you want red or white wine?"

"Whatever you're having," he calls back. "That stuff I had last week was nice."

I smile as I take it out of the fridge. "The stuff you drank without permission?"

"Uh-huh, that one. Went down well."

Harry storms back into the house, the door slams, and he stomps back up the stairs.

I frown. What *is* he doing? "I thought you were going to Brendan's house?" I call.

"I can't get there!" he calls angrily. "Someone took all my wheels. I'm going to go on the PlayStation."

"Okay," I call. Jeez, I wonder who took his damn wheels. Great. More money that I don't need to spend.

I take our wine and walk back into the living room to see Patrick and Tristan sitting together closely and watching their movie. Tristan has kicked his shoes off and has his feet up on the coffee table, and Patrick has done the same. I stand at the door and watch them in awe.

How has this happened? I did not expect my Friday night to turn out like this. He didn't mention anything about coming over tonight. And here he is, hanging with my kids and not running for the hills.

Wonders never cease.

Harry's door bangs open from upstairs, and I roll my eyes. God, this kid is a fucking drama queen. "Why is the internet not working?" he calls.

"I don't know," I snap. He's really beginning to piss me off with all this stomping around.

"Reboot it," Tristan calls.

"I didn't ask you." His bedroom door bangs shut again.

Patrick rolls his eyes at his brother's dramatics.

I take a seat on the other couch and curl my legs up underneath me, but I'm not watching the movie; I'm watching these two together.

They're talking and discussing things like long-lost friends, and I'm amazed at how well they're getting on.

Harry appears again. "The damn internet keeps dropping out," he yells.

"You're a big boy," Tristan says. "Go fix it."

Harry glares at Tristan and takes off again.

Ten minutes later we hear slamming upstairs and Harry yelling in frustration.

"Harrison," I call. "What are you doing up there?"

"This internet," he cries. "It's so crap I can't believe it." He marches down the stairs and checks the modem and walks into the living room. "I've had enough of this," he cries. "It's making me crazy."

Tristan watches him with a smile.

"What . . . is . . . so . . . funny?" Harry sneers.

"Tick. Tock," Tristan replies.

Harry's eyes widen, and Tristan winks at him.

I look between the two of them; their eyes are locked.

Huh?

"What does that mean?" I frown.

"Nothing," Harry snaps through gritted teeth. He marches upstairs and slams the door.

Tristan smiles into his wine and continues to watch the television, as if nothing has happened.

"What was that about?" I ask.

"I have no idea; the wizard has gone mad," he mutters dryly.

It's late. Harry and Patrick are in bed, and Tristan is talking to Fletcher in his room. They've been chatting for a while.

I creep up the hall and peer through the crack of the door. Tristan is lying on Fletcher's bed, throwing a tennis ball up in the air and catching it as they speak.

Fletcher is sitting at his desk, on the computer.

"So where did you go then?" Tristan asks.

"Back to my friend's house for a while."

I frown. What are they talking about? I lean in closer so that I can hear.

"So . . . Fletch." Tristan hesitates, as if choosing his words carefully. "You know how to put on a condom . . . right?"

What the fuck? How dare he ask that. Fletcher is nowhere near having sex.

"No, not really." Fletcher sighs. "What if I fuck it up and do it wrong? Can it come off midway?"

My eyes widen in horror.

What?

"Yeah, it can, and it's your responsibility to know this shit. Condoms are the boy's job. You need to practice before you get there."

I put my hand over my mouth. Oh my God.

My baby . . .

I quickly walk down the stairs. My ears . . . what the hell did I just hear?

I go to the kitchen sink and pour myself a glass of wine and chug it down.

I do it again.

I'm feeling overwhelmed and nervous and happy and terrified.

"Hey," Tristan whispers from behind me. "There you are."

I turn to him. "Thank you."

"For what?"

I swallow the lump in my throat. "For being here. It means a lot."

He leans in and tenderly kisses me. My eyes close at the feeling of his lips against mine.

We stare at each other in the semidarkened kitchen . . . and God, I want him.

I want all of him.

But this is wrong . . . this is Wade's house.

"I have to take a shower," I whisper.

"Okay." He smiles and softly kisses me again. His kiss has just the right amount of suction, and I feel it between my legs. Tristan being here feels special.

Too special.

I push myself off him and step back, and without another word, I rush from the room.

Half an hour later, I stand under the water in my shower. Guilt is coursing through my veins.

It feels real.

And I know it can't be, because he isn't my forever man.

My forever man died.

I screw up my face in tears. Wade.

I'm so sorry.

I haven't thought about my beautiful husband since Tristan came back into my life. My nightly ritual of going through my day in my mind with him and telling him I love him has fallen by the wayside.

I've lain in bed and thought about another man, the same man who's been downstairs with Wade's son.

Paris was about fun and finding myself again.

This time it's different. This time it's a closeness, a sense of belonging, and it feels a lot like love.

What kind of a wife am I if I can have feelings for someone else so easily?

This is Wade's house; these are *his* sons.

Tristan shouldn't be here.

I shake my head in disgust with myself. I'm just confused. He's the first man I've dated . . . fucked . . . what the hell are we even doing? There are no boundaries.

I need boundaries.

I get a vision of Patrick and Tristan sitting close together on the couch, watching movies and chatting, and my heart constricts.

Wade would have given anything to have watched a movie with Patrick, to know him. To get the chance to tell him that he loved him. I imagine Patrick and how much he would have adored his father. They would have been best friends.

I angrily swipe the tears away, terrified that I won't be able to stop crying when I need to. For five years I've cried here. It's the only place my kids can't see that I'm not coping. When the world gets too much, I go to my sadness sanctuary, the place where I can cry alone. I've cried buckets of tears in this shower. If the walls could talk, they would tell a very sad story indeed.

I close my eyes and take deep breaths, my ritual to stop the tears.

Breathe in . . . and out. Breathe in . . . and out.

It's okay. It's okay . . . stop crying. Stop crying. I shake my hands around and wash my face. I wash my hair and go through the process as I think of other things.

Other things I can deal with; other things don't hurt.

Nothing could ever hurt as much as losing him.

My eyes fill with tears anew.

Stop it.

I get out, dry myself, and then dress in my pajamas. I put my head around the corner and see that downstairs all is in darkness.

Tristan would be lying on the couch down there, waiting for me to come and say good night.

I can't.

I don't want him to see me like this. I'm so fragile that I feel like I'm about to break.

And maybe I am.

I turn off the light, get into bed, and stare up at the ceiling as tears run down my face and into my ears.

I've never felt so guilty before. I've never done anything to ever feel guilt. I'm having some kind of personal crisis, but . . . it will be better in the morning. Everything is always better in the morning.

Go to sleep.

My door opens, and I close my eyes. I feel the bed dip. "Hey," Tristan whispers. "Where's my good night kiss?"

The lump in my throat is so big that I can't speak. I screw up my face in the darkness.

Please go away.

He leans down to kiss me and stops. "You're crying."

"No, I'm not," I whisper through tears.

"Hey." He flicks the lamp on, and his face falls. "Baby, what's wrong?" he whispers.

I scrunch my lips together tight, because nothing I say will make sense. Not even to me.

His eyes search mine. "What is it?"

I shake my head, embarrassed. "I'm just getting my period—overemotional," I lie. "I'm sorry. It's nothing. I get like this sometimes."

He lies down beside me and pulls me into his arms and holds me tight, and the kindness of the act makes me lose it. I scrunch my face up in tears against his chest.

"Shh," he murmurs into my hair. "Are you okay, sweetheart?"

This isn't who you are. *Stop being so fucking nice!*

"Yes," I whisper.

He kisses my forehead as he holds me.

He feels so warm and here . . . and kind . . . and loveable . . . and *here.*

"I don't like you being upset," he murmurs. "I'm staying here with you."

"No, Tris. You can't—the kids."

"I'm not leaving you upset like this," he whispers.

261

"Baby, I'm fine. I'm just emotional. Hormones. It sucks being a woman sometimes. I'll see you in the morning?" I smile through tears.

He pushes my hair back from my forehead as he stares down at me. The air swirls between us, and I want to blurt out why I'm crying.

Because I think that I love him and that I'm going to lose him too.

He opens his mouth, as if he wants to say something, but he doesn't.

Unspoken words hang between us, a promise . . . a feeling . . . a *curse*.

"Good night, Claire."

I smile softly through tears, and I cup his face with my hand. I run my thumb over his stubble. "You're such a beautiful man, Tristan," I whisper.

He smiles. "Those hormones *are* making you crazy."

I giggle, and then he bends and slowly kisses me. The guilt comes back, and I screw up my face in tears against his.

"Claire." His eyes search mine. "Talk to me."

I shake my head, unable to speak. "Good night, Tris," I whisper. "Go to bed." I turn my back on him, and he sits and watches me for a while. Eventually he gets up and leaves. The door clicks quietly behind him.

I close my eyes and whisper into the darkness, "I think I love you." I cry into my pillow, and overcome with fear I jump up and put my wedding rings back on.

I need to feel the safety and protection of Wade . . . *my husband*.

I stare at the rings on my finger and feel a familiar comfort in their weight. "Wade," I whisper. "Help me. Help me through this. Why is this hurting so badly?"

It's as if the empty feeling that hurt my heart when he died is hurting again as something fills the void space.

Someone else.

Oh God. I screw up my face in tears and let myself cry.

I walk downstairs with a spring in my step.

Daylight, and a new day.

I cried for hours last night. It was sad, lonely, and long—and, I hate to admit it, cathartic.

Something that I needed to do.

I haven't dealt with the possibility of dating Tristan at all. It's been a shock to my system having him here with my children, and I have no idea what the outcome will be, but I have begun the process of working it out.

"Morning," I say as he comes into view.

He's stretching on the couch—just woken up, by the look of things—and he smiles sleepily up at me. "Good morning, Anderson." I smile. He only calls me Anderson when we are alone and he's flirting.

I smile as I look around. "Where are the children?"

"Who fucking cares?" He grabs me by the leg and tries to pull me down on him. In the process, he grabs my hand and notices something and then stops dead still.

My rings. I forgot to take them off.

Oh no.

His eyes flick to mine, and then without saying a word he sits up.

"Tris," I whisper nervously.

He throws his shirt over his head. "I've got to go." He pulls his jeans up.

"Where are you going?" I ask, half-panicked.

"Home."

I grab his arm. "What's the rush?"

He jerks his arm away from me. His hurt eyes hold mine. "I don't sleep with married women, Claire."

My heart drops.

He begins to throw his things together like a madman.

"What are you doing?" I whisper.

"What does it fucking look like? I'm leaving." He sits down to put on his shoes. "You know, if you had those rings on the entire time, it would be different." He rips the laces out of his shoes aggressively. "But you purposely put them back on."

"Tristan," I stammer.

"You're a fucking liar, Claire," he whispers angrily.

"I've never lied to you."

"What was last night?"

My eyes hold his.

"You told me you were hormonal." His chest rises and falls as he battles to contain his anger.

I look on, helpless to stop the train wreck as it happens before my eyes.

"But you were thinking about him," he whispers. "You were crying because you were thinking about him."

I drop my head in shame . . . it's true; I was.

He grabs his things and storms out the door. I hear his rented car pull out and drive down the street.

My heart breaks into a million pieces, and I want to run after him and beg him to stay.

But I won't . . . because he was going to leave anyway. I can't give him the life that he wants.

He was never mine to keep.

My forever man died.

Tristan Miles was just on loan.

Chapter 16

Tristan

I exhale heavily as I watch the numbers climb.

Hurry up.

Even the elevator is pissing me off today. It's Monday, and after the worst weekend in history, work is the very last place I want to be.

She dumped me.

The doors open, and I stride out and through the foyer. "Morning," I say to the girls at reception.

Sammia's eyes widen as she looks at me, and then she bursts out laughing. "What happened to your hair?"

"Bad product." I storm past.

She dives out of her seat and follows me up the corridor, determined to make fun of me. "What product is that bad?"

I dump my briefcase on my desk, and I take off my jacket. "The one I used, apparently. Now if you don't mind . . ." I gesture to the door.

She sits on the corner of my desk. "How was your weekend?" she asks.

I sit down and turn my computer on. "Ordinary. Yours?"

"Great. I had the most romantic weekend of all time," she gushes.

I roll my eyes.

"Don't you want to hear what I did?" she asks.

"No. I'm in an extremely bad mood, and it will be in your best interest not to talk to me for the rest of the year. I'm bad company."

"I seriously doubt that," she says as she watches me. "Do you need coffee?"

"Yes, please." I hit my keyboard with force.

She walks to the door and turns back, eyeing me carefully. "Are you okay?"

I type my code in. "Of course I am," I snap. "I'm always okay."

She gives me a stifled smile and disappears out the door.

Two minutes later, Fletcher appears at the door and says, "Hey."

"Hey, Fletch." I sigh as I gesture to the chair at my desk.

He walks in and takes a seat.

"How was your date?" I ask as I read through my emails.

"Pretty good."

My eyes flick to him. "How good?"

"Not that good."

"Fletcher." I turn back to my emails. "Ignore my previous advice about stepping up to the challenge. Stay the hell away from women altogether. They're more trouble than they're worth."

He frowns. "Why's that?"

"They just are." I bash my keyboard again. "Trust me on this one."

"What do you want me to do today?" he asks.

"We have meetings across town all afternoon. If you can, get started on the preparation for those," I reply. "Read through the minutes from the last meetings with these particular clients. I want you to know what's going on when we get there."

"Okay, sure thing." He gets up and walks to the door and turns back to me. "Do you know what's wrong with Mom?"

My eyes rise to meet his. "Why do you ask?"

"Because she sat on the balcony and stared into space for nine hours straight yesterday."

My stomach drops. I hate the thought of her upset. "I think she's missing your dad, buddy." I sigh.

He nods. "Yeah, probably." He shrugs. "Okay, I'll get started."

"Thanks."

I go back to my emails and stare at the screen. My mind goes back to Friday night.

There I was, sleeping alone on her cement lounge, pining to hold her in my arms.

And she was missing him.

My stomach twists in regret, because I know that no matter what happens between Claire and me . . .

I will never come first. Everyone will always come before me.

And it shouldn't upset me . . . but it does.

All my life I've been prepared to do a job that not many people could handle.

I take over companies and destroy them—take what isn't mine.

I hate that it applies to her too.

She will always be Wade Anderson's wife.

I let myself become too attached to her. From the moment I left Paris, all I have thought about is her. I've chased her, I've called her, I've booked hotel rooms and begged to see her every lunch hour, I've gone to her house and put up with shit from her children. And for the first time ever since I've been dating, I've done everything I could to try to make someone happy.

And she was missing him.

I feel stupid, but worst of all, for the first time, I feel hurt. I don't like it.

Sammia appears with a big slice of chocolate cake on a plate and a cup of coffee. "Here we go." She smiles sweetly. "Sugar for the fuzzy bear." She messes up my hair, and I swat her away.

"I am not a fuzzy bear," I snap, annoyed.

"Have you seen a mirror, Tris?"

"Shouldn't you be doing something right now?" I roll my eyes. "You know, like working?"

She giggles. "Now there's a thought."

"Sammia," we hear Jameson's voice call from reception. "Where are you?"

She sighs, and I smile into my coffee cup.

Sammia is Jameson's PA, and he's a taskmaster. He arrives at the door and breaks into a broad smile when he sees me. "For Christ's sake, Sammia, book him into a fucking barbershop today, please."

"Fuck off. It's not that bad," I huff.

"It's appalling. Have you looked at yourself?" he scoffs.

"Yes, but I can get a haircut, and you're still ugly. Both of you, get out of my office," I demand.

Sammia laughs, and they both disappear down the corridor. I walk into the bathroom and peer into the mirror.

My hair is the consistency of cotton wool and standing on end. "Fuck this," I whisper. I wet my fingers and pull them through my hair as I try to control it.

I go back to my desk and buzz Sammia.

"Hi," she answers.

"Can you book me in with a barber, please?"

"Already done. Twelve forty-five at Max's on Sixth."

"What would I do without you, Sam?" I ask.

"Probably call your own personal assistant."

I lean back in my chair and smile.

"And if you didn't have a habit of making them all fall in love with you, Tris, they could be on this floor instead of downstairs, and I wouldn't have to do all your crap."

"Stop with the dramatics. You love my crap. Addicted to it, actually."

"I am. Got to go. Your brother is on the rampage."

I chuckle and hang up. *Now, where was I?*

Oh, that's right . . . back to feeling like shit and swearing off women for all of eternity.

This is fucked.

Claire

I sit at my desk and stare into space.

I keep seeing Tristan's face and the way it fell when he saw the wedding rings on my finger.

I'm sad, but I don't know how to get around this. I understand why Tristan is hurt about my rings, and I didn't mean to leave them on. But then, on the other hand, how can I feel guilty for wanting to wear my wedding rings?

He was my husband; it's my right to put them on when I'm upset.

Is it necessary? No.

Is it calming for me? Most definitely yes.

Is it selfish when you're seeing someone else? Probably.

But it is what it is.

I want to call him, but I don't know what to say, because I don't feel like I should apologize for feeling guilty for falling in love with him.

Falling in love with him . . . God, can you hear yourself, Claire?

Am I really in love with Tristan Miles? Or am I in love with the happiness that he brings me and the way that he makes me feel?

But then . . . isn't that the same thing anyway?

And why would you let yourself fall for someone when you already know that it is going to end soon?

Is it?

Of course it is.

I can't let my boys become attached to him. I can't risk them being hurt again.

I can't lose another person I love . . . I wouldn't survive it.

I keep going around and around in my head and always end up at the same place.

I want Tristan.

I'm scared of Tristan.

I put my head into my hands on my desk. I'm so confused.

I pace back and forth in my office. I'm sure I've worn a threadbare trail in the carpet. This week has been a complete write-off. It's Thursday, and I've achieved nothing but an ulcer in my stomach from worrying.

Tristan hasn't called me once, and he's not going to.

If I want this, I know it's up to me. He's not chasing me this time.

Back and forth I walk. For some reason, I feel like today it's all coming to a head. I can't put it off any longer. I need to call him so I know where we stand. All this uncertainty is making me sick.

I can lie to the world all I want, but I can't lie to myself.

I like being with him.

I nervously dial his number. It begins to ring, and I close my eyes. "Please pick up."

"Hello," he snaps in a clipped tone.

I can hear the anger in his voice. "Hi, Tris."

"Hello, Claire. Yes, what is it?"

I frown. He's not going to make this easy. I should have known that. "Can I see you, please?"

"No, that won't be necessary."

"Tris." I sigh. "Please."

He stays silent.

"We really need to talk. I've had the most terrible week without you."

Silence.

"Can you book our hotel room?" I ask hopefully.

"I'm not sneaking around with a married woman, Claire," he fires back.

"No, baby," I whisper in a moment of weakness. "I'm not married. I'm missing you."

He inhales sharply. That's the first time I've shown him any semblance of emotion.

Damn it, and it was over the phone. "Please," I whisper. "We really need to talk."

"Fine," he snaps. "One o'clock."

"Okay." Excitement runs through me. "I'll see you then."

I hang up and smile. For the first time in five days, I have hope.

I nervously walk into the foyer just around one o'clock. I left work early so I wouldn't be late, and I walk over to our usual meeting spot by the elevator.

Tristan comes out of the restaurant. "Claire."

"Hi."

"I've got us a table in the restaurant." He's had a haircut, but he's still as sexy as hell. He turns and walks back into the restaurant without waiting for me.

No room.

"Okay." I follow him over to a table by the window, and he waits to push in my chair—even when severely pissed, he has to use his manners. It's so intrinsic to him that he wouldn't even realize he's doing it. I nervously sit down and wait for him to do the same.

He pours two glasses of water and calls the waiter over. "Can we have some menus, please?" He looks at his watch. "We'll have to be out of here in forty-five minutes, as I have a meeting. Make that happen, please."

"Yes, sir." The waiter takes off in a hurry.

Nerves dance in my stomach as I watch him. My Tris isn't here. I'm dealing with Tristan Miles the takeover king in all his glory.

He steeples his hands under his chin as his eyes come to me.

"Hi." I smile.

"I already said hello. What do you want, Claire?"

"Will you stop?" I whisper.

"Stop what?"

"Stop being aggressive."

"I am not being aggressive. What have I said that's aggressive?"

I roll my eyes. Maybe this was a bad idea. "I wanted to talk about Saturday morning."

He watches me, his hands under his chin, his pointer finger running up the side of his face. My eyes drop down to the hella expensive watch on his wrist, a reminder of how different we really are.

"What about it?" he asks.

"The way you left."

"I left because you lied to me."

"Tris," I whisper. I lean over and take his hand across the table. "You have to understand that grief is a weird thing." I pause as I try to articulate my feelings. "I can be fine and going along smoothly, and then something simple will bring up a memory, like . . . I can hear a song, and it will flip a switch, and I'm instantly taken back. It feels so recent and so raw that I can barely breathe. It breaks me. I have no warning that it's about to happen, and I can't stop it when it does."

He scratches the back of his head in frustration. "What has this got to do with me?"

I squeeze his hand in mine. "I was upset on Friday night because . . ." I pause.

"Because why?"

"Because I realized I have feelings for you. I wasn't crying tears of grief, Tristan. I was crying tears of guilt."

His eyes hold mine.

I feel stupid admitting this. It's been five years—I should have healed by now. My eyes well. "I thought we were just fucking," I whisper.

He frowns and leans forward. "Claire . . . I've never just fucked you. Never once have we just fucked," he whispers.

I blink, trying to get rid of these stupid tears. I wipe them away angrily. "Tris, I just don't . . ." I pause, trying to work out how to say what I have to say.

"You don't what?"

"I know that we have an expiration date."

"Why?" He frowns. "Why would you say that?"

"Because you told me yourself that all of your relationships have an expiry date." I give him a sad smile. "And besides, you are young and—"

"You are only four years older than me," he whispers angrily. "Don't use that as an excuse."

"You will want a family of your own soon."

"You are only thirty-eight, Claire. You could give me my own children, if that's what we decided. We could make it work, all of us together."

What?

My face falls in shock. "You've thought about this?"

"Of course I've fucking thought about this," he snaps. "I wouldn't be pursuing this if I didn't see a future."

I stare at him, lost for words.

"Claire, you need to talk to me. Right now. This is the time, because I'm just about to fucking walk out of your life."

I stare at him, and I know that I need to be honest about my feelings. The time for playing is over. This *is* something. I didn't imagine it at all.

"Tris. There are three other hearts connected to mine. If you leave me . . . you leave them."

Our eyes are locked.

"And I don't know if I could risk them ever losing . . ." I scrunch up my face at the thought of my children going through another heartbreak. "They wouldn't survive it. They are already broken, Tristan. My sons are damaged."

"What are you saying?" he asks.

"I'm saying you need to think about this."

"Claire, I make important decisions every day. Decisions worth millions of dollars. I am not flippant nor easily distracted. I've been with a lot of women, and this thing with you—it isn't going away. It's only getting stronger, and I know what I want."

My eyes search his. "What's that?"

"I want you, Claire. From the moment I left Paris, I have wanted you."

Hope blooms in my chest.

"I went away and thought about my preconceived ideas and what being with you means. Nobody else interests me in the slightest, and sure . . ." He pauses. "I'll admit it—the boys freaked me out at first . . . and I didn't handle that too well. But then I realized that they are a part of you, and if I want you, I have to want them. I have a long way to go with them, but we'll get there eventually."

I remember how fast he ran out the first day he met them. It was like a comedy skit, only worse.

He takes my hand. "Claire. When I'm with you, I don't want to be anywhere else. I would rather sleep on your lounge than be alone at my apartment."

I listen.

"Because I'm close to you . . . and . . . . I'm close to them."

My eyes well with tears once more at the mention of my children. *He gets it.*

"I want to try," he whispers. "I want to try the proper relationship thing—girlfriend, kids, house in the suburbs, and the mangy animals."

I smile over at the dreamy man sitting in front of me. "I'm a lot to take on, Tris."

"Claire." He pauses, as if searching for the right words. "The way you make me feel is worth anything," he whispers.

We stare at each other. The air swirls between us, and God, if I didn't love this man before, I just might now.

"Are you sure? You're sure?"

He rolls his eyes. "Positive."

"And you'll tell me straightaway if things change?" I whisper. "Because I completely understand if it all gets too much. I would never want you to stay if you didn't want to."

"You have my word."

I think on this for a moment. I had made plans in case it all worked out. "We need some time alone to work this out. I'm going to come and stay in New York with you for the weekend," I say.

He frowns. "How?"

"The kids can go to my parents' for the weekend. But Fletcher will need to take Monday off, if that's okay."

He comes around to my side of the table. "He can take the whole fucking week off." He kisses me, and it's soft and tender. I feel myself melt against him. We hug and hold each other tight. "I've missed you," I whisper.

He nips my bottom lip with his teeth, and I smile against him. "You're going to pay for putting me through this shit."

"I can't wait," I whisper. "Do you really have a meeting?"

"Fuck it—unfortunately yes."

My Uber pulls to a halt, and I pay the driver and get out as I peer up at the building in front of me. Tristan wanted his driver to come and collect me, but I didn't want to make a fuss. It was easy getting here.

"Hello . . . Ms. Anderson?" a voice from behind me says.

I turn in surprise. "Yes?"

"I'm Calvin, Tristan's driver. We met last month, on your arrival from Paris. He asked me to meet you and let you into his apartment. He's been held up in a meeting."

"Oh." I grip my overnight bag with white-knuckle force. Why am I so nervous? "Of course." I smile. "Thank you."

"Can I take your bag for you?"

"No, thank you. I've got it."

He nods with a kind smile. "Very well."

He leads me in through the fancy foyer, and we get into the elevator. He pushes the number fourteen.

I don't know what to say, so I say nothing at all. How many women has he shown up to Tristan's apartment in the past?

Stop it.

Why would that even cross my mind? And why would I let it bother me anyway?

Everyone has a past, even me.

We ride in silence to the fourteenth floor, and the doors open. I follow him down the wide, glamorous corridor, and he passes me a key. "This is the apartment." He opens the door with his own key and stands back to let me in. "Will you be needing anything else, Ms. Anderson?"

"No." I smile awkwardly. It's been a long time since I've been called *Ms.* "Thank you."

He turns to walk down the corridor.

"Oh, Calvin?" I ask.

"Yes." He turns back toward me.

"Did Tristan say how long he would be?" I ask.

"I'm going back to his office now to collect him, and in this traffic, he'll be another hour."

"Okay." I smile. Good—that gives me enough time for a shower. "Thanks."

I walk in and close the door, and I look around. I scratch the back of my neck in confusion. "Holy shit," I whisper. For five minutes my eyes drink in the visual sensation. Tristan's words from lunch come back to me: *I would rather sleep on your cement lounge than be alone in my apartment.*

"You poor, stupid man," I whisper out loud. "What could be better than here?"

I drop my bag off my shoulder with a thud. The apartment is gigantic. My house would fit in here four times. It's an old warehouse that's been converted. The perimeter has huge glass windows, the floor is polished concrete, and the place has a super-trendy industrial vibe. Huge colorful rugs soften the floor, and the walls have colorful abstract art everywhere. The furniture is modern and minimalistic.

"Wow." I walk through the living area. It has a huge slouchy navy couch. A three-seater and a two-seater and two one-seaters. A big chunky timber coffee table in the middle, and a gigantic television. I walk through to the kitchen—chunky timber and metal. An island sits in the middle with stools around it. I count them—nine in total. I look to the dining table and see that it seats eighteen. God, nine stools and eighteen chairs. How many friends does he have over for dinner at once?

I open the fridge and am surprised to see that it is fully stocked with healthy food.

Hmm, he must cook. Hell, I really don't know him at all, do I?

I walk down the hallway, past an office, a gymnasium, another living area, a bathroom. Then finally a bedroom, another bedroom, another bedroom. What the hell? How many bedrooms are there? Another bedroom, and then I get to two big double doors that open into the master suite.

My eyes widen, and I break into a stupid giggle. My kids' bedrooms would fit into his walk-in closet. Rows of expensive suits and shoes are all lined up. Everything is neat and in rows. It looks like a high-end men's boutique. The bedroom walls are dark navy, the linen and furniture are white, and a huge pop art abstract is on the wall in hot pinks. Huge palms tower in big white pots, and it looks just like a magazine. I run my hand through the leaves of the palm as I look around. "Wow," I whisper out loud. "Very impressive, Mr. Miles." I peek into the bathroom to see it's in a white stone; it's huge, with a circular bathtub sitting in the center. "Just fucking wow." I walk back out to the foyer and collect my bag in a rush. "Now to make myself utterly irresistible."

I raise my eyebrows at the challenge. "Like that's possible."

I lie back in the deep bath. The room is steamy, the water is hot, and my glass of champagne is ice cold.

Now this . . . is living.

Starting my weekend away with a bang. I mean, how could I resist?

I put my feet up on the end of the bathtub and slide deep into the water with a relaxed smile.

From the corner of my eye I see something, and I look up to see Tristan. His hands are in the pockets of his expensive suit, and he's leaning up against the doorjamb as he watches me. He gives me a slow, sexy smile. "Anderson."

I smile and slide down a little deeper into the water. "You're late."

He jerks his tie hard as he pushes off the door toward me. "And you look spectacular in my bathtub."

"Are you getting in?" I ask.

He smiles darkly as he tears his jacket over his shoulders. "I am most definitely . . . getting in." He begins to unbutton his shirt.

I giggle. "Dirty bastard."

"At your service." He throws his shirt to the side, and my stomach flutters at the sight of his chest. Wide and muscular, with a scattering of dark hair that dwindles down to a small trail that disappears into his pants.

I smile into my glass of champagne as I watch. This is one hell of a strip show.

He slides his zipper down, and my breath catches as I see that his cock is hard and sitting up above the waistband of his black briefs. He's hard from watching me.

What universe is this?

He kicks off his shoes and socks and slides his trousers down in one sharp movement, and I giggle like a schoolgirl.

"What is that laugh? I've never heard you do that before."

I smile bashfully, embarrassed that he caught that.

"Is that a rain giggle?" he asks with a raised brow as he steps into the water.

I frown. "Rain giggle?"

"You know, the one you do before you get dripping wet?"

I laugh out loud. "You idiot," I scoff. "I'm in a bath. I am dripping wet."

His eyes dance with delight. "Admit it, Anderson—some places are wetter than others." He sits down and pulls me over him as the water sloshes over the side and onto the floor. I laugh. For the first time in a long time, I feel so wild and free.

My legs straddle his, and his fingers slide through my open sex. He's completely right. I'm so fucking wet right now.

His eyes are locked on mine as he slowly circles his fingers through my sex. "Now this is how you should greet me every day. Naked and wet."

My mouth falls open. Oh God, that feels good.

We stare at each other as I float above him. It's as if we have both been waiting to touch each other all week, and we can't control ourselves any longer. Conversation is irrelevant when we are naked together. Our bodies speak for us.

He slowly slides a finger in, then two, and I wince as he pushes a third thick finger deep into my sex. He puts his mouth to my ear. "I want you to fuck my hand," he whispers. "You clench hard, and you fuck my fingers, Anderson."

My eyes roll back in my head. God, his dirty talk fries my brain. I could come just by listening to him. I begin to rock, and his eyes flicker with darkness. A sensuality runs between us. It's dark and uninhibited, and for the first time since we've been together, I want to let go of all control.

I want to be owned.

My Tristan.

I rock hard, and he clenches his jaw as he watches me, salivating as he waits for his turn. My eyes close, and I tip my head back in ecstasy. "So good," I whimper. "So. Fucking. Good."

He bites my neck hard as he loses control. Our bodies writhe together in pleasure, the water sloshing like a water rapid. "Condom," he whispers.

"No condom," I stammer. "I'm on the pill."

He stops still. His gaze meets mine, and his eyes darken. I can see the moment he loses control. "Get on my fucking cock." In one quick movement he lifts me and impales me.

He's deep, thick, and hard, and I cry out at his possession. "Tristan," I whimper.

His hands go to my hip bones, and he begins to slide me up and over his body.

Our eyes are locked. Our jaws hang slack. The feeling is overwhelmingly good.

Too good.

I can't hold it.

"I'm going to come," I whimper.

He slams me down hard. "Don't you fucking dare," he growls.

My knees are up around his shoulders, and his body slams into me deep . . . so deep.

"Anderson," he snaps to try to bring me back to the here and now.

I begin to shudder, and he clenches his jaw to try to stop it, but there's no chance; it's too good to stop.

Our movements are nearly violent, and the water is sloshing everywhere.

So big . . . so, so deep.

His eyes roll back in his head, and he slams me hard. I cry out, and he holds himself close. I feel the telling jerk as he comes inside my body. His cock quivers deep inside of me . . . so, so good to have his semen fill me. Perfection.

I see stars.

Perfect colored stars, in every shade of wonderful.

I fall against his chest, and he holds me tight. We pant as we cling to each other.

"So much for me playing hard to get," he whispers.

"You were playing easy to fuck." I smile against his chest.

He chuckles. "Yeah, I'm good at that game."

I smile. "The master."

Two hours later

I am crumpled and sleepy in Tristan's bed. That was one hell of a sex session.

He fucked me every which way—so good that I'm in an orgasm-induced stupor.

His hand roams up and over my hip, and he kisses the side of my face. "I'm going to get us some dinner."

"Hmm." I smile dreamily with my eyes closed.

"I had planned on cooking, but I seriously can't be fucked," he murmurs. "I'll get us some takeaway. I'm starving."

"Hmm."

He kisses me again and pulls me close and holds me tight. I smile at the feeling of him up against my body. "Back soon."

I come to my senses, and I sit up on my elbow. "Wait, where are you going?"

"I'll walk around the corner. There's a strip of restaurants. What do you feel like?"

"Umm . . ." I frown as I try to wake myself up. "Do you want me to come?"

"You don't have to." He climbs out of bed.

I watch him dress, and I know I really should make an effort. "Get me some clothes, and I'll come."

He walks into his closet and retrieves a pair of his shorts and a baggy sweater. He throws them on top of me, and they hit my head. "Not those." I smile. "My clothes."

"No, I'm not going looking for your clothes. We're going around the corner for two minutes. Throw them on." He grabs my hand and pulls me out of bed. He yanks the sweater over my head, and I bend and pull the baggy gray Nike basketball shorts on.

I grab my elastic band and pull my hair up into a messy bun.

I look a complete disaster, and I put my arms out wide. "Still want to be my boyfriend?"

He looks me up and down and smiles mischievously. "Come to think of it . . ."

I giggle as he takes me into his arms. He kisses me as I wrap my arms around his neck. "I like having you here," he whispers as he holds me close.

"I like being here." Our lips touch, and I smile. "Impersonating you could be my new hobby."

He chuckles as he pulls me by the hand. "I'm fucking starving, woman."

We ride the elevator downstairs, and luckily nobody is in the foyer. I glance down at myself and cringe. Oh my God, I look appalling.

He takes my hand, and we walk out onto the street. So different to where I live. I catch sight of our reflection in the window, and I have to bite my lip to stop my huge goofy smile. We are holding hands in public. We're really going to try this relationship thing.

Is this happening?

We turn the corner, and my eyes widen in horror. "Oh no, Tristan," I whisper. The street is busy and bustling. "I look ridiculous."

He puts his arm around me and pulls me close. "Shut up, Anderson. You look beautiful to me." He kisses my temple, and I smile against him. "Just fucked—suits you."

I smile up at my handsome date. He makes me feel beautiful. Never once since we've been together have I ever felt uncomfortable in my skin with him. Everything between us just feels so organic and natural. "What do you feel like, babe?" he asks as he looks along the street.

"Whatever. I like all food." I smile.

He leads me farther down the street. The restaurants are all trendy and hip. Beautiful people are everywhere. "Thai?" he asks.

"Uh-huh." I shrug. "Sounds good."

We go in, and he orders. The foyer is packed with people, so we go back out on the street to wait. He is standing behind me with his arm around my neck, and we hear, "Tristan."

We both turn to see a beautiful blonde woman. She's wearing a tight black leather skirt that sits just above her knees with sky-high stilettos and a fitted hot-pink top. Her perfect blonde hair is styled to perfection, and I think she just might be the most gorgeous woman I've ever seen.

He smiles broadly. "Melina, hi." He kisses her on the cheek as I stand back.

Her eyes come to me, and she looks me up and down.

"Melina, meet Claire," he introduces me. "My girlfriend."

Oh shit, he's telling people already? Can't I at least get used to it myself first?

Her mouth drops open as she stares at me. After a beat, she remembers her manners and puts her hand out. "Hi, I'm Melina . . . the ex-girlfriend."

Oh fuck.

The blood drains out of my face. I look like shit.

Her attention goes to Tristan. "I didn't know you were seeing anyone."

"Yes." Tristan smiles and puts his arm around my shoulders and pulls me close. "Claire and I have been together for a couple of months, very happy. How are you doing? Are you seeing anyone?"

I just want the earth to swallow me up . . . this is his ex-girlfriend . . . what the actual fuck does he see in me?

Her eyes come back to me, and I can see she's thinking the exact same thing. "No, still processing things." Her eyes turn back to Tristan. "I haven't seen you out in a long time."

"No, I haven't been out. I spend a lot of time at Claire's on Long Island," he lies.

I don't know what's going on here, but I feel like he's giving her a message of some sort.

"Long Island." She frowns as she looks between us.

"Yeah, well, Claire's got kids, so it's good for them out there."

Her eyes widen in horror. "You have kids?"

Oh hell, please earth . . . swallow me up. "Yes." I fake a smile. "Three boys."

Her eyes go back to Tristan in question. "Your mother didn't mention any of this to me."

He smiles casually. "Yeah, well, it's a bit awkward for poor Mom to be in the middle. You probably should start cutting ties with her."

Oh . . . realization hits. She wants him back and has been best friends with his mother to try to weasel back in.

She blinks, as if not able to believe what he has just said.

Awkward.

"I'm going to check on our order." I smile. "Lovely to meet you, Melina."

"Likewise," she says deadpan.

"I'm coming, babe," Tristan says as he grabs my hand. "Bye, Melina. Lovely to see you." He kisses her on the cheek.

I walk into the restaurant, and he comes in and stands behind me and puts his arms around my neck. I glance over to see Melina stopped still on the street, staring at us through the window.

"Jesus, Tristan," I whisper.

"Sorry," he murmurs into my hair. "I had to be rude. We broke up six months ago, and she's still calling my mother three times a week for coffee dates. Pisses me off."

She turns and walks up the street, and my stomach drops in pity for her. "She's beautiful."

"She is," he replies.

"Why didn't it work out with her?" I ask, distracted by her beauty.

He kisses my temple and holds his cheek to mine. "Because she wasn't you."

Chapter 17

I wake slowly. The room is semidark, and it feels weird not hearing a lawn mower.

The faint sound of traffic in the background is almost relaxing.

I look over to the man sleeping beside me. He's on his back. His dark hair and olive skin are a striking contrast to the crisp white linen, and his thick black lashes flutter, as if he's dreaming. His pouty big red lips softly part as he inhales.

I've never been with such a beautiful-looking man before. Everything about him is out of a catalog. Tall, dark, and handsome. A rippled and naturally athletic body . . . but it's what's inside that calls to me.

Underneath the fancy wrapping and the Miles Media surname . . . is a beautiful, gentle soul.

The man inside of this perfect body is who I want. The rest of him is just window dressing. I smile as I inhale deeply with hope.

This is a revelation.

I've found a man who ticks every box, and okay, there may be some issues with my children, but wouldn't I have that with any man I meet?

He wants to try, and God damn it, I'm giving it my best go.

I run the backs of my fingers through the hair on his lower stomach that leads down to his pubic hair.

The power of touch.

I never knew how much I needed it, craved it. And now that we've acknowledged that what's between us is more, I can hardly keep my needy hands off him.

Mine.

He's looking forward to the future, and for the first time in a long time . . . so am I.

His eyes slowly open on a deep inhale, and I smile over at him. "Morning."

He pulls me close and holds me tight. "Anderson, you're like a fucking rooster. Why are you awake so early?"

"Just admiring the view." I smile as I kiss his chest.

His naked skin up against mine is warm and hard . . . perfect.

He pulls out of my arms and gets up and goes into the bathroom, and I lie in bed wearing a stupid smile. I can't wipe it off my face.

After a while he comes back and lies on his side, facing me. His eyes are still sleepy, and it's obvious he wasn't ready to wake yet. "What?" he mumbles.

"Nothing . . . feeling happy."

He smiles sleepily. His eyes drift back closed.

I lean up onto my elbow and stare over at him. "How many women have you slept with, Tris?"

"Too many to admit to," he replies, eyes still closed.

"Oh." I think for a moment. What does that mean? How many is too many to admit to? Jeez.

"You wore a condom, though, right?" I frown.

"Yes, Anderson, I wore a condom. You don't have an STD. Go back to sleep."

I roll my lips to hide my smile. "You . . ." I frown as I try to articulate what I want to say. "You didn't wear a condom with your girlfriends, though, did you?"

"Yes, I did, actually." He shrugs. "Well, not my second girl-friend, but she was the only one apart from you."

"Oh." I frown. He has spoken of this second girlfriend before. "You loved her a lot, didn't you?" I ask.

"Is this a Saturday morning or a Spanish fucking Inquisition?" he mutters dryly.

I giggle. "I want to get to know you. I'm going to ask you questions all day long."

"Hmm." He frowns, unimpressed, eyes still closed.

"You ask me a question now," I say. "This is how we learn about each other."

He reaches over, drags my body to his, and kisses my forehead. "I don't care what happened to you before me. I only care about us." He pulls me tighter and kisses my temple again. "Go back to sleep, Anderson," he murmurs, eyes still closed.

I smile. I love him like this. All sleepy and docile. "I'm not tired. You go back to sleep. I'll keep watching you like a stalker."

"Hmm." He snuggles back into his pillow, unfazed by my comment. "You're a weird person."

I lean up onto my elbow again and smile at the resting god in front of me. I'm not even joking; I would pay good money to watch this spectacular blanket show. "It's okay, Tris," I whisper. "I've only ever murdered two men in their sleep before. You're completely safe."

He opens one eye. "The fact that that even crosses your mind to say is somewhat concerning, Claire."

I smile mischievously. "Shh, go to sleep, baby . . . nighty night."

He smirks, realizing that I'm not going to let him go back to sleep. He flicks the blankets back, exposing his naked body. "I suppose you can help yourself," he huffs, as if I am an inconvenience. "I am sleeping through it, though. Don't expect any input from me."

I laugh and kiss his chest as I work my way down his body toward his dick. "Yes, dear, whatever you say."

We walk into the restaurant hand in hand. It's nine o'clock on Saturday night, and we're only just going out for dinner in trendy downtown Manhattan. What is this ulterior cool universe? I'm usually tucked up in bed about now, too exhausted to even read.

I've been thinking about it, and I've come to the conclusion that when most people begin to see each other, it's a date and then a sweet goodbye. Casual at first, and maybe after a while a sleepover once in a while. It's slow and even tempered, and it builds over time. Tristan and I have done it all backward.

Our first meeting was a fight; then out of the blue he asked me out.

We met at a conference, had two hookups, then spent an entire weekend together. Then we didn't see each other for six weeks, had another fight in his office—this time, over my son. Reconnected, had a week of mind-blowing lunchtime sex and another sleepover on my couch, had another fight, then didn't see each other for another week, and now we are spending an entire weekend together again. It seems like we are all or nothing, but this time is different . . . we made a promise to each other of a possible tomorrow.

Being here in New York with him has been perfect.

We had a lazy morning, and he made me breakfast. Then we went for a walk and had lunch in a café on the edge of a park and read the papers. We've laughed and talked and kissed like schoolkids, made love, and had a late-afternoon sleep from which we didn't even wake up until seven o'clock. No rushing, no timeline to adhere to with the kids, nothing to cook or clean, nothing to wash, and nowhere we had to be.

We could just be us, together.

It's been a perfect Saturday.

Tristan leads me into the restaurant by the hand. "Hello, Mr. Miles," says the man at reception.

"Hello, Bill," he replies. Tristan casually glances over at me, and our eyes lock. He gives me a sexy wink.

My heart somersaults in my chest, and I bite my bottom lip to stifle my over-the-top smile. It's the strangest feeling. It's like a heavy dark cloud has been lifted, and happiness is literally beaming out of me.

I can feel myself glowing.

Tristan Miles makes me happy . . . deliriously happy.

We follow the waiter as he leads us through the restaurant to a table for two in the back corner. The restaurant is small and darkened, and candlelight flickers on all of the tables. The waiter pulls out my chair, and we both sit down. "Can I get you something to drink?" he asks.

Tristan opens the wine list. "What do you want, babe?" he asks, distracted.

"I'm easy," I reply as I go through the choices. Anything will be good, if I'm honest.

"Red?"

"Uh-huh."

"I'll have a bottle of the Malbec, please." He closes the menu.

"Excellent choice, sir. We have a batch from France."

"Thank you." He smiles as he passes the menu back. The waiter walks off, and Tristan's attention comes back to me.

"You come here often?" I ask.

He shrugs. "I used to. Mainly only now when my brother Elliot is in town. Nocello is one of our favorite restaurants in Manhattan. I used to be here a lot more than I am now."

I smile over at him. "You're close to Elliot?"

"Yeah, he's in town this weekend, actually."

"He is?" I ask, surprised.

"He and Christopher have flown in for an art auction that's on tomorrow night. I was going to talk to you about it, actually. Do you want to go?"

My eyes widen. "They flew in from London just for an art auction?"

"Yeah," he replies casually. "They fly around the world for art auctions. Elliot is into collecting art. He has a very impressive portfolio, actually. He started collecting back when we were kids."

"How do you start collecting art when you are a kid?" I frown.

The waiter returns to the table with our bottle of wine. He pops the cork and pours a little into a glass. He hands it to Tristan, who takes a sip and swooshes it around his mouth like the snob that he is. "Hmm." He rolls his lips. "That's lovely. Thank you."

The waiter then fills our glasses as I smirk over at my rich boy.

He comes from another world than mine. If I ever doubted it before, I know it now.

The waiter leaves us alone, and Tristan's eyes meet mine. "What?"

"Nothing." I smile dreamily over at him. "Carry on with your story. How in the hell does someone begin to collect art as a child?"

"Oh." He breaks into a breathtaking smile. "He bought a picture from a yard sale with his allowance when he was fourteen, and it ended up being very valuable."

I listen intently.

"Back in college, he would go to the art facility and buy paintings from the art students. He still has them all in storage. He has a real eye for evolving talent." He sips his wine, as if he has this conversation every day.

"And Christopher?" I ask. "He's into art too?"

"No, he's just Elliot's art wingman. He likes the thrill of the auctions. It's a game to him."

I smile into my wineglass. I love hearing the dynamics of his family.

"This auction tomorrow night is a big one."

"Why is that?" I frown.

"Elliot is obsessed with this artist, has all her paintings that have gone up for auction."

"Who is she?"

"We have no idea; her name is Harriet Boucher. She's an older recluse, apparently. We have searched and searched for this woman. She's been the topic of many a drinking session."

I smile as I imagine them stalking a reclusive artist. "And you think *I'm* a weird person."

He chuckles and sips his wine. "I suppose it does seem weird from the outside."

"So how . . ." I pause because I don't know how to articulate what I want to say.

"How what?"

"How was it decided what each of you boys would do in the company?" I shrug. "Like how were the positions given to each of you?"

He frowns and sips his drink, contemplating his answer. "I guess it was based on what we are individually good at."

I listen.

"Jameson is good at control. He is very . . ." His voice trails off. "You will meet him next weekend."

"When?" I frown. Oh God. I'm already dreading meeting that man.

"We have an industry cocktail party. I want you to come and meet my family."

I smile "Great," I lie.

Fuck, what will I wear? I sip my drink as I internally begin to go through my wardrobe. Nope, I have nothing . . . I'll have to buy something new.

God, I hate shopping.

"Elliot is into the graphics of the company. He oversees the visual representation of all things Miles."

I frown.

"Christopher manages human resources. He likes people. Managing staff is his thing."

"And you?" I ask.

"What about me?"

"How did you get to do the acquisitions?"

He smiles into his wineglass. "I'm good at numbers and taking calculated risks."

I listen, fascinated. "Meaning what?"

"Well, I can look at a company and its figures and do a due diligence report, and from that I know whether the company is worth anything moving forward."

"You know, now that I know you, I can't imagine you—and don't take this the wrong way—destroying companies."

He gives me a sad smile; his eyes hold mine, and understanding dawns on me.

On our first night together, he told me that he has insecurities, but just because I can't see them doesn't mean they aren't there.

This is his insecurity.

He's a good guy doing a job he's not proud of.

I get a lump in my throat as I imagine what he must feel as he tears a company apart in the name of profit. I smile over at him. "You know, Tris, out of all the people I have met in my life, you have been the biggest surprise."

"Why is that?"

"You're not at all who I thought you were."

"Who did you think I was?"

I reach over and take his hand. "Somebody that I could never have feelings for."

The air crackles between us.

"What are those feelings, Claire?" He picks up my hand and kisses my fingertips. "You keep hinting at these feelings, but you haven't told me what they actually are."

Our eyes are locked, and he knows that I know that I'm in love with him.

He wants me to tell him. He's waiting to hear the three sacred words; I know he is.

Those magical words swirl between us so often—the closeness and tenderness after we make love. I can almost hear them whispered in the air. I know he does too.

It's too soon.

I need to be sure. I need to know that this is going to work, because once I tell him that I love him, I can't take it back.

"You know, Tris . . ." I pause. "I don't want to sound insecure, because I'm not. I'm more than happy with who I am. But I do wonder what you see when you look at me."

He leans his face onto his hand as he watches me.

I feel suddenly uncomfortable. Why did I say that?

"You know what I see, Claire."

I frown.

"I don't see anything . . . it's how I feel."

I take his hand again.

"For the first time in my life . . ." He frowns, as if getting the wording right in his head.

"How do you feel, Tris?" I whisper.

His eyes meet mine. "Like myself."

Emotion fills my heart.

"I feel that when I'm with you, I'm who I'm supposed to be."

I smile softly.

"It's like . . ." He frowns. "It's like I've gone back to being a teenager, and you're reprogramming everything I thought I ever knew."

"Is that a bad thing?" I whisper, confused. "I don't want to reprogram you."

"No." He frowns. "Wrong choice of words. I mean, you're showing me what I want as opposed to what I was supposed to want."

"You mean my kids?"

"No," he whispers. "I mean you."

I frown.

"You're everything I never knew I wanted. Feminine but strong. Your beautiful body." He smiles softly. "Your selflessness with your boys."

I watch him as my heart somersaults in my chest.

"You put everyone's needs before yourself, Claire."

My stomach clenches.

"And for the first time in my life, you make me want to put someone before me."

I'm overcome with emotion. "Thank you," I whisper.

"For what?"

"For being everything that I thought you weren't."

He smiles. "No, thank you." He raises his glass to mine. "For being exactly who I thought you were."

I smile through tears. "Who, a bitch?"

He chuckles as he clinks our glasses together. "A raving bitch with a magical vagina."

I laugh out loud.

It's official—I do love this man . . . I really do.

I just wish I could tell him.

I straighten my dress. "Do I look okay?" I whisper as Tristan leads me through the crowd. We've just arrived at the auction and are weaving our way through the people to the other side of the room to meet his two younger brothers. I'm sick with nerves.

"You looking fucking hot, Anderson. Stop it," he whispers as he strides through the crowd.

God, this is a nightmare. Why did I agree to this?

We are in a trendy art gallery warehouse; the crowd is eclectic and buzzing with excitement.

Huge abstract paintings are on the walls, and people are gathered in front of them, admiring their beauty. Loud funky music is being piped through the space, and waiters are circling with silver trays and glasses of champagne.

This is another world, far from the school homework I'm usually doing on the dining room table on a Sunday night.

We get to a clearing. "There they are." Tristan smiles as he leads me toward two men standing and looking at a painting.

They are handsome and similar to Tristan: dark hair and tall and built—the family resemblance is strong. Dressed in jeans and sports jackets, they look as much like fashion models as their brother does.

"Hey." Tristan laughs as we get to them.

They both spin toward us, and their eyes light up. "Tris." They both laugh as they all shake hands.

"This is Claire." Tristan smiles proudly. "This is Elliot and Christopher, my two younger brothers."

"Hi," I breathe . . . oh God, this is hell.

Their eyes widen as they stare at me, and then, as if remembering their manners, they smile. "Hello, Claire." Elliot shakes my hand first. "Lovely to meet you." He's businesslike and emits a dominant power—quite daunting, actually.

"Hi."

Christopher smiles and leans in and kisses me on the cheek. "Hi, Claire. I've heard a lot about you. So lovely to finally get to meet you." Christopher is much more relaxed, it seems, and he looks like Tristan. He's my favorite—I can already tell.

"So . . ." Christopher smiles as he looks between us, making small talk. "What have you two been doing all weekend?"

From my peripheral vision, I can see Elliot looking me up and down as he stands back and sips his champagne. What is he thinking?

God, I just want the earth to swallow me up.

"Oh, you know." Tristan smiles as he puts his arm around me. "Bit of this and a bit of that."

Christopher laughs. That's code for sex.

And he's right; we've been at it like rabbits all weekend. It's a wonder I can walk.

Tristan holds his champagne glass up toward the painting we are standing in front of. "So this is Harriet Boucher?"

Elliot's eyes light up as he stares at the huge canvas in front of us. "This is her." He smiles at it in awe. "Spectacular, isn't it?"

Tristan scrunches up his nose, unimpressed. "Meh, it's okay."

Christopher laughs. "I could take it or leave it, to be honest too."

Tristan and Christopher begin to chat between themselves.

Elliot's eyes come to me. "What do you think, Claire?"

"Beauty is in the eye of the beholder," I reply.

He smiles softly as his eyes go back to admiring the painting. "Yes, it is."

"Tristan says that you love this artist?" I ask, trying to make conversation.

"I do." He gives me a lopsided smile. "Not love her as such, but I admire her work. She is by far my favorite artist."

"Why?"

He frowns, puzzled by my question. "I guess . . . hmm." He thinks for a moment. "Her paintings speak to me. I can't explain it."

I smile softly as I stand beside him and stare at the canvas. "How romantic."

His eyes come to me. "Really?"

"If I were an artist, all I would want in life is for my paintings to speak to someone."

He smiles and turns his attention back to the painting. "I suppose."

"So you know her?" I ask.

"No, I've never seen her. I go to every auction, but she never attends. She's elderly, from what I know."

"And you have a few of her paintings?" I ask.

"I've bought five at auctions, although there are thirty in circulation. It is my aim to own all of them at some stage. They never come up for sale."

"Are they all in storage?"

"No, her paintings are in my homes. They are personal to me."

I smile as I watch him. He's not intense like I first thought; he's deep.

A man in a suit comes out with a roll-out little table thingy. "We are about to begin the auction for Harriet Boucher," he calls.

The people in the room all turn and make their way over to where we stand. The crowd gathers in a semicircle around the painting.

Tristan puts his hand on the small of my back and smiles as he watches.

A woman comes and stands opposite us in the crowd. She's honey blonde and innocent looking. She has a ballerina look about her. Perfect posture and innately feminine.

Elliot's and her eyes meet across the crowd, and they stare at each other. I smile as I watch them; I can feel the electricity as it bounces between them.

Elliot leans into Tristan. "Black dress, red lips. Who the fuck is she?" he whispers.

"Never seen her before," Tristan whispers back.

Elliot turns to Christopher and whispers the same thing to him.

Christopher looks over at her and frowns. "No idea."

I smile as I listen to them. Tristan moves behind me and puts his arm around my waist as he pulls me close. He kisses my temple. "Do you want another drink?" he whispers.

"No, thanks." I smile. I'm too busy watching Elliot and this girl mentally fuck each other across the room.

The auctioneer begins. "The second auction for tonight is the painting *Serendipity* by Harriet Boucher."

I look at the painting. It's an abstract in greens and blues, and it almost looks like rays of light shining down from heaven. It really is magical. I can see why Elliot loves it.

"Do we have an opening bid?" the auctioneer asks.

"Two hundred thousand," Elliot says calmly.

My eyes widen . . . what the fuck?

"Two fifty," an older man replies.

Elliot glares at his competition. "Three fifty," he fires back.

Holy shit . . . this is a real art auction, the kind you see on cable.

"Three seventy," a woman calls.

Elliot rolls his eyes—another bidder. Tristan's eyes dance with delight as he looks on.

Christopher leans in and whispers something to Elliot. He nods once, as if understanding. "Half a million," Elliot announces.

The room falls silent.

The older man narrows his eyes. "Seven fifty."

Elliot clenches his jaw in anger.

Tristan begins to chuckle. "It's on," he whispers.

"One million dollars," Elliot fires back.

"One point one," the man fires back.

"Fuck," Elliot whispers.

Christopher leans in and says something to Elliot. He seems to think for a moment.

He's telling him what to bid. It seems that Christopher has a lot of pull in what Elliot does.

"Do we have another bid?" the auctioneer asks. "One point one is our last call."

"One point four," Elliot snaps.

The crowd lets out an audible gasp.

Elliot's jaw tilts to the sky in satisfaction, and Tristan smiles broadly.

I look among the Miles brothers. These men are wealthy beyond measure. They don't seem rattled at all—$1.4 million for a fucking painting . . . what the hell?

"One million four hundred and ten thousand dollars," the other bidder replies.

"One point five," Elliot fires back.

The man shakes his head. "I'm out."

The auctioneer turns to the woman. She shakes her head. "I'm out too."

The crowd waits and looks around.

"Do we have any more offers?" the auctioneer asks.

"One point five once . . . twice . . . three times. Last call." He brings down his hammer. "Sold, to the man in the navy jacket, Elliot Miles."

Elliot laughs in delight, and Tristan and Christopher shake his hand in congratulations. He looks up and around the room. "Where did she go?" he asks.

"Who?" Tristan frowns.

"The blonde," he replies as he scans the room. "She was right here."

"She left," I whisper. "As soon as you bid your last bid, she left. I saw her walk out the front doors."

Elliot turns and storms toward the door.

"Excuse me, sir," the auctioneer calls after him. "We need details."

"Go find her," he says to his brothers.

Christopher marches out the front door to look for her as Elliot talks to the auctioneer. Tristan goes looking for her too.

I smile as I watch. . . I just got a firsthand look at how the Miles boys operate.

They see something they want, and they go after it hard.

Impressive.

I straighten Tristan's tie as he looks down at me. It's Monday morning, and I don't want this weekend to end.

"There." I dust off his shoulders as I pretend to be happy about us parting. "You look extra handsome today."

He smiles softly down at me. "You know, I could get used to this sweet version of Claire."

"Extra handsome . . . for a bastard, I mean."

He smirks. "More your style."

We kiss, his tongue gently stroking mine. We linger over each other's lips for an extended time, and I run my fingers through his hair. We've had the most wonderful weekend. We went out after the auction last night, and I laughed and laughed with his brothers. They're as funny and smart as Tristan is. "When will I see you?" I whisper.

"Are you getting needy, Anderson?"

I smile. "A little."

"About fucking time." He pushes the hair back from my face as he stares down at me. "Tonight," he replies.

"Tonight?" I stare at him. "You don't have to come tonight. We have to ease the kids into this, and I know you hate the couch."

He rolls his eyes. "I'm coming tonight. I won't stay over."

"Okay, but remember, we're just friends at this stage to them." I hunch up my shoulders. "I really need them to be okay with this, Tris."

"They will be."

"Harry . . ." I wince.

"Is a nightmare," Tristan replies.

I widen my eyes. "Stop that. I'm allowed to call him a nightmare; you are not. Just like I'm allowed to call you a nightmare, and they are not."

He rolls his eyes. "However you put it. I'll see you tonight. Let's go out for dinner. The five of us."

"Really?" I frown. "That's very *Brady Bunch*."

He grabs my behind and brings me closer to his pelvis. I can feel a hint of hardness in his trousers. "Does the guy fuck the mother in the bathroom of the restaurant on *The Brady Bunch*?"

I giggle. "Surely not. And don't get any ideas. That is not happening. My children will never know that we have sex. Like ever."

He gives me a sexy wink.

"I mean it, Tristan."

"I wouldn't." He smiles.

"Why are you smiling, then?"

"Because I know what a horny fuckmaster two thousand their mother is."

I burst out laughing in surprise. "A horny fuckmaster two thousand?"

"Yes, it's the latest sex toy."

"And what does this toy do?"

"Deep throats like a champion. With a churning pussy that melts my cock."

My mouth falls open as I feign horror. "You will never see my deep-throating skills again if you keep going."

He smiles against my lips as he kisses me.

"I had a great weekend." I smile up at him. "The best."

"Hmm." His eyes close, and I feel his dick harden up against me.

"Didn't you say you had a meeting?" I ask.

"You must be a faulty model." He kisses me again.

"Why is that?"

"The horny fuckmaster two thousand doesn't speak. I specifically asked for one without a voice box."

I burst out laughing again. "Go to work, you fool."

I pull my dress over my head and smooth it down. It's navy and fitted and hangs just below the knees with spaghetti straps. I look at myself in the mirror.

The kids are back home from my parents' and are downstairs waiting for me to get ready so that we can go out to dinner. I haven't told them yet that Tristan is coming.

Not quite sure how to broach it with them, to be honest.

I smile as I go over the glorious weekend Tristan and I just had together. I'm on cloud nine.

I'm not fighting with the kids over him. I don't want that to be the big defining moment when they have to adjust to me dating again. I'm just going to ease him in as our friend, and then one day they will hopefully get along enough so that they like having him around.

Sounds easy in theory . . . right?

There is a knock at the door, and my heart jumps. He's here.

I hear footsteps running to the door. "Tristan!" Patrick yells in excitement.

"Hello." I hear his deep voice echo through the house.

"What are you doing here?" Harry barks.

"I'm coming to dinner. Where's Mom?"

"Mom only booked for four," Harry says.

"Well, that's funny," Tristan replies. "Because I booked the restaurant, and I booked for five."

I smile as I listen to the banter.

"This is a family-only dinner," Harry replies, unimpressed.

"Be quiet, Harry," Patrick snaps. "You're ruining everything."

"Yes, Wiz," Tristan says. "Good advice from your little brother."

I smile. He has a nickname for everyone. Even the cat is called Muff Cat—Muff won't do.

I walk around the corner and down the stairs. Tristan looks up, and our eyes meet. He smiles softly up at me as my stomach flutters.

"Hello," I say.

"Hi." He smiles dreamily.

The air circles between us, and I just want to run into his arms—but I can't, of course. My three bouncers are here to protect me.

"Thank you for coming," I say as I hit the bottom step.

"That's okay," Tristan replies. "I had nothing better to do."

Harry folds his arms with an exaggerated eye roll. "Oh great, this is all I need," he huffs. "The night is ruined."

"Don't be rude, Harry," I reply calmly. "Tristan is my friend, and I invited him to come with us."

"Who knows why," he mutters under his breath.

"We leave in ten minutes," I say. "Would you like a drink, Tristan?"

"Yes, please," he says. "Lead the way."

I walk out into the kitchen, and Tristan follows me. I take out two glasses and pour us each some wine. He clinks his glass with mine and gives me a tender smile. It feels so weird. Things are different; there's a closeness between us. "To drinking on Monday nights."

I smile and take a sip. "You're a bad influence on me, Mr. Miles. I never drink on a school night."

He narrows his eyes, as if thinking. "What *am* I exactly allowed to say to the wizard? Give me some boundaries to work with here."

"Nothing," I reply. "You will be the adult in the relationship; he's just a child. A confused, angry, naughty little boy. He's unsettled, and he doesn't like change. Like most kids, he acts up out of fear. He needs time to adjust . . . but he will come around and see how wonderful you are. I know he will." I put my hand on his as it sits on the kitchen counter. "You need to be patient with him."

"What, nothing?" He frowns. "Not one word?"

"No."

He rolls his eyes.

"Why? What would you like to say?" I ask.

"I don't know." He shrugs.

"Put yourself in my shoes for a moment. If this was your daughter, and I was coming into her house, what would you want me to do with her . . . be patient, or fight with her and put you in the middle?"

He sips his drink and looks at me flatly, clearly unimpressed with my boundaries.

"I just want you to ignore him, Tris. He's baiting you for a fight. And I can defend you if you're ignoring him and being the adult, but if you get into an open fight with a thirteen-year-old . . . I'm on his side. Every time."

Tristan rolls his eyes into his wineglass.

I smile sweetly. "First rule of being a mom: the kids always come first."

He leans into me. "When do I come first?"

"When we're alone," I whisper.

"What do I get for not strangling him?" he whispers.

"Me." I hold my hands out. "All of me."

He smiles, and the air crackles between us. "You drive a hard bargain, Anderson."

My eyes drop to his lips, and I'm so grateful that we're having this conversation. "I just wish I could kiss you right now."

"So . . . we can't even kiss?" He frowns. "What can we fucking do?"

"Not until they know we are dating."

He tips his head back and drains his glass. "That'll do me. Let's go." He walks out into the living room. "Come on, we're leaving," he calls.

I listen to him and Patrick as they talk. Fletcher is out there too now. I hear Harry stomp down the stairs. "I'm having dessert for dinner," he announces.

"Oh, good idea," Tristan agrees. "Me too. Let's all do that—sugar coma, here we come."

I smile. God. Harrison has no idea who he is trying to piss off here. Tristan can outdo anyone in any annoying contest. I walk out into the living area, and Tristan turns to me. "You got a coat, Mama? It's going to get cold out," he asks.

"I don't need one. I'm fine." I grab my bag and see Tristan disappearing up the stairs. "What are you doing?" I call after him.

"Getting you a coat."

I smirk. Control freak. He wants it to be cold now so that he can say "I told you so."

He reappears a few moments later with a cardigan for me. He flicks it over his shoulder and takes Patrick's hand. "Come on, let's go." We follow him out the front and over to his car. The lights flash as we approach it. He opens the front door and pushes the seat forward. "Climb in the back."

We all peer into the tiny back seat. "We're not going to fit into this sardine car," Harry moans.

"This is not a sardine car; it's an Aston Martin," Tristan replies through gritted teeth. "Nothing fishy about it, although I can always arrange a seat in the trunk, if you would prefer."

I roll my lips to hide my smile. "Climb in, baby. It's fine."

Harry rolls his eyes and climbs in.

"You get in the middle, Tricky," Tristan directs.

Patrick climbs in next.

"Now you, Fletch."

We watch as Fletcher squeezes his way into the back seat. Their shoulders are all bunched up, and their knees are around their chins. Tristan frowns as he peers in at them. "Great, they don't fit," he mutters under his breath as he slams the door shut.

"We can take my car," I offer.

"It will be fine this one time," he snaps.

We get in and drive to the restaurant. The boys whine and moan about how squashed and uncomfortable they are, and with every mile we travel, I can see Tristan's face becoming a little more red.

It's fun watching him fight to hold his tongue. Maybe he won't be so insistent on doing the family-dinner thing in the future.

We get to the restaurant, and the girl at the desk smiles broadly. "Hello, booking for Miles, please," he says.

"It's Anderson," Harry whispers loudly. "There are four Andersons and only one Miles. It's hardly a Miles booking, is it?" he huffs, as if outraged.

Tristan stares at Harry blankly.

308

I so wish I could read his mind. This is really quite comical. "That's enough, Harry," I remind him.

We are shown to our seats. "Your table."

"Thank you." Tristan smiles.

"Sit here." Fletcher pats the chair next to him. Tristan moves to sit next to him.

"I want to sit next to Tristan," Patrick whines as he taps the chair beside him. "Tristan, sit next to me, please."

Tristan comes over to my side. "To save arguments, I'm sitting next to Mom."

Harry rolls his eyes.

We all sit down, and as if he has been waiting all night to say it, Tristan blurts out. "There's a reason I wanted to have dinner tonight, Claire," he says loudly so that everyone can hear what he says.

I frown. "There is?"

The table falls silent.

"Yes." He straightens his tie, as if preparing himself for something. "I was wondering if you would like to go out with me next weekend."

My face falls.

"Like on a date?" Harry whispers, mortified.

"Yes," Tristan replies, unrattled. "Like on a date. I would like to be your boyfriend, Claire Anderson. What do you say?"

Chapter 18

"She says no. That's what she says," Harry snaps. "What a stupid question—as if she would go out with you, anyway."

My mouth falls open as I stare at Tristan. What in the world? This is not taking it slow at all.

He smiles sweetly. "Well?"

"I . . ." I look around at my children. Patrick is smiling hopefully, Harry is glaring at Tristan, and Fletcher looks like he's swallowed a fly.

"I . . . umm . . ."

"Well, you did say you were ready to have a friend again," Tristan says. "Someone to go to the movies and out to dinner with. A boyfriend, if you will."

I have no words; this man is the living end.

"And as I see it, you have four choices," he continues.

I frown. "I do?"

"Yes." He carries on with his sales pitch. "You can go out with that man you met in Paris." He pours us each a glass of water from the table jug. "However, that would mean that you all have to move to France." He sips his water with a casual shrug. "And of course, Muff Cat and Woofy can't move to Paris, so they would have to move in with me."

The boys' faces fall in horror.

"I am not moving to Paris," Harry snaps in an outrage.

"Me neither," Fletcher whispers angrily. "No way in hell."

"Me three," says Patrick.

Tristan's eyes dance with delight. I see what he's doing here.

"I don't know; Paris may be good for us." I smile.

"No way, Mom," Harry whispers angrily. "You can forget about it. I'm calling Grandma; she won't like this at all."

"What are the other choices?" I ask as I play along.

"You could go out with Pilates Paul," he offers.

"Oh, he's nice." I smile sweetly. "I do like him. Great choice."

Tristan looks at me deadpan. "He's boring, Claire," he mutters dryly.

"But so handsome, right?"

Tristan narrows his eyes, and I bite my lip to hide my giggle.

"I'm getting a headache," Harry says as he holds his temples.

"No, Mom," Fletcher snaps. "That's just embarrassing. He wears a pink sweatband around his head to Pilates."

"Yes," Tristan hisses. "Exactly my point, Fletch. He will bring the Anderson name into disrepute."

"He is weird, Mom," agrees Patrick. "You have to admit it."

I let out an overexaggerated sigh. "Okay, what is my other choice?"

"You could meet someone new who has kids."

I blink. This isn't what I thought he was going to say.

"But whenever he comes over, he will bring his children, and they will have to have a bedroom to stay in. So Harry and Patrick will have to share a bedroom from now on."

Harry's face is getting redder and redder; he's about to blow. "Why does Fletcher get his own room?" he demands.

Tristan sips his drink. He's loving this. "Because Fletcher is an adult, and he needs his own room. But then . . ." He pauses, as if thinking, for added effect. "Those other kids will use a lot of internet, maybe all the data."

I drop my head to hide my smile . . . oh, he's good.

"They'll also eat all of the food, and they won't have a skateboard or bike at your house, so you will have to share all of your things."

The blood drains from Harry's face as he listens.

"That's if they aren't girls."

"Girls?" Harry gasps as he chokes on his water. "No way. You are not going out with anyone with kids, Mom. I forbid it," he whispers through gritted teeth.

"Oh." I frown as I play along. "I kind of liked the idea of having more kids around."

"Or not," Tristan mutters under his breath.

"Well." I smile at the gorgeous, conniving man beside me. "What is my last choice?"

"Me."

"And why should I pick you to be my boyfriend?" I ask.

"That's a very good question, Claire," he says as he takes a piece of paper out of his suit coat pocket. "I have prepared a list of my attributes."

I roll my lips to hide my smile at his shenanigans.

He unfolds the paper and begins to read from the list of points he has written.

"I'm good looking."

Patrick smiles goofily up at Tristan. "It's true; you are." He bounces in his chair excitedly.

"Oh God," Harry moans. "Here we go."

"You don't have to move to another country and leave your pets homeless and vulnerable."

I laugh, and Fletcher rolls his eyes.

"You don't have to share a bedroom with anyone."

"I'm not doing that anyway," Harry cuts him off. "Don't get any ideas, Mom."

"I'm getting a bigger car," he continues.

"You are?" I frown. I put my hand out for the paper. "Show me where it says that on the list."

He pulls the paper out of my grasp. "That was a recently added point, Claire. Don't interrupt me."

I giggle.

"I'm fun." He straightens his tie.

I swoon across the table . . . you got that right, baby. You are so fun.

"You are not fun," Harry huffs. "You're boring."

Tristan flicks the paper down in disgust. "How am I boring? Name one time I have been boring."

"Right now. This is boring," Harry fires back.

"You're boring," Tristan mutters dryly. "Shut up, Wizard, and listen to my points."

"He's not boring, Mom," Patrick whispers, as if feeling the need to remind me.

"I live in New York, so I can come and visit you, and you can come to my house and visit me, if you like. Nobody has to move anywhere, and it's no big deal to visit."

They all listen intently.

"And," he adds, "I am an excellent cook."

I frown. "You cook?"

"Yes. Yes, I do." He flicks the paper in front of him. "My specialty is baking brownies and chocolate cake. They asked me to make a cookbook on chocolate desserts once, which I gracefully declined."

The boys' faces fall, and I struggle to hide my laugh.

"Well. I'm very impressed," I reply. "You do have some excellent assets."

"I do." He smiles proudly.

The table falls silent.

"I propose a vote," Tristan says.

"A vote?" I frown.

"Yes." He smiles proudly. "We all have to vote who your mom is going to have as a boyfriend."

"I didn't agree to this," Harry says.

"No, Wiz, you have to pick one for Mom. Think very carefully about it, and remember, majority vote wins," he says quickly as a disclaimer.

Tristan's eyes find mine, and I smile softly as I try to send him a telepathic message: *I love you.*

"All in favor of you moving to France, hold your hands up."

I go to put my hand up, and Tristan screws up his nose in a warning.

I giggle.

"Okay," he says, carrying on with the proceedings. "All those in favor of sharing bedrooms and internet, raise your hands."

Everyone sits still.

"All those in favor of *me* being your mom's boyfriend, raise your hand."

He puts his hand up. Patrick nearly touches the ceiling his hand shoots up so fast.

Fletcher frowns as he contemplates the question, and Tristan looks over and raises an eyebrow in a warning. Fletcher shrugs and sheepishly puts his hand half up.

"So . . . what are my other options?" I ask.

Tristan looks at me deadpan. "Pathetic Pilates Paul," he snaps.

"Oh, I do like him, though," I tease.

Tristan narrows his eyes.

"But I guess between you and him, I would prefer you." I raise my hand, and Tristan smiles and gives me a sexy wink.

Harry crosses his arms in front of him, outraged at such a vote.

"What's it going to be, Wiz?" Tristan asks. "Who are you voting for?"

Harry looks around the table as he weighs up all the options. "I'm voting for . . ."

We all hold our breath.

"I'm going with Pilates Paul."

My heart sinks. I was hoping he'd pick Tristan.

"Oh well." Tristan sighs. "How sad that you lost. Majority vote wins, and it's four against one." He sips his drink. "I can drop you at Pilates Paul's house on the way home, if you wish. I'm sure he has a spare pink headband for you."

Harry glares at him. Tristan smiles broadly back.

Tristan sits back in his chair, proud of how the vote went. "Well, I have to say I'm very relieved." He reaches over and takes my hand in his. The boys' eyes all nearly pop from their sockets as they watch. "What are you ordering, boys?" he asks casually, as if nothing is wrong. "I'm having the steak."

Over the next hour I sit as a spectator and watch Tristan interact with the boys. He chats and listens and laughs, and I really have to wonder how it is that he's so good with them. It's as if he has a world of experience with teenagers, when he actually has none.

Harry is obnoxious and constantly trying his hardest to ruffle him, but Tristan casually deflects his comments, as if he hasn't heard them. Patrick hangs on his every word and has his chair up so close to Tristan's that he is almost on his lap. His little hand rests on Tristan's thigh as they talk. And Fletcher—well, he and Tristan speak a language that nobody other than the two of them gets. They snicker and laugh at private jokes.

The waitress arrives with the hugest pile of ice cream and cake. It's shaped like a spaceship. "Here we go." She smiles. "Death by

Chocolate." She sets it down in front of Harry, and we all gasp as we stare at the mountain of sugar.

She sets our tiny little desserts in front of the rest of us. "Thank you." I smile.

"Well, well, well, Wiz," Tristan says. "I'll make a bet with you. If you eat every last bite of that, you get to pick what dinner I make tomorrow night."

Harry's eyes hold his, his interest suddenly piqued. "Anything I want?"

"Anything," Tristan replies.

"Cockroaches." He snickers.

The boys and I groan in horror.

Tristan cracks his knuckles. "My specialty, actually. Crumbed or fried?" The waitress walks past. "Excuse me," he calls to her.

"Yes."

"Can we have a pot of english breakfast tea with milk, please?" He gestures to me.

"Of course," she replies as she disappears into the kitchen.

I look over at the beautiful man beside me. He knows that I like granny tea with my dessert. He pays attention to the small things, and it's the small things that matter.

"But, Wiz," he adds, "if you don't eat all that dessert, every last bite, you have to cook what I want for dinner tomorrow night."

"Deal," Harry snaps. "Piece of cake." He gets to work on his mountain of dessert, and I watch my family around the table.

It's like Tris has always been here, and it's bizarre—in one dinner he has the boys all agreed that we're dating. They seem weirdly okay with him holding my hand . . . and he has opened them up to having dinner with us again tomorrow night. There's a reason Tristan Miles is the takeover king. When he knows what he wants, he goes and gets it. A charming, aggressive sales pitch that is second to none.

The master magician.

"Oh God," Harry moans from the back seat. "I'm going to be sick."

"If you vomit on us, I'm breaking your nose," Fletcher warns him.

Tristan smiles. His eyes flick up to the rearview mirror to a very full and sick Harry.

"Maybe you should punch him in the stomach now, Fletch . . . you know, just for fun."

"Oh no. Mom!" Harry cries. "Tell them to stop talking. I'm serious; I might throw up."

"Wimp," Tristan mouths to himself as we drive.

I look over at his pleased-with-himself face. "I'm quite sure this is some form of child abuse."

Tristan lets out an evil laugh. "Death by Chocolate," he says in a monster voice. "Prepare to die."

"Oh, stop talking about it," Harry moans. "I can't even think about chocolate anymore."

"Whatever you do, Wiz, don't think about fish milkshakes or slimy brains or anything gross."

Harry wails in pain.

"Tristan!" the whole car cries.

"If he throws up on me, I'm rubbing it on you," Fletcher calls.

"Yeah!" Patrick yells. "Me too."

"You do know"—I look over at the master teaser as he drives—"if he throws up, it is in your car. Who do you think is cleaning it up? Because it won't be me."

Tristan's eyes dart to me in horror. He didn't think of that, did he? He puts his foot down and steps on the gas. His eyes flick to the rearview mirror and Harry. "Hang on, Wiz. Nearly there, buddy."

An hour later, we walk out the front door and toward Tristan's car, parked on the street. He came in for a little while but is leaving now. Patrick is holding Tristan's hand. He hasn't left us alone for a minute. Surprisingly, Fletcher and Harrison are lingering too.

"So . . . I wonder where I can buy cockroaches." Tristan sighs. "Is there like a market or something?"

I smile. He lost the bet. Harry is picking what we eat tomorrow night. "I'm not eating cockroaches, Harrison," I say. "Pick something more food-like."

Harry twists his lips as he thinks. "Umm . . ."

"Something good," Tristan says. "I want to show off my culinary skills to your mother."

I giggle. Little does he know there is no need to show off—I am utterly impressed already.

"Mom likes pasta carbonara," Patrick says. His eyes widen, as if he's surprised that he remembers that piece of information.

"I do." I smile.

"It's Harry's pick," Tristan replies.

"Umm . . ." Harry looks over to me, and I know he wants to pick something horrible but now will feel bad if I don't get my favorite meal. "Fine." He sighs. "Carbonara it is."

"Okay," Tristan says as he looks among us. "Pasta it is." His eyes come to me, and I know he's internally navigating how to say goodbye with all our spectators.

"Tricky." He messes up Patrick's hair. "Fletch and Wiz. See you tomorrow."

They all stand and wait for him to drive off.

Go inside, will you?

He reaches up and tenderly touches my face. "Anderson."

My heart nearly explodes in my chest, and I want to throw myself into his arms. "Goodbye, Tris."

Patrick still has Tristan's hand in a viselike grip. He looks up the road with a worried face. "I don't want you to go home," he stammers.

"What?" Tristan frowns.

"What if there's a drunk driver?" He looks around in a panic. "It's very dark, and . . . it's not safe."

Drunk driver.

He's referring to the way his father died.

"Darling, it's okay. There's no need to worry," I say.

Patrick's eyes are filled with tears. "What if something goes wrong?" he whispers as he looks between us. "Bad things happen to good people, Mom."

My heart breaks.

Tristan drops to his knee in front of Patrick and looks up at him. "You're worried about me driving home?" He frowns as he pushes the hair back from Patrick's forehead.

Patrick fidgets nervously with his fingers and nods, ashamed.

Tristan stares at him for a moment and then stands. "Okay."

"Okay what?" Patrick replies.

"Okay, I won't go home."

I frown.

He takes Patrick's hand and begins to walk back into the house. "Come on. I'll sleep on the couch."

"Tris, it's okay. You don't have to," I reply.

He turns back to me. "Yeah, I do, Claire. I don't want him to worry about anything, least of all me." He turns, and with Fletch and Harry trailing behind them, they disappear into the house.

I blink . . . huh?

What just happened?

I stand in the dark and stare at my house.

I don't want him to worry about anything, least of all me.

Emotion overwhelms me, and I get a lump in my throat. It's been so long since I've felt like this.

It feels nice.

I toss and turn as I try to get comfortable.

Who fucking designed this piece-of-shit couch? They should be fired on the spot.

What if there's a drunk driver?

Patrick's words come back to me, and my heart breaks . . . that poor little kid.

He's so small, half the size of other kids his age; he has reading difficulties; and now I find out that he's so traumatized about drunk drivers that he worries.

God, what a nightmare.

I think about how excited he was that I was staying, and I smile to myself.

I hear the stair creak, and I glance up to see Claire tiptoeing down in the darkness. She's wearing a white nightdress, her hair is in a messy braid, and she looks as beautiful as ever. I scoot over to make room.

"Hi." She smiles as she sits beside me on the couch.

"Hi." I put my hand on her thigh. *Finally, I can touch her.*

She brushes the hair back from my forehead as she watches me in the darkness.

We stare at each other, and it's there between us, this magical spell she casts on me. It swirls in the air, steals my breath, and makes me ache for her.

She cups my face in her hand and stares at me for a moment. "I love you, Tristan," she whispers.

I get a lump in my throat as my eyes search hers.

"A . . . great deal, actually."

"It's about fucking time, Anderson," I whisper.

She smiles as she leans down and kisses me softly. Her lips linger over mine. Our faces meld together as we hold each other tight.

This is special . . . *she* is special.

"I . . ."

She puts her finger over my lips. "This isn't about how you feel," she cuts me off. "This is about me . . . loving you. I wanted to tell you, and I know it's premature. But I can't hold it in anymore. It doesn't matter how you feel about me, but I wanted you to know how I feel about you."

I smile up at the beautiful woman in front of me, and I tuck a piece of her hair behind her ear.

I do love you.

I pull her down to me, and we kiss more urgently. My tongue swipes through her open lips with a hunger for intimacy. "This needs to be celebrated."

"I know." She smiles against my lips. "But we can't." We kiss again. "Not yet," she breathes.

"Can you lie with me for a while?" I whisper.

"I can do that." She gets under my blanket and lies half over my body and kisses my chest.

We lie together in the darkness. It's quiet, and I can feel her heartbeat against my chest. It's not sexual or urgent but a closeness and a sense of belonging to each other.

A deep connection.

She's snuggled into my chest, and I smile into the darkness. *She loves me.*

For the first time in my life, I feel at home.

We walk down the bustling street. "That went well," I say. We just had a meeting across town, and a price was agreed to on a company we have been trying to get for over twelve months.

"It did," Fletcher replies.

"Watch what happens now," I say. "They will suddenly be urgent for the takeover to happen."

"Why is that?"

"This is what happens—they resist and resist so that by the time we take over, they are so over it that they just want to get out."

"No way," Fletcher gasps as he stops in front of a shop window. He takes out his phone and takes a photo of something.

"What?" I ask as I go back to see what he's looking at.

"That's Harrison's screen saver."

"What is?" I frown.

"The rocket. It's a model that you have to build."

"Huh?" I peer into the shop to see a huge red-and-gold rocket with all the bells and whistles on display. "Harry likes this kind of thing?" I frown.

"This is his ultimate. Mom won't buy it for him because she says he won't be able to do it. It's way too hard. He's asked for it two Christmases in a row."

I stare at the model as my mind races. Hmm . . . "Very interesting," I mutter under my breath.

"Wait till I send him the pic. He's going to go batshit crazy," Fletcher whispers.

I smile as I stare at the elusive spaceship. "That's a normal state for him, isn't it?"

Fletch shrugs. "I guess."

"Let's check it out." I walk into the store, and the bell goes off over the door. This *is* very old school.

"Can I help you?" an old man with white hair asks. He looks a little like Santa Claus.

"Yes, I was interested in the spaceship model in the window."

"Oh." He twists his hands together. "That's for experienced modelers only. I doubt you would be able to complete it."

I stare at him deadpan. Don't assume you know what I can do. "And what makes you think we wouldn't be able to do this?"

"Well." He gives me a condescending smile. "I can see you are not a modeler."

"How so?"

"Well." He holds his hands up toward Fletcher and me. "Your suits tell me you are in big business."

Fletcher and I exchange a glance. Don't piss me off, old man. "We'll take it," I snap.

"I must advise—"

"Wrap it up," I cut him off.

He raises his eyebrows. "Very well." He disappears out the back.

"Old wanker," I whisper.

"I know, right?" Fletcher whispers back.

Five whole minutes later he comes back with the biggest box I've ever seen. "That will be six hundred and twenty-five dollars."

"What?" My eyes widen. "For a toy?"

He gives me that smile again, and I imagine myself hitting him over the head with the gigantic box.

"Fine," I snap as I take out my wallet. "This better take us to the moon when it's built."

"*If* it's built." He smirks.

I raise an eyebrow at the know-it-all old man. "You know, it wouldn't hurt to brush up on your customer service . . . it's severely lacking."

He smiles sweetly. "We don't do returns, so when you realize I was right and you were wrong, don't ask for your money back, Mr. . . . Big Business."

I stare at the man over the counter as I imagine myself sticking the rocket up his ass.

Fletcher grabs my arm to distract me. "Goodbye," he says as he pulls me from the shop.

We stumble out onto the street with the huge box. "What's his fucking problem?" I whisper angrily. "I hate that old bastard."

"Yeah, well, I'm pretty sure he hates you too."

"Tristan, your mother is on her way down to your office." Sammia's voice comes through my intercom.

"Thanks, Sam."

I hit send on the email I've been writing. Then . . . knock, knock.

"Come in," I call.

My mother's warm smile comes into view, and I stand immediately. "Hello, Mom." I rush to her and kiss her cheek.

"Hello, darling." She hugs me. "I just came to check on my favorite son."

I chuckle. She says that to all four of us . . . apparently, we are each her favorite son.

"Take a seat. Do you want some tea?" I ask.

"Yes, please, that would be lovely." She sits down and crosses her legs.

I hit the intercom. "Sammia, can you ask someone to bring in some tea for Mom, please?"

"Sure can."

"Thanks." My attention turns back to my mother. "So . . ."

"So . . ." She widens her eyes with a smile. "I've had a hysterical Melina at our apartment all day."

"Oh God." I roll my eyes.

"Don't roll your eyes, Tristan. She's very hurt."

"Mom." I stand in exasperation. "We broke up six months ago."

"You were taking a break."

"There's no such thing as a break, Mom. That's what you say to try and make it less painful. As soon as you hear the word *break* . . . it means it's over. Everyone knows that."

She exhales heavily and looks at me.

"What?"

"She said you're seeing someone."

"I am." I lean my behind on my desk and fold my arms . . . here we go.

"Why haven't you told me?"

"Because you're still playing tea parties with Melina three times a week." I sigh. "And I don't need anyone's approval, Mom . . . not this time."

She watches me, and I know a million questions are on the tip of her tongue. "Who is she?"

I clench my jaw. I am not in the mood for this. "Her name is Claire."

"And *who* is Claire."

I smile. "Somebody . . . special."

She watches me intently. "It's serious, then?"

"Yes."

"She's divorced?"

"Widowed. Three boys. And yes, Mom, I'm in love with her," I snap.

Her eyebrows rise in surprise. "How old is she?"

My eyes drop to the ground.

"How old is she, Tristan?"

"Thirty-eight."

"So—" She cuts herself off.

"So what, Mom? What do you want to say?"

"Tristan." She pauses, as if choosing her words carefully. "If you end up with this woman, you won't have children of your own. She doesn't have much time—that's if she even wanted to."

"Probably not." I inhale sharply. I hate the cold hard facts.

"And you're okay with this?"

"I have to be, Mom. It is what it is, and I can't turn off my feelings for her. I tried that already. And perhaps she could, Mom. She's only thirty-eight, and you never know. We may be blessed with a child."

"Tris," she whispers. "It will take years for her to be ready to start again with another man. By then it will be too late. Deep down you already know that."

I screw up my face. The truth hurts. "Don't."

"How can I not worry, darling?"

"Mom." I shrug. "Trust me on this. Claire is nothing like anyone I've ever dated before. You will like her. There's a lot to like about this woman . . . everything, actually."

Her worried eyes hold mine.

"I'm bringing her on Saturday night."

She rolls her eyes.

"What does that mean?"

"It means . . . I'll see you on Saturday night." She stands.

"You're leaving?"

"Yes." She sighs.

I exhale heavily, annoyed with how our conversation has gone. "And cut ties with Melina, please. She's my ex-girlfriend. It's weird."

"Tristan, I'm friends with all of your ex-girlfriends. I can't just cut them off like you."

I roll my eyes.

"I just don't know how you can be so coldhearted to these women who love you. My heart breaks for them. Melina is absolutely devastated."

"She'll get over it." I look my mother in the eye. "She doesn't love me, Mom. She loves my money and my surname. Just like the rest of them did." I shake my head in disgust.

"Why would you say that?" she snaps.

"Because it's the truth. You be nice to Claire . . . she's important to me."

She marches to the door and then looks back. "I want my son to have his own family."

"And I will," I snap. "It just may not fit into your perfect little box."

She shakes her head and leaves in a huff, and I stare at the door she's disappeared through.

A knock sounds at the door. "Hello," I call.

Fletcher pokes his head around the door. "Hi," he says nervously. "I've got the tea you wanted."

"Hey, buddy." I fall into my seat, and I gesture to my desk. "Bring it in."

He walks in and with shaky hands puts it down onto the desk. He lingers, as if waiting, and my eyes rise to meet his.

"I heard what your mother said," he says softly.

I bite my bottom lip in anger. "I'm sorry. Ignore her."

"She doesn't want you to date my mom?" His eyes search mine.

I shrug.

"You don't want your own kids?" he asks.

"I do." I undo my tie with a sharp snap. "But I want your mother more."

Chapter 19

Claire

I exhale heavily and stare at the spreadsheet on the computer screen in front of me.

I can't believe I rejected Gabriel's offer of help. What was I thinking?

Obviously . . . I clearly wasn't.

God. I pinch the bridge of my nose. This is a nightmare. We just lost the biggest advertising campaign we had, and it's not getting any better. I'm going to have to let more people go this month.

Fuck's sake . . . we're running on skeleton staff as it is.

I don't know how we can possibly do what we have to do—and do it well—with the number of staff that we now have.

I put my head into my hands and let out a dejected sigh. This is hard. Harder than hard.

I don't know what I'm doing. How the hell do I keep us above water for much longer? If only Wade were here. He would know what to do. He was the brains of our business. Give him a problem, and he could work out a way around it. He saw problems as challenges or learning curves. Nothing was too big an obstacle for him.

But he's gone . . . and now it's just me.

God, I feel so out of my depth. I sit and stare at the computer screen for a long time.

Maybe if I stare at it long enough, the answer will come to me like magic.

What do I do?

What direction should I move in? I know something has to change . . . but what?

Stop.

Stop being so negative. I can pull us out of this. I know I can.

Reconfigure a few processes, move a few accounts. Streamline the advertising again.

It will be okay . . . it has to be.

Giving up this company is not an option.

I won't go down without a fight, and damn it, it *will* be okay. I'll make damn sure of it.

My office door opens in a rush. "Just this way," Marley says to someone.

A man comes through the door with the biggest bunch of red roses I have ever seen.

"Delivery for Claire Anderson."

"That's me," I reply.

The roses have huge heads with a deep perfume and are in the most beautiful crystal vase. He places them down on my desk. "Sign here, please."

I sign in the allocated box. "Thank you." I smile broadly.

"You're welcome. Although I have an admission. I didn't buy them."

Marley and I laugh. The joke isn't funny, but we are so excited that we would laugh at anything, it seems.

With a kind nod, he leaves us alone, and I open the card.

I'M A VERY HAPPY MAN TODAY.

#TOBELOVEDBYYOU

TRIS

XOX

An over-the-top smile beams from my face, and Marley snatches the card from me.

She reads it, and her eyes rise to meet mine in confusion. "What does that mean?"

I roll my lips.

"To be loved by you." She frowns.

I shrug.

Her eyes widen. "You love him?"

I give her a lopsided smile.

"You told him you love him?" She gasps.

I swing my chair back to my computer. "Yes, Marley. I admit it; I'm in love with Tristan Miles."

She falls into a seated position on my desk and stares at me for a while in disbelief.

"Well . . . holy fucking shit," she says as she puts her hands on her hips. "I was not expecting that."

"Me neither."

"So . . . what?" She stares at me for a moment as she tries to process the new information. "I mean, I knew you had that week of lunch fucks."

I smile at her analogy. "Sounds so romantic when you put it like that."

"You know what I mean." She smirks. "But what happened then? And more importantly, why the fuck haven't you told me about any of this?"

"I was just waiting to see what happened, and I didn't want to jinx it."

"Jinx it?"

"Well, sometimes when you put something out there, it doesn't turn out how you expect it to."

"So . . . this *is* turning out?" She frowns in surprise.

"Oh, Marley," I gush as I look at my beautiful flowers. "Tristan is just so . . ." I search for the right words. "Funny and sweet and understanding, and he sleeps on the couch at my house out of respect for my kids."

She screws up her face in disbelief. "Tristan Miles?"

"Uh-huh."

"Tristan Miles, the arrogant, gorgeous playboy?" she repeats, as if not believing me.

I smile with a nod. "Yep, that's him."

She frowns at me. "I'm so confused. I thought he was a hot player who had excellent fucking capabilities."

I laugh out loud. "He's all of those things, but there's more to him." I read my card again.

I'M A VERY HAPPY MAN TODAY.

#TOBELOVEDBYYOU

TRIS

XOX

"To be loved by you." I hold the card to my chest.

And he is.

Marley smiles as she watches me, and finally she says, "I love seeing you like this."

"Like what, all dreamy and starry eyed like a schoolgirl?"

"Happy."

I smile softly. "Thanks. I really am." I put the card carefully back into its envelope. I'll keep it in a safe place with the other card from the last lot of roses he gave me.

331

Everything from Tristan is special.

"I'm meeting his family on Saturday night at a black-tie dinner," I say.

"Oh jeez." Her eyes widen. "What are you wearing?"

"No idea. This is my worst nightmare."

"What do you have in your wardrobe?"

"Nothing. I haven't bought an evening dress in years. What the hell do you even wear to a black-tie dinner these days?"

"We'll go shopping. Don't worry; we'll find you something. You have to look amazing."

"I know." Nerves flutter in my stomach as I imagine meeting his parents and older brother, Jameson. I know their opinions are important to Tris. "I want to look understated sexy, not like mutton dressed up as lamb. Something age appropriate but not motherly."

"Definitely," Marley says as she thinks. "I'm going to google this."

"Dress sense doesn't come up on Google, Marley."

"No, but stylists do." She wiggles her eyebrows.

"I can't afford a stylist."

"What you can't afford is to look like a bag of shit. This is his announcement to the world that you and he are together. It's an important event, and everyone is going to be looking at you. Don't worry; we'll give her a strict budget to work with."

I stare at her as I process her advice. "Do you think? Isn't getting a stylist a bit over the top?"

"Claire, everyone in that ballroom is going to use a stylist, and besides, this is New York. Nothing is over the top. I got this. Leave it to me."

I pull onto my street and see the black Aston Martin parked in my driveway, and I bite my lip to stifle my smile.

He beat me home.

Tristan Miles is at my house . . . *with my kids.*

Wonders never cease.

I give a subtle shake of my head in disbelief as I go over the last few months. What a whirlwind.

I've gone from hating him to tolerating him to sleeping with him to loving him.

I pull into the driveway and park my car alongside his . . . and I do love him.

Regardless of what happens in the future, I love Tristan. I can happily admit it now.

I walk in through the front door to the sound of oohs and aahs.

"Oh my God, Mom. Look at this," Harry cries in excitement.

I turn the corner to see them all hunched over the dining table, a huge box front and center before them.

"Hello," I call.

"Mom, look what Tristan got us," Harry screams.

I haven't seen him this excited in forever. "What?" I ask as my eyes flick to the gigantic box.

"The rocket ship model." He gasps.

My mouth falls open. "The what?"

Harry reads the back of the box. "Holy hell, look at this," he cries as he points to something on the back of the box.

I blink as I try to keep up with what is going on here. "Tris, that model is stupidly expensive."

Tristan's eyes rise to meet mine, and he gives me a slow, sexy smile. "Anderson."

I smile as my stomach flips . . . I know that tone, and I know that nickname.

"What have you done?" I ask.

"I bought Wiz a present." He shrugs casually. "He won the bet fair and square and then didn't get to eat cockroaches. It was only right that I pay up."

I stare at him.

"And it's for the other boys as well. We're all going to do it together."

The boys all smile broadly as they lean over the box and read it out loud.

"Take it out of the box and lay it all out in the colored numbers. Keep the pieces in their individual bags, though. I'm going to change my clothes," Tristan says as he walks out into the living room.

The boys begin to chatter in excitement as they begin to open the box. "Get the scissors," Harry directs.

I see something from the corner of my eye, and I turn to see Tristan giving me a come-here curl of his finger. I glance back to the boys to see that they are completely distracted, and I give him a subtle nod.

He disappears up the stairs to my bedroom, and I wait for a few moments. "I'm going to get the washing off the line," I say, and then I go out the back door and walk around the front and come in the front door and sneak up the stairs.

I walk into my bedroom, and he pounces on me like a tiger. He flicks the lock on the door and pins me to the wall.

"Anderson," he whispers darkly. His lips take mine.

I smile. "Hi."

He grinds himself up against me, and I can feel that he's hard. He holds my face as he kisses me deeply.

"You seem very pleased to see me." I smile.

"Needy," he murmurs against my lips.

"Needy for what?" I breathe.

He bites my neck. "I need to be fucked, Anderson . . . and as my designated fuckee, you need to find a way to make that happen. Tonight."

I smile as his hand goes to my behind, and he drags my body over his. His teeth graze my neck, and I smile up at the ceiling. He's not joking; he really does need to be fucked. I can feel the need oozing out of him.

"How am I going to do that?" I whisper.

"I don't know. Get creative." He pushes me back against the wall hard, and my body weakens under his power.

"On the couch tonight—or in the laundry." He kisses me again. "Fuck me in my car out on the street, for all I care. I just need you to fuck me."

"Your car is too small," I tease.

He grabs my behind aggressively and bites my bottom lip, and I whimper.

"Don't dis the car." With his eyes locked on mine, he bends and slides his hand up my thigh and through the leg of my panties. The backs of his fingers slide through my dripping wet flesh.

He clenches his jaw as his eyes flicker with arousal.

We stare at each other as the air swirls between us. I've never had this before.

A physical attraction so strong that all else pales in comparison.

"Or you could fuck me now," he murmurs as he slides a finger in deep.

My eyes flutter closed. God, that feels good. "The children," I whisper.

"Are distracted." He unzips his trousers and falls into a seated position on the side of the bed and then brings me over to straddle him. He lifts my skirt and pulls my panties to the side and in one sharp movement slides home deep.

Our mouths fall open at the overwhelming pleasure. Our eyes are locked, and electricity crackles through the air like lightning.

He inhales sharply as we stare at each other.

"So . . . you love me," he whispers as his lips take mine.

I begin to slowly rock back and forth. Oh . . . this is good. The feeling of him inside of me is just too good.

I smile and kiss his lips with an open mouth. "I do."

He puts his mouth to my ear. "Fuck me like you hate me," he whispers.

His grip tightens on my behind, and he begins to move me aggressively over his cock.

Suddenly we are frantic. He's lifting me and bouncing me down hard onto him, and I'm trying to hold in my moans. But it's hard to stay silent when your whole world is in beautiful Technicolor. He puts his hands on the backs of my shoulders and begins to really bring me down hard onto his large cock, and sharp, shooting stars of ecstasy begin to make me shudder. His mouth hangs slack as he watches me. "Fuck me," he mouths. "Fuck me harder, Anderson."

I bring my feet up onto the bed behind him, bringing me into a squat.

We both fall still at the deep position.

He shudders. His eyes close, and I know this is it. The position he was craving.

"I hate you," I whisper.

He chuckles and bites my earlobe. Goose bumps scatter up my arms. "I hate you too," he whispers into my ear with a sharp nip. "Hate me harder."

I smile as he slams me down, and I shudder. He holds himself deep and does the same. I feel from the telling jerk of his cock that he's right here with me.

We fly to the moon and back, and waves of pleasure bounce between us as we both come in a rush, and then eventually . . . and slowly . . . we come back to earth.

Our hearts race, and he cups my face in his hands as he kisses me tenderly.

"Did you buy my children a spaceship so that we'd have time to sneak away and have sex?"

"Absolutely," he pants. "One hundred percent."

I giggle as I climb off him. I can't believe this—he cares if they like him. He doesn't want to be tolerated; he wants to be a part of us. This is the first night in forever that everyone has been happy together at the same time . . . including me. "Genius." I kiss him softly. "Now get out before they find you in here."

He flops back onto the bed, arms wide, his zipper undone with his dick hanging out, and I put my hand over my mouth to stop myself from laughing out loud.

He looks up at me. "What?"

"Too bad you have to go and build a rocket ship now . . . isn't it?"

He drops his head back onto the bed. "Fuck. Don't remind me." He holds his hand out, and I take it. He pulls me down on top of him. He kisses me softly as he brushes the hair back from my forehead. "It was worth it."

Ninety minutes later

"This is bullshit," Tristan snaps.

"Language," I remind him as I chop onions, and I smile as I look over at the four boys sitting around the dining table.

"What kind of imbecile packages things like this?" Tristan mutters.

They go through the bags and slide them from one place to another as they count.

"Not this way. That way," Harrison snaps.

"What are you going on about over there?" I ask. "You haven't even started it yet?"

"There are one hundred and forty—" Tristan mutters.

"Forty-five," Harrison interrupts.

"One hundred and forty-five ziplock bags of parts in this box, Claire."

The parts are all perfectly compartmentalized into color-coded ziplock bags. They are trying to locate a missing bag.

I smirk as I watch him lose his cool for the tenth time in twenty minutes. "If it's too hard for you . . . take it back."

"No!" the boys all cry in unison.

"Oh . . . we're taking it back," Tristan hisses through gritted teeth. "We're taking it back completely built, and I'm going to stick it in the old buzzard where the sun doesn't shine. I'm putting an engine on this mofo, and we're going to fly it through his damn shop window."

Patrick looks up at Tristan. "What, in the nighttime?" He frowns as he climbs onto his lap.

"Yeah, Tricky, that's it. Nighttime," he mutters, distracted.

"Why do you dislike this shopkeeper so much?" I ask as I continue to chop.

"He was a jerkoff," Tristan mutters.

"Tristan . . . language," I remind him.

He looks up and frowns. "*Jerk off* isn't a swear word. It's a verb, Claire . . . a doing word."

I roll my eyes, and Fletcher chuckles.

"If you can't say it in church, it *is* a swear word," Patrick announces.

"I'm pretty sure that priests know the meaning of the word," Tristan mutters dryly.

"Why didn't you look at the instructions before you bought it?" I ask.

"I would have, except these aren't instructions." He holds up a bound book. "These are directions on how to go insane. People have been institutionalized while reading this book, Claire." He flicks through the book in disgust. "Nobody can understand these instructions. The smartest man in the world couldn't."

I smile. So damn dramatic. "I thought you were the smartest man in the world," I say.

"Well, precisely. I am," he adds. "But how can I put something together when I can't even understand the stupid instructions?"

"Give me that," Harrison sneers as he snatches the booklet from Tristan. He studies the pictures and then frowns and begins to go through the bags again.

"Watch out, Tricky." Tristan taps his little lap sitter. "Hop up, buddy. I need a coffee." He stands and grabs a mug from the cupboard.

"You don't want a glass of wine?" I ask.

He looks at me deadpan as he begins collecting what he needs for his coffee. "Do I appear to be relaxed to you, Claire? Does this look like a relaxing moment in time?"

I smile as I stare at him. He's in navy boxer shorts, hair all messed up from nearly pulling it out. His sleepy orgasm glow is long gone, even though it was only a little while ago. I giggle.

"What?" he mutters as he pours the coffee into his cup.

"Maybe this model thing wasn't such a great idea?" I say.

"We'll get it," he says with renewed determination as he stirs his coffee. "If it's the last fucking thing I do," he whispers under his breath. "And it might be."

I kiss his shoulder, and it momentarily snaps him out of his stress. He kisses my forehead. "Stop distracting the genius at work," he replies as he goes back to the table.

I giggle and look up to see that Fletcher has just been watching our interaction.

He gives me a lopsided smile and turns his attention back to the model.

A frisson of guilt runs through me. Is it weird for him seeing me with another man?

Should I talk to him about this?

339

What would I say? Hmm . . . I'm going to have to think about this in great detail. I don't want to overdramatize it, but then I don't want to sweep it under the rug either.

"That's it!" Harry yells.

"What is?"

"The bags—they are the wrong colors compared to what's in the instructions. That's why nothing is adding up. It's all labeled wrong."

"What?" Fletcher frowns.

"The red parts are orange, and the orange parts are red. The black parts are white, and the white parts are gray. That's why we can't find all the pieces. The colors are all wrong."

Tristan punches his fist. "Why you . . . tick tock . . . old man."

"Yeah," Harrison growls. "Tick tock."

"Hmm." The stylist's eyes roam up and down my body as she circles me. "We have a lot to work with here." She fiddles with my hair and tucks it behind my ears. She messes it up with her fingers as she inspects me in great detail.

My eyes flick to Marley, and she gives me two thumbs-up, the universal symbol of "You can do this."

It's Wednesday, and I'm at the dreaded appointment with the personal stylist. "You're gorgeous, Claire; there is no doubt about it. Your bone structure is flawless, and you have a beautiful figure. But you don't dress accordingly. Why don't you show it off more?"

"Oh." I shrug bashfully.

"You need to wear more fitted things."

"I just don't want to look like I'm trying to be young," I reply meekly.

"You are young, Claire. You're only what? Early thirties?"

"I'm thirty-eight."

She smiles as she runs her hand down my shoulder and readjusts my bra strap. "I style eighty-year-olds. Trust me. You are young." She smiles as she stands back to look at me. "Now, what do you need?"

"I have a black-tie dinner on Saturday night."

"Okay." She holds my hair up and looks at it. "At what time is it?"

I frown, and Marley grabs my phone. Tristan sent me the invitation. "Seven p.m."

"Okay." She takes out her phone and makes a call. "Hello, Marcello."

She listens for a moment. "Hello, darling. Listen, I have a favor. Can you do hair and makeup for me on Saturday night, please?"

I frown, and my eyes flick to Marley.

"Oh . . . it's an emergency. I'm going to send you images of exactly what we need."

Emergency. I widen my eyes in horror, and Marley drops her head to hide her smile.

"Yes, we have a Cinderella here." She listens, and her eyes sweep up and down my body. "Okay great, I'll text you the address." She hangs up. "Okay, that's sorted out."

I smile nervously.

"Marcello will come to your place and do your hair and makeup late on Saturday afternoon."

I bite my lip to hide my smile. I've never had that before. "Is that necessary?"

"Oh my God, darling. Yes. It's necessary. Now . . . let's go shopping. I know exactly what you need."

"Okay, thanks, Barb." I smile. I rest my foot on top of Tristan's leg. It's Thursday night, and Tristan and I are having a glass of wine and watching television in the living room. The boys have miraculously done their homework, dinner is finished and cleaned up, and now they have a precious two hours to work on their model. This bribery of Tristan's is the best thing since sliced bread. Everyone is behaving and hustling to get things done quickly so they can work on it together.

It's like the freaking twilight zone or some shit.

"Are you sure that's okay?" I listen to my girlfriend as we speak on the phone. I'm arranging for Harry to stay at her place on Saturday night. Fletcher is staying here with two friends, and Patrick is taken care of, but it's Harry that I have to really check on.

"Of course, Claire, he'll be fine. We will get pizza and watch movies."

"Thanks so much. I'll see you then."

"Okay, see you on Saturday," she replies, and I hang up.

Tristan raises an eyebrow. "We good?" he asks hopefully.

"All good." I smile. "Who knew that Tristan Miles would be excited about locking in a babysitter?"

He chuckles and clinks his glass with mine. "Right?"

"Seriously, though, it is a relief. Barb is the only one I would leave Harrison with."

"What's gone on with Harrison in the past to make you so nervous about leaving him?"

I let out a big sigh. "He can be a nightmare."

"How? I mean, I know he's a bit mischievous and all that, but isn't that normal at his age?"

I sit back and sip my wine. "Oh hell, where do I start? He's been suspended from school. He disappears for hours at a time and then lies about where he's been, sneaks off to friends' houses without permission. He's fallen in with this party crowd but then denies he's been with them."

"Suspended from school—what for?"

I roll my eyes. "For some reason, he's under the impression that the teachers pick on him. One day he got a project back, and he thought he should have gotten a higher grade, and he got into a full-blown argument with his teacher."

"So . . . he was cheeky?" Tris frowns.

"No." I shake my head in embarrassment. "He opened the window and threw his assignment out of it in protest."

Tristan's eyes widen.

"But that's not the worst of it. It accidently hit a janitor who was walking past and scratched his head. They thought he needed stitches. It was mortifying."

Tristan bites his bottom lip as he tries to hide a smile.

"It was so embarrassing—you have no idea, Tristan."

He sips his wine as he pulls a straight face. "I can imagine."

I smile and rub my foot up his calf muscle. "Thank you."

His eyes hold mine as his fingers draw a circle on my shoulder. "For what?"

"For making the trek out to see me every night." I shrug bashfully. "I know you hate the couch."

He raises his eyebrows. "Well . . . I hate being at home without you more."

I smile and lean in and put my head on his shoulder. It's so nice having someone . . . wonderful, actually. He kisses my forehead, and we go back to watching television and our blissful silence. He doesn't even have to talk to me.

Him just being here is enough to make me happy.

"You know, as I was walking in here today, a bowerbird swooped at my balls."

I sit up with a frown. "A what?"

"A bowerbird."

"What's that?" I ask.

He rolls his eyes at my apparent stupidity. "Everyone knows what a bowerbird is, Claire. I suggest you google it."

I stare at him in question, and after a while he replies, "A bowerbird collects blue things, Claire." He raises an eyebrow as he waits for me to get it.

Oh . . . he's telling me he has blue balls. I smirk. "Whatever."

"Tristan," a voice calls out from the kitchen.

He smiles as his eyes widen. "Did you hear that?" he whispers.

"What?" I frown.

He raises his eyebrows as he waits for it, and eventually, the voice calls out again. "Tristan."

"That's the first time he's ever said my name."

"Harry's never said your name?" I frown.

He gives a subtle shake of his head.

"Tristan," Harry calls.

Tristan smiles broadly. "Yes, Wiz, what is it?"

"Can you help us for a minute, please?"

He raises his eyebrows in excitement at being needed. "Coming." He jumps up and makes his way into the kitchen. I listen to them talking about the diameter of a part that they are trying to work out. Tristan seems to think that it's put together backward, and they are in a deep discussion about the pros and cons of pulling it back apart and starting that piece again.

As I listen, I find myself smiling like a goofball at the television.

Happiness is to be loved by you.

"Let him in," Tristan says over the phone. He glances over at me and gives me a sexy wink as he hangs up. "Your hairdresser is here, Ms. Anderson," he teases.

"Oh God." I put my head into my hands in dismay. "This seems . . ."

"Normal." He kisses my temple as he walks past me and into the living area. "I'm going to go out for a while and leave you to it."

"Where are you going?" I frown. It feels weird being in his apartment without him.

"I'm meeting Elliot and Christopher at a bar to watch the game. I'll be back around six. We leave around six forty-five."

That will give me time to wash off the makeup and hair before he gets back if I don't like it. "Okay." I smile.

He kisses me softly. His lips linger over mine, and I hold him tight. "Do you need anything while I'm out?"

"Just for you to come home."

A knock sounds at the door.

He hugs me tight with a big smile. "Goodbye." He opens the door in a rush, and we are both taken aback.

The hairdresser is male . . . and hot. Like stupid hot.

He's European, in his early thirties, and has blue tight jeans and a black T-shirt on. He's muscular and fit looking.

Tristan's eyes flick to me in horror, and I smile goofily. I know exactly what he's thinking. "Hello." He holds out his hand to shake the man's. "Tristan Miles."

"Hi, I'm Marcello," the man replies in a heavy accent as he shakes his head. "I'm here to style Claire."

"Hello, that's me." I shake his hand.

He looks me up and down and rubs his hands together playfully. "Oh . . . this is going to be so fun."

Tristan looks at him deadpan and then at me. "No . . . this is going to be completely funless for you . . . or else," he mutters dryly.

Marcello laughs. "Oh . . . so possessive of his woman. I love that."

Tristan's jaw clenches, and I giggle as Marcello grabs my shoulders and turns me away from him. "Goodbye. She will be beautiful for you when you return."

"She already is," Tristan snaps, unimpressed. "And I'm not going anywhere. I'll be right out here." He flops onto the couch in disgust.

I giggle. He's actually ruffled . . . I love it.

"Through here." I guide Marcello to Tristan's en suite bathroom, and he puts his two big bags on the floor. He looks me up and down again. He sits me in the chair and gives me a broad smile.

"Let us begin."

Three hours later I stare at my reflection in the mirror. I hardly recognize myself.

My dark hair is set into Hollywood curls, and my makeup is out of this world. It's all gold and bronze with fanned eyelashes and big red lips. I look like a movie star or something. It's . . . just wow.

I'm in a black lace strapless bra and panties with a garter belt and a white dressing gown over the top. I'll put my dress on soon. Tristan is getting ready in the other bathroom. I heard him come home about half an hour ago. My eyes roam over my face and hair and down over my curves in the sexy lingerie, and I smile at my reflection. I've never seen myself look like this, and damn it, I'm going to make more of an effort moving forward.

Tristan loves me motherly . . . but hell, he deserves sexy. And I'm going to try my hardest to be that for him.

He loves me.

It's funny, you know—Tris has never said those elusive three words. But he doesn't have to. I already know that he loves me.

Every action, every message, every effort he makes to get along with my sons only cements our feelings. The tenderness in his touch is like an open book, and words are irrelevant between us.

Despite our different worlds and rocky beginning, we have a beautiful relationship, and I am utterly in love with the beautiful man that he is.

The door opens, and he comes into view. He frowns and inhales sharply, as if seeing me for the first time. "Claire," he murmurs, almost to himself.

He's wearing a black dinner suit, a crisp white shirt, and black bow tie. His dark hair has a slight curl to it, just enough to give it that perfect just-fucked style. He has the squarest jaw and dark-pink and full kissable lips, and his big brown eyes hold mine as he steps forward and takes me into his arms.

Without saying a word, he takes my face into his hands and kisses me. His tongue explores my open mouth, and his hands undo the tie on the dressing gown.

I smile against his lips. I love that he has to touch me.

He steps back. His eyes roam down my lingerie-clad body, and when they rise to meet mine, they are blazing with desire. "Fuck," he murmurs.

As if something snaps inside of him, he pushes me back to the counter and lifts me to sit on top of it. He lifts my foot onto the countertop, and he stands between my open legs as his lips take mine. "You look fucking edible, Anderson," he murmurs against my lips.

As he kisses me, I open my eyes to see that his are closed.

He's completely lost in the moment, right here with me.

His hand roams over my breasts and down my stomach, down over my garter belt, and down to my panties.

"Are you wet for me?" he asks.

He puts his hand down the front of my panties and finds that sweet spot between my legs. His eyes flicker with arousal as he slides three thick fingers deep into my sex.

My back arches as he holds me tight. "We need to go," I whimper.

He watches me as his fingers again slide in deep. "No." He pumps me hard. "You need to come."

My head tips back as his strong fingers get to work. The sound of my arousal sucking him in and out echoes around the room, and his dark eyes watch my helpless face.

He's rough, so rough . . . and I shudder as my foot on the counter lifts and hangs in the air.

His kiss is aggressive, his fingers strong. My legs are up on his chest.

But it's his eyes that get me . . . locked on mine, with such a tenderness behind them.

"I love you, Claire," he whispers. My heart collapses.

Sensory overload—the best kind of sensory overload. Emotional *and* physical.

He kisses me softly, with a strong pump of his hand, and all my senses crash as I come hard.

With one hand, he holds my face to his; with his other he tenderly lets me ride out the high.

"You love me?" I whisper.

"So much." He smiles against my lips.

My heart free-falls from my chest. *God . . . I love this man.*

He unclips my garter belt and then slides my panties down, and I hover somewhere in heaven as I watch him . . . and then he does the unthinkable.

He drops to his knees in front of me and spreads my legs.

My breath catches. What's he doing?

With his dark eyes locked to mine, he pulls me apart and licks me with his long thick tongue.

My body convulses. His eyes close in pleasure as he cleans me up.

My orgasm on his tongue.

I run my fingers through his hair as I watch him. He's in a black dinner suit on his knees before me—a new arousal takes me over.

Deep and dangerously dark.

Holy hell . . . Tristan fucking Miles.

Chapter 20

The limo pulls into the large circular driveway, and I feel the nerves in my stomach dance. As if reading my mind, Tristan leans in and kisses my temple. "You look beautiful, Anderson."

I blow out a deep breath. This meet-the-family thing is nerve-racking. The driver opens the door, and Tristan gets out and takes my hand to help me. The driveway and foyer are a hive of activity as the cars roll in one after the other. Beautiful people in black-tie attire are everywhere, and I am so glad that I let Marley talk me into getting that stylist.

My dress is black and fitted, and it has a big thick band that wraps around the top of it from the waist up, creating a strapless look. It's understated and sexy. Tristan loves it and told me I'm to wear it every day. He even made our driver take photos of us before we climbed into the limo.

He leads me up the stairs and into the ballroom. People are doing double takes as they see us together. "Hi. Hello. Hello, Roger," Tristan greets people as we walk through to the seating chart.

I smirk over at him.

"What?" he asks.

"You think you're a rock star or something."

"I am a fucking rock star, Anderson. When will you get with the program and realize it?" He gives me a sexy wink, and I smile broadly, happy to admit that I'm officially a groupie. He reads the board and looks for where we're sitting. "Over here."

My stomach flutters as I look to where he gestured and see his entire family sitting at the table.

Fuck . . . the blood drains from my face.

Meeting the family is always intimidating.

Meeting the Miles family is next-level terrifying. His father is one of the most respected men in New York, and his older brother, Jameson, is known for being one of the biggest assholes in the world. I catch a glimpse of Christopher and Elliot, and I feel slightly better—they're really nice and not at all what I imagined. I'm glad that I at least know them. "Hello." Tristan smiles broadly as we approach the table. "This is Claire Anderson." He presents me like a prized pig.

"Hello." I smile awkwardly.

"This is my father, George. My mother, Elizabeth. This is Jameson and Emily, and you know Elliot and Christopher."

They all stand. George shakes my hand. "Hello, Claire, lovely to meet you."

His mother kisses my cheek. "Hello, dear, so glad you could join us."

I smile awkwardly, and Emily grabs me into an embrace and chuckles. "I am absolutely thrilled to meet you," she gasps.

I giggle into the embrace . . . okay, she isn't what I imagined.

Jameson smiles and then leans in and kisses my cheek. "Lovely to meet you, Claire. I've heard so many good things." He gives me a genuine smile, and I breathe a sigh of relief. Oh, thank God . . . he's not as scary as I thought.

"Just so you all know, I am Claire's favorite Miles. Just putting it out there," Christopher says as he raises his champagne glass to me.

"Actually, I am," Tristan replies deadpan as he pulls my chair out.

I smile and take a seat next to Emily.

Tristan sits beside me and takes my hand on my lap for reassurance.

I love him.

"So, Claire," George addresses me as the group listens in. "You own Anderson Media?"

"Yes, I do."

"Very impressive."

"Thank you."

He smiles warmly. "I knew your husband. He was a good man."

"He was."

"I attended his funeral. It was a beautiful service."

I smile sadly, wishing the conversation hadn't gone this way.

Tristan squeezes my hand, and I gratefully squeeze it back.

Elizabeth changes the subject. "So you have children?"

Oh fuck . . . this is the night from hell. "Yes." I smile. "Three boys."

"How do they like Tristan?" Christopher laughs. "I hope they're giving him a run for his money."

"It would be payback if they did," George mutters dryly. "He was a coot of a kid."

The group laughs, and I feel a little more at ease.

"Do you want to go and get a drink?" Tristan asks me.

"Yes, please," I answer a little too eagerly.

"I'll come," Emily says. She's attractive and lovely—naturally beautiful and refreshingly unpretentious.

We stand and make our way to the bar. "What do you want, babe?" Tris asks.

"Fucking anything," I whisper back.

"Okay, drunk and disorderly in front of my parents, coming right up," he replies.

I grab his hand and pull him back to me as he goes to walk off. "On second thought, one drink. Don't let me drink any more than that. Being drunk here is my worst nightmare."

He and Emily chuckle, and he turns to her. "What do you want, Em?"

"Bubbles, please."

Tristan disappears to the bar, leaving me alone with Emily. "It's pretty nerve-racking meeting them, isn't it?" Emily says.

Relief fills me—she's normal. "God, I know. I'm so nervous."

She takes my hand. "Don't be; they're really lovely. Not at all what you think."

"Thanks." I smile gratefully. "So . . ." I frown. "You're married?"

"Yes, Jay and I got married three months ago."

"Oh, that's wonderful. Congratulations."

"Thanks." She smiles. "Still in the honeymoon phase. Tristan told me that you live on Long Island?"

"Yes, it's a ways out of New York but great for the boys."

"Oh, well, we live in New Jersey."

"Really?" I ask in surprise.

"We stay in New York maybe two nights a week at most. I wanted to get Jay out of the city and into a more relaxed lifestyle."

"He's stressed?" I frown.

"God." She rolls her eyes. "Massively. His workload is ridiculous. He's a lot better since we got married, and he works from home on Fridays now."

I stare at her in a state of shock. This is not what I expected at all. The Miles Media group has always seemed so invincible . . . never in a million years would I imagine the CEO is battling stress, although it's totally understandable that he is.

Tristan reappears with our drinks and puts his arm around me and kisses my temple. "Are you all right?"

I nod. "Thanks."

"Well, there's an ugly face if I ever saw one," I hear a deep English male voice say.

We all turn to see two men walking toward us. One is blond and gorgeous. The other is tall, dark, and handsome. "Hey." Tristan laughs out loud as he pulls them into an embrace.

My eyes flick to Emily, and she laughs too.

The three men laugh, and then Tristan introduces us. "Claire, please meet Spencer Jones and Sebastian Garcia, my friends from London. And you both know Emily. Jameson and Sebastian met in Italy at college."

"I've been trying to get rid of them ever since." Sebastian smiles with a wink.

Tristan puts his hand on my shoulder and pulls me close, and Emily laughs. "How are my favorite London villains?" she asks.

It's obvious she knows them quite well.

"Very well," Spencer replies. He has this boyish-charm thing going on. He turns his attention back to Tristan. "Where have you been?"

"I've been here," Tristan replies. He tips his champagne glass toward me. "With Claire."

Sebastian's eyes come to me, and then he snaps his fingers, as if remembering something. "Did you two meet in France?"

"This is her." Tristan smiles broadly. Wait . . . what? He's told them about me?

I glance over to Emily, and she hunches her shoulders, as if excited.

Sebastian glances over and sees Jameson talking to some men and walks up and grabs him in a headlock from behind. They laugh loudly. "Back in a minute," Tristan whispers, and he and Spencer join them.

The four men laugh as they talk, and I watch them for a moment. "Who are they?" I ask.

"They are the naughtiest men in all of England," Emily whispers. "And the most gorgeous."

"God," I whisper as I watch them. I have never seen such handsome men all in one place. All of them are freaking delicious. "You're not wrong."

"Spencer Jones is the world's biggest player."

"He's the blond?" I ask.

"That's him. Ridiculously good looking, isn't he?"

"The other one is more gorgeous. What's his name again?" I ask.

"Sebastian Garcia. His marriage just broke up recently."

"Really? He's a player too?" I frown.

"No, his wife slept with their gardener."

"What?" I frown as I look at the beautiful man. He's tall, dark, and European. "Is she mad?" I gasp.

"Apparently." She shrugs. "Must be absolutely off her fucking tree," she mutters.

I giggle, and Emily smiles and clinks her glass with mine. "It's so good to finally meet you," she whispers as she again takes my hand in hers.

"Oh, thanks." I smile. "Thank God you're normal. I thought you were going to be a supermodel taking selfies all night."

She bursts out laughing. "Ha. No, that would be Tristan's ex-girlfriends."

I cringe. "I don't really fit the mold, do I?"

"Thankfully not." She laughs.

I glance over and into the gaze of Tristan in his black dinner suit. His dark wavy hair and square jaw light up the room. He gives me a slow, sexy smile and a wink, and my heart somersaults in my chest.

I'm feeling like the luckiest girl in the world tonight.

He loves me.

Tristan's fingers trail a circle on my bare shoulder as I sit at the table and talk to Emily. It's been a great night filled with laughter, handsome men, and intelligent conversation.

Not at all what I expected.

From the corner of my eye I can see Elizabeth watching the two of us together. She hasn't had to look very hard—Tristan has been all over me all night. He's most definitely not shy with affection.

"The boys are going to a bar for a few drinks. Do you want to go?" Tristan leans in and whispers.

"Are you going?" I ask as I turn to Emily.

"Apparently." She smirks into her wineglass. "I've had enough champagne for a lifetime . . . but whatever."

"Me too." I giggle, but it will be nice to get to know everyone in a not-so-formal setting. "Okay, sure, sounds good."

We say our goodbyes, and twenty minutes later I find myself outside and waiting on the curb for a limo with Emily, the four Miles brothers, and Spencer Jones.

Everybody has had too much to drink, and we are cackling like schoolgirls. These guys are hilarious.

"Where the fuck is Seb?" Spencer frowns, looking around the crowd as people pour out of the function center.

"He's with two girls inside," Elliot replies as he types a message to someone on his phone.

"Jesus Christ," Spencer whispers. "If he doesn't hurry, we're leaving without him."

"I'm pretty sure he doesn't give a fuck," Elliot replies flatly.

Tristan takes his jacket off and puts it around my shoulders. He pulls me into his arms and smiles down at me. I have the urge to kiss him, but I won't . . . everyone is here. He leans down and kisses me anyway, and I smile against his lips. He knows what I want.

Sebastian walks out with a gorgeous girl on each arm. "The girls are coming with us," he announces.

"Hi, girls." Everyone laughs.

"What's your name?" Spencer asks the blonde as he picks up her hand and kisses it.

"Fuck off. She's with me," Sebastian says.

Spencer shrugs and turns to the brunette. "So . . . what's your name?"

"Also with me," Sebastian replies deadpan.

"Greedy prick," Spencer snaps as he drops her hand like a hot potato.

"Get your own." Sebastian winks to him.

We all laugh, and the girls cuddle closer into Sebastian. What the hell . . . *two* women?

Jeez.

I glance over to see Elliot and Christopher talking to a group of girls in the cab line. The women are all laughing on cue as the boys flirt up a storm. I imagine what these boys are like when they are out on the town together.

I wonder if Tristan has had two women before . . . of course he has. All these men have. Rich, funny, gorgeous, and intelligent.

The jackpot of eligible bachelors.

Tristan smiles goofily down at me and kisses me again. He really is quite tipsy.

And gorgeous.

Two limousines pull up, and Jameson opens the door. "Elliot, Christopher," he calls as he helps Emily into the car. We all climb in, and Sebastian and Spencer and the girls climb into the car behind us.

"Club 42, please," Tristan says.

"Sure thing." The driver smiles as he pulls out into the traffic. The boys are loud and joking, and laughter is filling the car.

The car accelerates, and I smile as I get a rush of adrenaline.

This is a fun night.

I giggle as I watch Tristan and Christopher together. They're like two peas in a pod.

They laugh at the same things, share private jokes, and finish each other's sentences. Similar looking, almost identical personalities, and nowhere near what I thought they were. Warm and friendly, not a cold soul sucker in sight.

From what I can tell, Elliot and Jameson are similar and look alike too.

It's late. Last time I looked, it was four o'clock in the morning, and we are now collectively drunk. We're in a small nightclub kind of bar, and the boys must come here a lot because they know all the staff and the DJ.

There aren't a lot of people left, and they've just called last drinks. I've had the best night ever. Emily and I have gotten on like a house on fire, and the boys are everything I never expected.

Kind and funny. Sarcastic like Tris, but lovely just the same.

"As I play the final song for the night," the DJ says into the mic, "with the Miles boys in the house, I had to play their anthem. 'Freak Me' by Silk." A tantric beat rings out.

Freak me, baby (ah, yeah)
Freak me, baby (mm, just like that)
Freak me, baby (ah, yeah)

The boys all laugh out loud and cheer. I'm instantly dragged to the dance floor, and the boys all begin to dance as if it's the best song in the world.

Tristan pushes me out and then twirls me. "What is this song?" I laugh out loud as I am bounced back to his body with force.

He smiles down at me as he moves us to the beat. "This was our boarding school anthem." He pushes me out again and then spins me and brings me back to him, and I can't contain my laughter.

"We played this song in our dorm every day for our entire schooling life. We all know it word for word."

I giggle and look around, and I see a very drunk Jameson dirty dancing with Emily as he sings to her. Elliot and Christopher have found girls somewhere and are singing to them. Sebastian is dirty dancing with his two girls, and Spencer has jumped up onstage and has dragged a waitress with him. They are slow dancing to the music. I listen to the words and laugh out loud as Tristan twirls me around.

Let me lick you up and down till you say stop
Let me play with your body, baby, make you real hot
Let me do all the things you want me to do

"This is the song you sang while at school?" I giggle. Sex maniacs, the lot of them.

"Yep." Tristan smiles down at me.

"Your favorite song was about licking women up and down?" I ask in horror.

"One hundred percent." He pushes me out and spins me hard, and I laugh out loud. He rocks us side to side as he holds my hand in his. "Still is." He leans down and kisses me softly, and his eyes twinkle with a certain something. "Speaking of which, let's go home, Anderson."

I smile up at the beautiful man in front of me. "I thought you'd never ask."

I hear a vibration on the side table, and I frown.

Bzzz . . . bzzz . . . bzzz.

Tristan lets out a deep sigh. "Who the fuck's that?" he mumbles. It stops, and we both relax.

It starts again.

Bzzz . . . bzzz . . . bzzz.

Tristan sits up onto his elbow and leans over to get my phone. He fumbles and drops it, and it slips between the bed and the side table. "Fuck off," he whispers.

My head begins to thump. "Oh God," I whimper. "What the fuck happened last night?"

The phone continues to ring, and Tristan puts the back of his forearm over his eyes. "Fuck off . . . whoever you are," he moans.

I wake properly and sit up. Shit. "Tris," I say. "The kids."

"Jesus." He stands and feels around for the missing phone. He's naked, and his hair is standing on end. I smile as I watch him. What a sight for sore eyes.

We can still hear my phone vibrating from its unknown location. He reaches in and pulls it out and holds it in the air. "Found the fucker." He frowns at the screen as he reads it, and then his face drops. "It's Barb." He passes it over.

"Hello," I answer. "What's wrong?"

"Hi, Claire."

"What is it?" My heart begins to beat faster.

"Harry's missing."

"What?"

"I got up to go to the bathroom just after three a.m. and stuck my head in to check on him, and he wasn't in bed."

I sit up in a rush. "What do you mean?"

"He snuck out, Claire, and he hasn't come back."

I begin to hear my heartbeat in my ears. "Why didn't you call me?" I stammer.

"I did, but you haven't been answering."

"Oh my God, I'm so sorry."

"We've looked everywhere and contacted all of his friends. We thought he would come back before we were supposed to wake up so he wouldn't get caught, but nobody has seen him."

My heart drops.

"What?" Tristan whispers.

"Harry's missing."

He screws up his face. "Huh?"

"I'm on my way." I hang up and jump out of bed.

Chapter 21

The hour-long car trip to Long Island has been a living hell. Tristan is quiet and has his hand protectively on my leg, and I'm staring out the window, trying to hold back tears. I've called Harrison no fewer than a hundred times, and I know his phone is probably about to go dead. Fletcher and his friends are all out looking for him. No sign.

"He'll be fine," Tris whispers.

"Where could he be?" I whisper. My eyes fill with tears as I lose the ability to hold it in any longer.

"Baby." Tristan puts his arm around me and pulls me close. "I'll find him. I promise you," he whispers into my hair. "I am going to kill him when I find him . . . but I will find him, regardless."

We pull onto my street, and I see my friends' and parents' cars all at my house. My heart drops in my chest. I shouldn't have gone last night. The car stops. "Thank you," I cry. I get out and run inside, and my mother's scared eyes meet mine.

"Mom," I whisper. "Where is he?"

"I don't know, love. We've looked everywhere."

I screw up my face in tears. "Oh my God." She pulls me into a hug, and the door bangs behind us. I turn to see Tristan awkwardly standing in the foyer, unsure what to do.

"Oh, Mom and Dad, this is Tristan."

Tristan smiles and shakes their hands. "Hello, nice to meet you."

"I'm going to kill that kid when I find him," my dad murmurs.

Tristan raises his eyebrows, and I know he's thinking *get in line*. "I'm going to call Fletch and see where he is," Tristan says.

"Okay."

He disappears out the front door.

"I'm going to call the police," I stammer.

"Good idea," Mom says.

"He'll be somewhere asleep, Claire," my dad reassures me. "Just give it another hour."

"He's here," Tristan calls.

"What?" I stammer as I run out onto the porch.

Tristan points, and we see Harrison pushing his bike up the street. It looks like it has a flat tire or something. He's dirty and wet and has a backpack on his back. He looks like he's been through a war.

I drop my head in relief, and then a sudden surge of anger rages through me like a rapid. I march down the front yard until I get to him. "Where have you been?" I cry.

He rolls his eyes.

"Why weren't you answering your phone?"

"I lost it," he barks with attitude.

"Where were you?"

"Out!" he yells.

"You . . . selfish little shit." Something snaps inside of me. "You are grounded!" I scream as I lose all of my control. "Get in that house, and do not come out of your bedroom ever again," I cry. I push his back to try to make him get there faster. At least when he's in there, I know he's safe. I can protect him from himself.

"Typical," he mutters under his breath as he storms past me.

"Harrison Anderson, you are in so much trouble!" I yell after him. "You've lost it—the phone, the internet. Every damn thing you own . . . is gone."

"I hate you." He storms inside and marches up the stairs. "I hate you all!" he yells. His bedroom door slams shut.

Tears roll down my face, and I'm shaking in anger. I am furious . . . beyond furious.

Fuming.

"We'll get going, love." Mom smiles sadly as she rubs my arm. "Glad he's home safe. Good luck." They turn to Tristan. "Nice to meet you."

"You too." He forces a smile, and they leave.

I begin to pace back and forth while I wring my hands. "What am I going to do with this fucking kid, Tristan?" I cry. "He's out of control and doesn't even care."

Tristan exhales heavily. "I'll go call Fletcher, let him know he's here." He disappears out the front door.

I dial Fletcher's number. "Hey, Tris."

"Hey, buddy, he's home," I say.

"Are you kidding me?" he growls. "I've been riding around all night looking for him. I'm going to kill him."

"Yeah, I know. Thanks. Hey . . . your mom is freaking out. Can you come home?"

"On my way."

I hang up, exhale heavily, and look out over the street. Where was he? I glance down and see his dirty backpack dumped next to the door, and I pick it up and go through it. Everything is sopping wet. Where the fuck was he? Did it rain here overnight? A sweater, a bottle of water, some wrappers from chocolate. I undo the zipper of the side pocket and pull out a crumpled, wet packet of cigars.

What?

I read the label. Not just any cigars—expensive ones.

Where the fuck did he get the money for these?

He smokes?

Jesus, what next?

He said he lost his phone. Is that a lie too, or did it just get wet? I dial his number again. "Hello," a woman answers.

I frown, surprised. "Hello, I . . ." I hesitate, unsure what to say. "You found my phone?"

"Yes, dear," the woman replies. She sounds elderly.

"Thank you so much." I hesitate. "It's actually a friend's phone. Can I come pick it up?"

"Of course. I am at Sixty Napier Street."

"Whereabouts is that?"

"Suffolk County."

I screw up my face. Suffolk County . . . that's at least fifteen miles from here. "Where did you find it?" I ask.

"On the street, in the gutter, just half an hour ago."

"Was it raining there last night?"

"Yes, poured all night. Luckily the phone was in the ziplock bag."

What?

This isn't making any sense at all. "Okay, see you soon." I hang up, scribble the address down, and walk inside to Claire. "I'm just going to the grocery store. I'll need to take your car. Do you want anything?"

"No, thanks." She sighs heavily, as if she has the weight of the world on her shoulders.

I take her into my arms and softly kiss her. "He's home now, babe. You can relax." I brush the hair back from her face.

She smiles up at me. "I love you."

"I love you too." Feels good hearing that. I smile and kiss her again. "Back soon."

Half an hour later I pull up to the address and knock on the front door. "Hello," the lady answers.

"Hi, I'm here for the phone. Thank you so much for answering my call."

"Oh, that's okay, dear." She smiles warmly. "I'll just get it." She disappears inside and then returns and hands it over. I stare at the phone in my hand. Carefully placed in a ziplock bag.

"Where did you find it?" I ask.

"Up on the corner of Elm and Second."

"Okay, thanks. I really appreciate it." I walk out and get into my car and put the street names into the GPS.

What are you up to, Wizard?

I pull the car up slowly at the corner of Elm and Second and stare at the huge black metal gates in front of me and read the sign.

SUFFOLK COUNTY CEMETERY

My heart drops. There's only one person I know who may be here.

Wade Anderson.

He was coming to see his dad.

Sadness fills me as the pieces of the puzzle click into place.

With a heavy heart, I turn the car on and do a U-turn. I need to get back.

It's just around six o'clock, and I finish up the dinner I've cooked for us—spaghetti bolognese. I need some carbs before I curl up and die. Claire fell asleep on the couch watching a movie, and Patrick and Fletcher are sitting on the bench talking to me.

My mind isn't here with them; it's up with Harrison in his room.

He's grounded, and I've listened to Claire take his every privilege from him this afternoon.

It's none of my business, and I can't intrude . . . but I feel for the kid.

I dish him up a large bowl of dinner, slather it in grated cheese, and put some garlic bread and a drink on a tray.

He's not allowed out of his room. I'll take him dinner before Claire wakes.

I make my way upstairs and knock on the door.

No answer.

I slowly open it to see him lying with his back to the door.

"I brought you some dinner, Wiz."

No answer. He ignores me.

Hmm . . .

I walk in and close the door behind me. I place the tray down on his desk and put my hands on my hips as I watch him. "You all right?" I ask.

"Get out." He sighs sadly.

I sit on the end of the bed, trying to work out what to say. "I found your phone."

His eyes flick to me.

"A lady found it, and I went and picked it up."

His eyes drop to the floor.

"Why don't you tell your mother that you go to the cemetery?"

He clenches his jaw but remains silent.

"Is that where you are whenever you go missing?"

His eyes meet mine, and I know that it is.

"How long does it take you to ride out there on your bike?" It's fifteen miles—must take him ages.

He stays silent.

"You got a flat tire last night, and you couldn't get home?" I ask. "And then it poured rain, and you were stuck in it for hours as you walked home?"

He still doesn't answer me.

"I'm not against you here, Wiz. I'm on your side." I put my hand on his foot. "I'm trying to work out what the fuck is going on with you. Why wouldn't you just ask your mother to take you there? Why do you lie about where you've been?"

"Because whenever she goes there, she cries for a week, and I can't stand seeing her sad."

God.

I drop my head, and we sit in silence for a while. "Where did you get the money for the cigars?" I ask.

His eyes flick to me in horror.

"You're not in trouble."

He stays quiet, and then eventually he replies, "I saved my allowance for six months."

I frown in confusion.

He turns away and looks at the wall. "They were for Dad," he whispers softly.

I close my eyes as a sadness fills my chest.

Poor fucking kid.

"Just tell your mom where you were. She won't be angry at you," I urge.

"What for? She'll just haul me back to the psychologist. I would rather her be angry than worried. I'm done with the shrinks."

We sit in silence for a while, and I don't know what to say. "Have your dinner, and then why don't you come down, and we'll build our spaceship for a few hours."

He stays still, staring at the wall. "No, thanks."

I put his phone on the bedside table. "Here's your phone." I turn toward the door.

"Tristan."

I turn back to him.

"Can you not tell her?"

I nod. "Sure thing."

I trudge down the stairs with a heavy heart and walk out to find Claire packing up the spaceship model and Fletcher standing nearby. "What are you doing?" I ask.

"Putting this in the Goodwill bin."

"Why?"

"Because he's lying, and I won't tolerate it. I'm not taking his crap anymore, Tristan. I'm done with it. There is no excuse for his behavior."

"Leave it on the table," I say.

"Tristan."

"I said leave it," I snap. How the fuck do I defend him without telling her what I know?

"Why are you suddenly on his side?" she snaps back. "What's gotten into you?"

"Just fucking ease up on him, will you?" I sigh. "Have your dinner, have a shower, and go to bed. The boys and I will clean up. Leave Harrison alone for the moment. You're tired and emotional. Things will seem better tomorrow; deal with it then."

Fletcher gives me a lopsided smile.

"Tricky, you ready for dinner?" I call.

Patrick comes bouncing in from the living room. "Yes, my favorite."

I sit in my car and watch Harrison as he walks up the road. I'm outside his school, it's just around three o'clock, it's finished for the day, and I have no fucking idea what I'm doing.

Well, I do, but I'm pretty sure Claire would go postal if she did.

Too bad . . . I have to do this. It's been eating at me all day. I drive the car up alongside him. "Wiz," I call.

He turns and frowns. "What are you doing here?"

"Get in."

"No." He keeps walking.

"Get in, or I'm telling her," I threaten.

He glares at me, exhales heavily, and walks around and gets into my car. "What?"

I hand him a packet of cigars, just like the ones that got wet. He frowns as he looks at them in his hand.

"Do you want to go see your dad?" I ask.

His eyes search mine, and he drops his head and stares at the cigars once more.

That means yes.

I pull out into the street, and after a very silent car ride, I park the car at the cemetery.

He climbs out, and I tentatively follow him through the tombstones. It's beautiful here, with green lush lawns, and immaculately kept.

WADE ANDERSON
BELOVED HUSBAND AND FATHER
FOREVER LOVED, SADLY MISSED

I put my hands into my suit pockets as I look on. Harrison wipes the nameplate clean with his shirt and straightens the flowers, and I can tell that he comes here often.

Alone.

I get a lump in my throat as I watch him.

With a shaky hand, he opens the packet and gets out a cigar and carefully places it on the grave.

"Here they are, Dad," he whispers. "Your favorite."

I clench my jaw. This is too much.

He takes one out and holds it in his hand, and then he passes one to me.

I frown in surprise.

I take it, pull out a lighter from my pocket, and flick it on. He stares at me for a moment, shocked. I bend and light my cigar and inhale deeply, and then I hold it alight for him. He does the same. He takes in a big breath and coughs as he chokes, and I chuckle as I blow out the thin stream of smoke.

I hold the cigar up and look at it. "Not bad." I smile. "You got good taste," I say to the tombstone.

Harrison fights a smile as he takes another drag. He puffs the smoke out like a dragon, and I can tell he doesn't normally smoke.

"This is Tristan," Harrison says to the tombstone.

I smile and dip my head in a greeting. "Mr. Anderson."

Harrison looks at me for a moment and then touches the tombstone. "You can touch it." He pats it, as if to entice me.

He wants me to shake hands with his dad.

I walk over and put my hand on the top of the cold hard stone.

Goose bumps scatter up my arms, and a weird emotion overwhelms me.

In some strange way, I feel like this is the changing of the guard.

The family he loved . . . is now with me.

In my care, for me to love.

"Nice to meet you, Wade," I whisper.

Claire

I watch the man in the expensive navy suit and perfect posture—the big-time city businessman who looks so out of place here. He slowly lifts the cigar to his lips and inhales deeply. He says something to the young boy he's with, then exhales the smoke in a thin stream. His hand rests on the boy's shoulder as they continue their conversation.

My heart constricts.

I lean up against the tree in the cemetery. Their silhouettes blur through tears as I watch Harrison and Tristan standing over Wade's grave.

If someone cut my heart open with a knife, it would be less painful than watching this.

The man whom I love, taking my son to see his dead father . . . smoking a cigar with them. And I know that Harrison is too young to smoke, and they shouldn't be doing this. I should be furious. I should be appalled . . . but then . . .

Wade loved cigars.

My chest shudders as I try to get a hold on my emotions.

This would be so special to Wade . . . having a cigar with his son.

I close my eyes, the pain unbearable.

I went to pick up Harrison from school so I could try to talk to him alone, and then I saw him getting into Tristan's car, and I followed them here.

This is the last thing I expected to see.

I don't want them to see me. I turn and walk back to my car, the tears streaming down my face. I get in, and without looking back, I drive home in tears.

I'm in love with a beautiful man.

I toss the salad in the bowl and glance at the clock. Seven o'clock. The boys have done their chores and are watching television.

My heart is bursting with love, and I am totally in awe of Tristan.

He did something, he did something very special for me . . . and for Wade—and to know that he has Harry's back when I didn't cuts my heart wide open.

I've just realized that he has a specialized skill that, no matter what, I couldn't give my boys.

Perspective.

This is what they've been craving. This is what they've been missing in their lives.

No wonder I was struggling so hard with them. I couldn't see the forest for the trees.

Harry didn't mention going to the cemetery, and I haven't brought up anything about the weekend. I'm acting normal because I'm not sure what to say. Whatever he and Tristan have talked about, he wants to keep to himself. If he wanted me to know, he would have told me.

The Aston Martin pulls up in the driveway. "Tristan's here!" Patrick yells as he runs for the front door.

Fletcher caught the subway home. I'm not actually sure where Tris has been since then. I watch through the window as Patrick opens Tristan's car door and talks a million miles per minute. Tristan listens and laughs. He's so patient with him. He passes him his laptop bag, and Patrick proudly carries it in. Fletcher goes to the door to greet him, and Harry stays sitting on the couch.

"Hello," Tristan says as he walks into the living room. His eyes find Harry across the room, and he gives him a nod.

Harry gives him a lopsided smile, and my heart soars.

It's going to be okay . . . it's all going to be okay.

"Hello, Anderson," he purrs in his oh-so-sexy deep voice.

I take him into my arms. "Hello, Mr. Miles." I lean up and kiss him softly, and he frowns, surprised I'm kissing him in front of the boys.

"Where have you been?" I ask.

"I had a meeting this afternoon and . . ." He hesitates as he thinks of a lie. "I had a busy afternoon."

"Oh." I smile up at my gorgeous liar. "Dinner's nearly ready."

"Good." He kisses me softly again. "I'm starving."

Chapter 22

Tristan

I stand in the elevator and turn up my nose.

What is that smell?

I got up and left early, trained with my personal trainer, and got dressed in the bathroom at the gym. I look around at my surroundings. This elevator stinks. What the fuck cleaning products are they using?

The doors open, and I stride out. "Morning," I say to the girls at reception.

"Morning," they all reply.

I can still smell it. Ugh, it's horrendous. Must have permeated my nostrils.

It's foul.

What the heck is it?

I walk into my office and begin to sniff around. Is it the carpet? I push the intercom. "Sammia, what is that godawful fucking smell?"

"What?"

"Can you smell something?"

"No."

"I can smell something."

"Maybe you wore too much aftershave."

I roll my eyes. "Whatever. Can you make sure my car is here to pick me up right at nine, please? I need to be early for my meeting this morning."

"Already booked, boss."

"Thanks." I walk into my bathroom and wash my hands. Maybe I touched something at the gym?

I take a seat at my desk and turn on my computer. I wince from the odor.

"Oh my God, this is intolerable," I mutter. I push the intercom again. "Sammia, can you come here for a moment, please?"

She sighs. "Fine."

I go back to my computer.

Moments later she walks in. "Yes?"

"What is that smell?"

She screws up her nose as she inhales. "Hmm . . . I can smell something."

"See. I told you."

She sniffs . . . and sniffs. She walks around and then leans in toward me. "It's you."

My eyes widen in horror, and I sniff the sleeve of my suit. "What?"

She leans in and sniffs again. "Smells like cat piss."

"What?" I explode. I jump from my chair and tear off my jacket. I glance down, and I see a faint mark on my shoes—my four-thousand-dollar fucking shoes. "That fucking Muff Cat has pissed in my overnight bag!" I scream.

Sammia puts her hands over her mouth and bursts out laughing.

I kick off my shoes, tear off my socks, and take off my shirt and tie and throw them into a pile on the floor. "Burn these fucking things. All of them!" I yell. "I don't have fucking time for this." I march out of the office and down past reception.

"Hell yeah." Mallory from reception giggles as she sees me shirtless. "Boom."

Sammia laughs out loud behind me. "I'll say," she chimes in.

"Not funny!" I cry as I storm into Jameson's office.

He's just arrived and glances up from his desk. "What the fuck are you doing?" He frowns.

"Give me your clothes."

"What?"

I hold my hand out. "That Muff Cat pissed on my clothes, and I have the most important meeting of the year. Give me your fucking suit."

He bursts out laughing.

"I'm not joking," I bark. "Give me your clothes and shoes. Right now."

Sammia and Mallory are laughing hard at the door.

"Not fucking funny, you two," I cry. "Sammia, call Claire and tell her the cat is going to hell. When I get ahold of that thing . . . tick fucking tock." I punch my fist hard.

The three of them burst out laughing again.

Jameson stands and begins to unbutton his shirt. "I thought Elliot and Christopher were coming in today. Take their suits."

"They won't be here until after ten. They have a breakfast meeting."

"Sammia, can you find Jameson some clothes, please?" I stammer.

"Do I have to?" She sighs dreamily.

He hands over his shirt, and we suddenly become aware of the three reception girls standing at the door watching, and we both glance over.

Sammia gives us a goofy smile and shrugs. "Don't mind us; this is the most exciting thing that's happened in the office for like . . . forever."

I glance at Jameson, and he rolls his eyes. What must we look like, both shirtless and half-undressed in the office?

"Fucking perverts," I huff. "Go watch some porn or something."

"This is better." Sammia sighs again.

"Jesus Christ," Jameson mutters under his breath.

The girls all giggle and slowly return to their desks.

Jameson hands over his shirt and tie and suit and shoes and socks, and I change into them. Elliot comes in the door unexpectedly, and his face falls when he sees Jameson sitting at his desk in only his boxer shorts. "What the hell is going on?"

"Claire's cat pissed on his clothes." Jameson smirks. "He has a meeting. Can you go and buy me a new suit?"

Elliot's brows rise in horror, and he looks to me.

"Don't fucking say it," I growl.

He bursts out laughing. "You fucking idiot."

I storm out of the office as I do my tie. "Goodbye," I call as I storm through the office. "This is not the morning I had in fucking mind."

"Good luck!" the girls all call. "I hope you don't run into any more cats out there."

"Shut up," I snap as I step into the elevator. "This isn't fucking funny."

It's just around four o'clock when Sammia's voice echoes through the intercom. "Tris, your mom is here."

I hit send on my email . . . great. "Send her in." I knew this was coming. I stand and go to the door and open it. Her lovely face comes into view, and I smile. "Hello, Mom."

"Hello, darling." She smiles as she walks past me. She takes a seat at my desk, and I hit the intercom. "Mallory, can you bring my mother in some tea, please?"

"Of course."

She smiles and stares at me.

"Yes?" I smirk.

"Claire's lovely."

"She is." I rest my elbow on my desk and steeple my fingers up over my temple.

She stays silent.

"But . . . ?" I ask.

She hesitates.

"Come on, Mother, you have come here for a reason today. What is it?"

"Tristan . . ." She pauses. "Why do you think you like Claire?"

"I don't like her, Mom. I love her."

She inhales sharply. "Tris." She stands and walks to the window and stares out over the city. "Ever since you were a child, you have had a very strong personality trait."

I frown as I listen.

"And so far in business, it has served you well."

I stay silent.

"But now I feel I must make you aware of it, because I fear it is affecting you personally."

"What are you talking about, Mom?" I sigh, annoyed.

She turns to me. "Tristan, you like to fix things."

I frown harder. What?

"You don't destroy companies; you buy them to fix them. It is your natural ability to sense when something needs you. You have always been like this, even when you were a tiny little boy. You are attracted to people who need help."

I stare at her.

"Think about it. The staff that you yourself hire always have an issue that they need to overcome."

My mind instantly goes to Fletcher.

"The companies that you want always are in trouble."

"That's my job, Mom."

"No, Tristan, nobody ever told you that you need to buy companies in trouble. You took that on yourself. Are you in love with Claire because she needs you to fix her?"

"No," I snap, annoyed.

"Her sons, do they have problems? Because I can guarantee the bigger the problems they have, the more you will be attracted to them."

I clench my jaw as I watch her.

"Every girlfriend you have ever had has needed fixing . . . except Mary."

My nostrils flair at the mention of her name. Mary was my second girlfriend. I grieved her for years after we broke up.

"You loved Mary, Tristan. With all your heart you loved her. But she didn't need fixing, so you felt that you had to leave her."

I drop my head and stare at the carpet as a piece of my puzzle falls into place . . . the world begins to spin . . . is she right?

"Why do you think you were so heartbroken breaking up with her? And yet you couldn't take her back," Mom says. "Could you?"

My eyes search hers.

"You are about to perhaps give up the chance to have your own children for a woman you think you need to fix. Those boys will never be yours, Tristan. They are hers and his."

I begin to hear my heartbeat in my ears. "I love Claire, Mom."

"I know you do, darling. There's a lot to love." She smiles softly and cups my face in her hand. "But before you go any further with her and her children, I need you to do something."

"What?"

"You do this for me, and I will never ever bring this up again, and I'll embrace Claire and her boys as if they are my own."

"What do you want?"

"I want you to go and see Mary."

I clench my jaw. I don't think I can. It hurts me just to think of her.

"After seeing her, if you can honestly tell me that you don't have any feelings for Mary and what I am saying isn't right, you have my blessing with Claire."

"Mary's probably married by now, Mom." I sigh.

"She's still in love with you, Tristan. She never got over you."

My chest tightens, and I frown in pain.

"I speak to her often." She hands me a card with her name and address. "She's expecting your call today."

Claire

I read the text and frown. That's weird.

Hi babe,
Something has come up tonight.
I'll see you tomorrow.
Love you
xoxox

He's never texted me before about not seeing me. In fact, he's never not seen me. From the day that Patrick asked him not to leave, he never has.

Uneasiness fills me. I spoke to him this morning in his limo, and he was going postal about Muff—no mention of anything going on tonight, though. I frown and text back.

Okay, have a good night.
Love you,
xoxox

It's late, ten o'clock, and I stare at my phone as I sit at the kitchen counter.

Tristan hasn't called me to say good night. Something feels off, but I can't put my finger on it.

Fletcher has been hovering around me all night, and I wonder what went on at the office today. He's now pretending to make a drink and not wanting to go to bed.

"How was Tristan at work today?" I ask.

His haunted eyes meet mine.

What is that look?

"Is something wrong, Fletch?"

He twists his hands in front of him, as if nervous. "Where did Tristan say he was tonight?" he asks quietly.

My stomach drops. "Something came up." My eyes search his. "Do you know where he is tonight?"

He nods, but he stays silent.

"You can tell me, baby. Nothing bad is going to happen. Tristan and I are adults."

He tentatively sits down beside me at the counter. "His mother came to see him."

I frown.

"I shouldn't have, but I listened at the door."

"Why?"

"Because last time she was there, I heard her warning Tristan that he wouldn't have his own children if he stayed with you."

My heart drops. "What did Tristan say to that?"

"He said he knew, but he wanted you more."

I get a lump in my throat, overwhelmed that he would make that sacrifice to be with me. "What did she say today?"

"She said that Tristan only wants things that he can fix."

I frown.

"She said that it's part of his personality, that he's drawn to people who need him."

He is—I already know that.

He drops his head and frowns, as if not wanting to elaborate.

"Go on, baby." I smile. "It's okay."

"She said that she thinks Tristan is still in love with his ex-girlfriend and that he only left her because she didn't need to be fixed."

My heart drops. I know which ex-girlfriend she's talking about. He's talked about her often.

"She thinks that Tristan is only with you because we are all so damaged, and he wants to help us."

Ouch . . .

My eyes fill with tears, and I blink to try to get rid of them before Fletcher sees.

We stare at each other for a moment.

"Where is he?" I whisper.

"He went to see Mary. He went to see if he still loves her."

I sit in the dark on the front porch in the seat swing and rock gently back and forth.

It's 12:40 a.m. I can't sleep. How could I?

It's quiet and still; only the creak of the chair can be heard.

Elizabeth is right.

In my heart of hearts, I know she's right.

Tristan isn't a soul sucker . . . he's a savior.

An angel in a perfect suit, he hides behind his asshole title.

He's a good man who takes no credit.

I rock back and forth as I think. He came in here like a white knight, against all odds, and even though he knew we weren't right for each other, he saw how damaged I was, and so he fought for us. He fought to save me.

He thawed me from my frozen state.

I get a vision of him and Harry at Wade's grave yesterday, and my heart breaks.

My boys are going to lose another man they admire and care about.

I screw up my face in tears. *I really loved him.*

It hurts to know why he loved me.

The tears roll down my face as I try to wrap my head around dealing with another loss.

He loved Mary, and he left her because he felt he had to.

I don't want that for him.

I want him to be happy and live his life with his true love. He deserves that.

We all deserve that.

I wipe my eyes and take out my phone, and I call his number. It goes to voice mail.

I frown as I prepare to push the words past my lips. "Hi, Tris." I smile sadly. "It's me." I pause as I try to get the wording right. "I hope everything went well with you and Mary tonight." My face crumples. "I just want you to know that I understand and . . ." I drop my head. "And . . . thank you." I screw up my face. "Thank you for trying with us. I appreciate it more than you know . . . but I'm letting you go." I wipe the tears as they roll down my face. "I want you to be with her. Your mother is right." I smile sadly. "She's the one you really love."

"No, she's not." The voice comes from behind me.

I turn to see Tristan standing behind me on the grass.

He puts his hands on his hips, indignant. "What fucking bullshit are you going on with, woman?" He frowns.

"What are you doing here?" I ask as I stand.

He puts his hands out wide, as if I'm a fool. "I'm coming home to sleep—what does it look like?"

"But . . . Mary?"

He takes me into his arms, and his lips softly take mine.

"Mary . . . ," I whisper.

"Was like seeing a sister. Nothing there at all. Just like I knew it would be. I went there to mollify my mother."

"What?"

"I love you." He kisses me softly. "And to be honest, I'm glad I went, because it proved something to me . . . my mother's got it all wrong." He takes my face into his hands, and I stare up at him through tears. "You and the boys . . . are saving me. Not the other way around."

His lips touch mine, and I screw up my face against his.

"I love you," he whispers. "I don't want to be anywhere else. In fact I've decided that I want to move in here."

Hope blooms in my chest. "You do?"

"I have some of my stuff in the car. I was actually at home packing a suitcase." He gestures out to the street, and I see a brand-new black Range Rover.

"What is that car?" I frown.

He shrugs casually. "I got us a new car."

I smile up at the beautiful man in front of me. "Are you sure about this . . . about us, Tris?" I whisper.

"Claire." He smiles down at me as he pushes the hair back from my face. "I love you more than anything. This . . . is where I want to be."

His lips take mine.

"And I'm going to kill Fletcher for listening through doors," he adds.

I giggle through tears.

"And the Muff Cat is going fucking down. I'm going inside to piss in its bed right now."

I laugh out loud as he drags me into the house. "And how dare you think I was in love with Mary?" he whispers. "I'm fucking your ass for that, Anderson." He slaps me hard on the behind as I take the bottom step.

I giggle. My man is home.

Tristan hovers in the kitchen, making his coffee, and I brace myself. I have to talk to the boys. I just want to make it a casual conversation as they sit at the counter eating their breakfast.

"So . . ." I frown as I swallow the sand in my throat. "I wanted to talk to you boys."

Tristan drains his coffee cup and rushes into the living room. He doesn't want to hear this.

"Yeah." They all keep eating their cereal.

"I was wondering if Tristan could move in."

They all stop eating and stare at me.

"It would mean that . . ." I pause, feeling faint. "It would mean that he would live here with us . . . and that he doesn't have to sleep on the couch anymore—that's all. It's beginning to hurt his back."

"Okay," Patrick says as he eats.

I look to the other two. "And of course, he would become part of our family now."

Tristan reappears through the door, and Harry's eyes rise to meet his. "Do you want to move in here?"

Tristan nods. "Yes."

Harry shrugs and keeps chewing.

"What does that mean?" I ask nervously.

"Yeah . . . okay."

I frown. "Okay what?"

"If he must."

Tristan's and my eyes meet. Surely it can't be that simple. I turn my attention to Fletcher. "I'll think about it." He glares at Tristan, and I remember what he heard yesterday.

"Okay," Tristan says. "Come on. We need to leave soon." He turns to Harry. "You get your grade back today, don't you, Wiz?"

"Yeah." Harry sighs. "I won't pass. I never do."

"I predict you're getting a one hundred," Tristan replies with a smile. "That assignment was on point. I checked it myself."

Fletcher goes up to get his things, and I follow Tristan out to the car. "Oh my God, Fletcher said no," I whisper.

"It will be fine. I'll talk to him today. He's angry at me; he'll be fine." He smiles down at me. "I love you."

I giggle up at my beautiful man. "I love you too."

"What?" Tristan's angry voice bellows through the entire house. "Thirty!" he yells. "A fucking thirty? Are you kidding me?" he cries as he holds the paper in the air.

"Tristan, language," I snap.

Fletcher and Patrick sit quietly on the couch as they watch, scared to speak.

Harry has just shown Tristan his grade for the space assignment they have done over the last week.

"There is no way in hell this assignment is a thirty!" he yells as he begins to pace. "What are these idiotic, stupid . . . incompetent assholes doing at this school?" he bellows.

"Mrs. Henderson hates me." Harry sighs.

"Will you calm down?" I say to Tristan. "Stop swearing."

"No. I will not," he growls. "That's it—tomorrow morning, nine a.m., I am at that fucking school." He punches his fist. "Tick . . . tock . . . Mrs. Henderson."

I roll my eyes. "Good grief, this is all I need."

Chapter 23

The thing about loving a powerful man is knowing when to stand back and let him take the reins.

Today I'm doing just that.

"What is he doing out there?" Patrick frowns.

I dip my head to peer out the window and onto the front porch to see Tristan pacing, hands on hips, muttering to himself. He's been up since five o'clock, dressed in his suit, and ready for battle.

Mrs. Henderson is going down . . . and to be honest I feel like calling ahead and warning her.

She needs to run.

It was his first official night here with me last night, and he didn't even come to bed until well after I was asleep, and he was up before I woke this morning. I missed the entire thing.

He stayed up and went through all of Harrison's past assignments and tests. He interviewed Harrison in great detail about the goings-on in class and when and why he has been sent out or suspended. I know that Harrison is a handful, and I've been sympathetic to the teachers about his behavior up until this point. But Tristan has assured me that there is more to this story than I realize. I'm pretty sure Mrs. Henderson is going to regret giving Harry such a low grade.

He sticks his head in the front door. "Are you ready?" he calls.

"Tristan." I stare at him.

He raises his eyebrows impatiently. "What?"

"You're not going to be passive aggressive to Mrs. Henderson, are you?"

He clenches his jaw. "Nope." He gestures toward the car impatiently, and the boys walk past him into the front yard. "I'm going to be *aggressive* aggressive."

I roll my eyes. "Can you not?"

"Claire." He pinches the bridge of his nose. "I will not for one fucking minute have him treated in this manner, and if you are asking me to bite my tongue . . . it's best you don't come."

"Christ Almighty," I mutter under my breath. "Can you just be calm, please?" I ask. "You're stressing me out."

"I'm stressing you out?" He points to his chest incredulously. "Don't come, Claire. Sit in the car. Because I am telling you right now: I'm not about to take shit from this fucking teacher."

Oh jeez. I brush past him and get into the car. It's big and black and has a new-car smell. Patrick and Harry bounce in the back. They love it and made Tristan drive them around the block ten times last night.

I watch Tristan leave the house and lock the door. He takes a deep breath, drops his shoulders, and undoes his suit jacket with one hand as he walks toward the car.

I smile as I watch him . . . Tristan Miles is here, the takeover king. The take-no-shit, get-what-he-wants man whom I used to hate is here batting . . . for *us*. Somehow, he has taken my naughty little boy under his wing.

I don't think I've ever loved him like I do right now.

He gets in and slams the door. "Harrison, you will be coming to the meeting with us, please."

Harry's eyes widen in horror. "But—"

"No buts. You need to learn how to defend yourself."

Oh jeez. I slide down in the seat in dread. I don't even want to come to this meeting myself . . . maybe I *can* sit in the car?

Ten minutes later we pull up at the school, and Tristan parks the car. We walk into the office. The receptionist does a double take as she sees him. Her eyes flick to me and then back to him, as if questioning what he's doing here with us.

She's a real bitch, this one, and I've had run-ins with her before.

"Can I help you?" she asks flatly.

"Hello, I'm Tristan Miles. I would like a meeting with Mrs. Henderson, the principal, the vice-principal, and someone from the parent-teacher association, please."

Her eyes flick to me, and I swallow the lump in my throat.

"When for?"

"Now." He stares at her deadpan, and I really wish the earth would swallow me up.

"What is this in regard to?" she asks.

"Harrison Anderson."

"About?"

Tristan glares at her. "Can you please just do your allocated job and book the appointment? This is a private matter."

Harrison looks up at Tristan and gives him a hopeful smile, and Tristan takes his hand.

I wither . . . oh crap.

Aggressive aggressive, here we go.

She glares at him and then twists her lips in annoyance. "That won't be possible. You need to book a meeting at least two weeks in advance."

"All right." Tristan fakes a smile. "I would like you to get the board of education on the phone for me immediately."

Her eyes widen. "What for?"

"I would like to make a formal complaint to them. It is your duty to contact them on my behalf in the instance of a crisis, is it not?"

She stares at him, shocked, and I drop my head to hide my smile.

He's such an arrogant ass.

He takes a seat in the waiting area, crosses his legs, and sits back, as if he owns the place.

"What are you doing?" she asks.

"I'm not leaving until I have that meeting or speak to the education board." He shrugs casually. "The choice is yours." He taps the chair beside him, and Harrison sits down.

"Just a minute," she says. She disappears into the principal's office. I know where it is—I've been there many times before.

I take a seat beside them, and I can't look at him—or I'll burst out laughing.

She reappears a moment later. "Mrs. Smithers, the principal, has had an opening. She can see you now. Mrs. Henderson is in class, so she won't be attending."

"Make that call. The meeting doesn't go ahead without her," he says as he lifts his chin defiantly.

She stares at him for a moment, as if doing an internal risk assessment.

He glares at her with a silent "don't fuck with me" attitude.

"Just a minute." She scurries back into the principal's office.

"No talking in here," Tristan whispers to Harry.

Harry nods. "Okay."

She reappears a moment later. "This way, please." She shows us into the office. Mrs. Smithers and the vice-principal are seated at the desk.

"Hello." He smiles calmly. "My name is Tristan Miles, and this is Claire Anderson, my partner, and I'm sure you know Harrison." He shakes their hands.

Their eyes flick to each other. "Take a seat, please."

Tristan turns toward the rude receptionist. "You will need to stay and take minutes, please."

Her mouth falls open. "What?"

"I want this meeting documented. Who will take notes," he replies as he looks among them, "if not you?"

I bite my lip to hide my smile. *Oh, he's something else.*

Mrs. Smithers nods. "Yes, okay. Sheridan, take the minutes, please." She passes her a notepad and pencil.

Mrs. Henderson rushes into the room all flustered. "I'm here." She falls into a seat and glances over at Harrison.

Mrs. Smithers links her fingers together on the desk. "How can I help you, Mr. Miles?"

"I would like to discuss the education of Harrison and, in particular, the grading system of his work." He pulls the assignment from the inside pocket of his jacket. "He got a thirty on this. Please explain to me why."

Mrs. Henderson shrugs. "It wasn't any good."

Tristan's eyes flicker with anger. "In whose opinion?"

"Mine, and as his teacher, what I say goes."

Tristan sits back, angered, and I wince . . . jeez. Here we go. "Is that so?" He smirks. "I would like this assignment independently graded."

"No, that's not possible, and why would you want to do that?"

"Because Harrison Anderson is being victimized by you because you have a personality clash with him."

"Oh please," Mrs. Henderson huffs. "I try and teach him, but there is nothing in his head."

The principal lets out an audible gasp.

Tristan smiles. "And there it is." He turns to the receptionist. "Did you get that?"

The receptionist nods nervously.

"You've just signed your termination letter, Mrs. Henderson." He smiles sweetly.

She glares at Harry.

"I've personally checked this assignment, and it is not a thirty—perhaps an eighty at worst. You grade him low on every test on some personal power trip."

"Oh, that is rubbish," she scoffs.

Tristan pulls out a folder from his briefcase. "I have every single test of Harrison's right here, and I would like an independent grader."

"He's rude, and he needs to repeat."

"He's gifted and tired of being discriminated against. Tell me, Mrs. Henderson, have you ever had his IQ tested?"

"No . . . but—"

"Do you think it's possible that you are intimidated by this child, and you purposely try and get him sent out of class so that he doesn't activate your own inferiority complex?"

"Oh, that's ridiculous," Mrs. Smithers retorts. "You are very rude, Mr. Miles."

Tristan turns his attention to her. "On another topic, Mrs. Smithers, I would like a report on what you are doing to help Patrick Anderson."

Her eyes widen. "For what?"

"He has dyslexia, and under state law your school receives special funding for extra help for him. Where is it?"

Oh, he's good.

"I don't appreciate you coming in here and slinging your accusations around," Mrs. Smithers snaps.

Tristan glares at her. "And I don't appreciate incompetence." He stands. "You will be hearing from the education board with regard to this matter." He takes Harry's hand. "Harrison won't be back. Nor Patrick, for that matter."

My eyes widen . . . what?

"And where are you going to send him?" Mrs. Henderson smirks sarcastically.

"They'll be attending Trinity School."

"Ha," Mrs. Smithers laughs. "He won't get in there. They won't take him with his behavior record."

"We'll see." He smiles at the people in the room with an eerie confidence. "You know, intelligent people scare stupid people." He turns to the woman taking notes. "Did you get that?"

She glares at him.

"What does that supposed to mean?" Mrs. Henderson snaps.

"What *is* that supposed to mean," Tristan corrects her. "Let's go; we are wasting our time here."

He marches out the door, leading Harrison by the hand, and we walk out through the playground. I had considered moving schools before but thought the boys had had enough changes to deal with. "Do you want to go and say goodbye to your friends?" Tristan asks him.

"Nah, my friends don't even go here anymore."

Tristan frowns down at him. "Who do you hang around with now? Where are your friends from?"

"Sports and the skate park."

"So . . . what about at school?"

"I sit alone every day."

I stare at him . . . and my heart breaks. God, this is worse than I ever imagined.

We climb into the car, and Tristan puts his seat belt on. "Good riddance, Mrs. Henderson, you stupid old bag." He pulls out into the traffic.

I smirk as I look out the window.

I'm in love with Superman.

My hero.

The boys all bounce in excitement on the couch, and Harry dials Tristan's number. "You need to hurry!" he cries before hanging up.

I smile as I sip my wine. The big game is on, and the boys are really into it. It's funny—they have never been into watching it before. Tristan has gotten them totally addicted. They all sit together on one couch and scream and laugh and yell at the ref.

Days of Tristan living with us have turned into weeks and then months.

Seven wonderful months, to be exact.

Our home is happy for the first time in a long time. The boys adore him, I am so happy, and even Muff is obsessed with my boyfriend. He follows him around, purring.

If I could just get over these work issues, my life would be perfect.

I'm losing control of Anderson Media. We have no advertising contracts left, and nobody is renewing. We're on skeleton staff, and I lie awake every night worrying about money. Tristan has no idea. I have no doubt he will be furious with me for not telling him when he finally finds out, but I don't want to tell him until I absolutely have to. He already does so much for me and the boys. He insists on paying for their private schooling. He drops them there every morning and has his driver pick them up every afternoon and bring them home.

Never in a million years did I think my sons would be picked up from the most exclusive school in New York every day by a limo.

And besides, I don't want to appear weaker than I already feel. If he knows about my situation, then I have to talk about it with him, and at the moment, he's my safe place, where nothing is corrupted.

I want him to be proud of me, like I am of him.

The door bursts open, and Tristan comes racing in. "What's happening?" he cries as he stares at the television.

"You missed the kickoff!" Harry yells.

Tristan throws his jacket off and marches into the kitchen. "Hey, baby," he says as he kisses me quickly.

I smile up at him, but before I have time to reply, he grabs a beer from the fridge and runs back out into the living room to the boys watching the game. "No!" he cries. They all begin to yell at something in the game.

I smile, and an unwanted resentment falls over me. I wish I could be so excited about something. I have this black cloud of fear hanging over me.

Everything that Wade worked so hard to build is disappearing before my eyes.

He wanted the boys to attend a public school in Long Island, and they aren't. He wanted them to grow up without excess money. I'm pretty sure having a limo pick them up from school every day blows that out of the water.

And now Anderson Media, the career that Wade worked so hard on creating—his biggest dream was to hand it down to the boys.

Now I'm losing it . . . I'm losing that too.

I exhale heavily as I go back to my laptop.

Wade . . . help me.

I'm tired. This week has been a never-ending roll of meetings with the board. We are in the final stages of staying afloat, and I don't know what to do. I look over to Tristan as he drives. "Where are we going?" I ask.

He smiles over at me like the cat that got the cream. He picks up my hand and kisses my fingertips. "I have a surprise for you."

The boys chatter in the back seat among themselves, and I try to calm my nerves. I'm not in the mood for surprises. I'm so anxious that I'm nearly suffocating.

If something drastic doesn't happen, if I don't get a big injection of funds from somewhere, the writing is on the wall—the liquidators will be moving in within the next six to eight weeks and taking my company from me. I will be forced into bankruptcy. The company insolvent.

I want to talk to Tristan about it, but I don't want him to worry or feel that he has to put the money in. I already declined the Ferrara offer; now my only other option is to sell to Miles Media, but then I know I'll hold that grudge against Tristan forever. He will always be the man who took Wade's dream from us, and I really don't want it to affect our relationship. Because I know if it does come to that . . . it will.

How could it not?

I think back to how hard Wade worked so that he would have something to hand down to his sons. And in the five and a half years since his death, I have effectively killed everything he worked for.

I'm sick to my stomach.

Tristan chats and laughs with the boys, carefree as he drives, and an unwelcome jealousy fills me. He has no idea what it's like to struggle.

He's never had to do it.

I know he works so hard and deserves everything he has, but it's . . . I can't even articulate what it is I'm feeling . . . resentment, maybe?

I don't know why I'm feeling like this now, but with the oncoming demise of Anderson Media, it's suddenly eating at me.

Maybe I'm just hormonal, or maybe it's because of the way we met.

From day one I have always known that Wade's company has been on Miles Media's acquisitions list. They wanted it, made no secret of it.

It's how we met.

I pushed it out of my mind for so long . . . but now that it's impending, it's all I can think about. Everything Wade wanted is coming to an end, and I just don't know how to stop it.

We pull up on the street in front of a grand house, and Tristan smiles over at me.

"What's this?" I ask flatly.

A man gets out of the car in front of us and smiles broadly.

Tristan waves. "Come on, boys, Claire."

"What are we doing?" I frown.

"Looking at this house."

"What for?"

"Because I want to buy it for us." He climbs out of the car, and the boys bounce out after him.

"What?" I frown.

He waves me out . . . fucking hell, I don't have time for this shit. I get out of the car and walk up to him as he talks to the man.

"Michael, this is Claire, my partner," he introduces me.

"Hello." I fake a smile as I shake his hand.

"And these are my boys, Fletcher, Harrison, and Patrick."

The hairs on the back of my neck rise. *His boys.*

They are Wade's boys.

"What a beautiful family you have." Michael smiles as he leads us up the path toward the house.

"Yes, I do." Tristan smiles proudly. He's holding Patrick's hand and has his other hand on Harry's shoulder protectively. Fletcher walks with them as they go into the house.

I begin to see red. Why is he showing me houses? I'm not fucking moving from Long Island. I own my house. I'm comfortable there . . . we're comfortable there.

It's our home.

It's what Wade wanted.

400

I begin to hear my angry heartbeat in my ears as I trail behind.

Calm down . . . calm down . . . calm down. *You're just stressed; calm the fuck down.*

The house is huge and set on a large plot of land in a leafy suburb about twenty minutes out of New York. Michael begins his sales pitch. "This is the foyer."

It's about the size of our current living room and has a grand sweeping staircase that splits into two near the top level.

Tristan smiles and takes my hand excitedly. "I'll show them around, Michael," he says.

My eyes flick to him in question. What? He's been here before?

How long has he been looking for a house on the sly? I begin to fume inside.

"Of course." Michael smiles. "I'll wait outside."

Michael disappears out the front door, and Tristan smiles proudly. "Pretty sweet, right?"

"Hmm," I reply as I look around.

"Out here is the kitchen." We walk through to a large kitchen, and I roll my lips in annoyance. "Wiz and I could cook up a storm," he says. Harry's eyes widen in excitement.

I hate it.

Wade has never lived here; his memories are in our current house.

I don't want new ones without him.

I don't want to erase everything that he stood for. Why doesn't Tristan get that?

My pulse begins to throb in my temples, and I feel like I'm about to explode.

I am now seeing red. I can't deal with this.

"This is the living area," he gushes.

The boys run to the back windows. "Oh my God, look at the pool," Patrick cries.

"It has a pool bar, Mom," Fletcher gasps.

"You're not old enough to drink," I snap.

"And look," Tristan says as he leads me through the house excitedly. "This could be your office." We peer into a room. It has a large window seat and looks out onto a leafy veranda. "And this could be my office, next door." He shows me into the office. "There's a bathroom down here. A second living area for the boys. A gymnasium."

The boys run through the house in excitement.

Fury begins to burn a hole in my stomach.

How dare he?

He leads me upstairs and down the hall. "Look at the master suite, Claire." He pulls me into the room, and I look around as I try to hold my sarcastic tongue.

It's beautiful and the size of half my current house.

"And the bathroom." He smiles excitedly. I peer in, and it has a huge white-marble bath like I've always fantasized about. "Look at the size of your closet, babe."

Something snaps deep inside of me. "It's not my closet, Tristan," I bark.

He pulls me into his arms. "But you like it . . . right?" I look around as I search for something nonbitchy to say.

I've got nothing.

The boys all scream in excitement as they look at the rest of the upstairs.

"I'm having this room," Harry cries.

"I want this one!" Patrick yells.

"I can see the pool from mine."

Tristan's eyes search mine. "What do you think?"

"About what?" I snap.

"Do you like it? I think I'll make an offer today."

"An offer for what?"

"To buy it for us to live in—what else?"

I screw up my face at his presumption. "I don't want to live here."

"Why not?" His face falls. "It's close to the boys' new school. You, Fletch, and I all work in New York. There's a yard for Muff and Woofy." He smiles as he pulls me into his arms again. "It's perfect for us."

"I'm not moving, Tristan," I insist. "I want to live in the house we are in."

"Claire," he says flatly, and I know he's about to give me his hard-core sales pitch. I can already tell he's made up his mind on this house, and when Tristan Miles decides he wants something, he doesn't give up until he gets it.

I'm shutting this down right now.

"I'm not moving," I snap. "End of story." I pull away from him and storm downstairs and out to the car.

"How was it?" Michael smiles as I walk out onto the street.

"Lovely," I reply.

"Can you see yourself living here?" He winks.

I glare at him as the last of my patience dissipates. "No. I can't, actually."

I get into the car and slam the door, and ten minutes later Tristan and the boys amble out of the house. I watch as he talks to Michael as the boys all listen, and then finally they get into the car.

The boys are all excited and talking about everything they have just seen.

Tristan gives me a sideways glance, annoyed with me.

"What?" I snap.

"Don't give me *what*," he growls as he pulls out into the street. "You didn't even look at it."

"I don't have to. I'm not moving from my home in Long Island."

"It's too small for us." He rolls his eyes, as if I'm an idiot, and my blood begins to boil.

"I want my boys to have room to have their friends over," he asserts angrily.

Something snaps inside of me.

Wade had plans for his sons, and I can't ignore them.

I won't.

"They are Wade's boys," I bark. "You need to stop calling them *your* boys."

The car falls deathly silent.

He narrows his eyes at me. "What the fuck is that supposed to mean?"

I glare out the front windshield and cross my arms, too angry to form words.

"You do know, Claire . . . that when we get married—"

"*If* we get married," I fume.

"I will be adopting the boys."

"What?" I explode. I stare at him for a moment in utter shock . . . what the fuck? He wants to adopt them. "That's not happening, Tristan."

"What?" he screams.

"They already have a father," I snap.

"I want them as my sons in the eyes of the law."

"Well, you can't fucking have them legally. You get to live with them—that's enough."

"Mom!" Fletcher cries from the back. "Stop it."

Tristan's eyes bulge from their sockets. His eyes flick between the road and me. "So you're telling me I can care for them, I can love them, but I can't ever call them my sons."

"They have a father," I repeat. "And they will remember and respect his wishes."

"He's fucking dead, Claire," he barks. "And I won't be punished because he's gone. I want them legally to be my sons."

I lose the last of my control. "It's never fucking happening," I splutter. "They are my and Wade's sons. Not yours. They will never be yours. I told you to find someone else and have your own children—you can't have Wade's."

He punches the steering wheel as he loses control, and we all jump. Patrick starts to cry.

"You're scaring him."

Tristan grips the steering wheel with white-knuckle force. His eyes fill with tears as he stares straight ahead.

Why did I say that?

Tears well in my eyes, and I angrily wipe them away.

We drive in silence the rest of the way, and he pulls into the driveway. He leaves the car going.

"Are you coming, Tris?" Harry whispers.

"No, buddy," Tristan replies as he stares straight ahead. "I'll call you later."

"No, Tristan," Patrick begs. "Please come in." He begins to cry. "Don't go." He grabs him over the back of his seat as he begs him not to leave.

Tristan closes his eyes.

I get out of the car, angry that my children would choose him over me. Surely they get my point? Don't they have any loyalty to their father?

"Get out of the car," I demand to the boys.

Fletcher gets out.

"Get out of the car," I snap. Patrick slowly gets out.

Harry sits tight.

"Get out of the car, Harrison."

"I'm going with Tristan."

405

I'm furious. How dare he say that in front of the boys and put me in the position where they think I'm the bad guy? I'm being loyal to their father . . . and so should they.

"You will do no such thing." I yank the door open and grab his arm as he fights me. "Let me go!" he screams as he kicks at me. "I want to stay with him."

Tristan pinches the bridge of his nose, overwhelmed by the situation.

I struggle to get him out as the two other boys watch in horror, and I slam the car door hard.

The tires screech as Tristan takes off like a maniac.

I turn to the boys. Tears run down their faces as they glare at me. "I hate you," Harry cries. "Make him come back."

He runs inside and slams the door.

"You ruined everything, Mom!" Patrick yells.

They turn and run inside after Harry.

I close my eyes . . . fuck, how the hell did that escalate to this?

Chapter 24

Love is stupid. Love is blind.

Love is a fucking bitch!

I have the shower on full bore to block out the sound of my heart breaking . . . I don't want the boys to see me cry. I stand under the hot water as the tears run down my face. The lump in my throat is big, the hole in my heart a giant crevasse.

Where the hell did that argument come from?

I had no idea any of that was on Tristan's agenda.

It shocked me—scared the hell out of me, if I'm honest. I get a vision of the hurt in Tristan's eyes, and my heart drops.

What have I done?

I pushed away the only person who has my back.

Tristan.

My beautiful Tristan, the man who loves me. The one who has cared for all of us . . . the man who would literally walk across fire to please me . . . wants to take on my children, and I just . . . can't.

I can't be that irresponsible and blinded by love.

Why would he want to adopt them? What benefit would it have for him?

If he's with me, he has them.

Letting him adopt them only gives him the power to take them if he doesn't need me anymore.

No woman in her right mind would allow a future partner to adopt her children by law. Not when they are already happy and stable. There is no reason for him to want it . . . other than if we break up.

He wants legal assurance that no matter what happens between us, he will always have them.

No.

I'm sorry.

I can't give him that.

Because I know that if we ever broke up, it would be because he cheated or did something to have caused it. I would never do anything to end us—I love him too much. And in that event, there is no way in hell I would be packing up my sons to go to his house every weekend to play happy family with his new girlfriend.

No woman would ever agree to this. No matter how in love she was. No matter who the man was . . . no matter what her sons wanted.

I screw up my face in tears when I picture their broken little faces as he drove off.

You did the right thing, whispers my conscience.

"Did I?" I reply. "Because it sure doesn't feel like it."

My shoulders rack with sobs; I have this sick, heavy, fucked-up lead ball in my stomach. I want to throw up or run away, and I want to go to him . . . but I can't do any of those things.

I stand for a long time under the hot water. With every minute that passes, along comes a little more guilt.

The vile taste runs through my bloodstream like poison. I'm sickened by what I said to him this afternoon, mortified that I could be so cold and hurtful. He's only ever loved us.

"I feel like I betrayed my best friend." I see the tears in his eyes when I said those horrible things, and I cry harder.

"Oh God, I'm done with this stress. Why is nothing damn easy with me?" I sob. "Why does everything have to be so fucking hard?"

I want to live in this house with my boys . . . and Tristan.

That's it. Nothing fancy, nothing different.

Why does he want things to change? It doesn't have to be like this.

The boys aren't talking to me. They're all in their bedrooms, the house is quiet and sad, and I know Tristan is alone and heartbroken in his apartment.

I slide down the wall and sit on the hard, cold tiles. I roll into a ball to try to protect myself from the pain.

But there is no antidote for this situation . . . I'm going to lose him.

Maybe I did already.

Sadness is heavy. Sadness is still.

I lie in the darkness and watch the time tick by: 11:53 p.m.

My mind goes to my beautiful man. What's he doing?

I can't do this. I can't lie here and do nothing.

I have to try to fix this. I can't go to sleep without speaking to him. I lean over and grab my phone from the side table and dial his number. My heart beats nervously as I wait for him to pick up.

It stops ringing . . . he declined the call.

My stomach sinks.

He's never rejected a call from me . . . ever.

I think for a moment, and I text.

I'm sorry about today,
I don't know what happened.
It spiraled out of control.
I'll call you tomorrow.

Goodnight,

I love you.

xoxo

I watch and see the read symbol come up. I smile . . . he saw it.

I wait as I hold my breath.

"Reply," I whisper. I hold my breath as I wait.

Nothing.

I watch and watch . . . and wait.

My eyes fill with tears. "Reply, baby."

But he doesn't, and I know he's not going to.

My heart drops to a new low, and the tears come hard and fast.

I've ruined everything.

I sit and stare at the figures on my computer, trying to miraculously find an extra $200,000.

I've sold our holiday home, I've sold all of our shares. Everything that Wade and I accumulated in our time together is gone.

And now to keep the man I love, I'm expected to hand his children over as well.

That's an unfair request. Surely Tristan must know that. How can he not see my point?

I feel like there's this big black cloud hanging over me and that I'll never truly be happy.

I must have been bad in my last life, because I feel like I'm being punished for something. I've loved two men in my life. One I lost to death.

The other . . .

I rest my hand under my chin and stare into space, wondering if I could have handled yesterday better.

There's no question I could have.

But . . . I stand by what I said. I don't want anyone to adopt my boys. I won't give over that power to someone else.

Even if that someone is the love of my life. It's not just Tristan—this isn't personal. This is sensible.

They are Wade's sons. They will always be Wade's sons.

My every instinct is telling me this is something that I should never do.

Always trust your gut.

A message comes through on my phone. It's from Tristan.

Can we talk?

Relief fills me. I write back.

Please.

He replies.

Our hotel,
1pm.

I smile, hopeful.

See you then.
I love you.
xoxox

At one o'clock I hold my breath as I walk into the foyer of our hotel. We've been here many times before. Always in excitement.

Today it's in dread.

Tristan stands over near the elevator, and my stomach flutters when I see him wearing his power suit and standing the way he does, straight and proud.

I know that if he really wants something, it's nonnegotiable.

"Hi." I smile.

"Hello." He dips his head, and in that moment fear runs through me.

He's not going to let this go.

I'm going to lose him.

We get into the elevator and ride up to our floor in silence.

Oh my God . . . no. Don't let this happen.

I stand behind him silently as he opens the door, and I walk in and take a seat on the bed.

He closes the door and walks straight to the bar and pours himself a scotch. "Do you want a drink?"

"No, thanks."

In slow motion he sips his scotch. His eyes hold mine.

"Tristan . . . what I said yesterday—"

"Yes," he cuts me off. "Let's talk about that."

Nerves begin to thump in my chest. "You need to understand where I am coming from. I love you. I want to spend the rest of my life with you." I pause.

"But?"

"But I made promises to my first husband. These children are his, and I need to honor his wishes."

He clenches his jaw; his eyes hold mine.

"We decided to live in that house for a reason."

"Such as?"

I smile, grateful that he's at least listening to me.

"Wade wanted that house. We could have afforded better, but he wanted that house. He wanted the boys to grow up in Long Island."

He stares at me, and I have no idea what he's thinking.

"He wanted the boys to go to a public school, and yet I let you take them out."

He screws up his face in anger. "You would keep them in a school that is no good for them, just to prove a fucking point?"

"No," I stammer as I begin to panic. "You were right on that one. I know you were—it was for the best."

I wring my hands in front of me. "I'm stressed out. I feel like I'm losing control, and I just want things to stay the same between us."

He puts his hands in his suit pockets and smiles as he drops his head in amusement.

Oh no . . . I know that look.

"So . . . what you are saying, Claire, is that you want me to step in and be Wade."

My face falls. "What? No."

"Yes, you do."

"I don't. I swear."

"You want me to live in Wade's house, with Wade's wife . . . with Wade's children."

I stare at him.

"What about fucking me, Claire?" he cries. "Where the fuck is my life?"

My eyes fill with tears at his anger. "Tristan," I whisper.

"I want my own wife, Claire, with my own children and to live in a fucking house that we choose together."

Tears overfill my eyes, and I swipe them away angrily.

"You told me when we met that there were three hearts connected to yours." He begins to pace. "Did you not?"

I stay silent.

"Answer me . . . fuck it!" he screams.

I jump. "Yes."

"So now that I'm in love with those hearts, and I want them as my sons"—he glares at me—"you tell me that I can't have them?"

His silhouette blurs. "Tristan," I whisper. "Please try and see this from my point of view."

"You're selfish, Claire." His eyes fill with tears.

I drop my head as fear overwhelms me. I'm going to lose him too.

"I deserve to have my own family."

"I know you do," I murmur.

"I want the boys as mine."

"Tristan." I shake my head. "I can't."

He clenches his jaw. "You know . . . my mother told me way back then . . . that they would always be another man's sons, that you would always be another man's wife." His eyes hold mine. "That you would never truly be my family—I would always be the stand-in."

I screw up my face in tears. He's so hurt.

He shakes his head. "I can't live with that, Claire."

"What are you saying?" I whisper.

His eyes hold mine. "I'm saying goodbye . . . I'm nobody's backup plan."

I try to contain my sobs. "No, Tris," I beg.

His haunted eyes hold mine . . . a silent beg for me to stop him.

We stare at each other, and this is it. The defining moment where I choose between my past and my present.

Regret hangs in the air between us, and I want to do as he asks. I want to concede to his demands.

Anything to keep him here with me.

But I just can't . . . and it's killing me.

Eventually, he turns and leaves. The door clicks quietly as it closes behind him.

I sob out loud into the silence.

He's gone.

The days are long . . . but the nights are endless.

Sleeping without him is a hell that I can't endure.

So I don't.

I pace . . . all night. Back and forth, back and forth . . . until my legs ache.

It's been nine days since Tristan left me.

Nine days in sheer hell.

The house is silent, the laughter gone. The boys are barely speaking to me.

Not only have I broken my heart; I've broken the four others that I love the most.

My sons' and Tristan's.

I stare at my computer. I have no urge to be at work . . . to be at home . . . to breathe.

My phone buzzes across my desk, and the name Fletcher lights up the screen.

"Hey, buddy." I smile. Hopefully he's talking to me again.

"Tristan is leaving," he whispers.

"What?"

"He's going to Paris."

"For how long?"

"He just transferred my internship to Jameson."

I stand as my eyes widen. "What?"

"He said he's not coming back, Mom. You really did it," he whispers angrily.

I screw up my face in tears, so close to the edge of the cliff I can almost feel myself hitting the bottom. "I'm coming," I stammer. "Keep him there; I'm coming."

I grab my bag and run.

Marley stands up as I run past her. "What in the world?"

"I'm out for the day," I call.

"Huh?" she calls after me. "But you have a meeting in an hour."

"Cancel it," I call as I run into the elevator. I hit the button with force. "Come on, come on."

I can't let him go.

He can't go.

The doors slowly close, and I tap my foot nervously. "Hurry."

I drag my hands through my hair as I begin to perspire . . . no . . . no . . . no, this can't be happening.

The elevator slowly goes down, and the doors open. A heap of people are standing there waiting. "Sorry." I slam the button to close the doors. "No time for you."

The door closes as their faces fall. I get to the ground floor and sprint through the foyer and run out into the street with my arm in the air. "Taxi!" I call as a cab drives past.

Another man is waiting on the curb for a cab too.

"Oh my God," I cry to him. "This is an emergency; my boyfriend is leaving me."

He winces.

"Because I'm selfish," I pant as I run up the street, arm stretched high. "Now he's flying to Paris without saying goodbye."

He rolls his eyes. "You are not getting my cab."

"I don't want your damn cab," I bark. A cab pulls up, and I dive into the back of it like a maniac. "I've got my own. The Miles Media building, please," I stammer.

"Hey!" the man calls as he watches me drive off. I give him a half wave.

"Bye."

I crane my neck to look at the traffic jam ahead.

"Can you drive fast, please? This is an emergency."

"Okay, lady." He swerves and turns down a side street.

My phone rings, and the name Fletcher lights up the screen. "Hello," I stammer.

"He's gone, Mom."

My face falls. "What?" I stare out the window. I don't believe this. "Which airport is he going to?"

"Hang on." He puts the phone down and asks someone, "Which airport?"

"JFK," I hear a woman reply. "Terminal two."

"JFK," Fletcher snaps. "Terminal two."

"Okay, I got it." I hang up. "Change of plans!" I yell to the driver. "JFK Airport. Terminal two. Please hurry; this is a life-and-death situation."

The driver does a sharp U-turn, and I hold on for dear life.

Thirty minutes later we arrive. I throw him the money and get out and run.

The check-in area is busy and bustling, and I look around frantically.

Where is he? Where . . . I turn a full 360-degree circle. Where is he?

I dial Fletcher's number.

"Hello," he snaps.

"Where is he? I can't find him. I'm at the airport. Call him, and find out where he is," I cry as I look around frantically.

"Okay. Sammia, call him and find out where he is." He comes back to me. "Stay on the line, Mom."

I hold the phone really close, and I hear Sammia talking to Tristan in the background.

"He's still in the car," Fletcher whispers. "He's just pulling up now."

I hang up and run out through the front doors, and I see the long black limo pulling in at the other end of the terminal. I kick off my shoes, pick them up, and run.

Tristan gets out slowly. He takes his luggage out of the trunk. Three suitcases.

He's leaving me.

I run as fast as I can through the crowd, and as I approach him, he glances up and sees me and stops what he's doing.

I throw up my arms in desperation. "What are you doing?" I cry.

He drops his head, his armor firmly in place. "Claire, don't cause a scene."

"Don't cause a scene?" I cry. "You're just going to leave us."

He stares at me and clenches his jaw. Damn it, I've hurt him.

I rush to him and take him into my arms. "Tris," I whisper. "I love you. I don't want you to leave. I'm just stressed about losing the business, and I said awful things."

He frowns. "Losing the business?"

I screw up my face in tears. "It's gone." I wipe the tears out of my eyes angrily. "I can't hold it any longer."

"What?" His expression abruptly changes. "Why didn't you tell me?"

"Because I didn't want you to know that I couldn't do it," I whisper. "I wanted you to be proud of me."

He stares at me, shock on his face.

"And then you wanted to change everything and the house and the boys, and I was overwhelmed and . . ." I shake my head in despair. This is all coming out wrong. "If you have me, you already have the boys—you don't need to adopt them."

His back straightens. "It's nonnegotiable, Claire."

My face falls. "What?"

"If I marry you, I want to adopt the boys."

"Why do you want to change things?" I stammer.

"Because . . . I want my own family."

"But I love you."

"It isn't enough."

My face falls.

Oh my God . . . this really is the end; my eyes fill with tears, and we stare at each other as everyone else in the airport disappears.

I take a step back from him to try to protect myself from what he's saying.

"I would give up having my own children, Claire, so that I don't lose yours."

A tear rolls down my cheek, and the lump in my throat nearly closes over.

"I love them. I want them as my sons. I want their surname to be Anderson-Miles."

I shake my head, unable to push the word *no* past my lips. "You just want to take them," I whisper. "You've already taken me over; you can't take over my sons. They are not up for grabs. You want power. I know how you work, Tristan—you always have to be in charge."

His face falls. "Is that what you think?"

I nod. What else could it be?

He drops his head; his face is solemn. "Goodbye, Claire."

"Why?" I cry. "Why do you want this so much?"

He turns to me like the devil himself. "Because I deserve my own family, God damn it. And I love them, and if you can't see that, I don't even fucking know who you are."

My heart drops.

He leans forward. "All this time . . . I thought you loved me," he whispers through tears. He pauses as my eyes search his. "Guess not."

"Tris," I whisper.

He turns and marches through the doors and into the airport.

"Tristan," I call.

He keeps walking.

"Tristan!" I cry.

The private doors open, and he walks through them without looking back. Security guards step in front of them to block me from running after him.

He's gone.

Fourteen days and fourteen nights . . . living without her.

Without them.

I sip my beer as I stare at the football game on the screen. I'm in the busiest American pub in Paris. People are everywhere. I hear their voices in the distance; the echoes of their jovial laughter fill the space. But I feel as if I'm hovering above them, not really here, not really there.

In a detached state, cut . . . to the bone.

If it were a physical injury, I would be in intensive care, barely clinging to life.

The heart hurts more than any injury ever could. It beats weakly . . . barely at all.

Every breath that I take feels like my chest is about to cave in.

Every exhale a struggle.

The walls have closed in, the dust has settled, and yet nothing has changed.

The world is spinning at a million miles per minute, but the silence without them . . . is deafening.

I never knew what it felt like to lose someone you loved. A heartbeat that once we shared, I can no longer hear.

I lost four pieces of myself on the same day.

My entire world.

I sip my beer as I stare at the television screen on the wall.

I want to talk to my boys . . . I want to kiss my girl.

And then I remember the painful truth.

That neither are mine—they will never be mine.

They belong to him.

My phone buzzes in my pocket, and the name Jameson lights up the screen. "Hey," I answer.

"You all right?"

"I'm fine, Jay." I sigh.

"Elliot and Christopher are on their way."

"That's not necessary."

"Hmm . . . I kind of think it is."

I stay silent.

"Where are you?" he asks.

"In a bar."

"Alone?"

"Yep." I roll my eyes and catch sight of myself in the mirror behind the bar.

I see him, the man whom the world sees, the heartless take-over king in the expensive suit.

The one who's dead inside.

This time, they're right . . . I am.

"I got to go." I sigh.

"Promise me you're all right."

"I'll call you tomorrow. I'm fine," I reply as I hang up. But I don't know if I'm fine. I don't even know what I am anymore, who I am . . . I frown and sip my drink.

This is an emptiness that I don't know how to fight.

The waiter wipes the bar. "Another one?" he asks.

"Yes." I nod once. "Keep them coming."

I read down the list of unopened emails, and I frown.

Anderson Media.

She emailed me from her work account. I click the email open.

Dear Mr. Miles,

I have fought all I can, I have nothing left to give. With no financial relief in sight,

I would like to accept your offer to acquire Anderson Media.

I would like assurance that all staff will keep their positions within the company or offered alternative employment.

Please find the attached financials and spread-sheets that you require for the due diligence.

Your first offer will be accepted.

Sincerely,
Claire Anderson

I stare at the email, void of emotion. How long has she been struggling to keep her business afloat?

Why didn't she tell me?

My mind goes back to the first time we met and how aggressive I was with her.

I was so hell bent on taking her company that I didn't care about anything else, no matter how much I was attracted to her—it was the company acquisition that I wanted.

I remember how determined she was to fight to the end.

The fire she had inside of her was so bright that I could feel it. It was the thing that drew me to her. Determination like that is so rare these days; it's not often I come across it.

That very same determination to be independent has now driven a wedge between us. It has all along, if I'm honest.

I had to fight to be in her life, and now I have to choose between what I know I deserve and what she wants. Both things should be the same.

It's heartbreaking that they aren't even on the same page. I exhale heavily as these depressing thoughts fill my soul.

How did it get to this?

What must it be like to lose something that you fought so hard for so long to keep? I imagine how gutted she must be. The timing couldn't be worse.

"Claire," I whisper. "Why didn't you tell me?"

I exhale heavily and click open the financial spreadsheets.

Time to separate business and pleasure . . . or in this case, business and heartbreak.

There will be no winner here.

"Can we go away with Uncle Bob this weekend fishing?" Harry asks.

I smile in relief. This is the first time Harry has talked to me all week. "Where's he going?"

"Down to Bear Mountain. He called and asked if Patrick and I could go."

"Oh." I stare at him for a moment. "You really want to go away fishing now?" I ask. Typical kids—don't understand that I need them close right now. "Is Fletcher going?"

"No, Fletcher said he didn't want to after working all week."

"I'll think about it," I reply.

He stares at me for a beat, as if waiting for me to say something.

"Do you want to talk about Saturday?" I ask.

He puts his hand on his hip with attitude. "Are you going to call Tristan and apologize?"

"I already went and saw Tristan, Harry."

His face lights up in excitement. "What did he say?"

I shrug as I search for the right words. "We decided that we're just going to be friends for the moment," I reply as I sip my coffee. He doesn't need to know the ins and outs of our conversation at the airport. I don't want to remember it myself.

He frowns. "So . . . he's not coming back?"

My heart drops. "No, honey. Remember, I told you that he had to go to Paris to work for a while." I take his hand and hold it in mine. "You need to understand why Tristan and I have a different opinion on the adoption thing."

He stares at me.

"Tristan isn't your dad, Harry, and although we all love each other, sometimes things don't turn out the way that we want them to. Tristan was my boyfriend, and going forward, I'm not sure where we stand with that. I'm sad too. This is affecting all of us. But he will always be your friend, Harry. Nobody will ever take that from the two of you."

"Dad's dead, Mom. And he's not coming back," he spits. "And Tristan wants to be my new dad . . . and you won't let him."

My eyes fill with tears at his cold attitude. "Harry."

"You ruined it," he blurts out like a poison. "You've ruined everything." He storms off.

"Harry, come back here!" I call after him.

He marches up the stairs and slams his bedroom door hard.

I drag my hand down my face. God, this is a fucking nightmare.

The first two months Tristan and I were together, Harry hated him with a passion, and now . . . he's the one who's unable to cope with all of this.

There are three hearts connected to mine.

I dial my brother's phone number and wait as it rings. "Hey, sis," he replies, and I can tell he's smiling.

"Hey," I breathe. I love my brother, and at times like this I just want to go and sleep on his couch so that I can be close to him. He makes everything seem better, and I have no doubt that's why my boys are seeking him out.

"How you doing?" he asks.

"Okay." I sigh.

"How you really doing?"

"Pretty crap." I smile sadly.

"Thought so."

"You really want to take the boys fishing this weekend?"

"Yeah, sure. When Harry called me—"

"Harry called you?" I interrupt him.

"Yeah, said he wanted to get away for the weekend with the boys."

I get a lump in my throat . . . he's really missing Tris.

425

"Anyway," he continues, "I'm happy to go. I could use some time with them too."

"Okay."

"I'll text Harry all the details and keep in contact with him," he says.

"Thanks." I sigh sadly. My heart feels like it's about to break from guilt.

"Hey . . . sis?" Bob says.

"Yeah."

"Are you sure you're doing the right thing with Tristan? Everybody seems pretty damn heartbroken over there."

My eyes fill with tears. "No, Bob, I'm not," I whisper.

"You might want to work it out pretty soon . . . before it's too late."

I get a lump in my throat. "I know," I whisper through tears. *Too late.*

A feeling I am all too familiar with. After Wade died, there were so many things that I had left unsaid . . . it was too late to tell him.

"You okay?"

"Uh-huh," I lie as I wipe my tears. "It's been a rough week. I'll survive." I smile sadly. "I always do."

"Bye, darlin'. Love you."

"I love you too."

I sit and stare at my phone for a moment until I can't stop myself anymore. I text Tristan.

I love you,

xoxo

I hit send and stare at my phone, and eventually the word appears.

Read.

He's read the message.

I wait . . . and I wait . . . and I wonder what he's doing right now. *Text me back . . . please.*

But he doesn't, and I cry because I know that it's probably already too late.

I sit in front of Fletcher's building in the loading bay. It's Friday afternoon, and I'm picking him up from work. The boys left to go on their fishing trip straight from school. It's just the two of us for three days.

I watch him walk out the front doors with Jameson. They're talking and laughing.

Does Jameson know about Tristan and me?

Jameson glances over at the car and nods his head. He turns his attention straight back to Fletcher.

He knows all right, and he's pissed.

The whole world thinks I'm doing the wrong thing . . . maybe I am.

I love Tristan. With all of my heart, I love Tristan. I would give anything to have him back in my life. But I can't give control to someone over my children; I just can't.

It's nonnegotiable.

And if he loved me, he would understand why.

This isn't an acquisition; this isn't just another takeover. These are my children.

Wade's flesh and blood, and I won't sign them over.

No matter how much it kills me.

And it might . . . I've never felt so sad. Well, that's a lie—I have felt this sad, but it was a different sad. It was grief, a deep dark hole of grief.

This time, my love is very much alive and well.

It's a torture that I can't explain.

I know Tristan is hurting, too, and I can't comfort him, and I can't get through to him.

He won't answer my calls. He won't listen to me.

And I said some horrible things that I wish I could take back, but in the end, I stand by my decision.

Why can't he see that?

Fletcher comes and gets into the car. "Hi," he says as he throws his bag into the back seat.

"Hi." I smile over at him. "How was your day?"

"Yeah, good."

I pull out into the traffic. "Let's go out for dinner, just the two of us."

"Ah . . ." He hesitates.

"You don't want to?" I frown over at him.

He scrunches his nose up. "Not really. I'm tired. It's been a big week at work. I just want to go home and chill, if that's okay."

I nod, saddened. "Okay, takeout it is."

The drive home is made in silence. I thought Fletcher was okay about Tristan and me, but maybe that's just because he was quiet. Now that I'm alone with him, I'm sensing more of his feelings.

He's angry.

With every mile we drive, the silence builds more animosity between us.

We get closer to home, and I pull into the bottle shop. "I'm just going to run in and get a bottle of wine."

Fletcher rolls his eyes, unimpressed.

I get out of the car and slam the door, annoyed. Since when is getting a bottle of wine a fucking crime? I walk around the shop as I mutter to myself angrily.

I've lost Tristan for standing up for my kids on behalf of their dead father, and now they aren't talking to me?

What a joke.

And no matter how much they love Tristan, they can't love him as much as I do.

I march back out to the car with a bee in my bonnet. Damn kids. I start the car, and we drive the two blocks home. Fletcher gets out and slams the door and marches inside.

Something inside of me snaps, and I storm in after him. I find him in the kitchen.

"What is your problem, Fletcher?" I snap.

"If you don't know what my problem is, then you're purposely ignoring my problem," he snarls.

I'm taken aback with his aggression. Fletcher never gets angry with me—never. "You are old enough to understand this, Fletch. I'm not the bad guy here. I'm acting on behalf of your dad."

"What?" he cries as he screws up his face in disgust. "You think that you're acting on behalf of Dad?" he scoffs.

I put my hands on my hips. "What is that supposed to mean?"

"Dad sent Tristan for us, Mom."

His eyes search mine.

"Don't you see?" he yells. "Dad was the one who found Tristan and sent him to us." His eyes well with tears. "What the hell would a man like Tristan Miles want with us . . . if Dad hadn't arranged it in heaven?" he cries.

My face falls. Pain sears my heart. The thought of my beautiful Wade searching for a new dad for his children breaks my heart, because I know it is something that he would do.

If he could send the best man on the planet to me, he would have.

He did.

The room begins to spin. Everything becomes foggy as I imagine Wade watching me from heaven with my broken heart . . . his children with their broken hearts . . . unable to help us.

"You're the only one who doesn't see it," Fletcher snaps.

"You think your dad sent Tristan for us?" I whisper.

"I know it, Mom. Harry and Patrick know it . . . why don't you know it?" he whispers through tears. "How can't you see it, Mom? When it's all we can see."

I drop my head and stare at the ground. Tears run down my face. They are hot and taste salty.

He runs out the front door, and it slams behind him. I put my face into my hands.

This heartbreak, this pain . . . I can't do it anymore.

Make it stop.

The sun peeks through the curtains, and I listen to the lawn mower next door. Every now and then it runs over a rock, and it makes a jarring sound.

Why do they have to mow their fucking lawn every Saturday morning and wake the entire neighborhood?

They don't even work. Why can't they do it during the week?

Why so early on the weekend?

I get up and go to the bathroom and peer through the side of the drapes at the perpetrator. I should storm down there and give them a piece of my mind.

But I won't, because this has been annoying me for years now, and I just smile every time I see them. They've had to put up with my hooligan kids throwing balls into their yard and riding their bikes across their lawn as a shortcut. I guess we're even.

I grab my phone and return to bed. I cried all night last night. I feel like I'm having a fucking breakdown or something. Things can't get any worse. I do feel a little better today, though, so that's something.

I go onto Facebook and scroll through. I go to Instagram and browse for a while, and then a video comes up from my brother's story.

He's dancing in a bar.

Huh?

I go back and watch it again. It must be old footage. He's out in the boondocks camping with the boys . . . where is this bar?

I read the caption: *dancing the night away.*

Huh?

I flick through to Bob's Facebook page and scroll down. Sure enough, he's posted a pic of himself getting on a plane, with the caption *Florida here I come.*

What?

I immediately dial his number. It rings out, and I call again.

"Hello," he answers groggily in a very hungover voice.

"Where are you?" I ask.

"Florida."

"Where are the boys?" I snap.

"Huh?"

"Where are the boys?"

"What do you mean? They canceled and said they couldn't go. I came here with my buddies."

I sit up in bed. "Bob, they're not here. I haven't seen them since Friday morning."

"What?"

"I thought they were with you?" I cry.

"I thought they were with you!" he cries back.

"Oh my God," I whisper as my eyes widen.

"What?"

"They've run away, Bob."

"Holy fuck, call the police."

Chapter 25

Tristan

I sit out on the balcony of my hotel room in Paris. I just got back from the hotel gym and am going in to the office this afternoon. I'm still working on the due diligence for Anderson Media. I want the deal closed early this week if possible.

The sooner I move on to new things, the better. I need to drag myself off the floor here. I can't go on like this.

I just want it over with.

My room phone rings, and I frown. Who would be calling me in the hotel? Nobody ever does. I walk inside and answer. "Bonjour."

"Mr. Miles?"

"Oui."

"Vous avez des visiteurs." (Translation: You have some visitors.)

I frown. "Qui est-ce?" (Translation: Who is it?)

"Juste une minute." (Translation: Just a minute.) He passes the phone to someone.

"Tris?"

I frown and screw up my face in confusion . . . what? "Harry?"

"Come and get us."

My eyes nearly bulge from their sockets. "I'll be right down." I run to the door and hit the elevator button.

They're here.

I watch the dial over the doors, and I tap my foot. Come on . . . come on.

The doors open, and I rush out and look around to see Harry and Patrick sitting on the lounge waiting for me. They look up and see me, and both come running at me at a million miles per minute. They nearly bowl me over as they grab a leg each to hug.

I put my arms around them and hold them tight. "Where's Mom?" I whisper into their hair.

"We ran away."

My mouth falls open in horror. "Your mother doesn't know you're here?" I gasp.

They both shake their heads. "Nope."

"Oh my God." I take out my phone. "She's going to be fucking frantic." I call Claire.

"Tristan," she cries in a panic. "They've run away."

"They just turned up here," I stammer.

"What?" she gasps.

"Patrick and Harrison just turned up at my hotel in Paris."

"What the hell?" she gasps. "Really?"

"Yes."

"They're okay, they're okay," I hear her tell someone.

"Where are you?" I ask.

"In the police station. Oh my God, Tristan," she cries in relief. "Oh my God. It's okay, Fletcher. They're safe," she says.

I flick the peak of Harry's cap. "You're in so much trouble," I mouth.

"I don't care," he mouths back with attitude.

433

"I'm on my way," she stammers. "Fletcher and I will catch the first flight out."

"Okay."

"Bye, Tris." She hangs up.

I look down at the two boys as they stare up at me. "What are you two thinking?" I snap. "Your mother has been frantic," I whisper as I gesture to the elevator. "You two are in so much trouble I can't even believe it," I whisper angrily.

They both smile up at me, and my heart constricts. I bend and take them both in my arms. "You little shits," I murmur into their hair.

"We came to get you," Patrick whispers into my shoulder. "We want you as our dad. We don't care what Mom says. It's up to us, anyway."

I grip them tighter in my arms, and I could just burst into tears. We hold on to each other tightly for a long time, and I'm quite sure everyone around is watching.

I take their hands, and we get into the elevator. "Do you know how dangerous that was? How the hell did you get on a plane, anyway?" I ask.

"With your credit card."

My mouth falls open. "You stole my credit card?" I gasp. "Oh my God. Harrison," I scold him. "You are unbelievable."

"No, I borrowed it. It was in Mom's drawer."

The credit card I had given to Claire for emergencies. The one she refused to use.

"You are grounded for life," I whisper as I hold his hand.

He smiles cheekily up at me, and I smirk down at him.

I fucking love this kid.

We get to my hotel suite, and I flop onto the lounge. They both sit nearly on top of me. They tell me how they lied to Bob and to Claire and sneaked out and caught the train to the airport and then somehow got on a plane without being stopped. They tell me every single detail about their last fifteen hours, and I can hardly believe it.

Patrick's little arms are tight around my neck as we converse, and Harrison's hand is on my thigh. They are animated and cutting each other off and so proud of themselves for actually pulling it off.

"Why did you come here?" I ask as I look between them.

"Because we love you," Harry says. "And we're staying with you until you come home . . . and you can't make us leave. You're our dad, and dads belong with their kids."

I pull them close and hold them tight. "I love you too," I whisper into their hair.

My heart bursts with love for these boys.

I smile. It seems all this lying makes for two sweaty kids. "And you two need a shower. You stink."

They moan.

"Where's Fletch?" I ask as I lead them into the bathroom.

"He wouldn't leave Mom alone for the weekend."

I smile proudly. *Always looking out for his mom.* "That's my boy."

It's just now 3:40 a.m., and the text I've been waiting for arrives from Claire.

Just pulling up at the hotel now.

She's here.
I text back.

Concierge knows you are coming,

435

They have a key for you.

A reply bounces back.

See you soon.

I begin to pace; my heart is in my throat. Claire's going to flip her fucking lid.

My God, that was so dangerous, what the boys did. Just wait till I get ahold of the airline responsible.

I take deep breaths. I'm nervous to see her.

It's been a long, lonely, and hellish few weeks.

The door lock clicks, and the door slowly opens. Fletcher walks in, and I pull him in for a hug. Then I see Claire, and my heart drops.

She's distraught, in tears, and pale. She looks like she's lost a lot of weight.

"Baby," I whisper.

She screws her face into tears, and I take her in my arms. She cries against my shoulder as I hold her tight. "Shh, they're okay," I whisper into her hair. "They're asleep. It's okay." I lead her by the hand into the bedroom, and she kisses both their foreheads as they sleep.

"I'm going to kill those two knuckleheads," Fletcher whispers.

"Get in line," I mutter as I watch Claire sob over them.

I turn to Fletcher and pull him into my arms again. "Good boy for staying with your mother," I whisper. I slap him on the back.

"Where am I sleeping?" he asks. "I'm exhausted."

"In the room next door."

"Good night, Mom," Fletcher whispers.

Claire wraps her arms around him. "Thank you so much, Fletch. Good night, sweetheart."

I close the boys' door, and we walk out into the living room. I'm waiting for her onslaught.

I turn toward her. "Claire—"

"I love you," she cuts me off. Her eyes are filled with tears, the pain in them unbearable for me to look at. "Whatever you want me to do," she whispers. "Wherever you want me to live. I'll do it."

Her eyes search mine.

"Just don't leave me again." She sobs. "I can't stand it. I can't do this without you, Tris." Her chest heaves with tears, and it's obvious she's been crying a long time. "Please don't leave me again," she begs in a whisper.

"Baby," I whisper as I pull her close. I've never seen her like this. "I'm not. I promise. I love you. We can do it your way." I hold her tight. "As long as I'm with you, it will be okay. I don't need papers; it's okay."

For a long time, she stays and cries in my arms. I hate seeing her like this. She's completely broken. She's usually always so strong. "Come on. Shower." I lead her into the bathroom and turn the hot water on. I slowly undress her.

She stands before me, weak and fragile. So not like my strong Claire.

My heart constricts at how much weight she's lost. I walk her in under the water, and her sad eyes hold mine. "Can you get in with me?"

I take my clothes off and step in, and we hold each other under the hot water. Her head is on my chest, my arms wrapped around her small frame.

This isn't like our normal showers together. This isn't about sex; it's about love.

My love . . . for *her*.

"I love you," I whisper.

She screws her face up into my neck. "Don't leave me again."

"I won't," I promise her.

She clings to me. This is going to take a while to get over. For both of us. But she's here. My family is here with me. We will get through this.

We have to.

I lie on my side and watch Claire sleep. She's utterly exhausted.

It's all caught up with her—the stress at work, our breakup, and then the boys going missing have her so wound up that she couldn't stop crying last night. Her body simply gave out. Enough was enough, and in the end, I gave her two sleeping pills so that she could finally relax enough to fall asleep.

I hear an argument from the other room, and I smile. Who knew that the sound of early-morning bickering could sound so good? I get up and go to investigate.

"I don't care if you didn't bring any other shorts," Fletcher snaps to Harry. "You're not wearing mine. No wonder I couldn't find any of my things to pack—they're all in your suitcase."

"Shh, Mom's asleep," I whisper as I walk into the room. "What's going on?"

"Harry stole all of my clothes," Fletcher whispers angrily.

"I did not." He looks to me. "All my shorts don't fit me anymore."

"It's too early for this." I sigh. "Give Fletcher back his shorts. I'll buy you new ones today, Harrison."

"Well, that's not fair," Fletcher snaps. "Why does he get new shorts?"

"Can I have new shorts?" Patrick asks from bed. "I've been growing lately, and I need all-new clothes."

Harry rolls his eyes. "Oh, stop it. You have not grown."

I look among the bickering boys, and a broad smile crosses my face. I'm actually grateful to be hearing them fight . . . who would have ever thought? "I'll buy you all new clothes today," I reply.

Their eyes widen.

"But right now, I want you to get dressed, go downstairs to the restaurant, and have breakfast," I say. "Eat something healthy from the buffet."

"Are you coming?" Patrick asks.

"I'm going to stay here with Mom. You'll be fine with Fletcher. Don't go anywhere else." I point to the two trouble-makers. "You come straight back up to the room when you're done. I mean it; you two are seriously grounded for life. Nowhere without an adult. Ever."

Fletcher gives a smug smile to his two brothers. He loves that I class him as an adult.

I make myself a coffee, and they shower and mess around, and about half an hour later they go downstairs for breakfast.

I hear the front door shut behind the boys, and I call out, "Tris?" I've been waiting for them to leave. I knew if I got up before they went, I would have to go to breakfast with them, and I want some time.

He appears at the door. "Hey." He's wearing nothing but navy boxer shorts. His beautiful body is on display.

I pull the covers back in an invitation.

He smiles and locks the door and climbs in and pulls me into his arms. "Are you all right?" he whispers.

I close my eyes as I lean against his chest. "God, I'm sorry about last night. I was a basket case."

"Don't be. You are so stressed; I'm worried about you."

I hug him tighter. Feels so good to be safe in his big strong arms.

He takes my face in his hands. "Why didn't you tell me before about Anderson Media being in trouble?"

I run my hand down over his washboard stomach. "I didn't want you to worry."

"Stop it. We need to talk about this." He pushes my hand away. "So . . . you took it all on yourself?"

"Tris." I sigh. "From day one you have been my knight in shining armor. Just for once I wanted you to be proud of me."

His eyes search mine. "I am proud of you; how could you ever think otherwise?"

I drop my head as sadness rolls in. "Because I'm not proud of myself for losing Wade's company, and I don't know how you could ever be."

He pushes the hair back from my face as his eyes hold mine. "It's your company too, Claire. Don't forget that. Wade may have started it, but you have flown the flag for five years alone."

Five years alone . . . just hearing those words brings tears to my eyes, and I blink to try to hide them.

I've felt *so* alone.

"Baby." Tristan pulls me close and kisses my forehead. "Let me in, Claire. I don't want you to have to go through anything alone anymore." He takes my face in his hands and stares into my eyes. "Okay?"

I nod through tears.

His lips take mine with a tenderness that rips my heart wide open, and I tear up again.

I've missed my man.

I slide my hand down his boxer shorts and run my fingers through his pubic hair.

His eyes hold mine, and I take him in my hand and slowly stroke him. I feel the blood rushing around his body, his cock hardening, and I stroke him again.

Our eyes are locked.

This is when we are at our best. Alone in bed, under the covers. Nobody here but us and the love that we share. "I need you," I murmur.

He takes my face in his hands and kisses me slowly. His tongue does a seductive dance against mine, waking my dormant body from its sleep.

I continue to slowly stroke him as he gets harder and harder. Our lips are locked. God, how did I think I could ever live without him?

No wonder my heart was broken. He makes it beat.

His fingers find the spot between my legs. "Open," he breathes against my lips.

I roll onto my back and spread my legs, and he leans up onto his elbow beside me.

He slides two thick fingers deep inside me. My back arches in pleasure. "That's it," he breathes. "I know how to relax you, baby."

His lips slowly take mine as he begins to pump me. The ripples of pleasure begin to build. I put my hands on his forearm as he works me, his movement getting rougher and rougher.

His dark eyes hold mine, and the bed begins to hit the wall with force.

Tristan Miles is the king of finger fucking. He gives it to me so good before we even get to the intercourse part. He has so much strength in his hand that I have no chance against him. No defense against his skill.

When he has me like this, he owns me.

Who am I kidding? He owns me wherever we are.

He pushes my legs back so they are bent against my chest, and he really lets me have it. The sound of my wet body sucking him in echoes throughout the room.

"Mmm," I moan as he watches me. My eyes are rolled back in my head, and I hover somewhere in subspace. "I need you," I pant. I grab the back of his head and drag him to me. "Fuck me," I plead.

With dark eyes, he rises above me, and I wrap my legs around his waist. He slides home deep. We both shudder, close to losing control.

We kiss, and it's slow and tender and moves in time with his body deep inside of mine.

"I missed you," he murmurs against my lips. I grip him tighter. I can't believe I nearly lost him.

I bear down and shudder hard. His eyes flutter with fire, and he pulls out and slams back in.

Oh . . . here we go.

He rises above me on straightened arms and begins to pump me with full force. His knees are wide, and my hands are on his behind. I feel him flex as he gets all the way in.

So good . . . so fucking good.

"Fuck," he growls through gritted teeth. "Knees up."

I bring my knees up to rest on his shoulders, and his eyes roll back. I smile up at him in wonder. "I love you," I whisper.

He kisses me aggressively, and then he lets me have it. Both barrels. The bed hits the wall so hard I think he might knock it down. He bites my neck, and I can't take it. I clench and convulse as I come hard. He holds himself deep as he does the same.

We move together slowly to completely empty his body into mine.

"I missed you," he whispers.

I hold him tight in my arms. "I missed you too."

We're back in Long Island now, and I look around at her bedroom and slide my hand up over Claire's hip as she sleeps. I inhale deeply and smile into her hair.

Today's the day.

"Morning." She sleepily sighs.

"I'm getting up, babe."

"Hmm," she murmurs with her eyes closed. "Why so early?"

"I'm taking the boys to the expo in New York, remember?"

"Oh, that's right," she replies. Her eyes are firmly shut. "Do you want me to get up to see you off?"

"No, I got it. The boys are already up. I can hear them downstairs. Stay here and sleep in."

"Okay." She smiles as she wraps her arms around me and holds me tight. "I love you."

I kiss her softly. "I love you too."

I climb out of bed, quickly shower, and make my way downstairs.

The boys are eating their cereal with huge grins on their faces. "Are we ready?" I whisper.

"Yeah, sure are," whispers Patrick excitedly.

I smile. "Hurry up. We need to go."

We walk down the mall in New York. It's snowing, and Christmas carols play loudly throughout the space. Patrick is holding my hand, and Harry and Fletcher are by my side. We've been looking for hours. Still nothing I like. "What if we don't find one?" Harry asks.

"We will."

"You should have had one made." Fletcher sighs with a roll of his eyes.

"I didn't have time."

The boys and I are looking for an engagement ring for Claire. We're finally going to be a family.

"When do you need it for?"

"Well, we leave in three weeks for Aspen, and my plan is to ask her on Christmas Eve," I reply as we walk. "I've got everything arranged. Now we just need the ring." Nerves flutter in my stomach. Finally.

My wife.

I've never wanted anything so badly. "Let's hope she says yes, eh?" I add.

"She better," Harry snaps as we walk. He takes my hand in his. "She's going to ruin the entire trip if she doesn't."

I chuckle. "Agreed. Two weeks' skiing in Aspen is going to be very uncomfortable if she says no."

I smile as I picture our first New Year's Eve together as a family, and I don't know if I've ever been this excited about a vacation before.

"Of course she's going to say yes," Fletcher scoffs. "As if she won't."

"I bet she cries." Harry smiles dreamily, as if imagining her face. "She always cries when good things happen."

"Remember, not a word to anyone about this." I widen my eyes at Patrick to remind him specifically.

If anyone is going to blab to Claire, it's him, but I didn't want to leave them out of this.

"I know," he says in disgust. "It's a big secret."

"You'll ruin Christmas if you tell," Fletcher adds.

"I won't," Patrick snaps. "Stop saying I'll tell, because I won't."

We keep walking and walking and walking. "Where is it, Fletch?" I ask.

He checks the directions on his phone. "Just around this corner."

We walk around the corner, and there it is.

NEW YORK DIAMOND TRADERS

"This is it."

We all stand still and stare at the sign.

"This makes me nervous," I whisper.

"Me too," replies Fletcher. "What if we get one she hates?"

"We won't." With renewed determination, I lead the boys into the jewelry store, and we look around.

"Can I help you, sir?" the man behind the counter asks.

"Yes," Fletcher interrupts. "We're looking for an engagement ring."

I smile, proud that he now speaks so confidently to strangers.

"For my mom," Patrick adds.

"Well." The salesman's eyes widen in delight. "How wonderful."

"Yes, it is." Harry beams happily as he swings my arm by the hand.

I smile as I watch the boys. They're as excited about this as I am. I'm so glad I included them in this.

"What are you after, sir?" the salesman asks.

"Gold." I look to Fletcher in question, and he nods. "Yes, eighteen-karat gold. A solitaire diamond, not too big and flashy, but the diamond has to be perfect."

"Okay. This way, please." He leads us over to a glass cabinet where diamond rings are displayed in rows.

"Thank you," I reply. "This could take a while."

"Of course. I'll leave you to it. I'll be just over here when you need me."

The boys and I all peer into the cabinet.

"Do you see any you like?" I whisper.

"Hmm." Patrick cranes his neck as he looks. "I'm trying to imagine if I were a girl."

"You wouldn't have to imagine too hard," Harry mutters dryly.

"That one." Fletcher points to a ring that sits on its own.

A solitaire diamond ring in a black velvet case sparkles perfectly in the light.

"Oh yeah," Harry whispers. "I like that one too."

"What do you think, Tricky?" I ask.

"Hmm." He frowns as he concentrates. "I think she might like a love-heart one instead. You know, for love."

Harry screws up his face in disgust. "She isn't ten," he scoffs. "Nobody likes love-heart rings."

"I think it would be nice," I reply as I stare at the ring in front of us. "But maybe Mom would prefer a round one." I shrug. "Good idea, though, Tricky." I rub his little head and mess up his hair.

He smiles up at me. "I suppose."

"Excuse me," I call to the salesman.

"Yes."

"Can we look at this one, please?" I point to the ring we like.

"Of course." He takes it out of the cabinet and passes it over.

We all stare at it in my hand. "Can you tell me about it?" I ask.

"Yes, this is a perfect-cut solitaire two-karat diamond. Eighteen-karat gold in a traditional setting."

I smile as I stare at it. I think this is it. "Can we have a moment alone, please?" I ask.

"Of course." He leaves us alone.

"What do you reckon?" I whisper as I pass it to Fletcher. He studies it carefully. "I love this one." He passes it to Harry, who inspects it in great detail. He nods in approval. He passes it to Patrick, who immediately drops it on the ground.

"Patrick, you idiot," Harry whispers angrily. "Watch what you're doing."

"It's slippery," Patrick stammers.

"Oh my God. I'm sorry," I stammer to the salesman as we all dive to the floor to retrieve it.

I pick it up and stare at it in my fingers, and a broad smile crosses my face. "This is it." I turn to the salesman. "We'll take it, please."

Snow is falling, and the boys all stare out the window of our chalet.

It's Christmas Eve, and we are sitting by the open fire, next to the Christmas tree.

This Christmas seems special . . . it *is* special.

My first with them.

Claire smiles over at me. "Thank you for bringing us here." She kisses me softly. "It's perfect."

"Boys," I call.

They all run to us and sit down, excited for what's to come.

"We have something for you." I smile.

Patrick puts his hand over his mouth so that he doesn't blurt it out.

Claire's eyes come to me in question.

I drop to my knee in front of her and hold out the ring. "Claire, will you marry me?"

The three boys all bounce on the spot in excitement.

Claire giggles and pulls me in to kiss her. "I thought you'd never ask." We kiss, and the boys high-five. "I've got a Christmas present for you too, Tris," she whispers.

I smile as I kiss her again, and then she takes my hand and puts it over her stomach.

"You're going to be a father."

My world stops.

She smiles through tears. "I'm two months pregnant."

I stare at her wide eyed; then I look to the boys, who are wide eyed too.

What the . . .

Claire giggles as my hand rests tenderly over her stomach. "Be careful what you wish for, Mr. Miles. Now you have four."

Two weeks later

I exhale heavily as I stand outside Jameson's office door. I drop my head as I brace myself.

I'm about to do something I've never imagined in my wildest dreams.

I knock twice.

"Come in," he calls.

Without a word, I walk in and hand him the envelope.

He frowns. "What's this?"

"My resignation."

"What?" His eyes hold mine. "Tell me you're joking."

"I'm taking over as CEO of Anderson Media. Fletcher and I are going to run it together."

His face falls. "I don't think—"

"The decision's already been made, Jay," I cut him off. "I'm going."

"What did Claire say?"

"She doesn't know yet."

He frowns. "You are leaving your family company to run someone else's company? That's madness."

I drop my head.

"I can't let you do this," he stammers.

"I'm going to run my sons' company . . . for them. I can build it back up so that by the time they are old enough to take it over, it will be booming."

His eyes hold mine, and he gives me a slow smile. "You're a good man, Tristan." He pulls me into a hug and kisses my cheek.

I want to blurt out that we are pregnant and not to be sad, because this is the beginning of something wonderful—a life with the woman I love and four beautiful children—but I can't. We've agreed to keep the pregnancy to ourselves for another month until Claire reaches her second trimester.

However, I'm well aware that this is the end of my time working with my brothers, and for that I truly am devastated.

It won't be the same not working with them.

My eyes well with tears as we hug. The ending of an era.

Eventually I pull out of his arms and walk toward the door.

"When will you be back?" he asks.

I turn back to him. "When my boys are men."

The End

ACKNOWLEDGMENTS

It takes an army to write a book, and I undoubtedly have the best army on earth.

To Sammia, Lindsey, and my Montlake team at Amazon, thank you for believing in me and my work—your support has been amazing.

Publishing with you has been a dream come true.

To my wonderful assistant of three years, Kellie, who we all know is the real boss around here. Thank you for everything you do: the travel, the covers, the books, my meltdowns . . . you handle it all with a beautiful smile on your face. I am so grateful for our friendship.

To my gorgeous beta readers, Rachel, Nicole, Vicki, Rena, Amanda, Nadia, and Lisa: you guys are the best. Thank you for everything that you do for me. You make me so much better.

To my family, the loves of my life. I love you. Xoxoxo.

To my beloved friends in the Swan Squad, thank you for your friendship and keeping me sane.

And last but not least, to my beautiful readers: it is because of you that I get to live this wonderful life, and words don't seem enough to express my gratitude.

Thank you so much for reading my books.

Thank you so much for your continued support.

Thank you so much for believing in my characters and stories as much as I do.

Dreams really do come true.

Tee

xoxoxox

Read on for the first chapter of T L Swan's backlist title *Mr. Masters*, available to buy now!

Prologue

ALINA MASTERS 1984–2013

WIFE AND BELOVED MOTHER. IN GOD'S HANDS WE TRUST.

Grief. The Grim Reaper of life.

Stealer of joy, hope, and purpose.

Some days are bearable. Other days I can hardly breathe, and I suffocate in a world of regret where good reason has no sense.

I never know when those days will hit, only that when I wake, my chest feels constricted and I need to run. I need to be anywhere but here, dealing with this life. My life.

Our life. Until you left.

The sound of a distant lawn mower brings me back to the present, and I glance over at the cemetery's caretaker. He's concentrating as he weaves among the tombstones, careful not to clip or damage one as he passes. It's dusk, and the mist is rolling in for the night.

I come here often to think, to try to feel.

I can't talk to anyone. I can't express my true feelings.

I want to know why.

Why did you do this to us?

I clench my jaw as I stare at my late wife's tombstone.

We could have had it all . . . but, we didn't.

I lean down and brush the dust away from her name and rearrange the pink lilies that I have just placed in the vase. I touch her face on the small oval photo. She stares back at me, void of emotion.

Stepping back, I drop my hands in the pockets of my black overcoat.

I could stand here and stare at this headstone all day—sometimes I do—but I turn and walk to the car without looking back.

My Porsche.

Sure, I have money and two kids who love me. I'm at the top of my professional field, working as a judge. I have all the tools to be happy, but I'm not.

I'm barely surviving; holding on by a thread. Playing the facade to the world.

Dying inside.

Half an hour later, I arrive at Madison's—my therapist.

I always leave here relaxed. I don't have to talk, I don't have to think, I don't have to feel.

I walk through the front doors on autopilot.

"Good afternoon, Mr. Smith." Hayley, the receptionist, smiles. "Your room is waiting, sir."

"Thank you." I frown, feeling like I need something more today. Something to take this edginess off. A distraction.

"I'll have someone extra today, Hayley."

"Of course, sir. Who would you like?"

I frown and take a moment to get it right. "Hmm. Hannah."

"So, Hannah and Belinda?"

"Yes."

"No problem, sir. Make yourself comfortable and they will be right up."

I take the lift to the exclusive penthouse. Once there I make myself a scotch and stare out the smoked-glass window overlooking London. I hear the door click behind me, and I turn toward the sound. Hannah and Belinda stand before me, smiling. Belinda has long blonde hair, while Hannah is a brunette.

There's no denying they're both young and beautiful. "Hello, Mr. Smith," they say in unison.

I sip my scotch as my eyes drink them in.

"Where would you like us, sir?"

I unbuckle my belt. "On your knees."

Chapter 1

Brielle

Customs is ridiculously slow, and a man has been pulled into the office up ahead. It all looks very suspicious from my position at the back of the line. "What do you think he did?" I whisper as I crane my neck to spy the commotion up ahead.

"I don't know, something stupid, probably," Emerson replies. We shuffle toward the desk as the line moves a little quicker.

We've just arrived in London to begin our yearlong working holiday. I'm going to work for a judge as a nanny, while Emerson, my best friend, is working for an art auctioneer. I'm terrified, yet excited.

"I wish we had come a week earlier so we could have spent some time together," Emerson says.

"Yeah, I know, but she needed me to start this week because she's going away next week. I need to learn the kids' routine."

"Who leaves their kids alone for three days with a complete stranger?" Em frowns in disgust.

I shrug. "My new boss, apparently."

"Well, at least I can come and stay with you next week. That's a bonus."

My position is residential, so my accommodation is secure. However, poor Emerson will be living with two strangers. She's freaking out over it.

"Yeah, but I'm sneaking you in," I say. "I don't want it to look like we're partying or anything." I look around the airport. It's busy, bustling, and I already feel so alive. Emerson and I are more than just young travelers.

Emerson is trying to find her purpose, and I'm running from a destructive past, one that involves me being in love with an adulterous prick.

I loved him. He just didn't love me. Not enough, anyway. If he had, he would have kept it in his pants, and I wouldn't be at Heathrow Airport feeling like I'm about to throw up.

I look down at myself and smooth the wrinkles from my dress. "She's picking me up. Do I look okay?"

Emerson looks me up and down, smiling broadly. "You look exactly how a twenty-five-year-old nanny from Australia should."

I bite my bottom lip to stop myself from smiling stupidly. That was a good answer.

"So, what's your boss's name?" she asks.

I rustle around in my bag for my phone and scroll through the emails until I get to the one from the nanny agency. "Mrs. Julian Masters."

Emerson nods. "And what's her story again? I know you've told me before, but I've forgotten."

"She's a Supreme Court judge, widowed five years ago."

"What happened to the husband?"

"I don't know, but apparently she's quite wealthy." I shrug. "Two kids, well behaved."

"Sounds good."

"I hope so. I hope they like me."

"They will." We move forward in the line. "We are definitely going out at the weekend though, yes?"

"Yes." I nod. "What are you going to do until then?"

Emerson shrugs. "Look around. I start work on Monday and it's Thursday today." She frowns as she watches me. "Are you sure you can go out on the weekends?"

"Yes," I snap, exasperated. "I told you a thousand times, we're going out on Saturday night."

Emerson nods nervously. I think she may be more nervous than I am, but at least I'm acting brave. "Did you get your phone sorted?" I ask.

"No, not yet. I'll find a phone shop tomorrow so I can call you."

"Okay."

We are called to the front of the line, and finally, half an hour later, we walk into the arrivals lounge of Heathrow International Airport. "Do you see our names?" Emerson whispers as we both look around.

"No."

"Shit, no one is here to pick us up. Typical." She begins to panic.

"Relax, they will be here," I mutter.

"What do we do if no one turns up?"

I raise my eyebrow as I consider the possibility. "Well, I don't know about you, but I'm going to lose my shit."

Emerson looks over my shoulder. "Oh, look, there's your name. She must have sent a driver."

I turn to see a tall, broad man in a navy suit holding a sign with the name Brielle Johnston on it. I force a smile and wave meekly as I feel my anxiety rise like a tidal wave in my stomach.

He walks over and smiles at me. "Brielle?"

His voice is deep and commanding. "Yes, that's me," I breathe. He holds out his hand to shake mine. "Julian Masters." What? My eyes widen.

A man?

He raises his eyebrows.

"Um, so, I'm . . . I'm Brielle," I stammer as I push my hand out. "And this is my friend Emerson, who I'm traveling with." He takes my hand in his, and my heart races.

A trace of a smile crosses his face before he covers it. "Nice to meet you." He turns to Emerson and shakes her hand. "How do you do?"

My eyes flash to Emerson, who is clearly loving this shit. She grins brightly. "Hello."

"I thought you were a woman," I whisper.

His brows furrow. "Last time I checked I was all man." His eyes hold mine.

Why did I just say that out loud? Oh my God, stop talking. This is so awkward.

I want to go home. This is a bad idea.

"I'll wait over here." He gestures to the corner before marching off in that direction. My horrified eyes meet Emerson's, and she giggles, so I punch her hard in the arm.

"Oh, my fuck, he's a fucking man," I whisper angrily.

"I can see that." She smirks, her eyes fixed on him.

"Excuse me, Mr. Masters?" I call after him.

He turns. "Yes."

We both wither under his glare. "We . . . we are just going to use the bathroom," I whisper nervously.

With one curt nod, he gestures to the right. We look up and see the sign. I grab Emerson by the arm and drag her into the bathroom. "I'm not working with a stuffy old man!" I shriek as we burst through the door.

"It will be okay. How did this happen?"

I take out my phone and scroll through the emails quickly. I knew it. "It says woman. I knew it said woman."

"He's not that old," she calls out from her cubicle. "I would prefer to work for a man than a woman, to be honest."

"You know what, Emerson? This is a shit idea. How the hell did I let you talk me into this?"

She smiles as she exits the cubicle and washes her hands. "It doesn't matter. You'll hardly see him anyway, and you're not working weekends when he's home." She's clearly trying to calm me. "Stop with the carry on."

Stop the carry on.

Steam feels like it's shooting from my ears. "I'm going to kill you. I'm going to fucking kill you."

Emerson bites her lip to stifle her smile. "Listen, just stay with him until we find you something else. I will get my phone sorted tomorrow, and we can start looking elsewhere for another job," she reassures me. "At least someone picked you up. Nobody cares about me at all."

I put my head into my hands as I try to calm my breathing. "This is a disaster, Em," I whisper. Suddenly every fear I had about traveling is coming true. I feel completely out of my comfort zone.

"It's going to be one week . . . tops."

My scared eyes lift to hold hers, and I nod.

"Okay?" She smiles as she pulls me into a hug.

"Okay." I glance back in the mirror, fix my hair, and straighten my dress. I'm completely rattled.

We walk back out and take our place next to Mr. Masters. He's in his late thirties, immaculately dressed, and kind of attractive. His hair is dark with a sprinkle of gray.

"Did you have a good flight?" he asks as he looks down at me.

"Yes, thanks," I push out. Oh, that sounded so forced. "Thank you for picking us up," I add meekly. He nods with no fuss.

Emerson smiles at the floor as she tries to hide her smile. That bitch is loving this shit.

"Emerson?" a male voice calls. We all turn to see a blond man, and Emerson's face falls. Ha! Now it's my turn to laugh. "Hello, I'm Mark." He kisses her on the cheek and then turns to me. "You must be Brielle?"

"Yes." I smile, then turn to Mr. Masters. "And this is . . ." I pause because I don't know how to introduce him.

"Julian Masters," he finishes for me, adding in a strong handshake.

Emerson and I fake smile at each other.

Oh, dear God, help me.

Emerson stands and talks with Mark and Mr. Masters, while I stand in uncomfortable silence. "The car is this way." He gestures to the right.

I nod nervously. Oh God, don't leave me with him. This is terrifying.

"Nice to meet you, Emerson and Mark." He shakes their hands.

"Likewise. Please look after my friend," Emerson whispers as her eyes flick to mine.

Mr. Masters nods, smiles, and then pulls my luggage behind him as he walks to the car. Emerson pulls me into an embrace. "This is shit," I whisper into her hair.

"It will be fine. He's probably really nice."

"He doesn't look nice," I whisper.

"Yeah, I agree. He looks like a tool," Mark adds as he watches him disappear through the crowd.

Emerson throws her new friend a dirty look, and I smirk. I think her friend is more annoying than mine, but anyway . . .

"Mark, look after my friend, please?" He beats his chest like a gorilla. "Oh, I intend to."

Emerson's eyes meet mine. She subtly shakes her head, and I bite my bottom lip to hide my smile. This guy is a dick. We both look over to see Mr. Masters looking back impatiently. "I better go," I whisper.

"You have my apartment details if you need me?"

"I'll probably turn up in an hour. Tell your roommates I'm coming in case I need a key."

She laughs and waves me off, and I go to Mr. Masters. He sees me coming and then starts to walk again.

God, can he not even wait for me? So rude. He walks out of the building into the VIP parking section. I follow him in complete silence.

Any notion that I was going to become friends with my new boss has been thrown out the window. I think he hates me already.

Just wait until he finds out that I lied on my résumé and I have no fucking idea what I'm doing. Nerves flutter in my stomach at the thought.

We get to a large, swanky black SUV, and he clicks it open to put my suitcase in the trunk. He opens the back door for me to get in. "Thank you." I smile awkwardly as I slide into the seat. He wants me to sit in the back when the front seat is empty.

This man is odd.

He slides into the front seat and eventually pulls out into the traffic. All I can do is clutch my handbag in my lap. Should I say something? Try to make conversation? What will I say?

"Do you live far from here?" I ask.

"Twenty minutes," he replies, his tone clipped.

Oh . . . is that it? Okay, shut up now. He doesn't want a conversation. For ten long minutes, we sit in silence. "You can drive this car when you have the children, or we have a small minivan. The choice is yours."

"Oh, okay." I pause for a moment. "Is this your car?"

"No." He turns onto a street and into a driveway with huge sandstone gates. "I drive a Porsche," he replies casually.

"Oh."

The driveway goes on and on and on. I look around at the perfectly kept grounds and rolling green hills. With every meter we pass, I feel my heart beat just that bit faster. As if it isn't bad enough that I can't do the whole nanny thing . . . I really can't do the rich thing. I have no idea what to do with polite company. I don't even know what fork to use at dinner. I've got myself into a right mess here. The house comes into focus, and the blood drains from my face.

It's not a house, not even close. It's a mansion, white and sandstone with a castle kind of feel to it, with six garages to the left.

He pulls into the large circular driveway, stopping under the awning.

"Your house is beautiful," I whisper.

He nods, as his eyes stay fixed out front. "We are fortunate."

He gets out of the car and opens my door for me. I climb out as I grip my handbag with white-knuckle force. My eyes rise to the luxurious building in front of me. This is an insane amount of money. He retrieves my suitcase and wheels it around to the side of the building. "Your entrance is around to the side," he says. I follow him up a path until we get to a door, which he opens and lets me walk through. There is a foyer and a living area in front of me. "The kitchen is this way." He points to the kitchen. "And your bedroom is in the back-left corner."

I nod and walk past him, into the apartment.

He stands at the door but doesn't come in. "The bathroom is to the right," he continues.

Why isn't he coming in here? "Okay, thanks," I reply.

"Order any groceries you want on the family shopping order and . . ." He pauses, as if collecting his thoughts. "If there is anything else you need, please talk to me first."

I frown. "First?"

He shrugs. "I don't want to be told about a problem for the first time when reading a resignation letter."

"Oh." Did that happen before? "Of course," I mutter.

"If you would like to come and meet the children . . ." He gestures to a hallway.

"Yes, please." Oh God, here we go. I follow him out into a corridor with glass walls that looks out onto the main house, which is about four meters away. A garden sits between the two buildings creating an atrium, and I smile as I look up in wonder. There is a large window in the main house that looks into the kitchen. I can see beyond that into the living area, where a young girl and small boy are watching television together. We continue to the end of the glass corridor, where a staircase with six steps leads up to the main house. I blow out a breath, and I follow Mr. Masters up the stairs. "Children, come and meet your new nanny."

The little boy jumps down and rushes over to me, clearly excited, while the girl just looks up and rolls her eyes. I smile to myself, remembering what it's like to be a typical teenager.

"Hello, I'm Samuel." The little boy smiles as he wraps his arms around my legs. He has dark hair, wears glasses, and is so damn cute.

"Hello, Samuel." I smile.

"This is Willow," he introduces.

I smile at the teenage girl. "Hello."

She folds her arms across her chest defiantly. "Hi," she grumbles.

Mr. Masters holds her gaze for a moment, saying so much with just one look. Willow eventually holds her hand out for me to shake. "I'm Willow."

I smile as my eyes flash up to Mr. Masters. He can keep her under control with just a simple glare.

Samuel runs back to the lounge, grabs something, and then comes straight back. I see a flash. Click, click.

What the hell?

He has a small instant Polaroid camera. He watches my face appear on the piece of paper in front of him before he looks back up at me. "You're pretty." He smiles. "I'm putting this on the fridge." He carefully affixes it to the fridge with a magnet. Mr. Masters seems to become flustered for some reason. "Bedtime for you two," he instructs, and they both complain. He turns his attention back to me. "Your kitchen is stocked with groceries, and I'm sure you're tired."

I fake a smile. Oh, I'm being dismissed. "Yes, of course." I go to walk back down to my apartment, and then turn back to him. "What time do I start tomorrow?"

His eyes hold mine. "When you hear Samuel wake up."

"Yes, of course." My eyes search his as I wait for him to say something else, but it doesn't come. "Good night, then." I smile awkwardly.

"Good night."

"Bye, Brielle." Samuel smiles, and Willow ignores me, walking away and up the stairs.

I walk back down into my apartment and close the door behind me. Then I flop onto the bed and stare up at the ceiling.

What have I done?

It's midnight and I'm thirsty, but I have looked everywhere and still cannot find a glass. There's no other option; I'm going to have to sneak up into the main house to find one. I'm wearing my silky white nightdress, but I'm sure they are all in bed.

Sneaking out into the darkened corridor, I can see into the lit-up house.

I suddenly catch sight of Mr. Masters sitting in the armchair reading a book. He has a glass of red wine in his hand. I stand in the dark, unable to tear my eyes away. There's something about him that fascinates me, but I don't quite know what it is. He stands abruptly, and I push myself back against the wall. Can he see me here in the dark?

Shit.

My eyes follow him as he walks into the kitchen. The only thing he's wearing is his navy-blue boxer shorts. His dark hair has messy, loose waves on top. His chest is broad, his body is . . .

My heart begins to beat faster. What am I doing? I shouldn't be standing here in the dark, watching him like a creep, but for some reason I can't make myself look away.

He goes to stand by the kitchen counter. His back is to me as he pours himself another glass of red. He lifts it to his lips slowly, and my eyes run over his body. I push myself against the wall harder. He walks over to the fridge and takes off the photo of me.

What?

He leans his ass on the counter as he studies it. What is he doing? I feel like I can't breathe.

He slowly puts his hand down the front of his boxer shorts, and then he seems to stroke himself a few times.

My eyes widen. What the fuck?

He puts his glass of wine on the counter and turns the main light off, leaving only a lamp to light the room. With my picture in his hand, he disappears up the hall. What the hell was that? I think Mr. Masters just went up to his bedroom to jerk off to my photo.

Oh. My. God.

Knock, knock.

My eyes are closed, but I frown and try to ignore the noise. I hear it again. Tap, tap. What is that? I roll toward the door, and I see it slowly begin to open. My eyes widen, and I sit up quickly. Mr. Masters comes into view. "I'm so sorry to bother you, Miss Brielle," he whispers. He smells like he's freshly showered, and he's wearing an immaculate suit. "I'm looking for Samuel." His gaze roams down to my breasts hanging loosely in my nightdress, and then he snaps his eyes back up to my face, as if he's horrified at what he just did.

"Where is he?" I frown. "Is he missing?"

"There he is," he whispers as he gestures to the lounger. I look over to see Samuel curled up with his teddy in the diluted light of the room. My mouth falls open. "Oh no, what's wrong?" I whisper. Did he need me and I slept through the whole thing?

"Nothing," Mr. Masters murmurs as he picks Samuel up and rests his son's head on his strong shoulder. "He's a sleepwalker. Sorry to disturb you. I've got this now." He leaves the room with his small son safely asleep in his arms. The door gently clicks closed behind them.

I lie back down and stare at the ceiling in the silence. That poor little boy. He came in here to see me, and I didn't even wake up. I was probably snoring, for fuck's sake. What if he was scared? Oh, I feel like shit now.

I blow out a deep breath, lift myself up to sit on the edge of the bed, and put my head into my hands. I need to up my game. If I'm in charge of looking after this kid, I can't have him wandering around at night on his own. Is he that lonely that he was looking for company from me—a complete stranger?

Unexplained sadness rolls over me, and I suddenly feel like the weight of the world is on my shoulders. I look around my room for a moment as I think.

Eventually, I get up and go to the bathroom, and then I walk to the window to pull the heavy drapes back. It's just getting light, and a white mist hangs over the paddocks.

Something catches my eye, and I look down to see Mr. Masters walking out to the garage.

Wearing a dark suit and carrying a briefcase, he disappears, and moments later I see his Porsche pull out and disappear up the driveway. I watch as the garage door slowly closes behind him. He's gone to work for the day.

What the hell?

His son was just found asleep on my lounger, and he just plops him back into his own bed and leaves for the day. Who does that? Well, screw this, I'm going to go and check on him. He's probably upstairs crying, scared out of his brain. Stupid men. Why don't they have an inch of fucking empathy for anyone but themselves? He's eight, for Christ's sake!

I walk up into the main house. The lamp is still on in the living room, and I can smell the eggs that Mr. Masters cooked himself for breakfast. I look around and then go up the grand staircase. Honestly, what the hell have I gotten myself into here? I'm in some stupid rich twat's house, worried about his child who he clearly doesn't give a fuck about.

I storm up the stairs, taking two at a time. I get to the top, and the change of scenery suddenly makes me feel nervous. It's luxurious up here. The corridor is wide, and the cream carpet feels lush beneath my feet. A huge mirror hangs in the hall on the wall. I catch a glimpse of myself and cringe.

God, no wonder he was looking at my boobs. They are hanging out everywhere, and my hair is wild. I readjust my nightgown over my breasts and continue up the hall. I pass a living area that seems to be for the children, with big comfy loungers inside it. I pass a bedroom, and then I get to a door that is closed. I open it carefully and allow myself to peer in. Willow is fast asleep—still scowling, though. I smirk and slowly shut her door to continue down the hall. Eventually, I get to a door that is slightly ajar. I peer around it and see Samuel sound asleep, tucked in nice and tight. I walk into his room and sit on the side of the bed. He's wearing bright-blue-and-green dinosaur pajamas, and his little glasses are on his side table, beside his lamp. I find myself smiling as I watch him. Unable to help it, I put my hand out and push the dark hair from his forehead. His bedroom is neat and tidy, filled with expensive furniture. It kind of looks like you would imagine a child's bedroom set out in a perfect family movie. Everything in this house is the absolute best of the best. Just how much money does Mr. Masters have? There's a bookcase, a desk, a wingback chair in the corner, and a toy box. The window has a bench seat running underneath it, and there are a few books sitting in a pile on the cushion, as if Samuel reads there a lot. I glance over to the armchair in the corner to his school clothes all laid out for him. Everything is there, folded neatly, right down to his socks and shiny, polished shoes. His school bag is packed, too.

I stand and walk over to look at his things. Mr. Masters must do this before he goes to bed. What must it be like to bring children up alone?

My mind goes to his wife and how much she is missing out on. Samuel is so young. With one last look at Samuel, I creep out of the room and head back down the hall, until something catches my eye.

A light is on in the en suite bathroom of the main bedroom. That must be Mr. Masters's bedroom. I look left and then right;

nobody is awake. I wonder what his room is like, and I can't stop myself from tiptoeing closer to inspect it. Wow.

The bed is clearly king size, and the room is grand, decorated in all different shades of coffee, complimented with dark antique furniture. A huge, expensive gold-and-magenta embroidered rug sits on the floor beneath the bed. The light in the wardrobe is on. I peer inside and see business shirts all lined up, neatly in a row. Super neatly, actually. I'm going to have to make sure I keep my room tidy or he'll think I'm a pig. I smirk, because I am one according to his standards of living.

I turn to see his bed has already been made, and my eyes linger over the velvet quilt and lush pillows there. Did he really touch himself in there last night as he thought of me, or am I completely delusional? I glance around for the photo of me, but I don't see it. He must have taken it back downstairs.

An unexpected thrill runs through me. I may return the favor tonight in my own bed.

I walk into the bathroom. It's all black and gray, and very modern. Once again, I notice that everything is very neat. There is a large mirror, and I can see that a slender cabinet sits behind it. I push the mirror, and the door pops open. My eyes roam over the shelves. You can tell a lot about people by their bathroom cabinet. Deodorant. Razors. Talcum powder. Condoms. I wonder how long ago his wife died. Does he have a new girlfriend?

It wouldn't surprise me. He is kind of hot, in an old way. I see a bottle of aftershave, and I pick it up, removing the lid before I lift it up to my nose.

Heaven in a bottle.

I inhale deeply again, and Mr. Masters's face suddenly appears in the mirror behind me.

"What the hell do you think you're doing?" he growls.

ABOUT THE AUTHOR

A psychologist in her former life, T L Swan is now seriously addicted to the thrill of writing and can't imagine a time when she never did.

She resides in Sydney, Australia, with her husband and their three children, where she is living out her own happily ever after with her first true love.